HELLFIRE

Paranormal Romance by Kate Douglas

"Crystal Dreams" in *Nocturnal*

Demonfire

Erotic Romance by Kate Douglas

Wolf Tales

"Chanku Rising" in *Sexy Beast*

Wolf Tales II

"Camille's Dawn" in *Wild Nights*

Wolf Tales III

"Chanku Fallen" in *Sexy Beast II*

Wolf Tales IV

"Chanku Journey" in *Sexy Beast III*

Wolf Tales V

"Chanku Destiny" in *Sexy Beast IV*

Wolf Tales VI

"Chanku Wild" in *Sexy Beast V*

Wolf Tales VII

"Chanku Honor" in *Sexy Beast VI*

Wolf Tales VIII

"Chanku Challenge" in *Sexy Beast VII*

Wolf Tales 9

"Chanku Spirit" in *Sexy Beast VIII*

Wolf Tales 10

Published by Kensington Publishing Corporation

HELLFIRE

The DemonSlayers

KATE DOUGLAS

ZEBRA BOOKS
KENSINGTON PUBLISHING CORP.

http://www.kensingtonbooks.com

ZEBRA BOOKS are published by

Kensington Publishing Corp.
119 West 40th Street
New York, NY 10018

All Kensington titles, imprints, and distributed lines are available at special quantity discounts for bulk purchases for sales promotion, premiums, fund-raising, educational, or institutional use.

Special book excerpts or customized printings can also be created to fit specific needs. For details, write or phone the office of the Kensington Special Sales Manager: Attn. Special Sales Department. Kensington Publishing Corp., 119 West 40th Street, New York, NY 10018. Phone: 1-800-221-2647.

Zebra and the Z logo Reg. U.S. Pat. & TM Off.

ISBN-13: 978-1-4201-1000-5
ISBN-10: 1-4201-1000-4

First Printing: September 2010

10 9 8 7 6 5 4 3 2 1

Printed in the United States of America

To Doug for . . . well, everything.
But most of all, for making me laugh.

ACKNOWLEDGMENTS

I remember thinking—back in my saner days—how much fun it would be to write books. What could be easier than sitting down and allowing the words to go directly from my brain, through my fingers, to the page, just the way my favorite authors did?

Little did I know how many hours of work went into their books—the books I devoured over the course of an evening. My sincere thanks go to the wonderful people who take my stories and make the books happen—to my fantastic agent, Jessica Faust of BookEnds LLC, my wonderful editor, Audrey LaFehr, her ever-patient and multiskilled assistant, Martin Biro, Kensington's truly talented art department, the publicists, sales personnel and production people . . . all of them so good at what they do, and so patient with those of us who love to write the stories but haven't got a clue how the rest of the process really works.

Thanks also to my great beta-readers—the ones who take my flawed first drafts, tell me what needs fixin', and do it without making me feel like a complete idiot. On this project, those intrepid souls were Rose Toubbeh, Karen Woods, Rhonda Wilson, Jan Takane, Treva Harte, Amanda Haffrey, and my agent, Jessica Faust. It really does take a village to create a book, and I'm blessed to exist in one of the very best villages around. Thank you, all of you.

I want to add a special thanks to reviewer Suzie Housley, who, way back when, read one of my very first e-published romances and said she just knew I'd make it. Suzie, I may not "be there" yet, but I'm working on it!

Foreword

The Legend of Lemuria . . .

Thousands of years ago, the continent of Lemuria disappeared beneath the sea, much in the manner of the lost continent of Atlantis. However, unlike the Atlanteans, Lemurians are not considered lost—legend says they relocated their entire society to a sanctuary deep within the dormant volcano known as Mount Shasta in the rugged mountains of northern California.

Much has been written about these tall and graceful beings, of their great intelligence and beauty, their advanced technology and supernatural abilities, but no actual proof of their existence has ever been discovered.

That doesn't mean, of course, that they're not really there, living in quiet splendor in their cities of gold, deep within Mount Shasta. Nor does it mean they've not had their interactions with humans.

Actually, Lemurians have maintained a peaceful and entirely nonviolent civilization in a separate dimension within the volcano for millennia, though many among them are beginning to recognize the importance of keeping Earth's population safe to protect their own secretive society— a society that has kept secrets even from its own citizens.

Now, when demonkind from Abyss threaten not only Earth but all worlds in all dimensions—including Lemuria— descendants of ancient Lemurian warriors are once again taking up arms in the ages-old battle between good and evil.

Chapter One

Ginny Jones wrapped a clean kitchen towel around her torn fingers and glared at the screeching cat she'd finally managed to shove into the carrier.

Her cousin Markus leaned over her shoulder and sighed. "Poor Tom. I sure hope he's not rabid."

"No shit, Sherlock." She glanced at the blood-soaked towel and then at Markus. "And what do you mean, poor Tom? Did you see what that stupid cat of yours did to my hand?"

Markus shook his head, sending his long dreads flying. "I don't understand. Tom's a sweetheart. He's never even scratched anyone, much less bitten before."

"Tell that to your neighbor. She's going to need stitches in her leg, not to mention what he did to me. C'mon. We have to get your stupid cat to the vet so they can quarantine him before animal control shows up, or they just might take him and put him down."

Markus grabbed the keys off the hook by the back door and picked up the carrier. Tom screeched, a long, low banshee wail that sent goosebumps racing along Ginny's arms and raised the tiny hairs on the back of her neck. Tom didn't sound anything like any cat she'd ever heard.

So, why did that screech sound so eerily familiar?

Something about it skirted the edges of her memory. She stared at Tom, glaring back at her through the slats of the carrier, but nothing clicked. She'd never seen a cat with eyes like his—they flashed blood red. When he snarled, she was almost certain he had extra rows of teeth.

She shivered again and wrapped her arms around herself. *Beyond weird.* Everything about the stupid cat was freaking her out, but then, so was this entire trip. Frowning, Ginny followed Markus at a safe distance through the backdoor to the garage and watched while he stowed the sturdy carrier in the rear seat of the Camry.

Tom howled again. Ginny shook her head. "I don't like this one bit. Shouldn't we maybe put him in the trunk?"

Markus ignored her suggestion and got into the driver's seat. "Get in. No cat of mine rides in the trunk."

Ginny stared at the red-eyed cat. Tom returned her stare.

Markus glared at her. "You scared of a cat? Damn it, Ginny. Get in."

She took a deep breath. She wasn't about to let herself act like a coward in front of her younger cousin. "Well, if he gets loose from the carrier, you're putting him back—and I'm outta here. I've bled enough for the cause." Ginny slammed the door and reached for her seat belt, wondering for the hundredth time what she was doing visiting her cousins in Sedona anyway. It wasn't like they were all that close, but for some reason she'd gotten a wild hair, packed her bags, and headed to Arizona without any plans or advance notice at all.

So far, her timing sucked. She'd barely parked the rental car at her aunt's house when the shit hit the fan. Old Tom, the fattest, laziest-looking cat she'd ever seen, had jumped up, shrieked like the devil was on his tail, and launched his porky butt off Aunt Betty's front porch.

He'd practically flown over the six-foot hedge between her aunt's house and the one next door—like a flying furball with fangs. He'd zeroed in on the poor neighbor lady who was just getting out of her car, arms loaded with groceries.

The bags had gone one way, the woman the other, but Tom latched on to her left leg and buried his teeth deep. It had taken both Markus and Ginny to pull the cat off the screaming woman, and then he'd taken off, still screeching. Aunt Betty had freaked out, grabbed the twins, and as far as Ginny knew, she was still hiding in the bedroom with the kids.

Markus—with typical teenage thinking—had gone after the cat with a big bass net like it was a four-legged fish. Ginny'd been the one who finally cornered Tom against the fence, but he'd gotten her good with claws and teeth before she'd managed to shove him into the carrier and latch the damned thing.

Not quite the entrance she'd imagined on the flight from Sacramento to Phoenix. If she had to go through a course of rabies shots, she was going to kill Markus, and anyone else who gave her grief.

Like Alton. Especially Alton.

Now why in the hell would she be thinking of her friend Eddy Marks's tall, drop-dead gorgeous, egotistical jackass college buddy Alton? They'd barely met, though Ginny kept associating him with her being here in Sedona, which made no sense whatsoever.

Neither did the fact he'd kissed her the first time she saw him. For some reason, her memories of that kiss were all fuzzy and dreamlike. She knew they'd locked lips, if only for a moment, but her memory should be sharper. A *lot* sharper.

He had perfect lips—full and warm and soft—and he was a spectacular kisser. She remembered that much, but little else.

Like *why.* She couldn't recall anything leading up to the kiss, or even what had happened directly after, which wasn't like her. Not one bit, but confusing memories of Alton were all jumbled up with boarding a plane for Phoenix. She'd rented a car and hung out in Phoenix for a few days, feeling confused and off-kilter before giving in to some weird need to see her aunt and cousins in Sedona. Early Tuesday morning, she'd finally hit the road for the two-hour drive across the desert to Sedona.

And now she was headed to the local vet's with a crazy cat, her stupid kid cousin, and a hand that was bleeding through the dishtowel she'd wrapped around the bites and scratches.

If this was a vacation, she'd definitely had better.

"Is it always this busy?" Ginny rewrapped the towel on her throbbing hand while Markus drove around the block again, looking for a parking space. All the slots at the vet's clinic were taken and there wasn't a single empty spot along the road.

Markus shook his head. "Never. Especially on a Tuesday morning. Weekends, maybe, but not today. I don't get it."

He finally pulled into the parking lot in front of a grocery store a block away. "I'll carry the cat." He glanced at Ginny and seemed to notice the blood-soaked towel for the first time. "Is that still bleeding?"

"Yes, it's still bleeding. Your sweetheart of a cat nailed me good." She got out of the car and started walking toward the clinic. Markus fell into step beside her with the carrier clutched in one hand. Tom had quit screeching, but his incessant yowling was almost as bad.

Markus was big for eighteen—at least six-foot-six with broad shoulders and legs like tree trunks. As tall as she was, Ginny had to look up at him. He might not be the sharpest tack in the box, but she figured if he couldn't protect her from a stupid cat, no one could.

Though, come to think of it, she was the one bleeding, not her cousin. She was still thinking along those lines when Markus grabbed the door to the clinic and held it open for her.

Ginny stepped into total pandemonium.

The small clinic reeked of sulfur, which made no sense at all. Usually vet clinics smelled like cat pee. This one was filled with crying kids, freaked-out grownups, screeching animals—most of them in cages, thank goodness—and a couple of staff members who looked as if they were ready to run and hide. Ginny turned and looked at her cousin.

Markus stared wild-eyed at a large cage holding a big blue macaw. The bird spread its beak wide and screeched. It sounded just like Tom. Markus swallowed with an audible gulp. Ginny took a closer look at the macaw. Teeth. Rows and rows of teeth.

Now, she was no expert, but Ginny was sure she'd never heard of birds with teeth. She blinked and refocused, but the macaw's mouth was still filled with way too many teeth—all of them razor sharp. A screechy howl caught her attention and she glanced down at a scrawny little Chihuahua that was, thankfully, wearing a muzzle.

More teeth. Not just sharp doggy fangs, but rows of shiny, razor-sharp teeth filled the little mutt's mouth. A lop-eared bunny in a cat carrier just like Tom's snarled and hissed and curled its lips back. More teeth. Every single animal in the clinic looked like something out of a cheap horror film, all of them snarling and screeching and trying to take bites with mouths filled with way too many rows of sharp teeth.

And just like that, memories crashed into the forefront of her mind. The big concrete bear chasing her that night back home in Evergreen, her best friend Eddy's dad, Ed Marks, and Alton—though she hadn't known him then, that tall, good-looking friend of Eddy's from college—rushing out of the darkness and attacking the impossible creature. Alton had saved her life.

She saw it like a movie on fast forward—Alton carrying a huge sword that glowed like a freaking Jedi lightsaber, jabbing it into the concrete bear like the bear was made of butter. Jumping up on the creature's back, riding it like a bucking bronco. And the sound! The bear'd been screeching and wailing.

Screeching and wailing, just like the animals here, in the veterinarian's clinic.

Ginny sucked in a breath as images flowed into her mind. Alton lopping off the concrete bear's head with a powerful swing of his sword, the glowing blade flashing by in a slashing arc.

The bear crumbling, just turning into a pile of rocks and dust and sulfuric stink, like it had never been alive at all. And the smell. That horrible stench.

Just like this vet clinic in Sedona.

She remembered Alton and Ed walking her home. How could she have forgotten that night? That was the night Alton kissed her! A girl didn't forget a night like that. It made no sense at all.

Except she was remembering now. Remembering it as clearly as if it had just happened. The bear, the battle . . . Alton's lips. Oh, Lordy . . . his lips, warm and full and so sweet, pressed against hers, moving over her mouth in a sensual whisper of sensation and seduction.

The noise, the screeching animals, the frantic humans, the stinky veterinarian's clinic, all faded away as Ginny pressed her fingertips against her lips and let the memories flow.

There'd been another night too. How the hell could she have forgotten? It was only a few days ago! She blinked as it came into focus. She and Alton, walking arm in arm down the street to her house. The two of them laughing and talking about lots of nothing—flirting, for crying out loud! Both of them standing on her front porch.

She sucked in a breath as the memories cleared. She'd been thinking of breaking all her rules about guys and inviting Alton in. He'd been just as bossy and arrogant as the first time they'd met, but she'd had fun with him, too, and even though they'd only met the night he'd saved her life, she'd been drawn to him on an almost primal level.

The chemistry had certainly been there—so intense the need she'd felt was almost painful. Even now, just thinking of him fired a slow burn of desire deep in her core.

How could she forget that he'd offered to stay the night on her front porch? Offered to sit out there to protect her. That was sweet, even though she didn't need any protection. Not in her little town of Evergreen on the slopes of Mount Shasta.

Safest place in the world.

She remembered saying good night. She'd kissed his cheek when she'd really wanted to drag him inside and take him straight to her bedroom. Her toes actually tingled, remembering. Her womb felt heavy, her breasts full, recalling now how she'd gone in alone and closed the door. Leaned against it, thinking of Alton. Hearing his voice.

Hearing his voice? How could she have forgotten his voice in her head, that sexy whisper . . . giving her orders?

Damn it all!

Telling me to come to Sedona.

Ginny clenched her hands into fists and bit back a scream that probably would have shut up every screeching animal in the room. It was him! This was all Alton's fault! Somehow he'd hypnotized her. That had to be it. He'd hypnotized her and made her forget the bear and his kiss and . . .

She growled. The macaw shut its big mouth and stared at her, but all Ginny could see was Alton. That insufferable jackass had sent her here. He'd saved her from a bear made of concrete with rows of sharp teeth, a bear that couldn't have been real, and he'd sent her down here to frickin' Sedona, Arizona, where the cats and bunnies and birds had the same kind of impossible teeth.

Ginny spun around and glared at her cousin.

Markus took a step back. "What'd I do?"

"Nothing. Not a damned thing." She sucked in a deep

breath and let it out. Something very weird was going on and Alton was involved, all the way from the tips of his sexy cowboy boots to the top of his beautiful blond head. "I have to make a phone call. You sign in. I'll be right back."

There wasn't a stitch of clothing covering her perfect body. She was tall and slim and her stylishly bobbed hair swung against her jaw with each step she took on gloriously long legs. If she hadn't been trying to kill him, Alton might have found her attractive. Instead, he wrapped both hands around the jeweled hilt of his crystal sword and swung with practiced ease.

The blade sliced cleanly through the juncture between her neck and shoulder. He watched with grim satisfaction as the mannequin's head bounced off the wall and rolled across the sidewalk. The jaws gaped wide, exposing row after row of razor-sharp teeth framed by perfectly painted pouty lips.

Alton stepped back out of the way, giving Eddy Marks plenty of space to aim the point of her crystal sword. She held DemonSlayer high, slashing through the demonic mist as it flowed through the hole in the mannequin's plastic neck.

The eerie banshee cry of the escaping demon sent shivers down Alton's spine. The screech ended abruptly the moment Eddy's sword sliced into the mist and it burst into flames. All that was left was a puff of foul-smelling smoke.

"Well done, my lady."

Eddy smiled at the sword in her hand. "Thank you, DemonSlayer." Then she sheathed her weapon and rose up on her toes to accept a kiss from her beloved Dax.

Alton couldn't help but think that Dax was one very lucky ex-demon, to find a woman like Eddy Marks, one brave enough to have gained immortality along with her own sentient sword. There weren't many women like her.

In fact, there were none like Eddy in his own lost world of Lemuria. As far as Alton knew, she was just as unique to Earth.

For some unfathomable reason, a fleeting image of Ginny Jones flashed through his mind—her body tall and lean with skin dark as night, and those gorgeous tiger's eyes of hers.

The image popped out of existence so fast it left him shaken. Blinking, he realized he was still watching Eddy and Dax.

"That was a new one," Eddy said when she finally peeled herself away from her lover. "Have you seen any others like her?" She nodded toward the mannequin lying on the sidewalk.

Alton dragged his gaze away from the two of them and stared at the mannequin. "Thankfully, no, but this isn't good. It was bad enough when demons were using ceramic and stone creatures as avatars, but plastic's a new medium for them. Can you imagine the chaos they're going to cause? There's no way to get rid of all the potential hosts for the damned things."

This latest demon invasion had begun less than two weeks ago. So far, demons could exist in Earth's dimension only as formless wraiths—smelly black mist without substance. They'd started out possessing ceramic, stone, and metal figurines, though they'd not managed to do too much damage.

This was scary, though, this move to plastic. The demon who'd possessed this mannequin seemed to have a lot more control than the ones who'd taken on the more primitive avatars. The creatures were somehow gaining power, even intelligence. It appeared they were actually evolving—and doing it way too fast.

Dax knelt down and ran his hand over the mannequin's body, as if he needed to see for himself what it was made of. "I want to know where these new demons are coming from. There shouldn't be so many. Not since Alton sealed the gateway from Abyss."

Eddy shoved her bangs out of her eyes and glanced at Alton. "Maybe they've opened a new one."

Nine hells. A new portal was the last thing they needed. Alton really didn't want to consider such a thing. He stared at Eddy and Dax and sighed. Just over a week ago he'd been a perfectly bored resident of Lemuria, wondering why nothing exciting ever happened. Then he'd helped two humans, a tiny will-o'-the-wisp, and a mongrel dog escape from a Lemurian prison in a separate dimension deep within Mount Shasta.

His life hadn't been the same since.

Exiled from Lemuria—a mythological world, according to humankind, which showed how little they actually knew—with a price on his head, he'd joined the battle against demonkind's invasion of Earth. Not that he was complaining about all the changes in his life, but was there no end to the damned demons?

Of course, Dax's and Eddy's lives had changed just as drastically. Dax the demon—kicked out of the hell of Abyss for good behavior—had become a demon slayer, working for the good guys to halt the demonic invasion of Earth. Eddy Marks was a newspaper reporter who had saved Dax's life without a clue what she was getting into. Alton knew the pragmatic journalist hadn't planned on becoming a demon slayer—or gaining immortality, a demon lover, and a sentient crystal sword that talked to her.

And Bumper was just a dog—a foster mutt Eddy had brought home from the pound to save from euthanasia. The dog barked. Alton leaned over and scratched her curly head. Bumper looked up at him, and Willow's thoughts flowed into Alton's mind.

I think that demon was the only one. Bumper and I checked.
Thank you, Willow. And Bumper.

He couldn't imagine Willow's life now, trapped inside a mongrel like Bumper. The tiny will-o'-the-wisp had been sent as Dax's companion, able to draw energy from the air to fuel his demon powers. In that last big battle on Mount Shasta when the demon ate Willow's tiny body, she'd managed to transfer her consciousness into Bumper just in time. While Dax no longer needed Willow for energy, Alton knew they all needed her as part of their team. Whether she looked like a tiny fairy or a curly blond pit bull, Willow had the soul and spirit of a warrior.

Just like his other companions.

Alton carefully sheathed his sword. HellFire, the crystal sword he'd had since reaching manhood, had finally, after so many millennia, gained sentience and begun to speak—proof that it finally considered Alton a warrior, a man worthy of respect.

They'd all earned that respect in the final battle with the gargoyle demon, which explained the crystal swords Dax and Eddy now wielded as well, replicates of his own sword.

DemonFire for Dax, DemonSlayer for Eddy.

Crystal swords, perfect for fighting the demon invasion that threatened to offset the balance between good and evil. Three warriors and their sentient swords, along with a mongrel hosting the mind of a bodiless will-o'-the-wisp.

They were all that stood between a demon invasion of Earth and the unsuspecting citizens of this world.

Alton was terrified they might not be enough.

Eddy's cell phone played "Ode to Joy." She reached for the phone and turned away to take her call.

A chill raced along Alton's spine.

Eddy stared at the phone in her hand for a long, long time. Then she slowly slipped it back into her jeans pocket. Alton and Dax were deep in conversation, and it looked like Bumper and Willow were right in there with them.

Bumper and Willow . . . BumperWillow. Eddy couldn't think of one without the other. Not anymore. Thank goodness she'd been able to get things straightened out with the shelter and they'd agreed to let her adopt her foster dog, Bumper, or they'd really have been in a fix. When the gargoyle had eaten the little sprite's body and she'd slipped into the closest available live host, at least she'd found one who loved and welcomed her.

The symbiosis between the brave little sprite and Eddy's funky mutt couldn't have been better, though after seeing how gorgeous Willow'd been before and how silly she looked as a pit bull crossed with a poodle, Eddy couldn't help but wonder if she ever had second thoughts about her choice of borrowed body.

But that was the least of Eddy's worries. Ginny Jones's phone call had just opened up a whole new can of worms.

"Guys," Eddy said, "we've got a problem."

Alton kept his arms tightly folded across his chest. He was afraid if he didn't hold himself contained, he would fly to pieces. Ginny was in danger, and it was his fault—all his fault—for sending her to Sedona.

He'd known there was more than one vortex in that Arizona town, but he hadn't even thought of the demons using one as a passage from Abyss to Earth's dimension. No, all he'd thought about was getting Ginny away from Evergreen and the demon invasion here.

Who in nine hells was he trying to kid? He'd wanted Ginny away, period. She was the most unsuitable distraction he'd ever seen and he wanted her gone because she was a danger to his own peace of mind. She'd have been safer if she stayed. This community was probably the safest one around for now, especially with the three of them keeping things under control.

He glanced at the headless mannequin lying in the alley. *Well, moderately under control.*

This was not good, but the problem in Sedona sounded even worse. Family pets with glowing eyes and multiple rows of razor-sharp teeth? Loving animals suddenly going berserk and attacking their owners? It sure sounded like demon possession to Alton, and he knew the others agreed.

Until today, they'd thought demons could only animate things of the earth—ceramic or stone, concrete or clay. Plastic was essentially more of the same, just a different material, but taking on living creatures as avatars took a lot more power, showed more intelligence.

Ginny could be in terrible danger, and it was all his fault.

Bumper whined. Alton looked at Dax and Eddy, and realized they were staring at him too. All three of them. What had he missed?

"Well?" Eddy planted her hands on her hips.

Alton blinked. "Well, what?"

She rolled her eyes. "Are you going? Is there a passage through the vortex that will get you to Sedona fast so you can check on Ginny? My best friend's in danger because of you."

He cringed. "I know. Yes, there's a passage, and yes, I'll go."

Eddy's sudden smile hinted at something more than mere concern for Ginny. "Be sure and pack some extra clothes," she said. "You might be gone for a while."

Eddy's dad, Ed Marks, gunned his old Jeep along the last steep stretch of dirt road. He'd offered to take Alton as far as he could up the rough flank of Mount Shasta, but they'd just about reached the end of the road. Alton knew he still had a long hike ahead of him before he made it to the portal.

The way was steep, the ground slippery with loose rock and scree that often meant slipping back two steps for every step forward, so the ride this far was welcome. Plus, he enjoyed spending time with Ed.

It shouldn't have surprised him, how much he liked Eddy's dad, but their close friendship had been an unexpected bonus. Alton figured it was as much his need for a father figure who treated him with respect as the fact Ed was just a hell of a nice guy. His own father still hadn't accepted that he was an adult, a capable man who could make his own decisions, but Ed saw Alton as a warrior, a brave companion to Dax and Eddy.

And he treated Alton like a man grown, which might have been silly under other circumstances. As an immortal, Alton was already centuries older than Ed Marks, something that didn't seem to bother Ed at all.

He wondered—would his own father ever see him as anything other than a disappointment? What would the ruling chancellor of the Council of Nine say if he knew his son's sword was now sentient, that Alton had proven himself as a warrior?

Fat chance of that ever happening. Now that he had a Lemurian death sentence hanging over his head for helping Dax and Eddy escape from their prison cell, Alton had to accept that going back to his world inside the volcano probably wasn't going to happen.

Still, it was something to dream of, his father actually learning his only son had accomplished what no other Lemurian in recent history had done—he'd established communication with his crystal sword. Even though the story of Lemurians as warriors and demon fighters was a huge part of their history, no one alive now—except maybe the reclusive Crone, a woman of legendary stature who had chosen exile for some unknown reason eons ago—could actually remember anyone strong enough or brave enough to bring their sword to life.

Yet Alton's sword spoke to him. Respected him enough to communicate, crystal sword to Lemurian.

In fact, as far as Alton knew, he was the only Lemurian alive today who'd actually taken part in battle using a weapon other than words. While his people took pride in being known as philosophers and statesmen, they'd lost their fighting edge—the very qualities that had kept their society safe for so long.

Just as they'd lost their strongest allies—their speaking crystal swords. The sword each young man received when he came of age had become nothing more than a fancy ornament.

Legend said the swords' sentience came from the spirits of demon fighters from long ago, the souls of powerful and brave men who'd bested demonkind in a war that had kept Abyss in line for millennia.

That didn't explain the sexy female voice in Eddy's sword, but it certainly accounted for the silence in every sword presented to every young Lemurian male. Why would any warrior's spirit want to speak with a man who didn't know how to fight and wasn't willing to risk his life for something of importance?

Their silence was understandable.

Alton had not only risked his life, he'd discovered an inner strength he hadn't known he possessed. He'd proved to both his sword and himself that he was a warrior, one willing to die for a cause he believed in—protecting the known worlds from the threat of demonkind. All civilizations linked to Earth, no matter what dimension, were at risk from the encroaching evil of Abyss.

The danger of reaching a tipping point, of the ages-old balance of good and evil finally slipping over to the dark side, was still very real, especially with the new threat of a demon king powerful enough and smart enough to lead the demon hordes to victory.

Gaining strength by the hour within his stone gargoyle avatar, the demon king had almost won. Dax's brave sacrifice and Eddy's strength and determination had bought a temporary victory when Eddy'd courageously risked death by wielding Alton's crystal sword. She'd beheaded the stone gargoyle and sent the demon king back to Abyss—for now.

But they knew he would be back.

Had he resurfaced in Sedona?

Alton stared at the trees they passed and thought about Dax and Eddy and the love between them that seemed to grow stronger each day. He would be jealous if he didn't love both of them so much. Eddy was brave and true, and Dax, a man who had begun as a demon, had shown more integrity and honor than anyone Alton had ever known in Lemuria. Dax and Eddy deserved the immortal love they'd found with each other.

So why did that make him think of Ginny Jones? She was nothing like Eddy Marks. Nothing at all. Ginny was mortal, her life no more than a tiny blip on Alton's life's screen. Plus, she was stubborn and opinionated and had no respect for a woman's place—a woman's role as the helpmate to her man. Not that Eddy was anything like the Lemurian women Alton had known, either, but she was Dax's problem.

Did that make Ginny his?

So long as she was in danger because of his screwup, Alton figured it must.

The engine revved and the Jeep's wheels spun as forward motion ceased. Alton glanced at Ed.

The older man shrugged. "This is as far as I can go, Alton. You'll have to hoof it the rest of the way." He slipped the gear into neutral but left the engine running. The trail wound upward from here, climbing through the last of the trees before it crossed areas of slippery scree, the shattered stones that littered the sides of the dormant volcano above the tree line.

Alton climbed out of the Jeep. He checked his scabbard to make certain his sword was secure, grabbed his pack, and slung it over his shoulder. "Thanks, Ed." He glanced around, orienting himself. It took a moment for him to realize where they were. Everything looked totally different in the light of day.

A harmless pile of rocks lay beside the road.

Harmless now, but they were the remnants of the gargoyle that had been the demon king's avatar, the one Eddy had destroyed with her singular act of bravery. She'd saved their lives—unfortunately, she'd missed the demon's soul.

Alton shook his head. "Hard to believe this is the same place where we fought the demon—and almost lost."

Ed slowly nodded in agreement. "I'll admit, I've never been so scared in my life. For myself, for my friends—the image of that monster twisting Dax's body and throwing him to the ground still wakes me up at night. I never thought I'd see the boy alive again." He cleared his throat, wiping a hand over his eyes. "The truth, though? Mostly, Alton, I was afraid for my daughter. Her bravery astounds me, even now."

Alton reached out and shook Ed's hand. "We don't need to worry about Eddy. She's a lot tougher than she looks."

Breaking into laughter, Ed threw the Jeep into gear. "That she is, son. Now you get. I'm worried about Ginny. She doesn't know what we went through here, so she doesn't have any idea what she's up against. You go take care of that girl." He winked, turned the Jeep, and headed down the hill.

Alton watched until the Jeep disappeared into the forest. Then he started the long hike up the hill. The entire mountain was an energy vortex, but there were only a couple of places where he could cross into the other dimensions and access the portal that would take him to Sedona.

Or the one that leads to Lemuria.

No. He couldn't think about home. He'd made his choice when he helped Dax and Eddy escape from their Lemurian prison cell. He'd walked away from everyone and everything he'd known and loved his entire life, but he'd chosen for the greater good.

He wondered if his friend Taron had had any luck convincing the Council of Nine to join the battle against demonkind. That was Alton's only hope of ever returning home. Taron could be persuasive, but were his powers of persuasion a match for the council's collective stubbornness?

The sun had moved to the west by the time Alton paused in front of a mass of tumbled boulders and knew he'd reached the portal. He wrinkled his nose against the stench of sulfur. There shouldn't be any sign of demons here, but their smell was all around him. That made no sense. He'd closed the portal to Abyss.

Unless they'd managed to open a new one.

Alton faced the lichen-covered rock, but before he stepped through, he removed his sword from his scabbard. As he wrapped his fingers around HellFire's jeweled hilt, he realized how much the sword's sentience had changed things. He no longer felt alone—not when he had HellFire beside him. Addressing the crystal blade, he asked, "Do you smell their stench as I do?"

The hilt vibrated in his hand. "I do," the sword answered. "I'm ready if you are."

With a nod, Alton stepped into the portal, walking through what appeared to be solid rock. The dark cavern he entered glistened with light from the various gateways leading to other dimensions: the green and turquoise that led to Atlantis, the gold and silver that would take him to Eden—and certain death should he attempt to pass into that hallowed land.

He stared at the gateway to Eden for a long moment. They'd been the first to recognize the demon invasion of

Earth, the ones to recruit Dax to fight demonkind, yet they remained in their insular world, unwilling to take part in the battle—and the demon king had been one of theirs.

Damn them.

He turned and stared at the portal that would take him home to Lemuria. Now, were he to attempt to pass, he feared he risked death as surely as if he tried to enter Eden's sanctuary.

Facing Ginny Jones and a whole passel of demonkind sounded a lot safer.

Alton turned his back on the gateway to his home world. The one that had once led to Abyss was still sealed shut. Why, then, did he smell the sulfuric stench of demons? Where was it coming from?

He held his sword high and used HellFire's glowing crystal blade to search along the stone walls. A small portal, tucked into a nook toward the back of the cavern, shimmered with the colors of a setting sun.

Sedona, Arizona. He recognized the multicolored hues of red rock and blue skies, but swirling within the portal's depths he sensed something else.

Demonkind.

Demons had passed this way, and not so long ago. Were they somehow making their way from Abyss to Sedona, and then north through the connected vortexes to Mount Shasta? He would have to ask Eddy and Dax about that.

After he got to Sedona.

He touched the cell phone Eddy had tucked into his pocket and wished it worked within the portals, but Eddy'd explained to him how they needed towers to carry the signal, and there certainly weren't any deep inside the volcano's energy vortex.

Alton took a step toward the portal, but he caught himself, pausing in midstep as a dark mist slipped through the multicolored gateway. Silently it flowed along the wall toward the portal leading outside to the flank of Mount Shasta.

Demon! This certainly answered part of his question.

His sword vibrated with power. Alton swung. The crystal blade connected with the black mist. The demon screeched and burst into flames. Crackling and sizzling, it disappeared in a puff of smoke.

Only the stench remained.

Alton stared at the spot where the demon had emerged. A shiver raced along his spine. This one had come directly from Sedona. His heart gave an unfamiliar lurch with the proof he couldn't deny. Ginny was in Sedona—and so were the demons.

Demons powerful enough to take on living creatures as their personal avatars. Creatures strong enough to kill.

Holding his sword aloft, Alton stepped through the portal.

Chapter Two

"Who'd you have to call?"

Markus's question snapped Ginny out of her convoluted thoughts. "Eddy. I called my friend Eddy Marks."

"I hope it was important." Markus backed out of the parking space he'd taken at the supermarket. Without Tom. The vet had insisted on keeping the cat for observation, which suited Ginny perfectly. Damned cat had really chewed up her hand. She peeked under the bloody towel and wished she hadn't looked.

"You were gone so long I had to take Tom in to see Dr. Buck by myself."

Ginny scowled at him. Her hand still hurt like the blazes and not once had Markus thanked her for risking life and limb to catch his stupid cat. "Well, Tom is your cat, cousin of mine, and I would really like to get back to the house so I can clean up the mess your *sweetheart* of a cat made of my hand."

Markus stared straight ahead. "Aren't you gonna ask me what the vet said?"

Ginny shook her head. "I figured you'd tell me if he had any idea what happened."

Markus curled his lip and made a snorting noise. "He says

they're all possessed. Idiot. I knew he was into crystals and vortexes and all that New Age stuff, but I thought it was just for show." He laughed. "He's dead serious."

"Possessed? By what? The ghost of Christmas past?" Ginny stared out the side window as Markus drove the few blocks home. *Possessed.* It sounded totally unbelievable, but how else do you explain a cat with four rows of teeth, glowing red eyes, and a scream like a banshee on meth? A scream that sounded horribly familiar.

Since her memories of that crazy night in Evergreen had resurfaced, Ginny'd had the bear's ear-shattering scream stuck in her head. A scream that was nothing more than a louder version of the strange howl coming from Markus's fat old cat.

Had the bear been possessed? Had some sort of evil entity turned a concrete statue into a slavering, screaming killer? Something had made it come to life. She hadn't imagined the damned thing, though until her memory had started coming back, she'd thought it was just a weird nightmare.

But all those animals at the vet's—the birds and bunnies, cats and dogs—every last one of them acted unnervingly similar. Screeching, trying to bite, flashing those rows of sharp teeth, and staring with glowing eyes.

Possession didn't sound all that crazy when you took it in context with what they'd seen today.

With what had attacked her just a few days ago.

With Tom's vicious attack this morning. Damn but her hand hurt, but then, so did her brain, just thinking along those lines.

Markus turned the car into the driveway and pulled into the garage. "Okay. So maybe he's not an idiot." He shut off the engine and turned in his seat to stare at her. "How else do you explain all those animals? They weren't normal. Birds don't have teeth. Rabbits don't hiss and snarl and screech like that little bunny we saw today. Something's making them act crazy. If they're not possessed, what's going on?"

Without waiting for an answer, he got out of the car and slammed the door. Ginny sat in the front seat for a few minutes, thinking of Tom and the other animals they'd seen at the veterinarian's clinic . . . thinking of the concrete grizzly that had attacked her.

Thinking of Eddy's friend Alton. Why did she know he was the reason she couldn't remember anything? Now that she was away from him, the memories were growing clearer by the moment. She recalled him saving her from the bear, walking with her, even laughing with her.

Most of all, she remembered his kiss.

What she couldn't remember was why he'd kissed her—or why she'd kissed him and then totally forgotten it. She hardly knew the man, and Ginny Jones did *not* come on to strange men. *Not ever.* But she knew one thing for certain—Alton was the only reason she'd come to Sedona.

None of this made sense, and Eddy hadn't been much help, either. She'd merely said to hold tight, that she was sending someone, but she wouldn't give Ginny any details about who or why or what the hell was going on.

Muttering under her breath, Ginny rewrapped the bloody towel around her hand and followed Markus into the house.

Covering vast distances via the vortex might be more disorienting than moving between dimensions, but the 1,030 miles between Mount Shasta in northern California and Bell Rock in Sedona, Arizona, took less than a minute down a dark tunnel lit only by HellFire's crystal light.

Alton entered a cavern very much like the one he'd just left in Mount Shasta. HellFire quivered in his grasp. Portals to other worlds glowed against the rock walls. He looked into one that seethed with shades of red and black. There was something inherently loathsome about it, something foul.

No doubt about it—this portal led to Abyss.

HellFire was drawn to the gateway between Abyss and Sedona like filings to a magnet. The sword's vibrations transferred to his hand, his wrist, up his arm. Anger flowed from the crystal. A powerful sense of purpose.

This, then, was the demon's newest entrance, the one that allowed them access into Earth's dimension. It was only a few feet from the portal he'd just crossed through. Obviously the demons had discovered a new route to Mount Shasta, coming through from Abyss here in Sedona and switching to the Shasta portal, bypassing the need for the more direct gate he'd closed between Abyss and Mount Shasta.

HellFire glowed brighter, stronger. Alton felt the pull increase as the sword tried to reach the portal to Abyss. "As you wish, my friend." He stepped close to the swirling gateway and aimed the sword. A burst of power shot down the length of the blade and the portal suddenly glowed deep red, then orange and yellow, hotter still, until the rock turned almost white and began to flow and melt beneath HellFire's attack.

Within moments, the portal had melted shut. The sword no longer vibrated. Breathing deeply, Alton lifted the blade away from the quickly cooling rock. What had been an active portal between Abyss and Sedona was now nothing more than a smooth black wall of cooling, melted stone within the Bell Rock vortex.

Alton sheathed his sword, passed through the Sedona portal, and stepped out on the rocky ground near the top of Bell Rock. It had been centuries since he'd last been to the Arizona desert. He'd forgotten just how beautiful it was. The sun was beginning to set and he stood for a moment, lost in the glory of a desert sunset and the brilliant reds and golds of the rugged, wind-shaped bluffs. The gentle breeze seemed to sing to him, a deep hum that resonated within his—

"Where the hell'd you come from?"

Alton spun to his left and blinked. Row after row of mostly gray-haired men and women, many of them wearing loose robes or colorful skirts, sat cross-legged in the dirt.

Well, crap and nine hells. He'd materialized out of the solid rock, right into the middle of a geriatric meditation group.

Straightening to his full height, Alton pressed his palms together, fingers extended beneath his chin, and bowed his head. His waist-length blond hair, unbound, flowed over his shoulders like silk and he knew his almost seven feet of height, aided a bit by his tooled cowboy boots, made him look pretty impressive to this group of humans.

"I come from within," he intoned. He kept his voice unnaturally deep and bowed his head once again. Then, biting back a powerful urge to laugh, he looked straight ahead and walked solemnly past the rows of brightly garbed folk.

Popping out of the portal in the midst of an evening meditation class of aging New Agers hadn't been an issue the last time he was here. Of course, it had been a while—give or take six hundred years.

He really needed to get out more.

Still chuckling, Alton found a well-traveled trail that took him down off the mountain and into a parking area. The light was beginning to fade. Only a few cars and one old, beat-up, but artfully decorated bus remained. He figured the bus must be here for the group he'd surprised up on top.

Maybe he could catch a ride into town with them . . . or not. Grinning at the thought of Lemurian royalty hitching a ride on a dilapidated bus painted with rainbows and flowers, Alton set his backpack down in the dirt and pulled out the cell phone Eddy had given him.

He carefully followed the steps Eddy had shown him,

found Ginny's number, and pushed the button to connect the call. He almost cheered when Ginny answered on the second ring, but he managed to control himself.

"Is this Virginia Jones?" he asked.

There was a long silence. Long enough that Alton wondered if he'd done something wrong.

"Who's this?"

Nope. That was Ginny. "This is Alton. Eddy Marks's friend."

"How'd you get my number?"

Definitely Ginny.

"From Eddy. Ginny, I'm in Sedona. Is there any way you can come get me?"

"Sedona? How the hell did you get to Sedona so fast? I just talked to Eddy a couple of hours ago, and there's no way you could have come . . ."

"I'm here, Ginny, and I'll explain everything once I see you. I'm in the parking lot at Bell Rock. Do you know where that is?"

"I'll be there in fifteen minutes. And you'd better have some answers for me because I've definitely got questions for you."

Before he could answer, the line went dead. Alton stared at the phone for a moment before calling one more number. Eddy's voice mail came on. He left a message and wondered where she'd gone, why she hadn't answered the phone. Then he tucked the little contraption in his pocket and leaned against a rock. Folding his arms across his chest, he waited impatiently for Ginny while the night grew dark around him.

Ginny hated to admit how glad she'd been to get away from Markus as she drove her little Ford Focus into the parking lot at Bell Rock. She'd barely seen her aunt and younger cousins all day, and she had the feeling Aunt Betty was as freaked about her as she was over the damned cat.

In fact, this whole trip was turning out just weird.

Then the headlights swept over a tall, breathtakingly familiar figure, and thoughts of Aunt Betty and Tom slipped out of her mind. Damn, she'd forgotten how gorgeous Alton was.

Why didn't she have any old college friends who looked that hot? She'd not seen his hair hanging loose before. On any other man, long silvery blond hair hanging all the way to his waist would look horribly effeminate. On this guy, it was flat-out sexy. Her fingers practically twitched with the need to run them through the silken strands.

A twitch she'd damned well better get under control right now. She knew for a fact she couldn't trust this jerk any farther than she could throw him, and as big as he was, she sure as hell couldn't throw him very far.

He pushed himself away from the rock he'd been leaning against and walked toward the car. He had that long-legged, self-confident saunter that made Ginny's stomach muscles clench at the same time it set her nerves on edge. She unlocked the door.

Alton opened the door and looked inside the little car. "Hello, Ginny," he said. Then he frowned, tossed his bag in the back, folded his lanky frame like a pretzel, and slid into the passenger seat.

Or at least tried to.

"Hi." She cleared her throat and hoped her voice wouldn't crack again, but the man literally took her breath even as he pissed her off. "You'll have to push the seat back. Little lever down on the side."

He fumbled with the catch and shoved the seat back as far as it would go. His knees still stuck up in front of him, but he managed to get the seat belt fastened and the door closed.

He was too close. Much too close. Too tall, too sexy, too

overpowering. Too . . . everything. The combination scared the crap out of her. She'd never dealt with a guy like him in her life. "How tall are you, anyway?" She checked the rear-view mirror. No one was coming, so she pulled ahead to the parking lot exit.

"Eddy measured me. I'm six feet, eight inches tall. But I'm wearing boots. I think they give me a couple more inches." He tilted his head and stared at her. "Why? Does it matter?"

"Matter?" Ginny glanced to her right and then back at the road. "No, it doesn't matter. I was just curious." She shot him another quick glance. He was still just as hot. "What matters is how you got here so fast. I just talked to Eddy a couple of hours ago. You haven't had time to catch a plane, and even if you did, how did you get to Bell Rock? Why not a bus station or an airport?"

"What happened to your hand?" He reached across her front and softly touched the thick bandage wrapped around her left hand.

"My cousin's cat bit me. The one with teeth like something out of a cheap horror movie."

"Will you be all right?"

Now that was a question she could answer on a lot of different levels. Sitting so close to him was doing things to her insides she didn't want to think about. He got to her on so many levels she didn't know where to start. Even the low timbre of his voice seemed to vibrate deep in her bones.

She reminded herself that same voice in her head was the reason she'd come to Sedona. She was not going to trust him, no matter how hot he was. Ginny took a big breath and let it out. "I'll be fine, if it doesn't get infected."

"Did you see a healer?"

"A healer? You mean a doctor?" Crap, she knew absolutely nothing about this guy, other than the fact he was Eddy's friend, and she'd trusted Eddy as long as she'd known her. As pragmatic as Eddy Marks was, Ginny couldn't picture her being close friends with someone into all that mystical stuff, but a *healer?* Next thing, he'd probably be offering herbs and magic crystals. She shook her head. "I haven't had time."

He nodded. "I will look at it later."

"You?" She laughed. "Dr. Alton?" She glanced at him one more time before looking back at the road. "What is your last name, anyway? All you told me was your first."

He hesitated a moment too long. Ginny shot him another quick look and he turned away. Then he looked back at her and smiled. "Artigos," he said. "Alton Artigos."

"That's different. What nationality?"

He shook his head. "I'm not sure. It's an old family name. Probably changed over the years. Greek, maybe?"

"Yeah," she said, watching the road ahead. "Maybe." It came to her, just how little she really knew about Alton Artigos—if that was his real name. She really needed to call Eddy and find out a little more about this guy. Working for the Siskiyou County Sheriff's Department had turned her into a total cynic when it came to men, but it was her dating history that had really taught her the truth—the nicest looking guys could hide some pretty ugly secrets.

Then he chuckled. She wondered what he was laughing about, but she remembered the sound of his laughter. They'd laughed a lot that last night when he'd walked her home from town.

Before he'd sent her to Sedona.

She really needed to ask him about that. In fact, she needed to ask Alton Artigos a lot of things.

They drove in silence through town. Ginny spotted a Burger King about the time her stomach rumbled. She didn't hesitate and pulled into the parking lot. "I haven't had a thing to eat all day. Let's stop here, okay?"

She turned off the ignition without waiting for his answer, and Alton followed her into the restaurant.

Alton wasn't certain what it was about Ginny Jones that threw him so totally off balance, but one thing he was sure of—walking behind her and watching the shift and sway of that perfectly heart-shaped bottom atop her long, long legs had suddenly become one of his favorite pastimes.

She was so tall and lean and moved with such a fluid grace that she mesmerized him. When he stood behind her in line, the top of her head came almost to his chin. Even Lemurian women were not as tall. He liked that about Ginny.

Liked the fact she looked him straight in the eye without backing down or turning demurely away as a Lemurian maiden should. Liked the intelligence swirling in her fascinating tiger's eyes.

"You want a Whopper? Cheese on that?"

Alton blinked. "A what?"

Ginny laughed. "Earth to Alton? I asked if you wanted a Whopper with cheese or would you rather have something else?"

He shook his head. He had no idea what she was talking about. "Whatever you're having." He dug in his pocket for the wallet Ed had given to him. He still wasn't certain if he had their currency straight in his mind, but . . .

"I'll get it. You can buy when we go somewhere expensive."

She smiled at him. He loved the way her eyes twinkled and her full lips spread into a wide smile. Loved the glossy, dark red color she'd painted on her full lips, and . . . *oh, my. Loved hamburgers and French fries.* The tray Ginny grabbed carried a raft of scents that made his mouth water. He'd had these once before when he'd been out with Ed Marks. Alton followed Ginny to a booth in the nearly empty restaurant. He slid into the seat across from her.

Ginny handed him a wrapped burger, picked up the two bags of fries, and dumped them out on the open paper. Then she proceeded to squirt a huge glob of red catsup next to the pile.

Luckily, he'd had similar meals and knew what to do with the fries. He dragged one through the catsup, popped it into his mouth, and sighed. It was so easy to forget demons when faced with a really good French fry.

This was fast becoming his favorite Earth meal. Lemuria had nothing like this. Nothing at all.

They ate in silence for a few moments. Then Ginny took a swallow of her drink and wiped her mouth with a napkin. Her golden eyes gleamed.

Alton swallowed and carefully wiped his lips with his napkin.

"Why did I come to Sedona?"

He hadn't expected that. Didn't think she'd make the connection between his compulsive suggestion and her trip.

"Because you have cousins here?"

"Cousins I haven't seen for years because we're not all that close. Then all of a sudden you walk me home one night and I have this overwhelming need to fly to Sedona and hang out with cousin Markus and the twin brats. Why? What did you do to me?"

Alton sighed. Eddy and Dax had suggested he bring Ginny in on everything, but he hadn't really thought of how he was going to do it. When in doubt . . .

Honesty generally worked best. He'd learned that the hard way when he was a kid and tried to lie his way out of trouble. Lying just got you into more trouble.

"I wanted to keep you safe and I wanted you gone. You were a distraction I didn't want or need, but my compulsion put you in worse danger. I'm sorry, Ginny. That was not my intent."

"You arrogant son of a . . ." She glared at him. "I knew you did something. I knew it! You hypnotized me, didn't you? I can almost hear your—"

"Not really hypnotism. More of a compulsion." He reached across the table and gently took her hand, the one that was wrapped in white gauze. "This never should have happened. It's all my fault."

Ginny looked at his hands supporting her injured one. Then she raised her head and stared directly into his eyes. "I don't understand. How could I be a distraction? I hardly know you. And what do you mean by a compulsion? How could you compel me to do something I don't want to do? Why did you want me to come here? And what is going on with the animals?"

Alton glanced around and realized the restaurant had emptied out entirely since they'd been eating. "I have a story to tell you that you will find unbelievable. Open your mind, please, and accept what I say. I'm not going to lie to you, Ginny. Your life is in danger. Many lives—an entire way of life—are in danger unless we prevail."

Ginny slipped her hand free of his grasp and sat back in her booth. She folded her arms across her chest and her dark brows knitted together in a very attractive frown. "Why do you sound like you're frickin' nuts?"

He smiled. Then the absolute impossibility of the situation caught him by surprise. He burst out laughing. "Maybe because I find myself wondering exactly the same thing?" He reached for her hand again, the uninjured one this time. She let him take it. He gently squeezed her fingers. Ginny didn't pull away, something that pleased him more than it should have.

He gazed directly into her beautiful eyes and tried his best to explain. "Just a little over a week ago, some strange things began happening in Evergreen. Eddy told me that it was right after she went out for coffee with you, that very night, that she first discovered Dax."

Ginny's eyes went wide. "She told me Dax was a friend from college. That you were a . . ."

Alton nodded. "I know. She had to come up with something quick, something to explain two men who couldn't possibly exist. In fact, Eddy found Dax unconscious in her potting shed. He was badly injured, a man on a mission, very much in need of help."

Ginny sputtered and he said, "Bear with me, Ginny, and I promise to answer your questions after I tell you everything. Will you just listen?"

Ginny stared at him a moment. "Okay. But that means I get to ask you a lot of questions."

He smiled. "I promise to answer all of them." He squeezed her fingers and took another sip of his drink. "Dax is not human. He was a demon, cast out of Abyss, the place you call Hell. He was hired as a mercenary and promised he would receive his place in Eden, your Heaven, should he prevail. His job was to fight a demon invasion in Evergreen. He enlisted Eddy's help and the two of them, realizing they couldn't stop the demons on their own, eventually came to my world—"

"Whoa!" Ginny shook her head so hard her thick black curls slapped her cheeks. "Not human? Your world? That's a little bit too much to—"

Alton held up his head. "Ask when I'm done. There's more."

She glanced at their clasped hands, raised her head, and glared at him. "If you're just puttin' me on, I'm gonna be so pissed."

He grinned. "Not putting you on, Ginny. I am not human, either. I am Lemurian, from the—"

"No." She shook her head so hard her dark curls bounced

and she covered her eyes with her bandaged hand. "Please. Do not tell me that Ed Marks was right and there really is a lost world of Lemuria. I don't want to hear that at all."

He really shouldn't be enjoying this so much. Gently he tugged her hand away from her eyes. "I know. Eddy's had to, as she puts it, eat some crow, though we never thought of Lemuria as lost. It's been in the same place in a separate dimension from yours, deep inside the volcano you call Mount Shasta for many thousands of years. Except when the volcano erupts. Eruptions tend to cross dimensions. Then we move everything to Sedona and wait until stuff settles down again."

He looked down at Ginny's long fingers nestled against his longer ones. Her dark, chocolaty skin against his fair color emphasized their differences as nothing else could. She was human. Mortal. He shouldn't feel this way about her. Attracted by her beauty, her sense of humor, her beautiful golden eyes.

He was the closest thing to Lemurian royalty they had. She was a 911 dispatcher in northern California. He was immortal, already thousands of years old. She was, according to Eddy, only thirty-one. He shouldn't be looking at her and hoping against hope that she would believe him, that she would fall in with his story, no matter how absurd it might sound to her.

He shouldn't care so much.

He raised his head and looked at her. She watched him warily, like an animal held in thrall by a predator's eyes. He didn't want her to fear him. Didn't want her to think he was nuts. "I would like to take you there, to Lemuria, someday. If I can ever go back."

"If? Why can't you?"

"When Eddy and Dax and Bumper and Willow found their way through the dimensional portal into Lemuria, they were arrested and put into jail. When I helped them escape,

I went against the edict of our ruling body, the Council of Nine. For ignoring their ruling, I most likely have a death sentence on my head, but I believed Eddy and Dax when they told me that the fate of many worlds rested on the battle they were fighting."

Ginny was shaking her head now. He couldn't lose her, but all of this had to be more than any mortal could accept. She tilted her head to one side, and it was almost as if he could see her mind processing what he'd told her, trying to figure out what, if any, of his tale was true.

"Those weird reports we had in Evergreen, the ceramic and stone figurines turning up in pieces around town, that big battle where people destroyed all the statues from the cemetery. Was that part of this so-called demon invasion? What about the garden gnome that ate Mrs. Abernathy's cat?"

He couldn't have stopped his smile if he'd wanted to. "And the gargoyle that was supposed to stay put on the old library building but kept flying away, and the bronze statue found in pieces inside Eddy's house. We discovered that demons from Abyss were slipping through a dimensional portal to Earth. Unable to exist in their natural form outside of Abyss, the demons needed avatars, but they had to be something of the earth. Stone figurines, ceramic, metal, concrete . . ."

"The bear? That bear that attacked me? It was a demon?"

He nodded. "Actually, it was a bunch of demons, working together. That's part of what makes this invasion even more sinister. They're working together, under the orders of a powerful demon we've been calling the demon king, for want of a better name. We thought it was marshaling demons as an army, but we discovered that it was actually bringing them to Earth's dimension as a source of power. They came through the portal and found avatars so they could remain, but once the avatars were destroyed, the demons turned back into wraiths. Their energy was absorbed by the demon king. Eddy was finally able to destroy the gargoyle a couple of nights ago. It was a horrible battle. We could have died if not for Eddy."

Ginny leaned back in the booth. Her hand slipped free of his. He flexed his fingers and thought of reaching for her again, but she was shaking her head, laughing as if he was telling her a really funny story.

"You're nuts, aren't you? I swear, Alton, you almost had me going, at least until you said Eddy was the one who destroyed the gargoyle. Eddy has the softest heart on Earth. She couldn't destroy anything, even if her life depended on it."

The images of that last battle flashed into Alton's mind. Like Ed, he still had nightmares. "That's quite possible, but in this case, Dax's and Bumper's lives—and her father's—depended on her. She took my crystal sword when I was injured—a brave act that put her in grave danger—and destroyed the gargoyle. The demon king survived and escaped back to Abyss, but Eddy not only saved my life and her father's, she gained immortality for herself and Dax, and even for Bumper. Of course, that's because Willow now resides within the—"

"Uh-huh. Immortality? A crystal sword? This I've got to see to believe." Ginny stood up and gathered the remains of their meal. "Alton, you're quite the storyteller, aren't you?"

She walked away with the tray filled with their trash. Alton checked the sword strapped across his back and thought of removing the glamour that kept it hidden from human eyes. Then he glanced up and saw the teenage employees watching him from behind the counter. Later. He couldn't do it here.

Ginny walked out of the restaurant without a single glance to see if he was coming. Alton followed her through the door.

She was halfway to the car when he noticed movement in the shrubs ringing the parking lot. A skinny animal that looked like a feral dog was slinking along the edge of the bushes, barely visible in the dark. It stalked Ginny, shadowing her as she walked toward the car. The scent of sulfur carried on the gentle breeze.

. Alton drew his sword and raced toward the creature. At the last moment, the animal turned toward him and screeched, a loud banshee wail that raised the hairs along Alton's spine. As it crouched low, its eyes glowed red. Light from overhead lamps glinted off rows of razor-sharp teeth.

It jumped, springing at Alton with impossible speed. Alton turned to meet it. He swung HellFire.

The sword balked at the last moment. Alton's arm jerked with the unexpected change in direction and he hit the beast beneath its ear with the flat side of the blade.

It toppled to the ground, unconscious but still alive. Ginny screamed and came running. The questions tumbled out of her, faster than Alton could answer.

"What was that? Ohmygawd! It's a coyote. They never attack people! What did you do? Where'd that sword come from? You didn't have it in the restaurant. I would have seen it! What happened?"

He wrapped an arm around Ginny's shoulders. She was shaking like a leaf. "It's okay," he said. "Hold on, just for a moment."

He held his sword up. "HellFire. You stopped my swing when I would have killed the demon. Why?"

The crystal sword glowed and he felt the power race from the hilt to the blade. "It is wrong to kill a living avatar. The death of an innocent creature will feed the demon's power. Touch my blade gently to the beast, over its heart. I will draw the evil to me."

Alton heard Ginny's soft gasp, but he concentrated on the sword, on gently laying the tip of the blade against the coyote's chest where he thought the heart must be.

A black mist began seeping out of the stunned animal. Alton

drew it forth with the crystal blade until the coyote shuddered and relaxed. The mist reeked of sulfur, but before it could escape, Alton slashed through the wraith with his blade.

The mist burst into flames. Ginny's short little scream cut off as the air filled with the stink of the dead demon and a puff of black smoke disappeared into the darkness.

Before Alton could explain what had happened, the coyote sat up, shook its head, and took off in a wobbly run toward the nearby fields.

Ginny stared at the sword in his hand. "That smelled just like the veterinarian's clinic. Oh shit. Everything you said? No. It can't be. Okay, bud . . . your moment's over. Explain."

Alton held the sword out in front of them. The light it cast was bright enough to leave shadows. "Ginny, meet HellFire. I've carried this sword since I was a very young man. It has only recently begun to speak to me. A couple of nights ago when Eddy destroyed the gargoyle, we fought a terrible battle, one where all our lives were at risk. Dax's borrowed body, his avatar, was killed, but because of Eddy's bravery, all of us achieved status as warriors. Dax was given his life back and he and Eddy were gifted with immortality when Dax made a deal with the Edenites. My sword replicated itself, creating two more exactly alike, so that Dax now carries DemonFire while Eddy carries DemonSlayer."

Ginny didn't say a word. She stared at the sword. Then she raised her head and stared at Alton, and he realized she was in shock. He did the only thing he could think of.

After carefully stowing HellFire in the scabbard once more and setting a glamour on the glowing sword so that others might not see it, Alton wrapped both his arms around Ginny Jones, pulled her body close to his, and kissed her.

Chapter Three

How could she possibly have forgotten what his kisses felt like? Ginny's memories hadn't even come close. His lips were full and soft, sliding over hers with warmth and possession.

Everything he'd said, all the crazy stories and the crazier things she'd witnessed faded away beneath the sensual glide of his mouth over hers, the warm, wet thrust of his tongue against her teeth and the sensitive roof of her mouth.

She'd never been kissed quite so thoroughly in her life, never felt her body go soft and pliant so that it fit against a man's with such perfection. His angles and ridges seemed to correspond perfectly to her curves and valleys. Where she left off, Alton began. When Ginny breathed out, he inhaled. Even their hearts beat in a synchronized rhythm, pounding at breakneck speed, faster and faster, yet keeping perfect pace.

One with the other.

Ginny moaned.

Alton groaned.

She plucked at his shirt. It pulled loose from his jeans and her fingers found warm, living skin beneath. His callused palm slid against her back, skin to skin, leaving a trail of heat and sensation wherever he touched her. His fingers wrapped around her ribs and softly stroked the full side of her breast.

She arched into him, silently begging for more. Her nipples puckered up against the lace of her bra as his fingers glided closer.

A car pulled into the parking lot. Lights flashed over them, dousing Ginny like a bucket of cold water. She ripped her mouth free of Alton's and backed as far away as his arms allowed, breathing in and out in harsh, explosive breaths.

He leaned his forehead against hers and she felt his laughter before she heard it.

"Nine hells," he said, gasping for air with each harsh breath. "Nine hells and then some. Woman . . . what you do to me!"

For the weirdest reason, his curse alone convinced her. No one said *nine hells*. Not anyone from this world. Still sucking air, she stared at his chest. If she concentrated hard enough, she saw the leather strap that crossed from one shoulder, over his chest, and around his waist on the opposite side.

"Turn around." Ginny stepped out of his embrace and planted both hands on her hips. Damn it all if he didn't do as she said. He turned slowly and she saw it then, the tooled-leather scabbard across his back with that damned crystal sword glowing through the design. The jeweled hilt stuck out of the top, glinting silver in the reflected parking lot lights.

"I can see it now." She walked around him until she stood directly in front of him again and folded her arms across her chest. "I couldn't see the sword before. Not at all. How come?"

Alton smiled and his green eyes twinkled. "It's called a glamour, sort of a spell I cast to hide the blade from curious eyes. If you really want to see it, or if you know of the glamour, the sword will be visible only to you. It's a simple compulsion, one that doesn't take a lot of energy but it works for most people."

He shrugged and laughter crinkled the corners of his eyes. "If it's any consolation, I learned early on that a simple compulsion doesn't work on you. For some reason, you're much too powerful. That's why I had to kiss you the night the demon's avatar—that bear—attacked you. I tried a simple compulsion to make you forget, but it wouldn't stick. I finally had to resort to a kiss."

"That's the only reason you kissed me? To make me forget?" She ran her tongue over her just-kissed lips, aware of a horrible hollow feeling in the pit of her stomach.

He at least had the good graces to look embarrassed. "That's what I told myself, and it did work, at least for a couple of days." He placed both his hands on her shoulders. His palms rested, warm and solid, against her. "Truth? I was looking for any excuse I could find to kiss you, Ginny. I'm not sure why, but I thought you were absolutely fascinating the first time I saw you, huddled down behind that filthy garbage bin, swinging a piece of scrap lumber at a concrete bear five times your size. Even then I knew you were special."

"You did?" That was the best she could come up with? Shit.

He grinned. "I did. I still do. I'm so sorry I got you into this mess. I sent you here because I wanted to keep you safe. I never imagined the demons would invade Sedona, but it looks like that's what's going on."

"Markus told me that's what the vet said—that the animals were possessed."

Alton nodded. "The vet is very perceptive. They're possessed by demons—which means the demon king can't be far away. I need to get Dax and Eddy here. BumperWillow, too. I can't fight a full-out invasion by myself."

"BumperWillow?" He'd mentioned someone named Willow, but wasn't Bumper that mutt that . . . ?

"Bumper is Eddy's dog and Willow is the will-o'-the-wisp who drew energy out of the air to drive Dax's demon powers. The demon king, when it was using the stone gargoyle as its avatar, attacked and ate Willow."

"Ick! How awful!" She didn't even know Willow, but—

"Yeah. It was pretty horrible and we thought she was gone, but she'd managed to slip her consciousness out of her little fairy body just in time. She hid inside Bumper. With her body gone, though, she's stuck there, sharing Bumper's body."

He laughed. "The two of them seem perfectly content with the situation, but since both of them are in there, we've been calling them BumperWillow. Dax doesn't need Willow to access his powers anymore, not since he got rid of the cursed snake tattoo and got the phoenix, but—"

"Whoa. You're losing me here." Shared bodies and cursed tattoos. She needed some quality time with Alton if she was ever going to make sense of any of this. The weird thing was, she believed him. It was too crazy a story for anyone to make up.

And there was that disappearing, talking sword, Tom the cat and his glowing eyes, and the coyote with way too many teeth. Too many visuals to ignore, but they still made her head spin.

She really needed to sit down.

Alton's arm went around her waist. Once again, he was much too close, his body too perfectly aligned with hers.

"Where are you staying?"

And that voice. She wanted to sigh. Just sigh and melt against him like a stupid damsel in distress, except she wasn't in distress and she was no weak-kneed damsel. And just because she believed him didn't mean she trusted him. "I just got here today," she said. "I was planning to stay at my cousins', but I don't think that's going to work."

She stopped and took a deep breath, stepped back out of his embrace, and planted her feet. She needed the solid feel of pavement beneath her sandals. Needed to know she was standing under her own power. She'd never been quite as pragmatic as Eddy, but even if she was a little more open-minded than her best bud, her head was reeling with everything Alton had said.

Crazy as all of it sounded, his wild explanation answered so many questions.

"You just got here today?" Alton tilted his head and looked at her with a frown. "But I sent you days ago. I checked your house over the weekend to make certain you were safe. You weren't there. I thought you were already in Sedona."

She shook her head. "I flew into Phoenix on Friday, but I hung around and shopped. I really didn't want to come here. I mean, we send cards at Christmas, but I'm not that close to my Aunt Betty, especially since my mom, her older sister, died."

She glared at him and tried to look fierce. "I couldn't get past the feeling that I had to be in Sedona." Then she lost it entirely and laughed. This was all just way too bizarre. "I finally gave up, rented a car, and drove the two hours to my cousins' house, where I was immediately attacked by their cat. Now I find out it's all your fault."

Alton groaned. "I am so sorry for that. Will you ever forgive me?"

She wanted to be angry with him, but how could she? He'd wanted to protect her. She couldn't think of another man who'd been as thoughtful. All the men she knew wanted something from her, whether it was sex or money or help for one thing or another. She'd gotten quite good at saying no to all requests.

Alton had only wanted to keep her safe.

"Let me think about it," she said, teasing him, but it was obvious he didn't get the joke.

He merely nodded his head and stared at the ground. She

bit her lips to keep from laughing again. "Alton? I was teasing. You're forgiven. There's nothing to forgive."

He raised his head and smiled at her and she was sure she felt it all the way to her toes. "Thank you, Ginny."

She shrugged. "You're welcome, I guess. Look, we need to find a place to stay. My Aunt Betty is already freaking out since their cat went nuts this morning. She doesn't need any visitors right now, and I couldn't take you there with me anyway. There's no room, and no way to explain you."

She grabbed her cell phone out of her purse and punched in her aunt's number. When Markus answered she told him she'd decided to stay in town. He sounded relieved when he promised to pass the message on to his mom. Ginny tucked the phone back in her purse after checking for messages.

Nothing. Not even a message from Eddy, but if what Alton said was true, Eddy probably had other things on her mind.

Like an immortal lover? Sheesh . . .

"C'mon." Ginny grabbed Alton's hand and tugged him toward the car. "Let's find a motel somewhere and figure out what we're going to do next." She glanced at him and caught the raised eyebrows. "Don't even think of it. I'm tired and we are not sharing a bed."

Alton laughed. "If you say so." He walked with her, hand in hand, to the little car.

She hardly knew the man and she was planning to stay with him in a motel room tonight. This was not the way she did things. So why was she smiling like a total idiot?

Because the world was suddenly not the world she'd always known. Because there were demons and magic and her best friend forever was now immortal.

And there's a man walking beside me who's not even human, yet he makes me feel things I've never felt in my life. Good things. If she added it all together, it still made no sense, but Ginny knew she couldn't have wiped that smile off her face for anything.

She just wished the little frisson of fear that accompanied it would quit coiling along her spine.

Ginny made him wait in the car while she got a room in a place called a Super 8. He wasn't sure what that meant, but she seemed to know what she was doing, which was a good thing. He wondered if he'd ever figure things out.

This dimension was nothing like Lemuria.

No, it was so much better, so much more alive, that he couldn't get enough of it.

Couldn't get enough of Ginny either, for that matter, which probably wasn't his smartest move, but she fascinated him. Everything about her, from her attitude to her tall, lean body, and her beautiful tiger's eyes that flashed with life and light. He loved her dark, dark skin and the subtle scent that was all hers, the soft fullness of her lips and the way she kissed. He leaned his head back against the seat and closed his eyes.

Damn, but the woman could kiss. Her lips were so soft and sleek and her mouth fit perfectly to his. He realized he was running his fingertips over his lips in a vain attempt to bring back that amazing sensation.

He wasn't even close. Feeling like a complete idiot, Alton folded his hands in his lap and gazed toward the office. Ginny stepped through the door and got into the car beside him. "The place is pretty full, but I got us a room in the back. Two beds. I could only get it for tonight. They're booked solid tomorrow."

He nodded. "That should give us time to figure out what we're going to do next. I really need to get in touch with Eddy, but I'm not getting an answer on her cell phone."

Ginny drove around the back of the motel complex. "Have you tried the house?"

He shook his head. "I don't have the number, but you're

right. Ed would know what's going on." Why hadn't he thought to get Ed's phone number?

Maybe because he still didn't quite understand how cell phones worked. Telepathy was so much easier. Unfortunately, he'd been unable to maintain his link with Taron back in Lemuria, and he, Eddy, and Dax had never established a very strong connection.

Come to think of it, he had no connection at all with Ginny, so maybe it wasn't all that great.

Ginny drove slowly through the parking lot, staring at the various doors they passed. "I'll call once we get in the room," she said. "I know all of Eddy's contact numbers." She pulled into a parking space and turned off the engine. "It's that one up there."

She pointed to a room on the second floor. Alton unfolded himself from the small front seat and got out. He grabbed the scabbard with HellFire and the pack with his extra clothes and followed Ginny's instructions on how to lock the car door.

She handed a little plastic card to him. "That's the key to get into the room. C'mon. I'll show you." She tugged a small bag behind her that rolled on wheels and he followed her to the stairs. She did something to the handle on the bag and suddenly she had a tote bag. He grabbed it out of her hand to carry it for her.

"Thank you." She smiled at him and went on up the stairs. Alton followed, pleased that he'd obviously done something right by carrying her bag. With human women, one never knew. They were terribly independent.

It had bothered him at first, when he'd watched Dax defer to Eddy on so many points, until he realized that Eddy knew more about this world and her decisions usually made more sense than something he or Dax might choose to do. It had taken some getting used to, women who were so self-assured, who had no problem taking the lead, even in battle.

He wondered what Ginny would be like if she were ever to fight beside him. The image of her striking out at that concrete bear when it had her cornered that night in Evergreen flashed through his mind.

Ginny would be an amazing warrior. Unfortunately, she was a mortal and no match for demons. Then he remembered that Eddy had been mortal when she'd bested the demon king, and she'd come through that battle in better shape than any of them.

He was still pondering that when they paused in front of a door that looked like all the others along this stretch. Ginny slipped her square of plastic into a slot on the door, waited until a light blinked, shoved the handle down, and entered. It all seemed relatively simple. Taron would love it here. His friend was fascinated by technology. There were so many amazing things humans used to make their lives easier—as well as a lot more complicated.

Alton followed Ginny into the room. It was fairly large with two big beds and a small table with two chairs sitting by the window. He really couldn't let himself think about the beds, not when he knew Ginny would be sleeping in one while he tried to sleep in the other.

It was going to be impossible, actually sleeping with her so close beside him, yet not with him. He put that out of his mind. No reason to borrow trouble.

He opened a couple of doors and found a closet and a bathroom. Everything they'd need for the night, though he could have done without the extra bed. Ginny tossed her purse on the one by the window and punched numbers into her cell phone. Alton left his bag on the bed by the door and slipped his scabbard off his shoulder. He left everything lying on the colorful bedding and went into the bathroom.

He still smelled the stench of demon on his skin and in his hair. While Ginny was on the phone, he took a quick shower. There were little tubes of shampoo and conditioner, similar to what he used in Lemuria, though at home they came in ceramic pots set into the walls of a natural hot spring in his private rooms.

He was scrubbed and out of the shower in a matter of minutes, but he'd forgotten to bring clean clothing into the bathroom. He ran his fingers through his hair and tossed the tangled mess over his shoulder. He'd comb it out later, maybe braid it the way he usually wore it. He'd hardly had time the past few days. Life in Earth's dimension was so much more complicated than Lemuria.

He glanced toward the closed door and listened. Ginny was still speaking to someone, so he wrapped a towel around his hips, grabbed his dirty clothing and walked back into the room.

Ginny's back was to him. He dug through his bag and found clean underwear and a new shirt. The jeans he'd been wearing would have to do for tomorrow. He didn't plan to sleep in them.

He dropped the towel and slipped on a clean pair of the soft pants Eddy'd called boxer shorts. After millennia wearing nothing but his flowing robes, he'd had a hard time getting used to such restrictive clothing, but the navy blue knit shorts with the narrow white stripes weren't too uncomfortable.

He was folding up his dirty clothes and stashing them in his bag when Ginny ended her call.

She stared at the phone for a moment. To think that just a few short hours ago, if anyone had mentioned demons she would have thought they were nuts. But the conversation she'd just had with Ed Marks had thrown an entirely new light on the situation.

She heard Alton behind her. She'd been vaguely aware of the sound of the shower, and the thought of him in there naked might, at any other time, have made her crazy.

Not now. There was just too much weird, unbelievable, and truly scary stuff going on—but when she turned around, she almost dropped the phone.

He was on the other side of the bed, his fair skin glowing and damp from the shower, his long hair hanging loose over his shoulders in thick, wet, streaky blond tangles. A fitted pair of knit boxer shorts hugged his slim hips and muscular thighs, but they didn't come close to hiding the rest of him.

He certainly looked human, though surprisingly muscular. She hadn't expected the ripple of muscle across his chest, the dusting of pale gold hair connecting two perfectly shaped, coppery nipples, or the hard ridges defining his flat belly. Water beaded on his skin and glistened in the perfect dip of his navel. A darker line of hair trailed down from the indentation and disappeared beneath the elastic band of his shorts.

Ginny swallowed. She raised her chin and caught Alton grinning at her, obviously well aware of what she'd been admiring. She felt heat rising from her chest to her cheeks. "I just talked to Ed," she said. Or tried to say. She cleared her throat. "Eddy and Dax are somewhere up near Grant's Pass, Oregon. There've been reports of cats and dogs acting crazy, sort of like what we've got here in Sedona."

Alton walked around the bed and sat on the side closest to her, totally unconcerned about the fact he was wearing nothing but his underwear. "I was afraid of that," he said. "There's a place I've heard of in southern Oregon. Eddy says it's just a tourist spot, but in Lemuria we've long been aware of it as a lesser vortex. It's similar to Mount Shasta—the same idea, anyway, though not as powerful. The demons must have created another portal to cross through from Abyss."

She would not look at anything but his eyes. It was impossible to carry on a conversation with all that beautiful bare skin so close—so clean and damp and utterly touchable. At least he had gorgeous green eyes. She could do this. Maybe.

"Where's their entryway here?"

His grin spread even wider and she was sure he knew what she was thinking. How much she wanted to look and touch and even taste. She was not going to go there. Absolutely not.

"Bell Rock," he said. "Though it might not be the only one. There are multiple energy vortexes in this area, but I found and sealed a portal in Bell Rock on my way here from Mount Shasta. We use the portals to move between dimensions— they're powered by the energy of the vortexes, and no, I have no idea what causes the power. They are what they are—and where they are. That's how I got here so fast, using the portal in the Shasta vortex. All of them connect on another dimensional plane. When I entered at Shasta and exited at Bell Rock, it was the equivalent of about a hundred yards down a tunnel. In reality it's over a thousand miles."

"I know. I flew here in a jet, remember?" She still couldn't believe she was having this conversation. It was just wrong on so many levels, beginning with the fact he was sitting here practically naked and they were talking about interdimensional travel. It would be so much easier if he'd just put his jeans back on . . . and if she could go back to thinking he was nuts. Unfortunately, everything was making such a weird kind of sense, she had to believe. Especially after talking to Ed.

Eddy's dad had sounded too concerned to be putting her on.

Alton nodded. "I know. And it's all my fault."

"You already said that. It's okay. You're forgiven." She sat on the bed and realized it was a mistake the moment she sat down. Their knees practically touched, so she slowly curled her legs under her and scooted back on the bed, like it was the way she'd planned to sit in the first place.

Except Alton's big grin said he knew exactly what she was up to. She decided to ignore him. Or at least ignore what she thought he might be thinking.

"So what now?" she said. "We've got demons taking over

animals in Sedona, possible demon issues in southern Oregon, and demons in Evergreen. Your entire army consists of one ex-demon and my best friend, both armed with talking swords, Eddy's dad, who has a bad hip and has to be in his late sixties, and a dog with a fairy stuck in her head. And you. I hate to be a killjoy, but that doesn't give me much confidence."

Alton laughed. "You forgot to mention my sword, or the fact that Eddy, Dax, Bumper, and I are immortal. We're not easy to kill. And Ed's hip is all better. That was part of the deal Dax made with the Edenites." After dropping that little nugget without more explanation, he sighed. "You're right, though. The demons are gaining strength and there are too few of us. I would like to study some of these possessed animals up close. Can you take me to the vet's clinic in the morning? With so many avatars caged, I might be able to destroy the demons within their hosts without harming the animals."

"You're kidding, right? You're just going to waltz into the clinic with your glowing sword and start killing demons?" He obviously didn't have a clue how the real world worked.

He shook his head. "Not quite. I want to be there before the clinic opens for the day. Hopefully a few staff members will have arrived early so they can let us in. I don't want to break your laws, but I'll use a compulsion to hide our presence. Once I have an idea how the demons are gaining control over their avatars, I'll know better how to fight them."

Maybe he did have a clue, after all. She'd forgotten about his ability to hypnotize people. Did that mean he was going to kiss everyone at the vet's? There'd been a couple of really cute assistants working there when she and Markus dropped Tom off, and . . . Ginny touched her fingertips to her lips.

Alton's soft chuckle had her blinking and staring at him. "What?"

"Your face is too expressive for your own good. No, I won't have to kiss anyone to compel them to forget my presence.

Remember? You're an exception, Ginny. I merely have to wave my hand in front of most people. You I had to kiss."

"You keep saying that like it's punishment." She tilted her head and cocked an eyebrow, well aware she was flirting with him. She never flirted. It just led to expectations she wasn't about to fulfill, but there was something about Alton. No. Flirting with him was an even bigger mistake, especially since they were sharing a motel room.

Before he had a chance to respond, she straightened up and said, "Tell me about your world. About Lemuria. According to Ed's books, you're supposed to have a horn in the middle of your forehead, wear long, white robes and lots of weird jewelry, and be close to twelve feet tall."

He flipped his long legs up on the bed, plumped the pillows, and leaned back against the headboard. He was so tall, he'd have to sleep crosswise, even on the queen-size bed, but he wasn't anywhere close to twelve feet tall.

He'd already told her his height. *Six feet, eight inches tall. Wow.* His green eyes twinkled with good humor and Ginny realized she was grinning right back at him.

"I've read all about your concept of Lemurians. Ed Marks had more than enough of our supposed ancient history. Not much of it, beyond our name, is right. Our name, and the fact that our world sank beneath the sea many thousands of years ago."

"That really happened?"

He nodded. "It did. I was still a child when the end came, but I remember our lives before, playing on the beautiful beaches, swimming in the sea. The island continent of Lemuria was a wonderful place to be a child."

"Wait a minute. You said it happened thousands of years ago. So how could you remember? You're what? Maybe thirty? Thirty-five?"

He got an odd, uncomfortable look on his face. Then he slowly shook his head and sat up, grabbed a comb out of his bag, and began running it through his long hair, tugging roughly at the wet tangles. After a moment he stopped. His shoulders rose and fell with the deep breath he inhaled and then exhaled.

He raised his head and smiled sadly at her. "I told you I was an immortal, Ginny. My world sank beneath the sea around twelve thousand years ago. I have existed, since my birth, for almost fifteen thousand of your years. Among my people, I am a young man. My father, who is much older than I am, remembers a time when we traded with the people of Atlantis, when our older members traveled among the stars."

He stared down at the tangles he'd snagged with his comb and sighed. When he raised his head, Ginny was almost certain there were tears in his eyes. "I've lived through the birth of your civilization, through wars and climate changes, earthquakes and volcanic eruptions. But never, in all my long years, have I seen a threat as terrifying as the one our worlds face now. Demons have always existed, but not like this. Not with the strength to actually offset the balance between good and evil. The strength to destroy your people. To end mine."

His pain arced between them, so powerful it was almost tangible. Ginny stood up and crossed the small distance between the two beds. She took the comb out of his hands. "Turn around, Alton."

He gazed at her a moment, and then he turned and sat in the middle of the bed with his legs crossed. She knelt behind him and worked the comb slowly through the long, silky strands of his hair, carefully removing the tangles one by one.

"You said Eddy and Dax went to Lemuria to see if your people would help fight. What happened with that? Why'd they end up in jail?"

He sighed. "It's a long, sad story. Lemurians were once great fighters. Your legends say we almost destroyed ourselves with thermonuclear war, but that's not true. We were a people of honor, armed with our sentient swords, and our fight wasn't with Atlantis or any other humanoid peoples. We fought demons and we kept balance between the worlds. Then, shortly before my birth, when Lemurians had the demon threat under control, my people began to fight among themselves. They came very close to destroying Lemurian civilization. By the time I was born, level heads had prevailed and our soldiers had become philosophers instead of fighting men.

"No one realized, though, that when our swords stopped speaking to us, it meant we had gone too far in our quest for peace through philosophical discourse. We had lost something important. Something that we, as a people, still needed—our strength in battle and our honor. When Dax and Eddy asked for Lemuria's help to fight demons, they were imprisoned. I think it's because the senators of the Council of Nine were embarrassed by their request. Embarrassed to admit they've lost not only the will, but the ability to fight."

Ginny finished combing out one section of his hair and went to work on another. "So why are you different? What made you decide to help total strangers?"

"I had been talking with my friend Taron. You would like Taron. He's like a brother to me, only Taron's a lot smarter." He laughed. "I was telling him how dissatisfied I was with my life. How I sensed there should be more, that our lives within the mountain were meaningless because we accomplished nothing. Essentially, I complained that we had nothing to fight for." He chuckled and turned to smile at her. "Don't ever tempt the gods. They often take your wishes seriously."

"So you met Eddy and Dax and just like that, up and left the only home you'd ever known?" She concentrated on a thick tangle and tried to imagine everything Alton had given up.

"It wasn't that simple. I went to the council and asked them to consider the captives' plea. I tried to convince them that the demon threat was real, that Taron, who discovered the threat even before Dax and Eddy arrived, had lost count of the demons passing through from Abyss into Earth's dimension. The council said it was not Lemuria's problem. That Earth must save itself and we should not get involved. What they don't seem to realize is that if Earth falls to demon rule, a tipping point could be reached. Lemuria and Atlantis could be next, and if they fall, even Eden might be lost. The battle between good and evil has gone on since time began, but we are faced with the fact that—this time— evil could very well prevail. If evil wins, the battle is over for all time. It's a terrible risk. One I couldn't ignore."

"Have you heard from your friend? From Taron?"

Alton shook his head. "No. I'm beginning to think that it might be worth the risk to return to Lemuria. We need help. My people were warriors once; maybe they can be warriors again. We need them. Our small band can't defeat demonkind on our own."

He reached across the bed for his scabbard and withdrew HellFire. The glowing blade fascinated Ginny, the sense of life she felt when she freed the sword from its sheath. She reached out and touched the blade, ran her fingers over the crystal. "It's warm," she said. "Almost like it's alive."

"I am alive. Haven't you been listening?"

She snatched her fingers back and stared at Alton. He looked just as surprised as she felt. Ginny turned back to the sword. "Well, Alton merely said you could speak. I guess I didn't realize the full ramification of that. I'm sorry."

She stroked the blade once again and ran her fingers over the jeweled hilt. "Alton, have you asked HellFire for advice? I mean, if the swords have been around for as long as you say . . ."

"Of course he hasn't thought to ask me. That would be too much to hope for."

Alton's snort disappeared behind the hand he pressed over his mouth. Ginny had to bite her lip. A snarky sword?

"HellFire, I apologize, but after carrying you for thousands of years with nary a word, I've not yet grown accustomed to conversing with you on a regular basis." Alton glanced at Ginny with raised eyebrows. Then he picked up the sword and held it across his lap. "Do you have any idea what we can do?"

"You and this woman must go to Lemuria. Speak with your father and the Council of Nine."

"Great. What if they throw us in prison, or worse, decide to kill me on the spot?"

The sword glowed a brilliant shade of blue. "They would not dare, not when you are accompanied by a sentient sword and a lost daughter of Lemuria."

Ginny felt a shiver run along her spine. She slowly pulled the comb free of Alton's snarls and stared into his green eyes when he turned to look at her.

"Lost daughter of Lemuria? Ginny?"

"Me?" Ginny cleared her throat and tried again. "You're saying that I . . ."

The blade glowed. "Descended from one who ventured forth from the continent before it disappeared beneath the sea. Her veins carry the blood of ancient Lemurian royalty, from a time before Lemuria was ruled by the Council of Nine. Her presence and mine shall ensure safety."

The crystal went dark. Ginny ran trembling fingers along the blade. Now it was merely cool and empty, like a beautiful piece of glass. "I don't believe that." She swallowed. "I'm not Lemurian. Look at me. I'm black!"

Alton still had a bemused expression on his face. "There are some among us who are darker skinned, though none as dark as you. Some of our men have crossed into Earth's dimension to consort with human women, but our fertility rate is so low, I never dreamed there might be children of such matings. Who's to say what woman that ancient Lemurian fell for." He laughed as he carefully slipped HellFire back inside the scabbard and set it on the little table by the window. "HellFire said you're descended from royalty. I knew you were special the moment I saw you. I just didn't know how special."

He turned around and pulled Ginny into his arms, but he didn't kiss her. No, he merely pressed his forehead to hers and stared deep into her eyes. "It explains why I couldn't use my compulsion on you. It doesn't work at all against Lemurians."

"I don't believe it." But she did. Deep inside, she knew the sword was telling the truth. Maybe that's why she'd never wanted to leave the little town of Evergreen, so close beside Mount Shasta. She'd felt drawn to the volcano. Always knew she wanted to live close by, even though she'd never believed any of that mystical stuff that people always talked about.

Maybe she should have been listening a little closer.

"What were your parents like?"

She blinked and stared at Alton. Shook her head. "I don't know. I was adopted. All I know about my mother is that she was an unwed teenager from Sacramento. I was adopted by a couple in Evergreen when I was a newborn, but they were a lot older. They've both been gone for a few years now."

"Then Markus isn't really your cousin? Your Aunt Betty . . . ?"

"Nope. Adopted family. Aunt Betty was my adoptive mom's baby sister. No blood line to me at all."

Alton scooted back against the headboard, dragging Ginny with him. He held her in his arms as if she weighed nothing at all, and she had to admit, she liked the way it felt to be cuddled by a man as big and powerful as he was.

"So," she asked, "now what?"

"I wonder if you were targeted? Tom the cat, the coyote. Do demons recognize you as Lemurian? See you as an ancient enemy?"

She shivered, thankful for Alton's embrace but not at all

happy about his suggestion. "I hope not. I'd rather think it was coincidental if you don't mind."

He chuckled softly. "If you like. Now we sleep, if we can. Then we pack up our stuff and get any supplies we might need, go to the clinic early, and check on the animals. Then we go to Bell Rock, hike to the top, and step through the portal into the mountain. Once we're inside, we'll take the gateway into Lemuria and hope HellFire knows exactly what he's talking about."

Ginny tilted her head and, for some unexplainable reason, kissed his cheek. "You're saying you'll believe a snarky sword?"

Alton laughed. "He is snarky, isn't he? I don't understand why. Dax's sword is very polite, and Eddy's is definitely a very brave and calm female, which is really weird, if the sentience in our swords comes from the souls of fallen warriors. Lemurian women don't fight. As far as I know, only one woman may have ever seen battle, and her story is more likely legend rather than fact." He shrugged. "For whatever reason, Eddy and Dax have polite, even friendly swords."

"But you got snark?" She cuddled close.

"I got snark."

Chapter Four

Ginny didn't realize they'd fallen asleep until she awoke hours later. She went from sound asleep to wide awake in a heartbeat, immediately aware she was cuddled next to Alton with her cheek pressed against his chest. The room was dark, and they were lying down instead of sitting up against the headboard.

Alton was warm and their skin damp with perspiration where they touched. She was struck with the intimacy, the fact she'd actually fallen asleep beside him on the bed. She was still dressed, but all he had on were his knit boxers, which left a whole lot of Alton exposed.

He slept soundly with one hand resting on her hip and she lay there for a moment, silently critiquing the sensation of waking up with such a tall and powerful man curled around her. She'd never once slept through the night with a man.

Not that the opportunity hadn't been there, but she'd never known any man before whom she cared enough about or trusted enough to let her guard down around him. For some reason, she trusted Alton, which made no sense. She hardly knew him. Even more bizarre, he'd already admitted he wasn't human.

Neither am I.

Oh, God. She'd avoided thinking about what HellFire said. That was going to take some getting used to. Was she just going to accept the word of a talking sword? For that matter, was she going to accept the fact a sword could talk?

Hard to ignore a talking sword. Especially a *snarky* talking sword. This was all just way, way too over the top.

Never in her wildest dreams . . .

Biting back an impending case of nervous giggles, Ginny carefully slipped out from under Alton's arm, grabbed her overnight bag, and quietly went into the bathroom. She hadn't had a shower since leaving Phoenix so many hours ago, and even though it was almost three in the morning, washing off the grime of travel was her number-one priority.

She showered quickly, towel-dried her hair, and resigned herself to the fact she'd have frizzy instead of smooth curls in the morning. Then she slipped into her cotton knit sleep pants and the soft cami top and padded quietly across the room to her own bed.

A blue glow on the little round table by the window caught her eye. Could HellFire be awake? She glanced at Alton. He snored softly, but he'd rolled over on his side and his back was to her. Before she could talk herself out of it, Ginny carefully grabbed the hilt and slipped the sword out of the scabbard.

Alton's warning slammed into her thoughts just as she pulled HellFire free. He'd told her she couldn't use his sword in battle without risking death. She stared at her fingers wrapped solidly around the jeweled hilt, at the way it fit her hand, and hoped the threat didn't extend to quiet conversation.

Nothing happened. She let out a soft, shaky breath. Then she quietly lay the glowing sword on the floor beside the bed and sat down next to it, out of Alton's line of sight.

The blade shimmered with a soft, blue-toned light. She ran her fingers along the crystal, careful not to cut herself on the razor-sharp edge. Whispering softly, she asked, "HellFire? Are you awake?"

I am.

The voice was in her mind! Clear as a bell and not nearly as snarky as it had sounded earlier. She answered with her thoughts and hoped she was doing it right. *May I ask you a question?*

You may.

Oh, this was just too weird, but she'd been afraid of waking Alton and she had so many questions! *You said I was a daughter of Lemuria. How can that be?*

There are very few who walk upon the earth with the blood of Lemuria in their veins. Only when like meets like does the blood run true.

She thought about that a moment. When like meets like . . . *Are you saying that both my birth mother and the man who fathered me carried the blood of Lemuria?*

The sword glowed brightly and then went dark. Ginny stared at it for a moment before whispering, "Guess that's an affirmative." Maybe she should have asked HellFire if she could ask *questions,* as in plural.

A snarky, literal sword.

Smiling at the thought, she carefully slipped the sword back into its scabbard and set it on the table. She started to crawl into her bed when Alton rolled over and blinked sleepy eyes in her direction. "Ginny? Is something wrong?"

"No. I felt grimy. I just took a shower."

"Come back to bed. We have a busy day ahead." He was lying on top of the covers, but he raised the sheet, inviting her to join him.

She glanced at her empty bed and shivered. She didn't want to sleep alone. Not with Alton so close, but at the same time, she had a feeling she could be making a terrible mistake . . . or not. With a last glance at the dark sword, she walked around the extra bed and crawled in beside Alton. He covered her with the sheet and tugged her close against his side.

Within seconds she knew he slept, but Ginny lay awake for a long time, wondering about the blood in her veins and the legacy she'd not known of until now. Wondering what it meant, and how this knowledge might change her life.

Alton awoke once more during the night. Ginny slept close beside him, tucked up under his arm with her nose pressed against his ribs. When he'd reached for her earlier and realized she'd gone, he never dreamed she'd come back to his bed.

The fact she'd fallen asleep in his arms in the first place had thrilled him more than it should have. He'd been afraid to move for fear she'd wake up and leave his side, but she'd come back. Awake and aware, she'd still slipped into bed beside him.

There might be a sheet between them, but she was closer than he'd expected, more relaxed beside him than he'd dreamed.

Her hair had dried into tight little curls. He inhaled and smelled the same shampoo he'd used on his hair. With the warmth of her body beside him and the clean scent of soap and shampoo tickling his nose, he drifted back to sleep.

It was light when Alton awoke again. Ginny stood beside the bed, dressing. He barely caught a glimpse of smooth, dark thigh and curved buttock when she slipped out of the soft pants she'd been wearing. Within seconds she'd pulled on a pair of pale blue underpants and a matching bra, followed by snug, faded blue jeans and a stretchy T-shirt. Her hair was pulled back in a tight ponytail this morning. She pulled the end out of her shirt and fluffed the frizzy black curls with a look of pure disgust on her face. While she was fiddling with her ponytail, he sat up in bed and waited for her to notice he was awake.

She turned around and bit back a short shriek. Then she glared at him. "How long have you been awake?"

He faked a big yawn and stretched. "Just now. Give me a minute and I'll be ready to go." He noticed the fresh bandage wrapped around her fingers and palm. "How's your hand?"

She shook her head. "Healing pretty fast, actually. There's no sign of infection." She held her hand up and showed him how she could flex her fingers in spite of the bandage. "See?"

"Good. I'm glad it's better. What time is it?"

"It's early. Barely six. I don't think the clinic opens until at least nine."

"Someone may come early to feed the animals," he said. "We can park nearby and wait."

Ginny drove through a fast food place and they bought a couple of breakfast burritos and cups of coffee. It was only quarter to eight when she parked the Focus down the street from the clinic.

Alton reached in his pocket for his cell phone. He'd remembered to charge it at the hotel, but there were no messages on it. He tried calling Eddy, but it went straight to her voice mail, so he left a message that they were at the clinic to check on the possessed pets, ended the call, and stuck the phone back in his pocket.

He'd thought about telling her of his plans to take Ginny to Lemuria. Thought about it, and discarded the idea. If Eddy said it was too dangerous, what would he do? He still wasn't sure it was the right move, but he had to do something. Had to find out if his people were going to help fight this battle that seemed to be growing more involved, more confusing, by the day.

* * *

They had a good view of the parking lot and employee entrance as well as the front of the clinic. Alton sipped his coffee and studied the building. Ginny nibbled on her egg burrito and studied Alton.

He filled the passenger side of the little car. Even though the seat was shoved as far back as it would go, his long legs were bent and his head nearly touched the top. Still, he seemed relaxed as he stared at the little adobe building that housed the clinic.

As big as he was, he moved like a man confident in his body. He'd slept the same way, on his back most of the night on top of the covers, his long hair like a tangled blond halo around his head. This morning he'd pulled it into two long, thick braids hanging forward against the sides of his face. The ends were tied with colorful twine he'd woven into the braid.

She thought about how her opinion of him was changing. He'd been so arrogant and overbearing when they'd first met. Cocky to the extreme. She still thought he was arrogant and cocky, but why didn't it bother her as much?

She'd need to think about that one. She had no patience for arrogant men, never liked their attitude or the way they treated her. She'd definitely had her fill of macho types while working as a 911 dispatcher. There were the ones who looked down on her, either because of her race or her gender or both, or the ones who thought she was the kind of girl to lie back and spread her legs merely because she was female and they were such hot stuff.

She'd certainly straightened them out in a hurry. In fact, she was damned proud of her reputation at work as a ball-buster, but at least it kept the jerks away. She had no patience for them. None at all.

She wasn't sure if Alton had backed off on the attitude that bugged her so much at first, or if she was just getting used to him. For whatever reason, Ginny was actually looking forward to spending the day with him.

She wasn't all that certain about going to Lemuria, but in the back of her mind she fully expected Alton would stop at some point and tell her it was all a joke.

What if he didn't? She wished she could get ahold of Eddy. There was an awful lot she really wanted to ask her best friend. So many questions Eddy might be able to answer.

An SUV pulled into the parking lot beside the clinic. Ginny recognized the veterinarian when he got out of the vehicle—the same fairly young man, with dark, shaggy hair, and a neatly trimmed beard, whom she'd seen yesterday. Though Ginny hadn't met him, she'd admired the way he calmly checked out the animals when she and Markus had brought Tom to him. He'd been equally patient with the stressed-out owners hovering over their pets. He seemed like a nice enough guy—tall and lean with such kind eyes. He'd acted competent, if a little confused by the strangely acting animals filling his clinic.

Yesterday? Ginny let out a deep breath. Not even twenty-four hours ago. How could so much have happened in less than a day? She couldn't wait to see what was coming next. Alton set his coffee on the dash and climbed out of the car. Ginny followed him across the street to the clinic.

"Good morning, Doctor." Alton nodded to the vet.

The man jerked away from the door he'd just unlocked. "Goodness," he said, tilting his head back to look up at Alton. "You startled me." Recovering quickly, he smiled and paused with his hand on the door. "We're not open yet. And even if we were, all my cages and pens are full. I can't take any more patients, at least until we figure out what's wrong with the ones we got in yesterday."

Ginny smiled. "My cousin brought his cat in yesterday. You have Tom here already."

Before the vet could comment, Alton added, "Ginny's cousin said you believe the creatures are possessed. I happen to agree with you. I would like the chance to observe the animals, if you don't mind."

The man blinked. He took a step back and Alton passed his hand in front of the vet's eyes. The man blinked again, smiled, and held the door. "Come in. Please. Take a look. I just need to get everyone fed."

Ginny glanced at Alton. He winked at her and waved her through the door. She entered the clinic with Alton and the vet right behind her.

The place was quiet. She'd expected banshee screams and the reek of sulfur, but it smelled like a regular veterinarian's clinic, sort of doggy and antiseptic with an overlay of cat pee. Alton glanced at her and frowned, but he spoke to the veterinarian. "Where are the affected animals?"

The vet didn't speak, but he led them through a set of double doors. Cages and wire kennels lined the room along both sides. As soon as they entered the room, dogs started barking, but they sounded perfectly normal. The veterinarian had to raise his voice to be heard. "Dogs are here, cats in the next room. I need to get everyone fed. Feel free to take a look."

He walked away without a backward glance.

"Wow. Just your everyday mind control, eh?" Ginny stared at him for a long moment with her hands planted firmly on her hips. "Definitely effective, isn't it? That's what you did to me?"

Alton smiled as he stepped close to a kennel holding a large German shepherd. "That's what I tried to do to you. Didn't work, remember?" He sighed dramatically. "And that is why I was forced to kiss you."

Ginny flashed him a flirty grin. "Hmm . . . should I apologize for being such a tough sell?"

Alton smiled down at her. "Never apologize, Ginny. Not for being who you are. You're really quite amazing." Then, after dropping that bombshell, he merely added, "Notice anything?"

She blinked. Talk about switching gears! Going back to the subject of possessed animals, she shook her head. "Other than the fact they sound like normal dogs? No stink of sulfur, either. Look at that guy. Normal dog teeth. Where'd the demon teeth go? For that matter, where'd the demons go?"

"I imagine they've gone back to the void, unless they could find new avatars after leaving the caged beasts. Let's go check the cats."

They found the vet staring at the rows of cages filled with cats. A couple meowed quietly. He turned to Alton and shook his head. "This doesn't make any sense. All these animals were screeching yesterday. Their teeth had changed, their eyes were glowing. Today they're regular cats. I don't get it."

"I'm not positive, but I imagine once the demons realized the animals were going to stay caged, they lost their value to the demons. Demons took possession of the animals to give themselves mobile avatars in this dimension. It's the only way they can stay here and move about. Caged avatars don't do them any good."

Obviously confused, as much from Alton's compulsion and his offhanded explanation of the patently impossible demon possession as he was by the perfectly normal animals filling his clinic, the vet stared at Alton and shrugged. "I still don't get it. Where are the demons now?"

Alton glanced at Ginny. "I wish I knew. They can't last long in Earth's dimension in their mist form, but they could have searched for new avatars. Wild animals or pets running free, not caged. I imagine you'll be seeing an entirely new group of patients, animals possessed by the same demons that once inhabited the creatures you've got here."

The vet scratched his head and stared long and hard at Alton. "How do you know this? When I told people I thought their pets were possessed, they looked at me like I was nuts."

"That's because the truth is often frightening." Alton stared at the rows of cats staring at him from their pens. His words had a sense of destiny to them, as if he was making a pledge as much as explaining himself to the vet. "I come from a long line of demon fighters. This is the job I was born to do."

Then he seemed to reach a conclusion. "I want you to remember my visit after I'm gone," he said, brushing his hand in front of the veterinarian's eyes. "You're going to want to keep me informed of any new and unusual activity."

The doctor blinked and shook his head. He smiled at Alton, but now his eyes were bright, focused. "What did you say your name was again?"

Alton stuck out his hand. "Alton Artigos. And this is my partner, Ginny Jones. We were talking about the animals you saw yesterday. As I said, the demons probably fled once they understood their avatars were caged, but I'd appreciate it if you'd let me know if you have another rush of animals like these. I forgot to ask—how long has this been going on? Is it a recent phenomenon?"

"It's just bizarre. Yesterday was the first day folks showed up with their pets acting so strange. I've never seen anything like this."

"Then how did you know it was demon possession?" Alton's question seemed to catch the vet by surprise.

"Why . . . I . . ." He shrugged. "I don't know. They felt wrong to me. They looked wrong. It seemed obvious, though I guess most people wouldn't phrase it quite the same as I did."

"Here." Ginny dug a business card out of her handbag. "My cell phone number is here. I'm so glad to see Tom looking normal and healthy. He was scary yesterday. He got me good." She held up her bandaged hand. It still hurt.

"He bit you?" The vet took her card. "That's not typical behavior. Normal, socially adjusted pets don't bite people." He blinked and stared at the rows of caged cats. "They're nothing like they were yesterday. I need to call their owners to come and get them. Strange. It's all very strange." With a last, somewhat confused glance over his shoulder, he walked out of a room filled with perfectly normal cats.

"What now?" Ginny tilted her head. She gazed up at Alton standing so quietly beside her.

He shook his head. "I guess we go to Lemuria. There's nothing for us here. I sure hope HellFire knows what he's talking about."

The little half smile he gave Ginny wasn't all that reassuring. Not when he'd told her he had a death sentence hanging over his head.

It was cool and overcast when Ginny parked the car in the empty parking area at Bell Rock. She stuffed a few things from her suitcase into her daypack while Alton checked to see what he wanted to take in his. There was no point in carrying any more extra weight than they had to.

After locking the car door, Ginny slung her pack over her shoulder and adjusted the weight. Alton grabbed his. It didn't weigh much at all, as he'd pared it down to the minimum, but he didn't take more than emergency overnight stuff. With any luck, he figured they could be back before sunset.

He wished he felt luckier. He stared up at the deep red sandstone of Bell Rock and tried to imagine what awaited them, but he had no idea what might happen once he and Ginny crossed into Lemuria. HellFire remained dark and silent, though the solid weight of the leather scabbard across his back was a surprising comfort to him. More so, now that HellFire had found his voice.

What would his people think of his sentient sword? As nervous as he was about entering Lemuria after the way he'd left—sneaking out with escaped prisoners in the gray light of early dawn—Alton couldn't help but feel a sense of achievement. His sword spoke to him, proof he'd gained status as a Lemurian warrior.

And, petty as it seemed, he hoped his father would be proud. It was not easy, living an immortal lifetime as a failure, feeling as if he'd always been a disappointment. He hated to think what his father had been thinking of him over the past week. All the chancellor knew was that his son had failed once again—he'd broken a Lemurian edict and, as far as anyone in Lemuria knew, Alton was nothing more than a common criminal.

He shivered, seeing himself as his father saw him. Seeing himself as someone even worse than a failure.

"C'mon, Alton. What're you waiting for?"

Jerked out of his black thoughts, Alton shook his head. "Nothing. Just thinking," he said, but before Ginny had a chance to ask him what he'd been thinking about, he took off at a brisk walk along the well-marked trail.

Leading Ginny up the bluff, he realized he'd not thought of his lack of accomplishment since leaving Lemuria. He hadn't dwelled on his supposed failings, on the fact he'd not measured up as the son his father wanted. Only now, knowing he would be facing his father in a very short time, was he suddenly swamped in self-doubt and insecurity.

Since he'd left Lemuria, he'd been filled with confidence and he'd acted bravely, with honor. He'd changed. He wasn't the same man he'd been just over a week ago.

He was a warrior. A confident fighter, one who'd met demons in battle, all because he'd chosen to take a stand for the right reasons and risk everything for a principle he believed in.

The self-confidence that had begun to ebb reappeared. He

walked tall, proud of himself, proud of the woman beside him—just as proud of the sword slung across his back.

Pride goes before a fall. He shook his head. Now was not the time to be thinking of old human sayings.

They followed the worn path that led up and around the towering red rock. It was still early and the threat of rain hung close in the dark and heavy clouds.

They crossed a large, flat area where the wind had scoured the rock smooth. Alton recognized it as the spot where the class had been meditating when he arrived from Shasta. A few fat raindrops fell, sending up tiny puffs of red dust as they hit. Alton grabbed Ginny's hand and tugged her toward a perpendicular bluff of deeper red sandstone. "This is the portal," he said, stopping in front of the smooth wall. "We pass through here."

Ginny shook her head. "How? There's nothing there but solid rock."

"Watch my hand." He pressed his palm against the rock, hesitated a fraction of a second, and his arm disappeared into the stone. Ginny gasped and her fingers tightened around his.

"That's impossible. Absolutely impossible."

He grinned at her, and then, because he really couldn't help himself, leaned over and kissed her. Her full lips immediately softened under his, so filled with invitation that it was harder to break away than he'd expected.

He finally ended the kiss and ran his tongue over his lips, tasting Ginny. "Actually, it's not," he said. "I just did it, and so will you." He held her palm against the wall. "Imagine a tunnel. It's dark and cool with light glowing at the other end."

She rolled her eyes in his direction with a look that let him know exactly what she thought of his instructions. Then she stared at the wall, closed her eyes a moment, and her hand disappeared all the way to her elbow. Immediately she jerked it back out.

"Shit! I did not see that."

He laughed. "Well, you would have if you'd opened your eyes."

"I did open my eyes, about the time my arm disappeared." She twisted and turned her arm, as if she needed to make sure her parts were still where they belonged. "That is just wrong."

"I hope not, because we're walking through before we get soaked." The storm was moving quickly across the desert. It looked like a dark gray wall coming closer by the second. Raindrops splattered all around them, faster now. Harder. "Hold my hand and follow me."

"I really don't want to . . . oh, crap."

He grabbed her hand and stepped through the portal. Ginny followed close behind and within seconds they'd cleared the gate. Alton turned her hand loose and pulled HellFire out of his scabbard. The glow from the crystal sword lit the dark cavern.

Ginny's eyes were tightly shut.

"You can open your eyes now. We're inside." He laughed and held HellFire overhead. Shadows danced off the shimmering walls. Thankfully, there was no sulfuric stench, no sign of demons having recently passed.

He turned and smiled at Ginny. She was staring at the shimmering walls, her eyes wide, lips parted in absolute astonishment. "What is this? What am I looking at? How can we be inside a solid chunk of rock?"

"We're not actually inside Bell Rock. It's merely a portal. It led us into another dimension using the power of the energy vortex in the rock." He pointed out the various gateways. "That will take you to Atlantis, the one next to it goes to Eden, though if you try to pass through uninvited, you will die. That melted splotch on the wall was a portal directly to Abyss, but I sealed it when I was here yesterday."

"Un-frickin-believable."

Laughing, he dragged her down the tunnel a short way. "If

you pass through that one, you'll end up in Mount Shasta. Takes just a couple of minutes to cover the distance. That's how we'll go home when it's time."

Ginny shook her head so hard her frizzy ponytail slapped the sides of her face. "This is absolutely unreal. Where's the one to Lemuria?"

"This way." He tugged her back to the main part of the cavern. The gateway to Lemuria beckoned with a golden glow. Alton tightened his grasp on Ginny and held his sword in front of them. "HellFire? You're sure this is safe? I don't want to expose Ginny to any danger."

"Every war is fraught with danger, but no one in Lemuria would dare cross a sentient crystal sword. Nor would they harm a daughter of Lemuria. Go."

Alton raised his eyebrows and glanced at Ginny. She looked like she was trying not to laugh. "If you say so," he said. Holding the sword high, he and Ginny crossed through the swirling gold portal and stepped onto the pathway that would take him home.

"What's that noise?" Ginny grabbed Alton's arm and planted both feet. She wasn't going to take another step until he explained the deep roaring sound that echoed throughout the tunnel they'd popped into once they passed through the portal. Gold light shimmered on the walls around them, but the sound seemed to pulse within her skull, so powerful, so all consuming that she was certain her heart had taken up its beat, that her breathing was locked to its cadence.

"It's energy—nothing more than visual and audio effects set up to protect Lemuria from invaders." Alton slipped his pack higher on his shoulder, grabbed her hand, and tugged her forward. "You'll see. It's pretty cool, actually."

"I'll believe that when I see it." Grumbling, Ginny wrapped her fingers around Alton's. They followed the pathway for a short distance. The roar grew louder with each step they took, until Ginny felt as if she'd become part of the noise, as if her own heartbeat contributed to the din. The tunnel ahead seemed to glow and shimmer in time with the echoing sound.

Alton stopped. His fingers tightened around hers and he turned to look directly into her eyes. "This is it, Ginny. Once we go through the veil, I'm a wanted man. I don't know what's happened since I left, what's waiting on the other side."

"You said your friend stayed behind. Is there any way to reach him?" She wriggled her fingers in the air between them. "You know, like telepathy?"

He shook his head. "Not until we pass through the energy veil. I'm going to try as soon as we're on the other side."

She stared at the pulsing golden wall in front of them. It reminded her of a waterfall, but it could have been molten metal. The air was cool, though. Melted gold would have to be really hot, wouldn't it?

Still, when Alton stepped through, she just about freaked, but he tugged on her hand and gave her no choice. She shut her eyes and followed him through the flowing wall of gold.

There was absolutely no sensation at all as they passed through. Within seconds they'd popped out on the other side into a long, wide tunnel that wound deep into the earth. Ginny planted her feet once again and stared around her, at the tunnel leading forward, at the flowing wall of gold at their backs. Not in her wildest dreams could she have imagined anything even remotely as unbelievable as all of this.

"C'mon. We might as well just go for it." Alton tugged her hand once again.

Ginny shook the tension out of her shoulders, squeezed his fingers tightly, and walked beside him down the wide tunnel. So this was Lemuria? She almost giggled as she thought of her friend, Eddy, and all the years they'd teased Eddy's father about his fervent belief that Lemuria existed. Eddy'd definitely had to eat some crow over this.

They passed a few smaller tunnels that led off to the right or left, but Alton kept to the main route. Suddenly he stopped.

"Nine hells," he cursed. He dropped his pack and his fingers flew as he unbuckled his scabbard and shoved the sword and scabbard into Ginny's hands. "They're coming for me. I reached Taron, but it's too late. He said there are armed guards on the way. Here's my pack. Take HellFire and find Taron. Use the sword. It should be able to lead you."

Ginny slung his pack over her shoulder and clutched the leather scabbard. "But, I don't—"

"Hide. They're almost here." Alton leaned over, kissed her hard on the lips, and shoved her into a narrow passage.

Ginny stumbled and almost fell, but she managed to slip back into the shadows as a group of soldiers dressed in weird blue robes descended on Alton. Heart thundering in her chest, she bit down on her fingers to keep from crying out as two men even bigger than Alton grabbed him roughly and twisted his arms behind his back.

He didn't look her way. Did nothing to betray her. He didn't fight his captors, either, even when they lashed his hands behind his back and tied his arms tightly all the way to his elbows. He never made a sound, though the pain had to be excruciating.

The one who appeared to be the commander of the small force shoved Alton forward with a muttered curse. Then they marched him quickly back the way they'd come.

It had taken less than a minute from the time the soldiers had arrived until Alton disappeared from sight. Ginny stayed behind, hiding in the shadows with Alton's sword clasped to her chest, praying that no one would hear the staccato pounding of her heart.

The sound of the men's heavy footsteps grew distant as the soldiers marched away with Alton. Ginny waited, paralyzed as much by fear as indecision. Should she try and find Taron? Or should she go back and try to contact Eddy and Dax?

No. She had to stay here. She couldn't leave Alton alone.

Trembling, alone in the dark passage in a strange, unfamiliar world, she tried to figure out how she could possibly rescue her Lemurian.

Chapter Five

Ginny had no idea how long she remained huddled in the dark corridor with HellFire clutched in her arms. She had to find Alton if she was going to be able to help him, but she wasn't ready to go after him yet—not until she was sure they were far enough ahead that she wouldn't stumble over the soldiers who'd taken him. They'd been heavily armed. Their swords didn't appear to be crystal, but a blade was a blade.

She held perfectly still, conscious of the distant roar of the energy field they'd passed through and the thundering beat of her heart.

Then another sound intruded. Footsteps.

Trembling, she squeezed back into the shadows and held her breath.

The whisper sounded just beyond her hiding place. "Ginny? Ginny, are you here? It's Taron. I'm Alton's friend."

Ginny let out a huge breath. Taron! Finally. She poked her head out of the opening. The man in the long, white robe walking softly toward her, studying the ground as if he searched for prints in the dust, was every bit as tall as Alton, though his skin looked almost tan, not nearly as fair. Instead of silvery blond hair, his was so red it was almost scarlet. He wore it pulled back from his face in a long braid that looped over his shoulder. His eyes were as emerald green as Alton's.

She slipped out of the shadows. "I'm here," she whispered. "I'm Ginny."

Taron's head snapped up and he grinned. "That you are," he said. "Exactly as Alton described you. Come quickly, before someone sees us."

She nodded, clasped the sword against her chest, and adjusted Alton's pack and hers over her shoulder.

"Here. Let me." Taron grabbed both packs, took her hand, and led her down the tunnel, in the same direction the soldiers had taken Alton. After about a hundred yards, he turned off to the left and followed a narrower route. They walked in silence along a tunnel that appeared to be lit from within. There were no visible lights, yet Ginny could see perfectly.

After about ten minutes, Taron turned down another, darker tunnel, then another and another until Ginny realized she was hopelessly turned around and entirely confused.

She couldn't have found her way back to the portal if she'd tried. She had to trust Taron, trust the fact that Alton trusted him. It wasn't easy, hanging on to a strange man she'd never met before, following him through unfamiliar tunnels deep within a mountain that actually existed in another dimension from the only world she knew.

Oh crap. She couldn't let herself start thinking along those lines. Not if she wanted to stay sane and help Alton.

Taron stopped in front of a swirling wall of light. "In here," he said. He let go of her hand and stepped through, the light swirled shut behind him, and he disappeared. Ginny stood, locked in place, staring at the light. She could do this. She had to do this. Just walk right into . . . what?

Suddenly a hand popped out through the mass of colors and light. A hand, part of an arm, and a swirl of light and color. *Crap, crap, crap* . . . Closing her eyes, Ginny latched on to the hand so tight her knuckles turned pink, and shut her eyes when Taron—at least she hoped it was Taron—dragged her through the doorway.

Because that's exactly what it was. A portal of sorts, one leading directly into what must be his private quarters. She'd stepped through a wall of light and color into a comfortable living area with furniture that could have graced any suburban family room back home in Evergreen.

She knew she must look bug-eyed to the tall Lemurian standing in the middle of the room with his arms crossed over his chest. At least he was smiling.

"So, you're Ginny," he said.

She swallowed. "So, you're Taron," she mimicked. Then she grinned at him. "Thank you. I had no idea what I was going to do next. I was terrified when they took Alton away, but he seemed to expect it. Do you know if he's all right?"

Taron nodded and tapped a finger to the side of his head. "We've been close friends for so long, our telepathy is very strong. I've been in contact with him. They've put him in a holding cell, but he's okay. He'll be going before the Council of Nine in about an hour, which is comparable to light speed in this place. He wants me to bring you with me once he's taken into the court. You're sort of his ace in the hole, to use a human saying."

Ginny let out a deep breath. "He said he has a death sentence hanging over him. What if . . . ?" She hugged HellFire close. When it came down to specifics, she hardly knew Alton, but if anything happened to him . . .

She couldn't think about that. She just couldn't.

"I think they've decided to drop the death sentence. Have a seat." He gestured toward a low couch. "There's really nothing we can do until he contacts me." Taron reached into a cabinet and pulled out two glasses. He reached into another and grabbed a bucket of ice and filled the glasses. Then he poured an amber liquid into each of them. "It's tea, nothing more." He handed one to Ginny. She sat with HellFire in her lap and a glass of what had to be the Lemurian version of iced tea in her hand.

Taron seemed perfectly relaxed when he dropped into a chair across from her. If he wasn't worried, maybe everything would be okay. She hoped.

He took a sip of his tea and set the glass on a low table beside his chair. Then he leaned forward, planted his elbows on his knees, and rested his chin in his hands. "I've been arguing with the council ever since Alton left. I think the capital crime he was charged with has a lot to do with Alton's unhappy relationship with his father. Artigos hates to admit an error, and he has to know he acted precipitously by sentencing the two humans to death without a trial. That's not the way we as a people behave. I don't want you to think that."

Ginny nodded. "Alton said as much. That's why he helped them escape. He said it was wrong—that Dax, once a demon, had acted with more honor than the Council of Nine."

"He's right, and most of the council agrees. It's been a rough week for Alton's father. He is not a man to admit an error, and having the son show more honor in his actions than the father has been difficult for Chancellor Artigos to accept."

"You're not kidding it's been a rough week." Ginny sipped at her cup of tea. It had a totally unfamiliar but wonderful taste. And it was cold and refreshing. A good thing when she needed to keep her head clear and her thoughts in order.

"How are Dax and Eddy? And that little sprite, Willow?"

Ginny shook her head. "Good, as far as I know. I'll let Alton fill you in on the details since he was there and I wasn't, but I did hear that Willow is now living inside Bumper the dog since a demon ate her body."

Taron leaned back. "Nine hells. Really? Is she okay?"

Ginny shrugged. "As far as I know, she's fine. According

to Alton she slipped her consciousness out of her body before the demon swallowed." She waved her hand in the air and laughed. "Sorry. It's all still beyond me, but Alton said Willow is happy inside Bumper and they're both just fine."

Taron suddenly focused on the sword clasped in Ginny's hands. "Isn't that HellFire you're holding? Alton's sword?"

Ginny nodded. "It is."

Taron shook his head. "But how can you handle it without risk? We're taught from birth that only a man may wield a sword, and only the one he's gifted when he comes of age. I don't understand how you can hold it without harm."

Ginny stared at the sword in her lap. HellFire glowed a soft blue through the leather scabbard, proof he was listening to them. She carefully slipped the sword free of the leather and set it on the couch beside her. "HellFire? Did you hear Taron's question?"

Taron's soft gasp caught Ginny by surprise. "The sword speaks?"

"I do."

"Nine hells. He's sentient." Taron moved closer and knelt beside the couch, but he kept his hands folded tightly across his chest. Obviously he wasn't willing to risk touching the blade.

Ginny shrugged. "Alton told me he started talking after a big battle they were in with a demon. It was up on the side of Mount Shasta and Dax was actually killed before the Edenites brought him back to life, but then Eddy grabbed HellFire and destroyed the demon's avatar, which Alton said was enough to send the demon back to Abyss. The problem is, he's not going to stay there, or at least we don't think he is, because now we've got demons in Sedona and—"

"Whoa." Laughing, Taron held his hand up to stop her rapid-fire flow of words. "You're going to need to go slower. So Alton's actually been in battle? He's fought demons in Earth's dimension?"

Ginny nodded. "He said that's when HellFire finally started talking, though Eddy's sword and Dax's started speaking as soon as they appeared."

"Wait a minute . . . Eddy and Dax have crystal swords, too?"

Again, Ginny nodded. "That's what Alton said. He told me that HellFire replicated himself, except Eddy's sword is female, which I think is just cool." She laughed with the tale she was telling. Bizarre didn't even come close.

"Anyway," she said, stroking her fingers along HellFire's glowing blade, "now you've got me curious, too. HellFire, how is it I can hold you and speak with you when you belong to Alton?"

The blade shimmered brightly, then dimmed just a bit.

"You are a daughter of Lemuria. Your loyalty to Alton is pure. You hold him in your heart. Alton, son of Artigos, is a warrior true. You stand beside him, not behind him. You honor the warrior, therefore you honor Lemuria. You are worthy of bearing crystal."

Taron sat back on his heels. "Amazing," he said. Then he scrambled to his feet, crossed the room, and opened a closet door. Reaching inside, he pulled out a scabbard similar to the one holding HellFire. Inside was a sword of the same design.

The blade was dark. There was no sense of life to it when Taron removed it from the scabbard. He held it up and let the light shine off the crystal blade, but there was no fire from within. Nothing like HellFire's inner glow.

Taron studied his sword, turning it to catch the light before setting it on the couch beside Hellfire. "Each male carries a crystal sword." His rough voice, barely above a whisper, sent a shiver along Ginny's spine.

Clearing his throat, he continued in that same harsh rasp. "Mine will glow, but has never spoken. Swords never do—not anymore—but we've all heard the stories of their sentience, of swords coming to life. They're supposed to be the souls of fallen warriors come back to be our brave companions in battle."

He turned to Ginny and his eyes sparkled. "Did you know that legend says a sword dies if the warrior who bears it is killed in battle? The blade turns black, like obsidian. If a warrior acts in a cowardly manner, the blade shatters. All my life I've heard of swords coming to life, heard of them speaking . . . but until now, I've never actually heard one speak."

He stared at Alton's sword with pure longing written in his eyes, on his face. Finally Taron sighed. "May I touch you, HellFire?"

"You may. But only the blade. Do not touch my hilt."

Taron raised his head and his eyes twinkled. "Wouldn't think of it," he said, but Ginny noticed that his fingers trembled when he ran them the length of the crystal blade.

His sword remained lifeless and silent. Taron stroked HellFire for a moment. Then he quietly returned his own sword to its leather scabbard and once again stowed it in the closet. "One day I hope to join Alton in the battle against demonkind. For now, though, I've discovered that my strengths lie in another direction. My powers of persuasion are better than I'd realized. My arguments are what swayed the council to drop the death sentence."

Ginny replaced HellFire in the leather scabbard. "Does that mean your people will join the fight?"

"Not yet, but I see more and more of the men leaning in that direction. It's not going to be easy to change thousands of years of inaction, even with Alton's sentient sword. We are no longer warriors."

"Alton is. If he is, so are you. So are the other men. I don't think it's something you lose, not if it's born inside of you." Ginny stood up and started pacing. She couldn't sit still, not when Alton was a prisoner. Not when demons were taking over pets and wild animals in the town of Sedona and somewhere up in Oregon. Not when she hadn't been able to reach Eddy and had no idea if her friend and Dax were safe or not. And what about Evergreen? Was her town okay? Now that she was free of Alton's compulsion, she remembered all the weird stuff that had happened in her hometown just last week.

How could she ever have forgotten that horrible bear with all those teeth? Or Alton's bravery? He'd leapt up on the bear's back and risked his own life to save hers. She'd never seen anyone act so bravely—or foolishly—in her life. And he hadn't even known her. He'd acted purely on instinct.

A warrior's instinct.

For that matter, Alton hardly knew her now. They were still essentially strangers, yet she was here, hoping to help him, somehow, hiding out in another dimension deep within a dormant volcano—only she wasn't really in the volcano as she knew it on Earth. She'd entered through Bell Rock in Arizona—yet here she was, same place, same Mount Shasta she saw outside her window in Evergreen, California, only a different dimension, and it was all so unbelievable it made her head hurt.

But she was here for Alton, just as he'd been there for her. She needed to think about that, why and how he'd suddenly become so terribly important to her, but not now. Now she needed to act. Ginny raised her chin and looked into Taron's bright green eyes. "Alton's the bravest, most honorable man I've ever known," she said. "How can they treat him like a criminal?"

"That's what I've been trying to tell them, how I've attempted to sway Alton's father, Chancellor Artigos. He's the head of the Council of Nine and his feelings, one way or another, will affect how the other senators decide to vote. I've tried to convince him that Alton has acted honorably to protect our world, that the other men should be following his example, not censuring him for it."

"Alton says they've forgotten how to fight." Ginny paused in her pacing and glared at Taron. "Is that true?"

He shook his head. "I don't know. There are no warriors still living, none beyond Alton. The men living today were but children when the first demon wars were fought. They only remember fear and hardship. The oldest surviving member of our race, the only one who might remember, is a female, who, for some unknown reason, has chosen to exile herself from Lemurian society."

"I thought Lemurians were immortal. Doesn't that mean you live forever?"

Taron sat on the arm of the couch while Ginny paced back and forth. "Immortality means we have the potential to live forever, but our elders reach a point where they no longer find joy in life. When that happens, they choose to leave their physical bodies and become spirit."

"Like ghosts?" At least this conversation was taking her mind off Alton. A little. She wondered how long it would be before he called Taron to bring her. She wished she shared his ability to use telepathy. Not having contact with Alton was making her crazy.

"In a way," Taron said. "Much of our history is more legend than known fact. Most of our records disappeared when Lemuria sank beneath the sea, but we're taught that the swords our warriors once carried held the departed spirits of ancients. That Alton's HellFire, for instance, might have fought demons in the DemonWars thousands of years ago. Legend says there are spirits within the swords, but they don't want to converse with a man they don't respect."

Ginny nodded. "That's sort of what Alton said, why he was so frustrated even after battling demons, when HellFire wouldn't talk to him. Then when HellFire finally acknowledged Alton and started talking, he was"—she glanced at the sword, now tightly bound within the leather scabbard, and whispered—"sort of snarky. Like he was really pissed about being stuck in Alton's sword." She covered her mouth to keep from giggling.

"Snarky?" Taron glanced at the sword and grinned. "Alton got a snarky sword?"

"Yep. And what's really bad is that, according to Alton, Dax, the ex-demon, got one with a really classy voice, but the best is Eddy's. She's got a female sword that chatters away with her like they're girlfriends."

"But where did theirs come from?" Taron stopped in front of the scabbard Ginny'd hung over a straight-backed chair.

"Alton said after the battle with the demon, when Eddy used his sword to destroy the avatar, HellFire replicated himself."

"Nine hells. The council's going to have a fit." Taron paused and gazed off toward the door. Then he smiled. "Alton's being taken before the council now. Are you ready?"

Ginny straightened up. "I am," she said. And she realized as she said it, that she *was* ready. Calm, self-confident, and sure of herself. Sure of the role she would be playing—whatever that role might be.

She grabbed the leather scabbard and held HellFire in her arms, close against her chest. Taron picked up both packs, and when he stepped through the swirling doorway of lights, Ginny followed. She kept her eyes wide open this time, and her hands didn't tremble at all.

In the past, when he'd come before the Council of Nine in the huge cavern they called the great hall, Alton had been intimidated by the sheer age and power of the group, not to mention the icy stare he usually got from his father.

Of course, in the past, he'd usually been dragged up before the eight senators and his father, the chancellor, for some minor transgression or another. This was a first. He'd never actually been arrested before and brought here in chains. Never had to stand before his father as a wanted criminal with a price on his head.

He hadn't been told anything, though Taron had assured him that the death sentence—unofficially, anyway—had been lifted. He certainly hoped so. Dying wasn't on the list of things he hoped to accomplish with this trip home to Lemuria.

No, he wanted his peoples' help. The combined worlds needed their help. He had to bring together enough strong young men—men of the aristocracy, like himself—who wielded crystal swords and were willing to fight. Men brave enough to go up against the demons invading Earth's dimension.

Men willing to fight the powerful demon king when he returned from Abyss. There was no doubt in Alton's mind the demon king would be back if he wasn't already, and when he returned, Alton wanted his army ready with men who still carried the blood of demon fighters in their veins. Men like his friend Taron.

And women like Ginny—only there were no Lemurian women like her, even if she did have Lemurian ancestors. Lemurian women would never fight. Their lives were spent keeping the home calm and peaceful for their mates, not training and preparing for battle. He certainly couldn't see Ginny in the traditional, subservient role like that. Ginny was a warrior. She'd been one surprise after another. She was tough and strong and, for whatever reason, she believed in him. She trusted him.

Damn, but he hoped she was okay. Taron said she was fine, that she had HellFire and seemed to be holding up well, but Alton hated that she'd been frightened. Hated to think of her being treated with any kind of disrespect. At least he knew Taron would watch over her. So would HellFire.

He actually felt a connection to his sword. What a great

surprise that had been, to think that even though Ginny carried the sword safely locked away in its leather scabbard, he remained aware of and connected to his sword's sentience. The feeling was so powerful, Alton actually felt that if he called HellFire to him, the sword would come.

He hoped he had no need to test such a theory. No, this was not the time for theatrics. He merely wanted to get the council talking about the possibility of actually engaging in the war. He didn't expect immediate action—not from Lemurians—but he wanted to know they'd not closed their minds to the idea.

Now, though, as he stood in front of the empty dais, there were soldiers on both sides of him, traditionally dressed in the blue robes and stout sandals soldiers had worn for as long as Alton could remember. He'd seen images, though, of warriors of old, and they wore pants and boots. Tightly fitted, protective pants that allowed for freedom of movement, and high-topped leather boots for quick maneuvering and protection.

A robe would tangle too easily in a man's blade.

It was obvious to him now, since he'd actually been in battle himself, that the robes and sandals his people wore were a part of their nonviolent tradition. By dressing in a manner of scholars, not warriors, they made a physical display of the type of men they were.

Alton looked down his long legs at the blue jeans he now found so comfortable and practical, at the sturdy western-style boots covering his feet, and he felt like a warrior. His plain black cotton T-shirt made an informal statement as well. He had taken on the trappings of a warrior. He no longer wore the garb of a Lemurian scholar.

He was not the same man who had left Lemuria like a common criminal less than two short weeks ago.

The door behind the dais opened. Alton raised his head

proudly. He had no reason to bow before the council. No reason to act in a subservient manner.

He was a warrior. He had battled demons, and his sword spoke to him. With those thoughts in mind, Alton held his head high and smiled grimly as the nine members of the council entered the room. And when his father glowered at him, Alton merely dipped his chin in a show of respect.

Nothing more. He would not prostrate himself before these men. He had no reason to feel shame. What he'd done when he freed Dax and Eddy, Willow, and Bumper was right. It was done for the good of Lemuria. He stood proudly behind his decision.

Just as Ginny now stood behind him. He didn't need to turn around to know she was there, to know that she carried HellFire for him. He sensed Ginny, sensed her dismay that he was standing here in chains, but he heard the sword!

HellFire was in his mind, as was Taron. He wished he shared that telepathic connection with Ginny, but even without it, he knew she stood proudly behind him, supporting him. He felt her confidence and it lifted him. Gave him even more courage than he'd had mere moments ago.

Gave him the courage to stand tall and stare directly at each member of the powerful Council of Nine as they sat in judgment of his supposed transgressions.

His father stood. As the ruling chancellor, it was his place to pronounce sentence, but that should come only after a trial. In the past, Alton might have lowered his eyes beneath his father's critical gaze. Now he looked directly into his narrowed eyes and saw the man who had raised him.

Saw how much he had aged. Had Alton's actions brought about this change? If so, he regretted only his father's reaction, not the choice he had made to free prisoners unjustly held.

Chancellor Artigos stared directly into Alton's eyes, as if daring him to look away. Alton held his father's glare and returned it without rancor. Calmly he stood with his feet apart as far as the chains would allow, his hands bound behind his back with a chain that linked his wrists and stretched down to the one holding his ankles together.

Alton's father cleared his throat. Then he looked away. Startled, Alton realized the father was the one unable to meet the son's eyes.

"Before the proceedings begin," Artigos said, "I wish to make a declaration." He nodded to a scribe who sat to one side of the dais. "Strike Alton's name from the Artigos line. He has brought shame to our family. He is no longer my son."

Ginny's soft gasp and Taron's shock vibrated through Alton. He refused to react to his father's bald pronouncement, even as his heart stuttered in his chest. He'd never imagined his father taking such a terrible step. Never imagined it, but realized it made no difference to the choices he'd made. The choices he would continue to make.

Alton stared at his father—with nothing more than his will he forced the older man to look his way. Artigos had already turned to walk back to his seat at the center of the Nine, but he paused and stared back toward his son.

Alton raised his head as he spoke. "I imagine, Chancellor Artigos, that it is much easier to condemn a man who is not of your line. What you don't seem to realize is that it makes it that much easier for me to defy your unjust ruling. We are at war, Chancellor. Your denial of that war will not make it go away. Your refusal to accept my actions does not make them wrong. I have met demons in battle and they are a fierce and deadly threat. A threat to all of Lemuria, to all of the inhabitants of all the worlds connected through the dimensional gates. Denying that threat doesn't make it any less dangerous to our tightly linked societies."

"Guards? I would have you remove this man from our presence."

Maybe this *was* a time for theatrics, after all.

Before the soldiers at either side of him could react, Alton spun about and shouted, "HellFire!"

As if she'd read his mind, Ginny had already released the sword from the scabbard. She tossed it into the air. Alton turned his back and stretched his hands away from his body as best he could. The sword spun overhead, glowing with white fire as it twisted in midair, appeared to pause a moment, and then dove straight for Alton's back.

Screams and gasps of surprise filled the huge cavern. The crowd surged back, away from the dais. The guards stumbled over themselves, scrambling to get out of the way. Alton stretched the chains tight. HellFire flew true and the blade cut through the links as if slicing through butter.

Then it hovered in the air, defying gravity, awaiting Alton's hand.

Spinning around, Alton grabbed the sword with both hands, slashed through the chains holding his ankles, and spun once again in a perfect pirouette that put him between Taron and Ginny with the glowing sword clasped over his head.

He held the sword high and the light that burst forth from the crystal blade was blinding. The senators scrambled for safety, hiding ingloriously behind their chairs and beneath the long table. The guards had formed a loose circle between Alton and the dais, but it was obvious they were in awe of the glowing sword and unwilling to mount an attack.

After a moment, Alton lowered the sword, though the blade still shimmered with its own inner fire. Holding it firmly in his right hand, he reached out for Ginny. She slipped her hand into his, and with Ginny on his left and Taron walking beside him on the right, Alton led them up the nine steps to the dais.

The chains had fallen away entirely. He left them in a small pile on the floor. Alton's father was the only one still standing, obviously too shocked to move. "Sit down, Father."

Alton stepped forward and pulled the chancellor's chair out for him.

Artigos sat.

Alton retrieved Ginny's hand, squeezed her fingers tightly, and then he turned and gazed out over the huge crowd that had gathered in the great hall. All wore white, so that only hair color and faces set them apart. He saw friends he'd not seen in years. He saw his mother standing off to one side, her hands clasped nervously in front of her, and he couldn't help but wonder what she thought of his father disowning him. Had she been warned that would happen? Did she approve?

Did it really matter, in the overall scheme of things? Alton gazed down at the sword in his hand and looked to his left, at Ginny's broad smile. Taron stood beside him at his right, and Alton knew he could ask for no stronger allies. He held HellFire aloft once more. A brilliant beam of light flashed from the blade, encompassing Alton, Ginny, and Taron.

A unified gasp filled the great hall.

You're on, my friend. Alton's fingers tightened around the jeweled hilt.

HellFire spoke. Once more, gasps of surprise filled the room. Light blossomed and pulsed, until the entire sword glowed like a beacon as HellFire's words, somehow magnified, filled the huge cavern. "Lemuria is at a crossroads," he said in a strong, true voice. "Ignore the danger facing you now, and deny your descendants a future. Demonkind will rule into eternity unless you put aside your cowardly ways and take up the sword again. Discuss if you must, for that is the way of Lemuria, but you cannot ignore the threat that grows more powerful by the day."

The glow dimmed. Silence followed the sword's brief yet powerful warning. Alton took the scabbard from Ginny, fastened it across his shoulders, and carefully slipped HellFire into the sheath. Then he turned to face the Council of Nine.

The men had scrambled out of hiding and now sat in their respective seats as if nothing had sent them scampering.

Again, Alton squeezed Ginny's hand and tugged her forward. "Gentlemen, this is Virginia Jones of Earth. Ginny carries royal blood of Lemuria in her veins. You will treat her with respect." He grabbed Taron's hand next and placed it against his own heart.

"Because of Taron, we were warned in advance of the demon threat. Because of his powerful love of our world, he has stayed to argue the need for Lemuria to enter the fight. He, too, deserves your respect, as well as your thanks. Because of him, we may yet have a chance to prevail."

He released Taron's hand and once again faced his father. "You have disowned me as your son, but you will always be my father. I am sorry to have been such a disappointment to you, Father, but you were the one who taught me the importance of putting love of country ahead of all else. My love for Lemuria is worth more to me than my father's love. I regret it is a choice you have forced me to make."

Chancellor Artigos stared into his son's eyes with an expression of frigid disdain. Seeing his own future in that cold image, Alton realized there would never be a true meeting of minds with this man. Where Alton was open to all that was possible, his father saw walls. Where Alton's dreams were limited only by his idealistic imagination, Artigos would be forever trapped by boundaries and rules and the need to conform.

Alton could no more exist within his father's dark and hopeless world than Artigos could understand Alton's passion, his intensity, his powerful expectation of a future world free of the taint of demonkind.

They had reached an impasse. Alton finally acknowledged the painful truth—if he wanted to survive with his spirit intact, it was time to move beyond his father's narrow view, time to abandon his desire for the man's approval.

It wasn't going to happen. Alton accepted that now.

A rumble of voices caught his attention. Alton turned toward the sound and saw the crowd parting, but even from his vantage point on the stage, he couldn't see who or what they parted for. Holding tightly to Ginny's hand, he turned his back on Artigos, and watched and waited as the crowd slowly surged and separated, like a wave flowing across the cavernous room.

Finally a tiny woman, stooped with age and wrinkled beyond belief, came into view. Taron's soft curse had Alton looking away from the small figure approaching them to see what Taron knew.

"It's the Crone," he said, slowly shaking his head. "It has to be. I've heard of her, but she's not shown herself for thousands of years."

A chill spread over Alton's spine and raised the fine hairs on the back of his neck. He knew of the Crone, of the story of how Lemuria's only warrior woman chose to live in exile until her successor appeared. He grasped Ginny's hand tighter as the Crone reached the nine steps and slowly climbed them, one by one.

She was tiny for a Lemurian, barely five and a half feet tall. Her back was bent with age and her white hair hung in long tangles almost to her knees. Instead of the plain white robes most Lemurians wore, hers was a shimmer of amethyst that glowed with a dark light. Alton realized there wasn't a sound in the huge room. All attention was focused on the old woman and her painstaking climb up the steps.

Taron was the one who stepped forward and offered his arm.

She looked up at him and smiled. As wrinkled and aged as she appeared, her smile was that of a young woman, filled with the joy of life. Alton realized he was smiling back at her as she clutched Taron's arm and ascended the last few steps.

When she walked across the stage area of the dais, it was

Ginny she saw, Ginny who was the focus of the Crone's attention.

She paused in front of Ginny and tilted her chin to look up at her. Her smile grew even wider and her eyes twinkled. Golden eyes, just like Ginny's. "Finally, you have come," she said. "I have waited a long time for you, my dear. Give me your hand, child of my lineage."

"Yes, ma'am." Without any hesitation, Ginny held out her hand. The Crone took it between both of hers and brought it to her face. Ginny didn't take her eyes off the old woman, and Alton couldn't take his eyes off either of them.

"You are indeed a child of Lemuria. I felt your power the moment you entered our land." The Crone raised her head and studied Alton for a moment. "She is of my line, of my blood, and the power of the ages runs through her veins. Royal power. There is an ancient prophecy . . ." Her golden eyes twinkled and she laughed. "More ancient even than I, and believe me, I am very, very old." Then, still chuckling, still clasping Ginny's hand, she looked at her and began to recite—

> *Tall and dark as raven's wings,*
> *yet in her veins runs blood of kings.*
> *Her tiger's eyes and heart are bold,*
> *her hand a crystal sword will hold.*

The Crone paused and smiled, nodding as if at some private joke. Then she added, almost as an afterthought,

> *My gift to you, oh daughter mine,*
> *Long life to battle demonkind.*

The Crone raised her hands. She placed her palms on either side of Ginny's face and pulled her close. Then she kissed her full on the lips. Ginny trembled. Alton lunged forward as Ginny's eyes rolled back in her head and she began to sway.

Alton grabbed her as she slowly crumpled to the ground. The Crone, smiling once again, tipped her head to both Ginny and Alton, and backed away.

Stunned, Alton grabbed Ginny up in his arms and held her close against his chest. Her eyes were closed, her body limp. The Crone stood still for a moment at the edge of the stage, gazing at the two of them, still smiling as if she held a wonderful secret. Then she collapsed and fell slowly to the ground, folding in upon herself.

There was a collective gasp. All who could see the raised dais watched in horror as the old woman crumpled to the stage and her frail body and violet robe turned to dust.

Ginny struggled to consciousness in Alton's grasp. A breeze sprang up out of nowhere, lifted the dust particles, and dispersed them into the air. Nothing remained but a few ragged pieces of the Crone's violet gown.

Ginny shook her head and blinked. Then she looked from Alton to Taron. "What the hell just happened?"

"I'm not certain," Taron said, slowly shaking his head, "but I think the Crone just gave you immortality."

"Holy shit. Put me down. Please!" Alton lowered her legs to the ground, but she swayed as if they were made of rubber until he wrapped his arm tightly around her waist and supported her.

He glanced over his shoulder and cursed. "Nine hells. It appears HellFire has something for you, too." He slipped his scabbard off his back and pulled HellFire free. Directly behind his sword, a crystal blade glowed—but instead of the brilliant blue of HellFire, it shimmered purple, like a black light. "I imagine this one is yours." He held the scabbard out for Ginny.

She looked at him wide-eyed, without saying a word. Then she reached for the sword, wrapped her fingers around the silver and jeweled hilt, and pulled it free. She held it aloft, turning it slowly this way and that. "I don't understand. I'm not a warrior. I don't even like violent movies. I've never been in a battle. Why me?"

The sword vibrated in her hand and the glow deepened, shimmering with an eerie pulse of life. A vibrant yet familiar woman's voice rang from the depths of the blade. "I am DarkFire. You are the warrior woman of prophecy. You will have need of me in the days to come, as I have needed you."

Then the sword went dark.

Ginny raised her head and gazed at Alton. "It's the Crone's voice. A younger version, but I swear it sounds just like her." She shuddered, stared at the sword for a long time, and then shook her head hard enough to send her ponytail bouncing. She looked directly into Alton's eyes. "You said things could be a little dicey if we came back here, Alton. Just what is the Lemurian definition of 'dicey'?"

He stared at the dark blade. He'd never seen anything like it. Of course, he'd never seen anyone like Ginny, either. He leaned close and kissed her. "You have the spirit of the Crone within your sword. She's ancient and her knowledge of demonkind could prove to be invaluable. You are a warrior, Ginny. You fought the demon bear with nothing but a broken scrap of wood and your courage. You have Lemurian blood in your veins."

He paused and ran his fingers along her cheek. "Ginny, listen closely." *Do you hear me? You have me in your mind, just as I have you. Somehow you've received all of the gifts of your heritage. You truly are Lemurian.*

Chapter Six

Eddy sheathed DemonSlayer and leaned against the thick trunk of the redwood tree, sucking one deep breath after the next into her tortured lungs. Dax sat on the ground beside her with his head between his knees, breathing just as hard.

Even Bumper looked exhausted, standing with her feet spread wide and her head hanging low. Her curly blond coat was matted with twigs and other bits and pieces of the forest floor.

The air reeked of sulfur. A couple of dazed squirrels sat on the ground beside Bumper, oblivious to the small group of demon hunters.

Only moments ago, they'd sported rows of razor-sharp teeth and clawed talons. Now they were just typical gray squirrels suffering a demon-possession hangover.

Eddy finally caught her breath enough to nudge Dax with her toe. "Do you think we got all of them?"

"For now." He rolled his head back against the tree and smiled up at her. The sight of his sexy grin was enough to make her heart stutter in her chest. "This is a small vortex with just the one portal from Abyss and the one linking us to Shasta. The one to Abyss is sealed tight. You did well."

Eddy ran her fingers over the jeweled hilt of her sword.

This was the first portal she'd ever sealed on her own, and she'd decided immediately it was a chore she'd never grow tired of. In fact, sealing the gateway to Abyss had given her an amazing sense of elation—and power. Wielding Demon-Slayer made her feel like a warrior, but sealing the demons' gateway had been something else altogether—something only a crystal sword could do. Now, instead of backing Dax up with a crowbar or a baseball bat, she was truly armed for battling demons.

What a rush.

Bumper barked and Willow's voice blossomed in Eddy's mind. *There are no more demons nearby, but I'm worried about Alton and Ginny. We haven't heard from them since Alton left for Sedona.*

Eddy nodded. "I know, but we've been out of cell range since he left. I figure he can't possibly get into too much trouble in just one day. Still, we need to head back." She glanced at the two spaced-out-looking squirrels and laughed.

"At least no animals were injured in the making of this battle," she said, mimicking the disclaimer for a television commercial. "I'm glad we figured out how to force the demons out without hurting their hosts."

Dax nodded. He flicked his fingers toward the two dazed squirrels. "Get, you two. And don't play with demons." The squirrels ran up the closest tree, sat on a thick branch, and chattered indignantly at Dax as he slowly rose to his feet. "We need to contact Alton and see how he's doing. When you last talked to Ginny, it sounded as if the demons were possessing animals in Sedona, too."

Aching in every muscle and bone, Eddy shoved away from the tree. "We need to check on Dad and make certain all is okay in Evergreen first."

"And sleep," Dax said. "We've been awake for over twenty-four hours. We all need time to recharge." He rubbed

Bumper's curly head. She butted his hand when he stopped, blatantly asking for more. Willow didn't say a word.

Too tired to agree with Dax, Eddy merely nodded. They gathered up their packs and hiked quietly through the woods to the vortex. This one had long been a popular tourist attraction, but it was closed for the day. Luckily they'd arrived early, before the spot had opened, because the portal was in full view of the main attraction. Now, though, with the day growing late, it was easy to slip through the portal in the hillside that led to their gateway.

Once through, they'd still have to hike down the mountain to the road where Eddy'd parked her dad's Jeep. Dax was right. They were exhausted. Even immortals needed a few hours' sleep a night. Holding on to Dax's hand, with Bumper following close behind, Eddy stepped through the gateway to Mount Shasta.

Alton took Ginny's hand and walked down the steps from the dais to the stone floor of the great hall. Taron walked beside them. They didn't look back at the eight senators or Chancellor Artigos.

Neither did the soldiers try to stop the man who had been brought before the Council of Nine in chains. What had just occurred was unprecedented. HellFire's speech, Alton's warning, and the Crone's prophecy and death—and rebirth in the heart of a crystal sword—would be discussed, dissected, and argued for many years to come.

If they had that many years. Alton paused halfway across the room and turned to his friend. "I would give almost anything to have you come with me, Taron, but I believe your place is here. We have to convince them. *You* have to convince them. What happened today helped, but knowing the way they argue a point to death . . ." He shrugged helplessly. "It isn't going to be enough."

Taron nodded. "I agree. What are your plans? Will I see you again before you leave?"

Alton slapped Taron's shoulder. "Definitely. We both need food and rest." He tightened his arm around Ginny's shoulders. "And I should speak with my mother. Come to my rooms for the evening meal. We'll talk tonight, but Ginny and I must be away by daybreak."

"I'll be there." Taron glanced toward the dais. "I think I should meet with the senators and your father now, while they're too deeply in shock to argue."

Alton laughed. "As if that ever happens. Later, my friend. Thank you for rescuing Ginny."

She reached for Taron and laid her fingers on his forearm. "And for being Alton's friend. That can't be easy." She laughed and winked at Alton. "In fact, I've already discovered just how difficult it can be."

"Alton, have I told you how much I like this woman of yours? Thank you, Ginny. I agree. He's a pain in the butt." Laughing, Taron slipped their packs off his shoulder and handed them over, then he turned away and walked back toward the dais where the nine council members were already in heated discussion.

"Come with me." Alton adjusted his pack on his shoulder, grabbed Ginny's hand, and dragged her across the crowded floor of the plaza. Lemurians watched them pass, but no one tried to stop them or engage them in conversation. For all the questions people must have had, no one was willing to break protocol and ask.

Protocol. Alton glanced at Ginny and felt his heart twist deep in his chest. What was protocol when you'd suddenly discovered someone like Ginny? All of his obligations had changed from the first moment he saw her—yet his sense of duty had never been stronger or more clearly defined. What he did now, he did as much for her as for Lemuria.

Interesting thought, that. Ginny *was* Lemuria, in so many ways. The future of his world—a piece of its past.

Smiling with the surge of knowledge, he raised his head and caught the answering smile of a tall, fair, and breathtakingly beautiful woman waiting for him under a carved stone arch. Alton knew the resemblance between him and his mother was strong. He'd never been happier than he was at this moment, to know he favored her and not his father.

He stopped in front of her and tugged Ginny close. "Mother, I would like to present Ginny to you." Still holding on to Ginny, he took his mother's hand in his, connecting the women who mattered most in his life through his grasp. "Ginny, my mother, Gaia. I find it terribly apropos that she's named after Mother Earth, since it appears that is where my destiny lies."

Gaia leaned close and kissed Alton's cheek. Then she took Ginny's hand in hers. "It's good to meet you, Ginny." She sent a twinkling glance at Alton with eyes as green as his. "I have a feeling, my son, that your destiny lies more with this young woman than with the world that carries my name."

Alton couldn't have wiped the grin off his face for anything, nor did he want to. Ginny flashed a quick yet questioning look at him. He winked at her, and Ginny seemed to relax a little.

Smiling, she turned back to his mother. "It's good to meet you, ma'am, though that destiny thing remains to be seen. Alton and I hardly know each other. We've been sort of busy since we met."

"Fighting demons is rather time-consuming." Alton wrapped a possessive arm around Ginny. She might not have figured it out yet, but he wanted his mother to know his feelings, even though he wasn't all that sure of them himself. So much had happened in so little time.

"Will you be staying, my son?" From the look of sadness on her face, it was obvious his mother already knew his answer. She'd tried for years to make peace between him and his father. After today's events, even she must know it would never happen.

He shook his head. "No, Mother. Ginny and I will be meeting with Taron tonight and leaving early in the morning. The threat to Lemuria is more dangerous and immediate than we realized. I need to be where the battles will be fought. I need your help as well. If there is any way you can convince Father . . ."

Gaia slowly shook her head. "Oh, Alton. There's no changing that man's mind." She touched her fingers to his cheek. "When he was young, he was as open and idealistic as you are now, but he lost his idealism and his soul somewhere along the way. It was as if he changed overnight, but suddenly he was no longer the man I'd fallen in love with. Don't ever let that happen to you, my son. Keep your mind open to the promises that exist in all our worlds." She sighed. Her brilliant green eyes sparkled with unshed tears. "Most important, beloved son, keep your heart open to love."

Her fingers fell away from his face. "Your father forgot what love was long ago. He remembers only duty, and even that sense has become stale and perverted over time."

She leaned close and kissed Ginny's cheek. "Bless you both. Be safe. Come back to me soon and tell me how it goes in the worlds outside." Then she stood up on tiptoe and kissed Alton's cheek as well. "I love you, my son, and I am very, very proud of you. In spite of your father's cruel pronouncement, never, ever doubt my love for you. You are always my son. Only a very brave man would have the courage to make the choices you have made."

Before Alton could say anything at all, Gaia turned away. Her back was straight, her head high as she walked through the archway to the living quarters she shared with her mate.

Alton tried to imagine all the thousands of years his

parents had been together. How lonely his mother must be. Yet even after all this time, she still remembered hope and love, still clung to promises made.

His father clung to nothing more than his sense of self-righteousness. What a miserable legacy for a man to leave. Shaking his head over all of life his mother had to live without, Alton drew Ginny into his arms and hugged her close.

Shock didn't even come close to describing her state of mind. Not only was she clutching a crystal sword in her hand and hearing Alton's voice in her head, but the fact was, Ginny felt different.

Was this how immortality felt? She couldn't explain it. Wasn't even certain she wanted to, but her steps felt lighter, her body stronger, and the hand holding the sword . . . *Wow. Just wow.*

She glanced for the millionth time at the way her fingers curled around the silver and jeweled hilt as if she'd carried a sword all her life, and wondered how it could possibly feel so right in her grasp. The grip, perfect. Balance, perfect.

Alton stepped through a swirling wall of light and Ginny followed without hesitation. Energy portals? No big deal. She'd been through them before.

But she'd never been to Alton's home. She stopped dead in her tracks, aware of the sudden intimacy, the sense they were entirely alone. At least until she glanced at DarkFire in her hand and then at HellFire strapped to Alton's back.

The giggles hit her without warning. Within seconds she was doubled over, laughing so hard she couldn't catch her breath.

"Ginny? Are you okay?" Alton planted his big palms on her shoulders and his gaze was so serious she laughed even harder.

"I'm . . . I'm . . ." Tears streamed from her eyes and her

legs felt like rubber. She did what any normal woman would do under similar circumstances—she sat on the floor, right in the middle of the room.

DarkFire shimmered in shades of lavender across her lap. Alton squatted down in front of her, concern in his eyes, in his body language, in every careful move he made.

He probably thought she was nuts. Well, wasn't she? Ginny forced herself to take slow, even breaths. She scrubbed at her streaming eyes, sniffed, and bit back another wave of giggles before they escaped.

"Ginny?"

She flattened one hand over her eyes, waved him off with the other. "Just a minute."

Another breath. Then another. Then one big, deep one that she held inside and slowly released. Alton handed her a glass of water and she smiled gratefully. She sipped slowly and finally got herself under control.

"Okay," she said. "I think I'm okay. Just a minor meltdown. No big deal, considering."

Alton plopped down beside her, leaned close, and kissed her cheek. "Actually, I think you're handling everything quite well. It's not every day that a human finds out she's descended from Lemurian royalty, is granted immortality, and gets her own crystal sword."

He laughed and stroked her damp hair back from her forehead. "Actually, the fact that two crystal swords have now been presented to women and a third to an ex-demon is totally unheard of." He ran his fingers along DarkFire's amethyst blade. "As is the color of your sword. I wonder what the color signifies? I also need to make certain our scholars know of the blades that went to Dax and Eddy. I imagine they're already deep in discussion over yours. Maybe they understand the significance of the swords going to women."

Ginny swallowed more water. "Maybe the significance

is that there aren't enough male Lemurian warriors. Dax obviously earned his sword, but so did Eddy. Maybe, in order to win this war, women need to take up arms."

Alton shook his head. "I hate to think we've come to that. I was raised to believe women are the weaker sex. Eddy, and now you, are showing me differently. For whatever reason, if the spirits of ancient warriors inhabit the swords, those women in your swords had to come from somewhere. I need to learn more of the Crone's history. Who she was and how old. I've never seen a Lemurian old enough to actually look old before."

Ginny ran her fingers along the blade of her sword. "Are you in there, DarkFire? Can you tell me what your name was? I can't imagine your mother naming you Crone."

"Ginny!" Alton snorted. "You can't ask your sword things like that!"

"Why shouldn't she?"

The voice really did sound like the Crone's.

Ginny flashed a cocky grin at Alton. "Thank you, Dark-Fire. Will you answer my question?"

The blade glowed brightly, then dimmed just a bit. The sword spoke. "I was called Daria in my youth. I fought alongside men during the DemonWars. In those days long ago, Lemurian women were expected to take up arms in the fight to save our way of life from demon rule. Many women warriors carried crystal, and many lost their lives in those horrible battles, but they fought bravely, though our numbers were sorely depleted when the wars finally ended. Then the dark times came and the women warriors were taken away. Only I, because I chose exile before the purge, remained free. I have waited all these years for the one who would fulfill the prophecy. The one who would call me DarkFire and carry me once more into battle. You are that woman. The DemonWars are upon us once again."

The dark light in the blade dimmed. Ginny raised her head

and looked into Alton's serious gaze. "I think DarkFire just answered a few of my questions. The 'dark times' must refer to when Lemuria sank beneath the sea. What do you think?"

Alton shook his head. "I've never heard any of this, but crystal doesn't lie. The Crone, Daria, must have been a fighter during the DemonWars. It's hard to believe, but it explains so much. I wonder exactly what she meant by 'the purge,' and why this knowledge was kept from us?"

He stood and held his hand out for Ginny. "I have a scabbard that might work for DarkFire. I always wondered why my grandmother left me a scabbard that was too small for my sword. Now I wonder if it was hers."

He opened a closet and rummaged through for a few moments before dragging a cloth bag out of the back. Then he lifted out a beautifully tooled leather scabbard and handed it to Ginny.

"It's beautiful. Alton, are you sure you want to give this to me?" She ran her fingers over the leather, which felt as supple and fresh as if it were newly tanned. "Your grandmother's? It must be ancient."

He nodded. "She chose the spirit world shortly after I was born. I don't remember her, but my mother gave that to me when I received my sword. My father insisted I use the scabbard from his father, and since this one was too small, I put it away."

He ran his fingers over the leather. "I never dreamed I was saving it for you, Ginny, but that must be the way of it." *You are the woman warrior of the prophecy. I can think of no better demon fighter to carry this into battle.*

Ginny blinked back the sudden rush of tears. *Will I ever get used to your voice in my head?*

I hope so. Come. I don't know about you, but I could really use a long soak in a hot pool.

Ginny nodded. Carefully, she slipped DarkFire into the leather scabbard. The fit was perfect, as she knew it would be. Then she took Alton's hand as he tugged her to her feet, grabbed her bag, and followed him down a dark hallway that led toward the back of his rooms.

She felt strangely disconnected, as if her feet moved independently of her mind. Was this her way of accepting and adjusting to so many changes? She clung to Alton's strong hand, hating the weakness in herself that had her counting on him to guide her. She was not one to blindly follow, yet what choice did she have? Until she understood her new reality, she'd have to follow his lead.

They emerged in a naturally formed cavern with a small pool on one side. Candles burned in sconces along the wall. Their dim light reflected off spring-fed bubbles churning in the middle of the pool. Dark water overflowed and trickled out through a narrow crevice at the far end of the cavern. The air was hot and humid, the steam coming off the roiling water an invitation that was seductive beyond belief.

Ginny drew up short at the edge. There was only one problem. She hadn't brought a suit and she wasn't all that sure about getting naked with a guy she hardly knew.

Alton's eyes twinkled. "You know me better than you think. Don't worry. I may look, but I promise not to touch." He cocked one eyebrow in her direction. "I was a good boy last night, wasn't I?"

Ginny shook her head, laughing. "Yeah. You were a perfect gentleman. I'll admit, such behavior was highly unexpected." She glanced at him, unwilling to tell him the entire truth, the fact she couldn't think of a single guy she'd ever known who would have been as well behaved. She'd never once felt threatened by him, even when they'd slept all curled up together.

Even though he'd obviously been aroused, he'd not pushed the issue at all. She'd trusted him then. She trusted him now, but as tightly strung as she felt, it was herself she was a little concerned about. She flashed him a cocky grin she was far from feeling. "Anyway, I'll trust you, but you'd better be good. I've got a sword now, big boy."

"And a fine sword it is," he said, but she thought his laughter sounded forced. He stared at her for a long moment, but his thoughts were hidden from her. Then he set his sword and scabbard aside and pulled his shirt over his head, removed his boots and slipped his blue jeans over his long legs.

Ginny caught herself staring and quickly turned away. She gently placed DarkFire beside HellFire, slipped out of her shirt, sandals, and jeans, and with her back to the pool, unhooked her bra and removed it. She curled her fingers in the elastic waistband, closed her eyes, and quickly shoved her blue panties down over her hips.

She should have felt embarrassed, undressing like this in front of him. She didn't. No, she felt powerful. Not merely feminine, but very, very powerful. After everything that had happened to her today, how could she not?

Turning with complete confidence, Ginny walked across the stone floor and sat on the edge of the pool. Not until she'd slipped into the warm, bubbling water did she raise her head and look into Alton's eyes.

He watched her with a secretive little half smile on his lips. She frowned, more curious than she wanted to be. *What?*

You're beautiful. More beautiful than any woman I've ever seen. Beautiful and strong and nothing like I first imagined.

Oh? She laughed, and glided across the pool until she stood directly in front of him. The water came just to the tops of her breasts. She figured her dark skin against the dark stone pool made her almost invisible and that helped her relax. She wondered if she was all teeth and reflecting eyes when she smiled at him, which made her smile even wider. "So," she said, staring into his twinkling eyes, "are you going to tell me what you first imagined?"

Alton threw his head back and laughed. "If you like, but

it'll probably get me in trouble. I thought you were brave and beautiful and a complete pain in the ass. I remember thinking that Dax had chosen Eddy, which made her his problem. I wasn't sure I wanted you to be my problem."

She knew she was asking for it. Couldn't help herself. Couldn't stop the words, the body language, the unwelcome need rushing through her arms and legs and the very soul of her. She drifted closer. "So, what's the problem now?"

"That I'll never, ever get enough of you." He reached for her. She shoved her worries aside. Forgot the promises she'd made herself. She didn't hesitate, didn't think about appropriate behavior or whether she should be the one to behave. Didn't even worry about her longtime hands-off policy with men or the fact she'd once thought him arrogant and rude.

No, she did the only thing possible. She kicked off from the sandy bottom of the pool and floated into Alton's waiting arms.

He was naked. Ginny was naked. The water was warm and bubbling with natural effervescence springing forth from deep within the world's crust. Alton's blood thundered through his veins, powered by a heart that couldn't have beat faster or harder if it tried.

She slid against him like a wet seal, all sleek woman and perfect curves. When the taut, puckered points of her breasts connected with his chest he thought he might lose it altogether. He'd never felt so aroused, so terribly in need.

His intentions flashed from *well behaved* to *wanting Ginny now* in a heartbeat, and when she wrapped her gloriously long legs around his waist and settled her warm and perfect sex against his belly, he didn't even try to bite back his groan.

Part pleasure, part pain, all need. Desperate, clawing need growing stronger each second, more powerful with every point of connection. Her long, strong arms around his shoulders, her fingers buried in his hair, muscular thighs clasping his waist, and the erotic tickle of dark pubic curls caressing his belly.

He searched for her thoughts and found only sensation. Her mind was spinning in a riot of color and light, of fire and ice and song without words. Pure sensation, pure desire and need.

She raised her head and found his mouth with hers. The warm, wet brush of her lips sucked him into everything Ginny was feeling, deeper into her mind, her thoughts without words. Their teeth clicked, tongues twisted and danced as Alton turned his head *just so,* as Ginny's lips molded *that way.* He ran his hands along her spine, tracing each vertebra with flying fingers, cupped her firm bottom in the palm of his hand, and lifted her against him.

His cock strained hard and hot, trapped tightly between her body and his, but he didn't try to force entry, didn't shift his hips in search of that next step, that final thrust that would lead to penetration and that much-desired connection. Her sex felt swollen and hot against the underside of his erection, her body strained close against him, undulating with a slow, sensual rhythm that called to him, enticed him—took him to the edge.

He wanted her as he'd never wanted anything in his life.

But he'd promised and they were too new. They both understood their situation was too precarious, their worlds at risk and now was not the time, no matter how much his body argued he take her, that he make love to her.

Somehow he managed to hang on to that one point of sanity—the words they'd spoken, almost in jest, the promise he'd made to behave. That stupid, idiotic promise he'd give anything to break right now.

Ginny was the one who ended the kiss, the one to finally break their connection. Her chest heaved with each labored breath as she rested her forehead against his breastbone. He felt her shoulders shaking, her whole body trembling, and his breath caught.

"Ginny? Are you okay? Sweetheart, what's wrong?" Gently he touched the line of her jaw with his fingers. Lifted her chin.

She raised her head. Tears streamed from her eyes.

Tears of laughter?

"Aarrrgggh!" He lifted her high, tossed her into the pond, and dove after her. They both came up laughing. Standing in front of him, Ginny shook her head like a wet dog. She sent water flying in all directions, took a deep breath, and grinned at him. Then she raised her arms and looped her hands over his shoulders.

She was still giggling. "I am so sorry, Alton. I really am. I tell you to behave and then I act like a damned hussy."

He kissed her nose. "Hussy works for me."

"Well, it doesn't work for me." She shook her head slowly, but at least she was smiling. "I don't do sex with guys I hardly know." She chuckled and glanced away, obviously embarrassed to say the words out loud. "I rarely have sex with guys I know. That's not me and it's not smart."

"I agree, but there's something about you . . ." He kissed her again, a mere meeting of lips that wasn't nearly enough. Leaning his forehead against Ginny's, he took a deep breath while he gave his heart a chance to find its normal cadence. "Like I said before, from the first time I saw you, I was interested."

"I know the feeling." She kissed him back, a gentle press of lips to lips that left him wanting so much more.

Obviously, Ginny felt the same way, as reluctantly as she pulled away. She shook her head. "Damn." A short, sharp laugh punctuated her soft curse. "That's not easy. Oh, Alton . . . I don't want to rush into anything. So much has happened in the last day since you called me from Bell

Rock. . . . I feel as if my life has been tossed into a vortex and it's still spinning."

"For what it's worth, it's really good to know that at least you're interested."

She snorted in a most unfeminine manner. "That's probably the understatement of the year. Keep that thought in mind."

Alton was the one laughing now as he tugged her toward the edge of the pool. "I'll be lucky if there's room to think of anything else. C'mon. Taron's probably already drinking my beer."

"Lemurians have beer?"

"Of course. We got it from the Atlanteans. Where do you think humans learned to make it?"

Taron wasn't drinking Alton's beer when they slipped in through the back door. No, he was pacing a hole in the floor.

He jerked to a stop when Alton opened the door and Ginny stepped into the room ahead of him.

"Where in the nine hells have you been?"

Alton kept his hand planted on Ginny's shoulder. "Bathing. What's up?"

"Your father. What else?" Taron flopped down on the long, low couch that stretched along the back wall. "He's trying to convince the other members of the council that you staged everything, that the talking sword's a fake and that thing where it cut your chains was all sleight of hand. He's got them doubting their own minds, searching for records of the Crone to prove she's only a myth, that she didn't exist. And he's still trying to get you arrested."

Alton shook his head in obvious frustration. "What is with that man? He's had it in for me for as long as I can recall."

Ginny felt the tension in his body, sensed it in his

mind, though his actual thoughts were a jumble of disconnected words.

She really needed to work on this telepathy thing.

Alton's fingers tightened on her shoulder. "Taron, what about the soldiers you've talked to? What's their feeling? Is anyone willing to join the fight?"

Taron shook his head and stared at his clasped hands hanging loosely between his knees. "Not yet. A couple, maybe, but most of them are afraid of the chancellor's power and they all think he's just a little bit insane. They saw how easily he wrote off his only son." Taron waved his hand around the room. "You realize you're going to lose your rooms here, don't you? He's having the eviction notice prepared. He's talking total exile from Lemuria if he can't get the death edict reinstated."

"I should have figured as much. Damn." Alton took a deep breath and his fingers tightened on Ginny's shoulder. "I was hoping we could get some rest here tonight, but we probably need to get out while we can." He let out an explosive breath and rubbed Ginny's shoulder. "Now that you have my grandmother's scabbard, there's not a damned thing here I want to keep." The look he gave her spoke volumes. "I'm sorry, Ginny."

She covered his hand with hers. "It's not your fault, Alton. You have nothing to be sorry for, but I agree with both you and Taron. We should leave while we can."

"Do you want me to take you home? To Evergreen?" Alton ran his fingers over her shoulder and down her arm. He left a trail of shivers behind.

She'd never had a man affect her as he did. Never responded so quickly to any man's touch, but as much as her body loved it, that thinking part of her wasn't so sure.

She sighed. Attraction was one thing, demons another. They'd better keep their priorities straight. "Why would you want to do that? The demons are in Sedona. Isn't that where we should go?"

Alton cupped her shoulders in his hands and stared into her eyes. Damn. His were so green they didn't look real. More like those fake, glittery glass eyes in stuffed animals, the kind that seemed to look right through you.

The way Alton was looking through her right now. Seeing inside Ginny where she kept her most private thoughts, her deepest needs.

"It's going to get really ugly when we go back, Ginny. There's no doubt in my mind there are demons in Sedona. We're going to be on our own unless we can reach Dax and Eddy and get them to join us. I brought you here hoping we'd find people willing to help, but we're going back the way we came. Just the two of us."

Ginny shook her head. "No, we're not the same. Not at all. I'm going back with an entirely new identity. I'm Lemurian, Alton. Just like you. I've got DarkFire. You've got me. That makes us another team that didn't exist before. I can be more than just moral support for you now."

She flexed her arm and made a muscle. There wasn't much of one, but it made him laugh. "See?" she said, pumping her muscle. "No demon's gettin' by me."

Alton shook his head, but at least he was still grinning. "Taron, it looks like it's up to you to convince the council. They can't deny what happened out there, just as they can't continue to deny the demon threat is real, that it's going to affect the safety of Lemuria sooner rather than later."

Taron took Alton's hand and the two men grasped each other's forearms. "Be safe, Alton. You're the brother I wish I'd had. I don't want to lose you."

"You are my brother, Taron. You always have been. Always will be. I wish you luck with our hardheaded council."

Taron laughed. "Wish me luck with the one who denies being your father. His is the hardest head I have to deal with.

Take care, my friend. I promise to do my best." He turned to Ginny. "You, too, Ginny. Be safe. Take care of Alton for me. I'm not at all worried about you, but that guy is something else altogether."

Ginny rose up on her toes and surprised Taron with a kiss to his cheek. He blushed to the roots of his brilliant red hair.

"I promise, Taron. I just wish there was a way we could keep in touch." She glanced at Alton. "Can we plan to meet in a few days? I think we need to know how things are going here. If there's any change in the council's decision."

"Bell Rock?" Alton hugged Ginny close.

Taron nodded. "Bell Rock it is. Three days from today, at sunset. I'll meet you at the portal within the vortex." He held his vermillion braid in one hand. "I'd rather not risk exposure in human society."

"Agreed." Alton leaned over and kissed Ginny. "You're already thinking like a warrior. Planning ahead. I like that."

A soft chime rang—three crystal-clear tones. Alton glanced quickly toward the doorway. Taron looked at Alton. "Are you expecting anyone?"

He shook his head and grabbed Ginny's arm. They both gathered up their things and slipped into the hallway that led to the pool, out of sight of the door. A moment later, Taron called to them. "It's okay. Hurry."

A large man in a blue robe stood uncomfortably in the front room. Ginny recognized him immediately as one of the soldiers who'd brought Alton to the great hall in chains. She squeezed Alton's hand but kept her eyes on the guard.

Alton asked, "What's going on?"

The guard nodded his head toward Ginny and Alton. "I am Roland of Kronus, Sergeant of the Guard. I've come to warn you. Chancellor Artigos has convinced the council to hold you under house arrest until they've had time to discuss the current situation." He looked at Taron and shrugged. "We all know what that means. Months of discussion, no action while the demons gain a stronger foothold. You need to leave immediately, but the route to Sedona's Bell Rock is guarded."

"How about the one through Mount Shasta?" Alton was slipping his scabbard over his shoulders as he questioned the sergeant.

Grinning, the man nodded his head. "I'm covering that one. Hurry. Those charged with your arrest are on their way, though they promised to take their time. You're going to have to get through the veil before my troops are in place. I'm not sure where all their loyalties lie." He turned toward the swirl of light and color, poked his head through, and then popped back into the room. "It's all clear."

Ginny buckled her scabbard in place and grabbed her pack. Taron gave her a quick hug and propelled her toward the portal. Alton looped his pack over his shoulder and grabbed Ginny's hand. Without another backward glance, they followed the sergeant of the guard into the tunnel.

Chapter Seven

Sergeant Kronus moved quickly, running in the opposite direction Ginny and Alton had taken earlier. This way was dark, the walls close on either side. Their pounding footsteps echoed eerily against the walls. After a short race down the hall, they turned in to an even narrower passage. Alton seemed familiar with the route. Ginny kept her mouth shut and her feet in motion, but she'd never been so thankful for all the miles she was used to jogging or the hours she'd spent at the gym.

Finally they slipped out through a narrow tunnel that appeared to be nothing more than a crack in the walls between two passages. The sergeant looked both ways and then stepped aside. Alton tugged Ginny through the opening. "Thank you, my friend. Can you come with me? We could use a warrior like you."

Roland shook his head. "My wife and child are here. I can't leave them, but I want to know our world and their future are safe from demonkind. If I can help from here, I will. I know what I saw today was true. You did not fool me with sleight of hand—I heard your sword speak and I believe the warning. Good luck to you." He turned to Ginny. "And to you as well. My grandmother fought in the

DemonWars before she disappeared. Her brave story is part of our family's lore and Lemuria's shame. Daria the Crone was a great and powerful warrior. The council can deny our history all they want, but the truth is known to the common people. I wish you well."

He turned and slipped back through the opening. Alton's eyes were shining when he grabbed Ginny's hand once more and tugged her across the passageway, down another and another until she heard the roar of the golden veil and knew they were close to the vortex.

Alton drew his sword and used HellFire's glow to light the way along the dark tunnel they entered. This one took them perpendicular to the main passage with the golden wall marking the boundary between Lemuria and the energy vortex where the portals were located.

They popped out beside the curtain of gold. Alton held his finger to his lips. Ginny looked back toward Lemuria and saw the same man who had helped them just moments ago, marching into place with his troops. He studiously ignored their hiding place and set his men to look back along the tunnel, toward Lemuria.

Alton grabbed Ginny and the two of them slipped into the shimmering gold. Within seconds they were through, but something felt wrong. Ginny glanced over her shoulder at Alton. He was slipping HellFire into his scabbard.

She pulled DarkFire out of hers.

"What's wrong?"

She shook her head. "I don't know." She wished she could explain the strange sense of danger that seemed to wrap her body in cold chills. "Something's wrong. Can you smell sulfur?"

"A little." Alton sniffed the air. "Okay. A lot." He drew Hell-Fire once more. Ginny stood back, scanning the space around them as he used the glow to check the nooks and crannies around the cavern. The various portals glowed as they should. There were no dark wraiths, no sign of demon mist.

This cavern was different than the one they'd entered from Bell Rock. Ginny followed Alton into the main part where sections of rock pulsed and swirled around them. "Where are we?"

Alton pointed toward a shimmering area along one wall. "These are all dimensional portals, powered by the Mount Shasta vortex. If we go toward the back of the cavern, we'll be able to take the same one I traveled before to Bell Rock. We're literally at a crossroads, here. The choice is yours— back to Sedona or home to Evergreen?"

Ginny flashed him a grin. "I've still got a week of vacation. I choose Sedona."

"Fighting demons is not necessarily my idea of a vacation, but I highly approve of your choice. Thank you." Alton adjusted the pack on his shoulder and held his sword high for light. Ginny followed him down the tunnel. She almost ran into his back as Alton skidded to a stop.

The portal was there, glowing in reds and golds, but it was almost lost, buried beneath the swirling black mist pouring through from Sedona. Not just one demon, but what looked like an entire cloud bank of demon mist gathered in front of the portal.

Cursing softly under his breath, Alton stepped directly into the mist.

Ginny held her sword in a white-knuckled grasp and stared at the pulsing cloud of demons. DarkFire shimmered, brilliant purple flashed. Beneath her dark light, demons suddenly glowed in fluorescent brilliance. The shapeless black wraiths took on details not visible before—incandescent eyes and phosphorescent teeth glimmered in grossly malformed faces. Twisted arms and legs protruded from misshapen bodies with scales and fangs and protruding spurs of bone.

Hideous creatures, ugly beyond belief, yet they flowed almost gracefully in their mist form, without true substance, light as air yet charged with corruption.

Ginny saw them truly for the first time and recognized evil in its purest form. Then she sucked in one terrified breath, clasped DarkFire tightly in her hand, and plunged into her first-ever fight against demonkind.

He'd not seen the likes of this before—such vast numbers of demonkind pouring through the gateway from Sedona. Their thick, sulfuric stench was suffocating. The naturally cool air in the cavern dropped several more degrees as demon after demon spilled out of the portal, bringing the chill of evil with them.

Had they come directly from Abyss, merely using a previously undiscovered portal around Sedona as their gateway, or was Sedona entirely overrun with the bastards? Was something driving them out? Or even worse, was something luring them here?

Had the demon king reappeared near Evergreen?

He'd have to worry about the details later. The sense of malevolence surrounding the massing demons made his skin crawl. Alton stepped directly into the black cloud and slashed HellFire through the thick collection of demonic souls.

Sparks flew. The ear-shattering screams as several creatures exploded beneath the crystal blade made his head spin. His eyes watered from the disgusting stench while his sword twisted and danced through the roiling black mist, but he swung with care—he sensed Ginny beside him, but he couldn't see her through the thick wall of demon mist.

"Ginny? Are you okay?"

"I'm great," she said.

Damn if she wasn't laughing!

He glanced to his right. The dark flash of her unusual crystal blade and the horrific screams told him DarkFire had cut through more of the demon wraiths. The air began to clear, enough that Alton could finally see Ginny as he destroyed the demons surrounding him.

She moved with the grace of a dancer, reaching high for demons trying to escape overhead, twisting and diving for the ones that slipped out along the ground. But it wasn't Ginny's beauty that caught Alton's eye. Not this time.

Caught in the fluorescent glow of Ginny's sword, the demon wraiths had come to life. Where he saw only black mist as formless clouds, DarkFire illuminated their true nature. They might be wraiths without true substance, but beneath her dark glow, demonkind showed their true form— and they were hideous, inherently evil, and ugly beyond belief.

Yet Ginny didn't hesitate. She danced and swung her amethyst blade and the demons fell, one by one, screeching as their lost souls exploded in bursts of dark purple sparks.

Alton clenched his jaw. He had to concentrate on his own battle as more of the filthy creatures flowed through the portal, but it was different now that their image was so firmly planted in his mind. They had to be stopped, but how? He couldn't close this portal or he and Ginny would lose their route back to Sedona, but he had to know—where in the nine hells were the bastards coming from?

"Behind you!"

He spun around. A tower of black wraiths hovered at his back, pulsing with a sense of evil. Not one demon, but many, connected within their swirling black consciousness, coming together to attack.

Taking on form and substance even to his eyes—a head, arms, legs. Even a thick body floating in and out of sight.

Ginny swept DarkFire over the massed wraiths and their

true nature glowed in all its incandescent fury, a monstrous blend of many creatures into one.

Alton struck the middle with HellFire and watched the roiling mass collapse as the ones in the center burst into stinking sparks. Immediately, the demons reformed, billowing up and out and taking shape once more. A thick, oily cloud rippled and flowed, coming together again in what seemed to be an unprecedented, organized attack.

Demons in this dimension, limited by their mist form, were generally nothing more than wraiths. He'd never known them to function outside of Abyss without an avatar. Away from their world, they existed as formless, mindless beings of energy that appeared as black, stinking mist until they'd commandeered something to animate—or they looked that way to anyone without a sword like DarkFire.

Was that something new, that demon shape within the mist? Had DarkFire evolved because the demons were changing? So many questions without answers, but one thing had always been consistent—the demons' need for an avatar. In the past it had been something of the earth—stone or ceramic or various metals. In Sedona, they'd graduated to living creatures, though he'd not heard of them taking on a human host.

In Evergreen, they'd taken on plastic, but at least none of their avatars, so far, had given them the natural weapons that kept them alive and able to fight on Abyss.

On their own world, they were massive, multi-limbed creatures with scales and claws, huge fangs, and armored hides. Poisonous and powerful on Abyss, it took them time to gain strength in Earth's dimension, to function as corporeal beings.

Before, they'd needed a borrowed body of some kind—an avatar. Something to give them form and function, to house their wraithlike souls before they could begin the slow evolution from mindless demon mist to living, functioning creatures.

At least that was the way things had been. These already appeared to show intelligence while still in their mist form. Under DarkFire's light their demon shapes appeared. Had they always held that form in Earth's dimension, or was it something new? A more powerful aspect of evil?

They were obviously evolving, beginning to work together. There was a pattern to their fight. Instead of trying to get away, they were actually mounting an attack. They'd managed to cooperate in a rudimentary fashion last week in Evergreen, but he and Dax had thought maybe the demon king was directing them for his own purpose.

There was no sign of the demon king here, yet the towering creature began to reform. *Demons working together.* Showing intelligence. Merely using the Sedona portal to reach the portal in Mount Shasta should have been beyond them, at least in the beginning.

Dax had explained it, how demons crossing from one dimension to another lost what little intelligence they had. It took time and experience in Earth's dimension before they could begin to act with true cognitive thought. Only the demon king had shown actual intelligence, the ability to plot and plan.

Demonkind was changing. Evolving almost before their eyes.

Alton swung HellFire through the demon wraiths that formed the legs. Sparks flew, demons screeched, and the stench of sulfur burned his nostrils.

The entire creature collapsed.

Just as quickly, it reformed. New demons flowed into position to build a new set of legs. This time, when Alton swung his sword, the creature of mist opened its black jaws wide. It screeched in defiance—the sound of many voices working as one—and twisted out of the way.

Alton leapt forward and slashed HellFire through the body of the beast. More wraiths exploded and disappeared, but this made no sense. What in the nine hells was it trying to do? As mist, it had no real weapons. A beast of cloud, no matter how foul, had no way to cause damage.

There was so much they didn't know, and as soon as they thought they'd figured something out about demonkind, the damned creatures appeared to evolve into something different, breaking their own rules.

At least they still died beneath HellFire's fury. Alton swung his sword and watched with great satisfaction as the demons he touched with the crystal blade exploded on contact.

He heard Ginny's grunts and soft curses. The screech and howl of dying demons added its discordant song. Yet still they came. Even more wraiths poured through the gateway from Sedona, but why here? What drew them and where were they going? Were they headed for Evergreen or Lemuria?

Either choice was bad. Somehow he had to stop the demons' access. He'd closed off their gateway from Bell Rock to Abyss. Were all these demons already in Sedona? Were they using the power of the vortex to move from one part of Earth's dimension to another, or were they somehow new demons, fresh from Abyss, coming in through an undiscovered portal?

Alton slashed through the last of the demons and the beast disappeared in a puff of stinking black smoke. Alton coughed and his eyes watered. He stepped back, took a deep breath, and turned to check on Ginny.

The only thing left in the cavern was the stench of sulfur. He raised HellFire. The brilliant glow of crystal illuminated the entire cavern. There was no sign of Ginny. The only sound he heard was the blood pounding in his ears, the harsh intake of one breath after another. A chill raced along his spine. "Ginny?" he shouted. "Ginny! Where are you?"

Panic ripped through him. He searched for her thoughts,

for any sense of her. Breathing hard enough to hyperventilate, Alton forced himself to find calm, to take slow, even breaths and narrow his searching mind to Ginny and only Ginny.

He listened for her thoughts. They really needed to work on their newly discovered telepathy. He could barely pick her up when she was next to him, but . . .

There! In the next room, the main cavern they'd just left. He glanced once more toward the Sedona portal. It was clear of demon mist for the moment. He spun around and raced through the tunnel, skidding as he rounded the turn into the main cavern.

Ginny had her back to the Lemurian portal. Framed in its golden glow, she fought a gathering of demons. Beneath DarkFire's purple glow they snarled with shining teeth and struck with shimmering claws, though they were still only harmless mist. DarkFire flashed through the insubstantial wraiths with unbelievable speed and blinding grace. With a flick of her wrist, Ginny caught one of the demons as it launched itself in her direction.

It exploded in a burst of flames and sulfuric stench.

She fought like an expert swordsman—feet dancing, her bandaged left hand raised behind her, DarkFire grasped firmly in her right as she twisted the blade through demon after demon.

Mesmerized by her grace and beauty, Alton stood in the entrance to the cavern and stared.

"You just gonna stand there watching, or you gonna help?" Ginny flashed him a bright grin and lunged for yet another snarling wraith.

Alton joined her. Standing shoulder to shoulder, the two of them blocked the portal to Lemuria and protected Alton's world with their crystal swords. They found a perfect rhythm, swinging right and left, slicing through the dark wraiths—visible now as malignant demons in DarkFire's purple fluorescence, black, smoky ghosts under HellFire's blue light—and watching the bursts of sulfuric flame with growing satisfaction.

"Who goes there?"

With sword upraised, Alton spun about as four Lemurian guards stepped through the portal. "Roland! Have you come to help us?" Alton quickly turned his back on the four and slashed through yet another wraith.

"Hey, Roland!" Ginny waved her bandaged hand and leapt forward. With a feral grin on her face, she caught two wraiths with her dark crystal blade and watched the demons explode.

"What are these things?" Roland stepped up beside Alton and slashed his steel sword through a dark ghost. The black smoke merely divided along the blade and reformed on either side. "My sword doesn't stop them!"

Alton cut through another demon. Sparks flashed and it disappeared. "I was afraid of that. Only crystal seems to kill them." He lunged forward once more. Another demon died. "Why are you here? I didn't think the guard ever left Lemuria."

"Right after your escape, orders came down for your arrest. I'm sorry, Alton, but they were directly from Artigos. He truly has disowned you. I was told to bring you back for trial, even if it meant finding you in Earth's dimension."

Ginny spun around with her sword raised high. Roland took a quick step back.

"You've got to be frickin' kidding me!" she said. "We're out here protecting Lemuria from a demon invasion and you're going to arrest us?"

Her voice rose on the last word. Alton glanced her way, caught her eye, and winked. She glared at him in return.

"To your left! Quickly!" Roland pointed and Alton caught yet another demon. "Those are my orders." He glanced over his shoulder at the other men. They stared wide-eyed at the battle going on in front of them and didn't say a word.

Roland turned back to Ginny. "I didn't say I intended to follow them."

"What? You're going to ignore the chancellor's direct orders?" Alton faced Roland and stopped dead in his tracks, ignoring the billowing cloud of demonic mist beginning to take shape and form behind him. "Then what do you intend?"

Roland dipped his head. "I intend to do as my Lord Taron asked—warn you not to return to Lemuria until he brings the council around to his way of thinking. Already favor is turning against your father. He has angered many by his disavowal of your birthright as much as his denunciation of the Crone. She is a much beloved figure among the common people. He has publicly denied her sacrifice and called it nothing more than show."

"What?" Ginny's sword flashed and DarkFire spoke. "Who in the nine hells does he think he is?"

Roland blinked. Then he suddenly dropped to one knee. "Lady Daria." He looked up at Ginny. "I recognize her voice. I knew this wasn't some kind of trick."

"Of course it's not a trick." The sword glowed with each word. "Stand, Roland of Kronus. I remember your grandmother. She was a brave warrior and true to her people. As are you."

Roland stood up. It was only then that Alton realized the other three soldiers with him had gone to their knees as well.

"Alton!"

Ginny's cry spun him around. A massive black beast towered over them, so tall its head touched the ceiling and the span of its arms could have gathered all six of them at once.

Ginny held her sword high and dark light illuminated the beast. Beneath DarkFire's light, it was a horrifying blend of many demons, a monster writhing with dozens of foul creatures melded together.

Ginny lunged toward the abomination. DarkFire slid

through the middle, leaving flames and sparks in her path. This creature appeared to have more substance than any they'd seen before and all its many parts were screeching and howling, creating a horrifying cacophony that echoed within the cavern.

Alton slashed through the neck, expecting the head to tumble, but in spite of the flames from the demons he killed, the mist reformed and the beast remained intact.

It shrieked and circled on thick legs. Members of the guard spread out around it, but their steel swords had no effect. Slashing through the roiling mist, they passed through harmlessly without doing any damage.

Alton and Ginny fought on, cutting and jabbing, attacking and retreating and yet the creature remained upright, its many voices undiminished. When Ginny withdrew, it appeared as nothing more than roiling mist in the shape of a beast, but when she slashed out with DarkFire, the purple light illuminated the many foul demons still forming the arms and legs, the thick body and huge head.

They continued to fight, tiring now but driven to beat this thing before it crossed into Lemuria. Each crystalline strike brought forth howls and shrieks and flashing sparks. As more and more demons were destroyed, the beast grew smaller, though the wraiths remained connected, changing within the fluid structure to take the places of those Ginny or Alton killed.

Finally, it was no more than waist high when Alton's sword slashed from top to bottom and Ginny cut from right to left. Fire flashed and the last wraith disappeared.

Panting, Ginny leaned against the wall with DarkFire hanging loosely in her grasp. Her body trembled as she sucked in great, deep breaths. The four soldiers of the guard stood in stunned silence while Alton walked back along the tunnel and searched for more demonkind, but the trail was clear and there were none to be seen.

He hurried back to the main cavern. "I don't get it. The demons were trying to go through the portal into Lemuria. What could they possibly do in mist form?"

"Creatures such as these would cause terrible panic among our people." Roland glanced at the sword in his hand and shook his head. "My weapon was useless against them. Those who carry crystal have forgotten how to fight. They don't have the balls to defend our world." He glanced at Alton and blushed a deep red. "Present company excepted, sir."

DarkFire glowed once again. Ginny turned to Roland. "Hold your sword out, Roland."

He frowned, but he did as she said. Ginny touched the crystal point of her sword to Roland's steel. His began to glow as the other three soldiers gathered close. Within seconds, it was too bright to look directly at the blade.

Then, with a sound as clear as a bell, the blades rang as if they'd come together in battle. Ginny stepped back. Roland gasped and held his sword high. The crystal facets glowed in the reflected light of the surrounding portals, but where Ginny's sword was dark, Roland's blade glowed with crystalline purity.

Once again DarkFire pulsed with light. "Your blade carries the spirit of Hesta, your grandmother. She cannot speak, not yet, but she will."

Roland stared at DarkFire as if neither Ginny nor Alton existed. "Only the aristocracy may carry crystal." His words faded on a sigh of wonder. He held the sword high, turning and twisting it so that light cascaded from the facets.

DarkFire flashed and her voice echoed off the cavern's walls. "That is the council's law. Do you serve the Council of Nine, or do you serve Lemuria?"

With that final question, DarkFire's glow faded. Ginny stared at her sword until the blade no longer cast its own dark light. She carefully stuck it inside her scabbard. When she looked at Roland, her golden eyes were shining. "Well, Roland? How do you answer DarkFire's question?"

Roland's dark eyes flashed from Ginny to Alton. Open-mouthed, he gaped at his stunned and speechless men. They watched the crystal sword he clutched in his hand with wonder and obvious envy. "I serve Lemuria," he said. His voice was barely above a whisper.

Alton's eyes burned with unshed tears. He was flooded with a sense of loyalty and pride for his world he'd not felt for hundreds of years. This was the spirit of Lemuria. These were Lemurian soldiers. He cleared his throat and quietly asked, "Who do you serve?"

Roland held his sword aloft and repeated his vow, stronger this time. "I serve Lemuria." He glanced at his men. They held their blades aloft, steel to his crystal. All of them, this time together, said it again. Loudly and with great pride.

"We serve Lemuria."

Light burst from Roland's crystal sword. One of the men gasped as cold fire traveled from the linked blades along each man's powerful sword arm, then back up to the points. The light flashed again, every color of the rainbow. This time, everyone in the cavern gasped.

Four perfect crystal blades shimmered. Light from the golden portal into Lemuria reflected from their many facets.

Alton stared at the crystal, almost mesmerized by the light. Then he shook himself and stepped forward. He held his hand out to Roland. The Sergeant of the Guard stared at Alton's hand for a moment and then clasped it in his.

"I am not Lemuria's ruler," Alton said, well aware his heart was pounding in his chest and sweat trickled down his spine. He'd never seen anything like this. Never heard of common soldiers bearing crystal, but then he'd not known of the women warriors of Lemuria, either. Times were changing and the threat against his people grew by the hour. With the power of the swords, maybe they did have a chance against demonkind. He looked into Roland's clear gaze. "I have no authority other than that as a citizen of Lemuria, but I would ask you to return to Lemuria with your story. Show the councilmen your swords. Explain the threat as only an honest soldier can."

Ginny grabbed Roland's arm. "You have to make them understand, Roland. Imprisoning Alton serves demonkind, not Lemuria. Once you convince them, come back. Join us. You're armed with crystal now and we need you on our side."

Alton stepped aside and left the path to the portal clear. "Go to Taron. He'll help you. We need soldiers who carry crystal. That's the only way we're going to win this fight."

Roland glanced at his soldiers. The others held their swords proudly, ready to follow whatever orders he gave. Without exchanging a word, Roland turned to Alton. "They have to believe us. We carry crystal. Everyone knows if you're not meant to wield a crystal sword, it will turn on you."

He stared at the beautiful sword in his hand, slowly shook his head, and spoke with great reverence. "I carry crystal with Hesta's spirit still locked inside. We'll go to Taron, but first we're going to the barracks. Once the men see what's happened, we'll have the entire guard on our side."

They marched through the portal to Lemuria. Alton watched them go with a powerful sense of pride. Common soldiers, yet common no longer. They'd shed millennia of dust from their sandals with their decision. Old ideas, tired philosophies, and eons of inaction.

Their army was growing. One brave soldier at a time.

Ginny shook her head and wondered if she'd ever experience anything even close to normal again. "Do you think they'll be okay? I have a feeling your father's out for blood."

Alton turned away from the portal and threw an arm over her shoulders. His casual hug felt so good and she was absolutely beat. All she wanted to do was lean against him and just let Alton carry her burdens . . . for a little while, at least.

"Roland's decision to go to the other men first is a good one," Alton said. His fingers idly stroked her arm. Ginny wondered if he had any idea what his touch did to her.

Obviously not. He was all business.

"If Roland has the guard behind him," he said, "the council will at least have to hear him out. The fact he now bears crystal will carry a lot of weight with the other members, even if my father refuses to acknowledge its importance."

He leaned over and kissed the top of her head. "I'm just glad you're safe. When I realized you were gone, I panicked."

She wrapped her arms around his waist and hugged him. "I'm sorry. I didn't meant to frighten you, but I missed a couple in the other room and followed them in here. I thought they'd be heading out through the portal to Mount Shasta, but they were gathered together in the middle of the cavern. There were more than I expected. They'd already formed a huge creature all morphed together, and they were headed straight for the Lemurian gate. I didn't have time to call for help."

"You did really well, Ginny. Your first fight, and it was a big one. How did you know what to do?"

His praise had her heart pounding in her chest and a lump forming in her throat. All of a sudden, the enormity of the past hour's battle, the meeting with Roland, and the changes in her life hit her at once. It took her a minute before she felt she could speak. Then she merely reached over her shoulder and stroked the hilt of her sword. "DarkFire," she said. "She was in my head, telling me how to swing, what to do. I never once felt like I was on my own."

"You never were," Alton said. He tilted her chin up and stared into her eyes. Ginny was almost positive he was going to kiss her, and it wouldn't be just a quick little peck to the lips. She ran her tongue over her lower lip. Alton's focus shifted and he stared at her mouth. "I was with you, too, Ginny. I'll always be beside you."

He leaned closer. She felt the clench of muscles deep in her belly. Her eyes drifted closed.

A dog barked. Blinking, Ginny spun around. What was a dog doing inside the vortex? It barked again, closer this time, and then a flurry of blond curls scrambled out of the darkness. "Bumper? Isn't she Eddy's mutt? What are you doing here?" The curly blond dog raced past her and leapt at Alton, all wiggles and yips and wet doggy kisses.

Alton! Alton! You're here! What are you doing here?

The dog was talking? Ginny slapped a hand to her forehead, where the voice seemed to echo in her mind. She stared at the silly-looking mutt as Alton slipped his arm from Ginny's waist and dropped to his knees, laughing and hugging the frantic dog.

"That's Willow you hear," he said, dodging doggy kisses. "Remember? I told you she's inside Bumper now."

Feeling as if she'd been hit with maybe one too many impossible things, Ginny glanced up as Eddy and Dax stepped out of the shadows. Finally—someone familiar! Arms wide, Ginny raced across the cavern. "I don't believe this. Eddy! What are you doing here?" She grabbed her best friend in a hug, but her eyes were on Dax.

"Me?" Eddy laughed and hugged her tight. "What are you doing here?"

College buddy, my eye! Ginny hugged her best friend ever, but her mind was absolutely seething with questions. She wasn't about to let go of the one with all the answers.

Chapter Eight

Dax grabbed Alton's arm and dragged him to one side. "What are you doing here?"

"I was going to ask you the same thing." Alton shook his head, but he kept his eye on Ginny and Eddy. After what they'd just been through, he wasn't letting Ginny out of his sight.

"Demons are thick in Sedona," Alton said. "We needed some answers and I figured we'd better look for help, so I took Ginny with me to Lemuria."

Dax frowned. "How'd that go?"

Alton grinned at him. Then he burst out laughing. Both women stopped hugging and looked his way. Ginny had a huge smile on her face. When Alton held his hand out, she reached for him and wrapped her fingers around his. He looked into her shining eyes and was immediately caught up in their depth and unexpected heat. He cleared his throat and squeezed her hand.

"Well," he said, dragging out the word for emphasis, "I'm still a wanted man. Ginny is Lemurian. She's immortal. She's got her own sword, a different kind of crystal that shows the real demon beneath the demon mist. Other than that, it was just your typical trip to another dimension."

"What? Ginny?" Eddy gaped at Ginny. "What do you mean, you're Lemurian?"

Ginny merely shrugged and glanced at Alton.

Alton wrapped his arm around her shoulders and hugged her close. "It appears Ginny is descended from Lemurian royalty, from a time when we still had a king and a queen. HellFire was the first to tell us. Then the Crone, an ancient woman I always thought was more myth than reality, presented Ginny with her own sword—along with the details of her Lemurian birthright."

Eddy laughed out loud. "Ginny, you got some 'splainin' to do."

Ginny flashed her a bright grin, let go of Alton's hand, and carefully withdrew DarkFire. "It was so weird," she said, staring at the darkly glowing crystal blade. "As soon as we got to Lemuria, Alton was arrested, but his friend Taron took me with him. We all met up again in this huge underground plaza, and after HellFire cut through Alton's chains, this really old woman walked through the crowd, and it was like Moses parting the Red Sea. She met us up on the dais and spoke a prophecy that she insisted was about my coming to Lemuria. Then she kissed me, walked away, and turned into dust."

She grabbed Alton's hand and squeezed his fingers. Shaking her head in disbelief, she said, "Next thing I knew, Hell-Fire had birthed a twin, except my sword glows with this weird light and she's definitely female." She held the crystal sword out for Eddy and Dax. "Meet DarkFire. She carries the spirit of the old woman known as the Crone, whose real name was Daria. She was a woman warrior who fought in the Lemurian DemonWars."

"Hello." The sword's voice was soft, almost melodic.

Eddy's eyes opened wide. "Woman warrior? I didn't think Lemurian women were soldiers."

"Then who is the voice of DemonSlayer?"

Alton's soft question seemed to catch Eddy by surprise. She reached back and touched the pommel of her sword, rising above the leather scabbard. "I hadn't thought of that," she said, stroking the smooth metal.

Dax grinned. He dipped his head, acknowledging Ginny's sword. "It appears they were. Greetings, DarkFire."

The sword pulsed in brilliant shades of lavender and purple.

"Ginny, this is so cool." Eddy reached out and touched the crystal blade. "Hard to believe, but cool. It's good to meet you, DarkFire. I had no idea there were women warriors in Lemuria."

"Ginny will tell you my story. DemonSlayer will tell her own when the time is right. For now, beyond you, Edwina Marks, Ginny is the only woman warrior among our kind, the only one willing to take up the fight against demonkind." The blade darkened. After a moment, Ginny returned it to her scabbard.

Eddy blinked. "How the hell did she know my name was Edwina?" Then she yawned and slapped her hand over her mouth. "Oops. Sorry . . . we've been up since yesterday. There was a nasty infestation in southern Oregon, but Ginny! I want to know everything! How did you find out about, well . . . everything? You're coming back to Evergreen, right?"

Ginny glanced at Alton. He shook his head. "No," he said. "Not yet. We have to see what's happening in Sedona. There were hundreds of demons pouring through the portal from Bell Rock just before you arrived. There shouldn't be any. I closed the portal there when I first arrived, so they must have opened a new one. Sedona's full of vortexes that can power the gateways."

Dax nodded. "Makes sense. We'll try and join you once we check in with Ed and get some sleep. We've been fighting a small invasion north of here, but I think it's under control."

Alton grabbed his arm. "They're changing, Dax. It's like they have a sense of purpose. They massed and tried to get through the portal to Lemuria. If Ginny hadn't stopped them, they might have made it."

"At least we've got some Lemurian soldiers on our side." Ginny glanced at Alton. "You tell them what happened. I'm still not sure."

Alton nodded and quickly described the battle, Roland of Kronus and his sword's amazing transformation from steel to crystal. "DarkFire sort of replicated herself," he said.

"Sort of?" Dax frowned and glanced from Ginny to Alton.

"It was amazing," Ginny said. "She created a sword for Roland, much larger than she is, out of his own sword. She turned his steel to crystal."

"She said it holds the spirit of Hesta, Roland's grandmother, who was also a woman warrior." Alton shook his head. "Why didn't we know there were women who fought for Lemuria? What happened to them? Roland said their story was known to the common folk. Why not the rest of us?"

Dax shrugged. "We need to find out. Did his sword speak?"

Alton shook his head. "Not yet. He still has to earn his sword's respect in battle, I guess. But when he held his sword up for his men to swear loyalty to Lemuria, not to the council, the other three soldiers' steel blades all turned to crystal."

"Wow." Eddy shook her head. "That just happened? Here?" She swept her hand wide, encompassing the cavern.

"Right here," Alton said. "About two minutes before you guys showed up."

"Well, crap." Eddy grabbed Dax's hand. "Our timing sucks." She yawned and leaned close to her ex-demon lover.

Dax brushed her short hair back from her face and she snuggled against his shoulder. Even Alton could tell she was ready to fold from exhaustion. "We can catch up on all of this after you get some rest. Ginny's got her cell phone with her."

"Okay, 'cause I want details." Eddy sighed and stared at the portal Alton had sealed just one week ago, the same gateway that had allowed so many demons into the tiny community of Evergreen. She seemed every bit as frustrated as she was tired.

"Did Dax tell you that the ones we fought in Oregon had taken on living animals as avatars?" Eddy clung even tighter to Dax's arm. "They're evolving even faster than last week. It's as if something is pushing them, enabling them in ways we haven't seen."

Alton nodded. "We saw the same thing in Sedona. They're taking on animal form there as well. Household pets and wild animals, though if the animal is caged, the demon goes in search of another host that's still running free."

"Wow." Ginny barely whispered the word, but everyone immediately glanced her way. Ginny held up her hand. She'd removed all the bandages. "Look. It's all healed. I had some really deep scratches and bites."

Eddy grabbed her wrist and turned Ginny's hand. Pink flesh against her dark skin left bright patterns from the healed wounds. "What happened to you?"

"Tom the demon-powered cat happened." She shrugged, obviously fascinated by her healed hand. "My cousin's cat was possessed and went crazy. I was helping Markus catch him and he—the cat, not Markus—attacked me. I had some pretty ugly bites and scratches, but I haven't had time to see a doctor." She looked at Alton. "How'd this heal so quickly?"

He ran his fingers over the newly healed flesh and smiled. At least this was some good news. "More proof you're Lemurian. We heal fast. Broken bones take longer, unless Willow can still do her healing stuff from inside Bumper. . . ." He glanced at Dax.

Dax shrugged. "Don't know. Haven't needed any healing since . . . well, since Willow and Bumper became more closely acquainted."

Eddy laughed and grabbed his arm. "That's a nice way of putting it, dear. We can discuss this later. I need sleep and we still have a long hike down the mountain to Dad's Jeep."

Ginny gave her a quick hug. "Call me after you catch up on your rest. Girl, we really need to talk."

Eddy hugged her back and then turned and gave Alton a long, slow, assessing look. Laughing, she shook her head. "You're not kidding," she said. She hugged Alton, grabbed Dax by the arm, and whistled for the dog. "C'mon, Bumper-Willow. Time to go home."

The three of them passed through the portal. Alton watched them leave. Then he held his sword high and searched the nooks and crannies and corners of the cavern. There was no demon sign, at least for now. Finally he glanced over his shoulder at Ginny. "You ready to go?"

She nodded, but she was still staring at her healed hand. "Ya know, the sword is really cool and I love the telepathic link, but for some reason, this just blows me away!"

Alton grabbed her arm and tugged her toward the portal to Sedona. "Well, let's hope it blows you this way. I want to get back before dark."

"Where are we going to stay?" Ginny planted her feet. "I don't have all that much money that I can pay for hotels and meals in restaurants for very long."

Alton reached into his pocket and pulled out a small leather pouch. He'd totally forgotten about it. "I grabbed this when we were in my rooms in Lemuria. Hold out your hand."

Ginny spread her fingers wide. Alton dumped a small pile of diamonds into her palm.

"Holy shit. Talk about bling! Are those for real?" She picked one up with her free hand and turned it, catching the light from Alton's sword in the diamond.

"Definitely real. We'll sell a few as we need cash, but just a couple of those should be good for more than the time we'll need to be in Sedona."

Ginny carefully helped him pour the stones back into the bag. Then she burst out laughing. "You're just full of surprises, aren't you?"

"Oh, I hope so," he said, tugging her hand and pulling her close. "Now let's get to Sedona and find a place where we can get comfortable."

"At least we can each afford to have our own rooms now, right?" She glanced up at him out of the corner of her eye. He was certain he saw her lips twitching.

"I don't think so," he said. He tugged her close and they paused in front of the portal to Sedona. "It's dangerous. I need to keep you close. Besides, we have to work on our telepathy."

Ginny poked him in the back. "I've heard lots better lines than that, Alton."

They were both laughing as they stepped into the tunnel.

The stench of demon was faint, but enough sulfur lingered that it was obvious demonkind had come this way. Alton held HellFire high and carefully checked the full length of the tunnel between the two vortexes—one in Mount Shasta, California, the other in Sedona, Arizona.

A thousand miles' distance in Earth's dimension, yet only a matter of a few yards when passing through interdimensional portals. "Look." He held the sword close to the wall. "I didn't even notice these before. I wonder where they go?"

"What are they?"

He shook his head, studying the pale wash of light and color in the stone. "Portals, but they're very low energy. They don't appear to draw much from the vortex, which means they probably don't cross vast distances."

"I know of at least four energy vortexes in Sedona." Ginny stepped up close and stared at the wall. "According to my cousin Markus, they're scattered all around the area." She shook her head, laughing softly. "Of course, I always thought vortexes were fake—something to attract tourists. I never imagined they were real." She gestured at the smaller portals. "Maybe these are just for moving around Sedona." Then she touched the wall and gasped when her fingers disappeared into the rock. Immediately she yanked her hand back. "I will never get used to that. Never."

"Four?" Alton walked back along the tunnel. "I only know of one other, at Cathedral Rock, though I've not used it before." He flashed her a grin. "It's powered by feminine energy as opposed to the masculine energy of Bell Rock."

"Well, I don't know if they're boy vortexes or girl vortexes, but Markus told me there's one out north of town in a place called Boynton Canyon, and another one in town, near the airport."

Alton turned and stared at her. "Girl vortexes and boy vortexes?"

"You said masculine and feminine. What else would it mean?" She looked so serious, she almost got him.

Almost. Laughing, he turned away from the tunnel and grabbed Ginny's hand. "Let's go. We can come back and check on these tomorrow, after we've eaten and gotten some sleep. It's been a long day."

Ginny linked her fingers with his. "Agreed." She skipped a step to catch up to his longer stride. Chagrined, he matched his steps more closely to hers when she punched his arm and added, "Then you can tell me more about little girl and boy vortexes . . . after we find a room."

He couldn't stand it. Alton stopped dead in his tracks, turned, and wrapped his arms around her. He drew in a deep breath, absorbing her scent and wondering if he could ever get enough of her. He nuzzled the top of her head and held her close. She molded her body to his as if they'd been perfectly designed to fit together. "Ginny?" he asked, breathing deep once again of her natural perfume. "What would I do without you?"

But he didn't give her time to answer. Instead, he lowered his head as she tilted her chin and raised her lips to his. Once again, the connection was perfect, the fit as if they'd been designed for each other.

Her lips were full and soft and slightly moist. The way her fingers clutched at his biceps and slipped easily around his neck was the most amazing thing he'd felt in his life. All the reservations he'd had, the fact she was mortal and human and he a Lemurian of the ruling class no longer applied.

She was more royal than any son of Artigos could ever hope to claim. More beautiful than any woman he'd ever seen. The question now was, could she be interested in an exiled Lemurian warrior, one whose own father had publicly disowned him?

Not only was Ginny royal, she was immortal, descended of one of the women warriors of Lemuria, an unheralded group of heroes unlike anything he'd heard of in his long, long life.

She was also the one who broke the kiss, who took a step back and then sucked in one deep breath after another. "Okay. I think we really need to back off a bit and find something for dinner because I am starving. Then we need to find a decent room." She pointed at the pocket where he'd stuck the pouch of diamonds. "No. Let's change that request. Not just decent. I want gorgeous."

She flashed him a sly grin, but with her lips moist and swollen from their kiss, it was more erotic than anything he could possibly imagine. "In fact," she said, cocking one hip and planting her hand firmly on the perfect curve, "it appears you can afford the best, and after the day I've had, I can honestly say I'm worth it."

"I couldn't agree more." Feeling unbelievably light-hearted, considering the demon invasion going on just beyond the portal, Alton tugged Ginny along behind him as he stepped through the gateway and out onto the rocky side of Bell Rock. The sun was beginning to set and a fresh breeze lifted Alton's long braids.

Ginny's little Ford Focus sat all alone in the parking lot below them. The meditation group wasn't here this evening, and the air was free of demon stench. Of course, the wind would have blown it away by now if the demons they'd battled earlier had come through this portal.

"What now?" Ginny stood beside him, clutching his hand tightly in hers.

"Now we find food and a place where we can stay for a few days, and we get some sleep. Then we need to go out and about and see what we've missed in the past hours."

Ginny stared at the colorful sky where the sun had just disappeared behind dark cliffs. "Hard to believe it's only been a few hours. In the span of one day, my entire life has changed." She turned and studied Alton while the wind blew little dust devils through the shadows. He tried searching her thoughts, but her mind projected a blank wall to him.

She might not be that great at her newfound telepathy, but she'd certainly figured out how to keep her privacy barriers in place.

Alton grabbed Ginny's hand and, with a light tug, drew her alongside for the walk back to the car.

It was dark by the time they pulled into a gorgeous resort in Boynton Canyon, northwest of Sedona. It wasn't all that far from the vortex Ginny'd heard about, but at this point all she was interested in was a long, hot shower and a comfortable bed.

They'd grabbed a couple of tacos at a fast food place. After they ate, Alton found a jewelry shop owner willing to accept his story of wanting to sell a couple of diamonds he'd inherited. Of course, it had taken that weird power of his that compelled the jeweler into not asking too many questions.

Which, of course, made Ginny wonder if she'd inherited the same power, except she was too blasted tired to worry about it tonight. They'd walked away with a check for more money than Ginny'd ever seen at one time—more than she earned in an entire year as a 911 dispatcher—and it was still only a fraction of the value of the few gems Alton had traded. He didn't seem to mind a bit that he'd gotten the short end of the deal. At this point, Ginny didn't care either . . . she was hot and tired and dirty and just wanted a room, though it still felt weird, taking so much money from a man she barely knew.

She'd stopped at an ATM to deposit the jeweler's check in her account. That was another thing. It was Alton's money, but he'd just handed the check over like it was nothing. Of course, she was the one with the credit card and the bank account.

There was no such thing as banking on Lemuria. What was the need for personal wealth when everything was free? Still, it helped her relax a bit over swiping her card to pay for the beautiful little adobe house the resort called a casita that was going to cost them almost seven hundred dollars a night.

She paid less than that for a whole month's rent on her duplex in Evergreen, where she even had a view of Mount Shasta out the kitchen window.

Here she looked out on towering red bluffs—or she would, the concierge assured them—once the sun came up in the morning.

They had one bedroom with two beds, a nice little kitchen, a sitting room, and two large bathrooms. There was a second bedroom available, but the door to it was locked. Ginny'd thought about renting the entire casita so they could each have their own room, but it seemed like a waste of money . . . they'd shared a room the night before without any problem.

Who was she kidding? She didn't want Alton that far away.

She grabbed her bag and headed into the bathroom closest to the bedroom and closed and locked the door behind her. She needed to pee, she needed a shower, and she needed to think.

Not necessarily in that order.

When she joined Alton on the deck a little while later, she was clean and every bit as confused as she'd been while standing under the spray.

She'd at least come to one conclusion: There was no denying the attraction she felt to the tall, slim man sitting so comfortably in the semidarkness. For some reason her convoluted feelings for him made her angry, but even her anger confused her. Too many changes. Too much, too fast.

A couple of candles flickered on a small table beside the deck chair where he sat. He faced away from her as he gazed out across the desert. The light flickered off his blond hair and etched his strong features with light and shadow.

He wore his long white Lemurian robe and his hair hung free, still damp from his shower. He should have looked more feminine with his fair skin and flowing mane, with the soft fabric that molded his chest and shoulders and draped over his long legs, but she'd never seen a sexier, more masculine sight in her life.

He rested his chin on his big, bony knuckles and stared out into the darkness. His long, narrow feet were bare, with one ankle exposed beneath the hem of the soft robe. He reminded Ginny of a Grecian god contemplating the fate of the world.

The image almost made her laugh. In some ways, he was a god, and more likely than not he actually was contemplating the world's fate. Immortal, pure of heart, brave and kind. The gods she'd read about could take a lesson or two from this man. Still, she wondered what he contemplated, staring so solemnly into the darkness?

She cast out a thought, still not quite certain how this new telepathy thing worked. *Alton?*

He spun around. "Ginny. I didn't hear you." Then he smiled at her, and the desire in his eyes took her breath.

She walked slowly across the deck. Even though she wore nothing fancier than a comfy old pair of cotton sleep pants and a soft cami top, Ginny grew more deeply aware of herself as a woman with each step she took. A desirable woman. A woman of power unlike anything she'd known before, and she wasn't thinking entirely of her newfound immortality and her crystal sword.

No. This was also about the subtle strength that seemed to spring from her core. Her allure as a female of worth, of value. She walked with the knowledge this beautiful man— a man she liked and admired more every moment she was with him—wanted her. That simple fact strengthened and empowered her new reality.

Alton pulled a bottle of wine out of a bucket of ice, poured some into a bell-shaped glass, and handed it to her. It felt almost dreamlike to take the glass from him. A couple of hours ago she'd been fighting demons with a crystal sword deep inside the Earth. Now she stood on a small deck overlooking the Arizona desert and sipped chilled wine from a crystal goblet.

Definitely surrealistic. Alton patted the space beside him and she sat close, leaned back, and propped her feet on the deck railing in front of them.

The desert night stretched out before them—a blanket of black velvet scattered with diamonds. They sat together in silence, sipping their wine, staring into the night.

Alton slipped his arm over Ginny's shoulders and she leaned close against him. "It feels so good to be clean," she said. She sipped the icy pinot grigio he'd poured for her. "I reeked of sulfur. I've come to the conclusion there's nothing more disgusting than smelling like dead demon. Yuck."

Alton laughed. A coyote howled somewhere nearby. It was a nice, normal howl without any hint of banshee scream.

For some odd reason, the purity of the sound made her feel like crying. Ginny glanced at Alton. He was staring at her. "It's nice to hear something that sounds so normal," she said.

He nodded. "I wondered if that was a natural sound. We don't have anything like it in Lemuria. What is it?"

"A coyote. The same kind of animal that was stalking me last night. The one that was possessed. That's the way they're supposed to sound."

He nodded and took a sip of his wine. "We have no animals in Lemuria. Did you notice? No birds. No bees or butterflies or mosquitoes. Neither fish nor fowl," he added with a melodramatic flair.

He sounded terribly sad.

"No pets? You don't have dogs or cats?"

Alton shook his head. "We've given up so much to live as we do within the mountain, part of, yet apart from, the Earth that was once our home. I remember swimming with dolphins as a boy before our continent was destroyed. Watching birds against a blue sky. Catching frogs with Taron."

"You and Taron have been friends for a long time, haven't you?"

Alton nodded. "He was the only boy my age and we were the best of friends. Like brothers, as we are today. Our people have very few children. We are so long lived that we would quickly overpopulate our world if we could easily breed. Only a very small percentage of our women ever conceive, and then only once. There seems to be a natural law that allows conception only when someone has passed to the other side. It's all about balance."

"But is that really living?" She hadn't noticed many women in that huge auditorium. A few, but they'd stayed in the shadows, much as Alton's mother had. "What do your women do if they don't have children to care for? I didn't see any woman council members. Do women have jobs?"

Alton stared out into the darkness. "No. A woman's job is to care for her man, to raise a child if she is blessed by the gods. We have many more men than women, so if a man is lucky enough to find a wife, he treasures her and protects her. She keeps his home a calm and peaceful place where he can find comfort in her warmth and her loving company."

Ginny stared at him for a long, slow heartbeat. Was he serious? "You're kidding me, right? Making a joke?"

He frowned. "Why would I joke about this? That is a woman's place, to care for her man. To defer to him in all ways."

"Well, crap!" She snorted her wine. Coughed. Embarrassed, she giggled and glanced away. When she looked back at Alton he stared seriously at her, obviously perplexed.

"I'm sure glad that's not our way," she said. She grabbed his hand and squeezed to make her point. "I'd go frickin' nuts, Alton. Tell me why? Why did your women let this happen to them? They were once warriors. Brave soldiers. *Equals.* I carry a sword with the spirit of a female demon fighter. At one time, they fought beside their men. Why did they give up their equality? What happened to them?"

He shook his head, but at least he was smiling. "I have no idea, though I wouldn't be surprised to learn my father had something to do with it. Women fighting in the Demon Wars? That's a part of our history I've never heard before, but your sword and Daria the Crone are proof the women warriors existed. My father is a terribly chauvinistic male who clings to power. He has surrounded himself with similar men on the council. It surprises me my mother's spirit isn't broken, but I can't help but wonder what role he and the others on the Council of Nine might have played in subjugating women."

"I bet DarkFire can tell me." She started to rise. Alton stopped her with a soft hold on her wrist.

"Later. Sit with me. Enjoy the quiet. I imagine, sometime in the near future we'll wish we had this moment back."

Ginny sat. "You're probably right." She ran her fingertips along the side of his face. "Just don't ever expect me to defer unless it's something I would have wanted to do anyway."

Alton laughed and grabbed her hand. Kissed her fingertips. "I was right the first time I saw you. I knew you were going to be trouble."

Ginny glared at him, but she had to fight the twitch in her lips to keep from smiling. "Drink your wine, Alton."

"Yes, ma'am."

Alton lay awake in the bed beside Ginny's and stared at the shadows a small nightlight cast against the ceiling. Ginny'd slept soundly for the past few hours. It had been an unspoken yet mutual agreement to choose separate beds. He'd sensed Ginny's desire for him even as he'd struggled to bank the power of his own heavy arousal, but they were both exhausted, both overwhelmed by all that had happened over the past thirty hours. Tonight was not the night for any more excitement.

Ginny had gained a legacy. Alton had lost a father. He hadn't allowed himself to think of his father's proclamation today, but now, lying alone in the darkness, the words echoed hollowly in his mind.

Strike Alton's name from the Artigos line. He has brought shame to our family. He is no longer my son.

How could any man of honor disown his own child? Granted, there'd been no love lost between the two of them; not that Alton hadn't tried. He'd played by his father's rules most of his life, and when that hadn't garnered him any love or attention, he'd changed course and broken those same rules.

It never seemed to matter, one way or the other. Now, though, when he'd finally taken a position he could be proud of, his father had disowned him. It made no sense. None at all. What made even less sense was how much it hurt. He was a man grown. A good man who'd made a difficult choice to help save his world.

He shouldn't be so easily affected by a father's love—or lack of same—yet he was. He couldn't believe how badly it hurt. He'd given up all that was dear to him, and for what? To be treated now as a common criminal. He needed to get past this foolish need for a father's approval. It was never going to happen, and he might as well accept it.

The bed dipped. The covers lifted and Ginny's sleep-warmed body snuggled against his. He tucked her close beside him and murmured, "What are you doing here? I thought you were asleep."

She grumbled and rubbed her face against his bare chest. "I was, but you woke me up."

"How? I've been quiet as a mouse."

She pushed and he rolled over to his back. She rolled with him, sprawled across his body and wrapped her arms around him. He stroked her spine and she purred like a warm, sleepy kitten.

"You were not. You were thinking really loud. And besides, what do you know of mice? You told me you don't have any animals in Lemuria."

"Thinking loud?" He chuckled and nuzzled the soft skin where her slim throat dipped and curved toward her collarbone. "I didn't mean to. And you're right. We don't have animals now, but I remember them. Remember? I told you we had them before our world sank into the sea."

Kate Douglas

"Even mice?" She lifted her head and stared into his eyes, blinking owlishly.

He kissed her nose. "Even mice," he said. "Ginny? You need to go back to your bed."

She rested her cheek against his chest. "Why? You make a wonderful mattress."

"And you make a perfect blanket, but if I hold you like this much longer, I'm going to make love to you. And if I do that, you're going to be really angry with me tomorrow."

"Why? Are you a really horrible lover?"

He chuckled and felt her slim body bounce against his. "No. I think I'm an adequate lover, but I know you don't take sex lightly and neither do I. I don't want you feeling any misgivings come morning."

Chapter Nine

Ginny raised her head and looked at him again, only this time she was clear-eyed and obviously wide awake. Running her fingertips along the line of his jaw, she whispered, "No misgivings. No regrets, and no way am I going to miss this chance."

He frowned. Turned his head and kissed her fingers. "I don't understand. What changed your mind?"

She kissed him. As kisses went, it was nothing more than a simple little peck to his lips. But as kisses can, it sent a surge of heat spiraling from lips to groin while firing all parts in between.

"You changed my mind," she said. "Lying here in your bed wondering why that bastard of a father of yours would disown you, while I'm lying in my bed wondering why I was over there all alone when the most honorable, decent, wonderful, brave, and beautiful man I've ever met was within my reach."

She cupped his face in her hands and looked into his eyes with so much feeling, so many emotions in those beautiful tiger's eyes of hers that Alton felt a tightening in his throat and a burning in his eyes.

"I can't say I love you, Alton. I've never been in love, so

I don't even know what it feels like, but I know that I care about you. I admire you, I want you and I need the connection that making love with you will give me. Does that make sense? Can we do this without being in love and not fracture whatever it is we've got so far?"

"Ah, Ginny." He closed his eyes and wrapped his arms around her, holding her so close he felt her heart beating against his chest, felt the rush of air in her lungs and breathed in the air she exhaled. "I want you. I need you like I've never needed anyone in my life, but you have to be absolutely certain. I know this isn't something you take lightly. I don't think you take anything lightly, but I swear, if you come to me tonight I promise to make it good for you. I promise we'll find that connection you're looking for. Is that enough?"

She sat up, straddled his waist with her long legs bent close against his hips, and tugged her camisole top over her head. There was barely enough light to see her, but her dark skin glistened where the dim glow from the nightlight caught her curves and valleys.

Watching as Ginny slowly unveiled herself, Alton's heart pounded so hard and fast he felt light-headed. She leaned down and kissed him, and again it was just a tease, the light touch of her full lips to his. "Is that ever enough? Alton, you amaze and confound me, but I want this like I've never wanted anything before. However . . ." She sighed, a movement so slight that he barely felt the brush of her turgid nipples across his chest. "What I don't want is to get pregnant." She laughed, but there was a shaky, nervous sound to it. Abruptly, she sat up and pressed her palms to his belly. "Do Lemurians use condoms?"

He chuckled, but it was over her nervousness, not the question she'd asked. She always seemed so self-assured—he found it rather refreshing that she hesitated now. He rested his hands on her hips, over her soft cotton pants, and spread his fingers across her firm bottom. Then he shook his head. "We don't, but only because it's so difficult for our women to conceive. But for you, Ginny, I will do whatever you ask."

She nodded. "I have some in my bag. I always keep them with me, just in case. For what it's worth, I regularly throw them out because they never get used and go out of date." She gnawed on her full lower lip for a moment. "I was a mistake. My mother gave me up for adoption because she was an unwed teenager who got pregnant when she shouldn't have. That's one family tradition I don't plan to continue."

"You're not a mistake, Ginny. Never a mistake." He ran his finger over her dark cheek, across her damp lips. Then he trailed it along the line of her jaw, down her throat to a point between her breasts. She had absolutely lovely breasts, small and perfectly round with dark, dark nipples. He ran his thumb over the left one and watched it tighten into a taut little point. When Ginny moaned, he repeated the same touch on her right side. "Were you to conceive, my beautiful Ginny, I would cherish our child, but now, with demonkind threatening our worlds, is not the time to take such risks with innocent life. When the time is right, and if the gods are willing, I hope you will someday consider taking a chance with me."

She nodded. Then she clambered off of him and reached for her bag, dug out a small packet, and clutched it in her hands. Wearing nothing but her sagging sleep pants hanging loosely around her hips, she glanced over her shoulder and smiled. The long line of her spine called to him. The soft curve of her bottom. The sleek muscles from shoulder to fingertips.

He wanted to touch her, to taste every part of her, and he knew he was fast losing his control. He tried to remember the last woman he'd been with, but it had been too long ago, and obviously not at all memorable. "Come here, Ginny." He held out his hand and she took it, but for all her brashness and blatant self-confidence, she was once again shy and hesitant. He tugged.

She stepped to the side of the bed. Alton slipped his fingers beneath the waistband of her cotton pants and cocked an eyebrow. She huffed out a breath. Then she shimmied out of the pants and stood there gloriously naked, yet still much too unsure of herself. Alton threw the covers back and sat up. He turned and sat on the edge of the bed and tugged Ginny close until she stood between his legs, caught in his embrace. Standing while he sat, she was exactly his height. Their lips came together so naturally there was nothing to do but kiss her.

She parted her lips beneath the gentle prodding of his tongue. He ran his fingertips along her spine and traced the perfect curve of her bottom, pulling her closer until he held her—between his thighs, in his arms, with his mouth. Connected, yet not. Not nearly close enough.

He still wore his knit boxer shorts, but Ginny suddenly ended the kiss and hooked her fingers in his waistband. "I don't think I should be the only one naked, do you?" Laughing, obviously a bit more confident now, she tugged and he lifted his butt so she could slide his shorts over his hips, over his painfully swollen erection, and down over his long legs. She knelt to tug them over his feet and stayed there, kneeling in front of him with her tiger's eyes twinkling as she studied the length and breadth of his cock.

Her steady perusal was more erotic than fingers stroking or tongues licking. Arousal spiraled through him like a living creature taking over his senses. When Ginny reached out and stroked her fingers along his full length, Alton groaned and his hips jerked. His sac tightened close against his body and he felt another hot rush of blood to his groin.

She flashed him a big smile as she slowly circled his broad glans with the tip of one finger. Slowly, she stroked down his full length. Her gentle touch left fire in its wake.

When she wrapped her fingers as far around him as she could and began the upward journey once again, he caught her wrist in his hand. "Do that again and this entire evening could end quite soon."

She laughed, leaned close, and kissed the very tip. As her lips connected with his damp flesh, a shock raced from his penis to his balls and back again like a circuit connecting.

"Ginny." He barely croaked out her name. So much for smooth. "Enough. Please." He was not going to beg. Didn't want to, but . . .

She held the packet between her thumb and forefinger. "Should I help you put this on?"

He nodded. Breathing heavily he leaned back, supporting himself with his hands. At this point, it was the best he could do. Ginny tore the packet open with her teeth and brought out a flimsy disk made of some kind of plastic. He'd heard of these but still wasn't quite certain what she intended to do with it.

She placed it on the head of his penis and slowly rolled the covering over his full length, smoothing it over his sensitive skin until it covered him in a clear sheath.

So this was the protection he'd heard humans used. He groaned as she stroked it. Merely putting it on was arousing.

Anything that Ginny Jones did to him was arousing. He'd been fighting his growing desire for her since the first night he'd seen her, caught behind that Dumpster with the demon trying to get to her. Fighting the feelings, yet never once imagining they'd ever actually make love.

"Come up here, Ginny." His voice sounded unnaturally hoarse as he grabbed her fingers and tugged her close. She crawled up on the bed as he spun around and tangled his legs with hers. He didn't know where to touch first, what to kiss next. She was dark perfection, all warm and willing woman. She was in his bed, in his arms, and the night stretched out ahead.

* * *

Ginny felt as if she moved in slow motion even as her heart pounded so hard and fast she was afraid it would beat right out of her chest. She'd tried opening her thoughts to Alton's, but his mind was a dark jumble of need and desire, almost frightening in its intensity.

She couldn't believe they were doing this—that she was naked with a man she hardly knew, a veritable giant of a man who could physically overpower her if he wanted, yet she wasn't afraid of him. Never of him. Alton was every wonderful thing she'd ever dreamed of in a man. She hardly knew him, yet she felt closer to him, more familiar with him than she had with any man she'd ever known.

Like she'd known so many. She'd had sex exactly twice in her life, and both times it had been a disaster. Both men had led her to believe they cared for her, but they'd cared only for themselves. She'd learned her lesson. She liked men just fine. She had lots of guys for friends, but not as lovers. Never as lovers.

Until now. She should be terrified. She wasn't. Not with Alton looking at her as if she were some sort of goddess. Not with his gentle touch, his wonderful kisses, his sweet and loving smile. He was so big, though. So tall and broad with wide shoulders and long arms and perfectly formed legs.

He was big everywhere. She bit back a giggle. Thank goodness the condom stretched as well as it did. Then he ran his fingers over her thigh and cupped her bottom, and she quit worrying about his size or his muscles or the fact they were going to make love right now, right here, tonight.

He leaned over her and trailed kisses from her knee to the crease between her thigh and groin. He teased her with his tongue before moving higher and taking first one nipple and then the other between his lips. Her muscles quivered and jumped beneath his gentle touch, and her body trembled.

While his mouth was making her crazy, his fingers were walking a trail along her inner thigh to the moist center between her legs, slipping between her softly swollen folds and dipping inside. She shivered as much with anticipation as nerves when he touched her so intimately. Neither of her lovers had explored her body.

Neither one had touched her heart.

She arched against him and whimpered as two fingers brushed her inner walls and curled against her tightly clenching muscles. The rough pad of his thumb found her clit and her hips bucked as wave after wave of sensation rolled over her.

She clenched the crisp sheets with both hands, and her heels pressed down on the mattress. The trembling spread until her knees and thighs shivered and her body quivered on the very edge of orgasm.

Alton suckled her breast and his fingers slowly thrust in and out, taking her close but not close enough, taking her high but not over the top. She heard a noise, the sound of whimpering, and realized she was making those soft, silly little cries. When he slipped his fingers free of her, she cried out and arched her back, reaching for him.

Alton settled himself between her thighs and pressed the broad head of his penis against the mouth of her vagina. Slowly, so very slowly, he pushed forward, withdrew, then slipped forward again just a little bit more. Filling her, stretching her so much her inner walls burned, taking her someplace new, some dimension so intense, so unbelievably sensual she felt the tears rolling from her eyes, trickling into her hair.

When he filled her completely, he paused and gave her a moment to adjust to his size. The burn eased until she was filled with a delicious sense of fullness. Her muscles quivered and rippled around him. He traced through her tears with his fingertip. "Ginny? Are you okay? I'm sorry, sweetheart. I didn't mean to hurt you." He sighed and his breath shuddered out of his lungs. "We'll stop. Right now, we'll end this."

"Don't you dare." She grabbed the thick fall of his hair. Wrapped her fingers in the strands and practically growled. "Now, Alton. Fuck me now."

"Praise the gods," he whispered. And then he began to move.

She'd never experienced anything even remotely like this. He was big and strong and powerful and long. There was so much of him. Big hands, long arms, long hair, broad shoulders, and those wonderful hair-roughened legs rubbing against hers as he thrust hard and fast and so deep. So very deep, touching the mouth of her womb on every forward press of his hips, sliding in and out with so much strength, so much gentle, loving strength.

Ginny raised her hips to meet him. She grasped his shoulders and thrilled with the ripple of those long, lean muscles beneath her fingertips. He took her to the edge and held her there, making love to her as if she were someone fragile and small, then turning loose and thrusting hard and fast until she gasped with each deep penetration.

Each time she came close to her climax, he slowed the pace, teasing her, making her whimper in need and overwhelming pleasure. She'd never been played so well—played like a fine instrument wielded by a master.

Finally, he reared back on his heels and carried her with him. Ginny wrapped her legs around his waist and he held her close. His big hands lifted her bottom, holding her against him as he rolled his hips forward, tilting her perfectly so the thick length of his cock rode over her clit on every thrust.

He picked up the pace, driving into Ginny harder. Faster. So deep she felt the pressure inside when he touched the farthest reaches of her channel. So perfect she wanted to cry, but it felt too good, so good she almost laughed, amazed how her emotions seemed to fly from one extreme to the other.

Once more he thrust deep. His groan vibrated through her body. He filled her again and she flew. Flew high and far in a cascade of sound and light, of hearts pounding and breath rasping out of billowing lungs.

She'd been so close for so long, hanging on the precipice of completion, shocked now by the intensity, by the sheer force of pleasure that had her crying out and arching her back, driving herself down hard as Alton rammed into her, shouting something totally incomprehensible.

Or was that hers? That cry of unbelievable ecstasy?

He tightened his arms across her back and tumbled them both to the bed. Connected. Caught in the pulsing rhythm of muscles clenching and releasing, of hearts thudding, of lips parted to catch as much air as possible.

Lying on her side, facing the most beautiful man she'd ever seen, Ginny slowly blinked herself back to the here and now. *Amazing. Absolutely amazing.*

She'd never experienced anything like this in her life.

Alton opened his eyes and smiled at her. "You okay?"

She nodded. Took a moment to catch her breath. "Adequate lover, eh?" She chuckled. "That's all? Just adequate?"

"I hope so." He kissed her. "I do hope you were satisfied."

She had to bite her lip to keep from giggling with the sheer bliss of utter satiation. "If you were any more adequate, I think you might kill me."

He nodded sagely. "Don't worry. I promise we'll get better with practice."

She nuzzled the soft hair on his chest and drew in a deep breath filled with the scent of clean male sweat. Her body rippled with orgasmic aftershocks. She felt him begin to stir deep inside. "That's good to know," she said, planting a kiss at the base of his throat. "Especially since I think lesson number two is about to begin."

It took Ginny a moment before she realized why she was awake. Struggling out of a deep sleep with Alton's long arm draped over her chest and his perfect patrician nose buried in her hair, she thought seriously about ignoring the irritating noise coming from her backpack, of just rolling over and going back to sleep.

Then recognition kicked in.

It was the new ring tone on her cell phone. She'd downloaded it Tuesday morning before she'd left Phoenix and headed to Sedona. So this was Thursday? Only the third day since . . . crap. So much had happened in such a short time it made her dizzy just thinking about it. Shaking her still-muzzy head, she crawled out from under Alton's arm and left the big Lemurian sleeping soundly as she reached for her pack.

The phone quit ringing just as she pulled it out and checked the number. She had no idea who it was who'd called. A moment later the phone beeped. Whoever called had left her a message. Yawning, she sat on the floor beside the bed and checked her voice mail.

There was only one message. *Markus?* Now why would her cousin be calling at . . . she rolled her head to one side against the edge of the mattress, squinted, and looked at the clock beside the bed. *Six o'clock in the morning? Sheesh.* Ginny punched in her code. An icy shiver rolled down her spine as she listened to Markus's frantic message. His final anxious words left her mind spinning.

Ginny? What in the hell's going on?

She let out a deep breath and leaned against the bed. "Alton? Alton, wake up."

He groaned. Ginny grinned. It appeared she'd worn her more than adequate lover out last night, though if they hadn't run out of condoms, he might have lasted even longer than he had. Of course, if they'd made love any more than they had, she doubted she'd have been able to walk this morning.

Not that she was complaining.

Alton snorted, groaned, rolled over, and started to snore. Ginny stood up, yawned again, and made a quick trip to the bathroom. While she was in there, she decided to shower. Whatever was going on with Markus would just have to wait until she was clean and a little more awake.

She stepped out of the bathroom a few minutes later and caught Alton sitting up in bed with her cell phone in his hand. "It keeps beeping," he grumbled. Then he dropped the phone and his irritated frown turned to a welcoming grin, which was a really nice compliment, considering she didn't have so much as a stitch on.

"Good morning." He held out his hand and she sashayed across the room until she was close enough for Alton to curl his fingers around her bottom and pull her up against the edge of the mattress.

Amazing how one night of really good sex with a talented and definitely more-than-adequate lover could take away a girl's self-consciousness. Ginny leaned close and kissed him.

He drew her closer until she was straddling his long body with only a thin sheet between them. His hair was tangled and mussed, but the disheveled look only added to his sex appeal. She leaned close and slipped her hands into the thick strands, sliding her fingers across his skull as she brought him close for a kiss.

They'd barely touched, lips to lips, her hands tangled in his long hair, his firmly grasping her hips, when her phone beeped again.

"Not that I'm complaining, but that's what woke me," Alton grumbled. "It won't stop beeping."

Another message? "Damn. I forgot about Markus!" Ginny scrambled out of Alton's embrace, grabbed the phone off the bed, and checked the messages. Markus's deep voice had risen a note this time, and his frantic plea added a layer of guilt.

Ginny! Where are you? I'm getting worried and all hell's breaking loose!

She raised her head. Alton nodded and stroked her hand—the one holding the phone. "He's right, you know. All hell is breaking loose. Let's check on your cousin. We can hike up to the vortex and check on the portal later."

Ginny laughed as she hit redial. "If you want the truth, I wasn't even thinking of the hike to the vortex." She glanced at the tented covers over Alton's lap. "And don't try and tell me you were, either."

Markus answered the phone as Alton swatted her on the butt and headed to the shower.

"Markus?" she said, eyeing Alton's perfectly shaped rear. "What's up?"

Ginny brought him a cup of coffee in the bathroom as Alton carefully plaited his long hair in a single braid down the middle of his back. He wrapped a towel around his hips and reached for the welcome cup. He'd certainly developed a taste for the hot brew during his week at Ed Marks's house.

He took a swallow and sighed. It had to be his imagination, but he was sure the stuff got his synapses firing with the very first sip. "What's going on with your cousin?"

Ginny perched on the counter beside him. "Markus said he picked Tom up yesterday morning after the vet called and said he was okay, and everything was just fine until last night when Tom let out a shriek and so did Markus's little sister. Markus was afraid the cat had gone crazy and attacked her, but he said when he went to check, the cat was fine and Jamilla was holding him in her lap and petting him."

"So what's the problem?"

"That's the weird part. Markus said Tom was purring, but then he yawned. The teeth were back. All those extra rows of sharp teeth, and his eyes were, as my dear, demented cousin said, 'freakin' evil.' But Tom was acting perfectly normal."

"What do you make of it?" Alton turned and propped his hip on the bathroom counter. He loved to watch Ginny when she was thinking through a problem. She'd frown and nibble her lower lip. Her body would be so still it amazed him, that Ginny, who was generally in perpetual motion, could remain motionless.

"They can't be smart enough to use subterfuge, can they?" She raised her head and frowned. "I'm still getting used to the whole concept of demons invading Earth, but it's easier to handle when I think they're just stupid clouds of mist. The idea of demons taking over a creature's body and then acting as if everything is just fine is pretty scary. That's consciously using deception, which means they're thinking it through. I hate to think they're getting that much smarter this fast."

Alton focused on the strands of his braid to keep from reaching for her. "They're generally brainless—evil but not too bright—when they're away from Abyss. Not smart enough to be devious. I agree with you." He raised his head and looked into her beautiful eyes. "Deception requires a certain amount of intelligence, so if Markus is right, we've got more of a problem than I thought."

"He sounded scared. Markus is almost as big as you. It takes a lot to scare him."

Alton chuckled. "I look forward to meeting this large cousin of yours." He tied off the end of his braid with a rubber band and caught himself staring at the little red loop. Now that was something else humans had that was lacking in Lemuria—rubber bands. So simple yet entirely practical, and a lot less trouble than tying a piece of twine around the end. He held the braid up and studied the way the little band held everything in place. Such a simple yet perfect solution. The more time he spent on Earth, the more he loved it here.

And it wasn't just the rubber bands.

He'd been right all along—humans didn't always think things through, but they acted with passion. They felt more emotion in a single day than some Lemurians experienced in a lifetime, and he was quickly learning the importance of feeling, the visceral need to experience emotions with all their pain, if only for the chance to know the glory.

He'd experienced the glory of passion just last night. Making love with Ginny had rocked his world. In fact, it had shaken him to his very roots, to the point where he had to shove those feelings aside or he'd not be able to function.

And function he must. His role here had changed. It was no longer imperative that he fight demonkind to protect Lemuria. No. His focus now was to protect the people of this world.

To protect Ginny. A sense of urgency gripped him. "Let's go." He shoved away from the counter, tugged Ginny's hand, and led her into the bedroom. They'd have to check out the Boynton vortex later. First order of the day was Tom the cat.

Demons behaving well was just wrong.

Markus was waiting on the curb when they drove up in Ginny's little rental car. Ginny hadn't been kidding—he was one big kid. He was only a couple of inches shorter than Alton, but he probably outweighed him by close to a hundred pounds. With skin as dark as Alton's morning cup of coffee and long black hair hanging in strange coils that Ginny called "dreads," he cut a pretty imposing figure for such a young man.

He eyed Alton suspiciously. When Ginny got out of the

car, Markus stalked around the front to meet her on the driver's side. "Who's the blond dude?"

Ginny just laughed. Obviously she wasn't the least bit intimidated by her cousin. "The blond dude is Alton. He's here to help. Alton, meet Markus, owner of the devil cat."

"Not funny, Ginny. He's freaky. Bad enough that I don't want Jamilla or Jamal playing with him. Mom's scared to death. She was ready to call the pound last night to come pick him up, but I couldn't let her do that. He's my cat. I've had Tom for ten years, ever since he was a kitten."

For just a moment, Alton thought the big guy was going to break down and cry, but Markus just shook his head and turned away. "He's not right. He—" Markus abruptly stopped talking and stalked toward the house.

Ginny grabbed Alton's hand and they followed him in. "Can you see DarkFire? I tried to set a glamour on her the way you told me. Is it working?"

He squeezed her fingers. "I can see her, but she's very faint. I doubt Markus can see her at all. You're learning quickly."

She flashed him a huge grin that made his heart soar and reminded him how much he was rethinking so many rules he'd been taught while growing up. It was almost as if the basis for everything he'd learned denied the man he truly wanted to be. He'd discovered very quickly that he was a creature of emotion, just like Ginny. He felt passion, he understood fear and sadness, yet he'd spent his life trying to believe what he'd been taught—the dangers of acknowledging emotion, the necessity for remaining in control at all times.

Following Ginny into the house, he felt a shiver of excitement, a sense of adventure just waiting up ahead. There was no doubt in his mind—being out of control was totally new, more frightening than anything he'd ever experienced in his life, and definitely entertaining.

Markus pointed to a fat, gray cat sleeping on an old couch

in a sunbeam by the front window. Tom didn't look at all threatening and certainly not dangerous, but the stench of demon clung to him. Alton felt a pulse of energy from Hell-Fire. He turned Ginny's hand loose and walked past Markus without waiting for the young man's permission.

Squatting down on his haunches in front of the couch, Alton reached for the cat. Tom raised one eyelid and glared at him out of strangely luminescent eyes. Then he blinked, sniffed the air, and growled. His ears lay flat against his broad skull.

Alton glanced at Markus. "Is that a normal sound for your cat to make?"

Markus shook his head. "Not like that."

Alton stood up. "Markus, stand back, will you? Ginny, draw DarkFire."

Her head snapped up. She looked at Alton as if to reassure herself he'd really said what he'd said. Then she shot a quick look at her cousin. "Are you sure?"

"It's all right." Alton drew HellFire from his scabbard, ignoring Markus's soft curse. He turned the blade, making sure to catch what light he could on the crystal facets so that it glowed even brighter than usual. He almost laughed. He'd never realized before what a flair for showmanship he had.

"Markus, what you're going to see and what I'm going to tell you are top secret." He turned and caught Markus in what he hoped was a commanding glare. Markus didn't move a muscle. Nor did he shift his gaze from the glowing sword in Alton's hand.

"Ginny and I are working for a secret government agency that's aware of the demon invasion. You can't tell anyone what we're going to do right now. Do I have your promise?"

Markus kept staring wide-eyed at the glowing blade on HellFire. He nodded, but when Ginny stood up and drew DarkFire from her scabbard, he stumbled back another couple of steps. "Holy shit. What the fu—?"

Ginny flashed him a look that shut him up in midcurse. "You heard Alton. Stand back."

What now?

Alton struggled to keep from laughing. She was a natural. For that matter, so was he. This was not the way things were done in Lemuria. *I'm going to hold the sword to Tom's heart. When the demon is forced out, it's all yours. Make it look good.*

Tom seemed to suspect something was going on. The cat rose to its feet and snarled. Alton glanced toward Markus. "I'm not going to hurt your cat, but you have to stay out of the way."

Markus nodded and backed up a few more steps. He kept his gaze glued to the two shining swords, not his beloved cat. Alton dipped the blade beneath Tom's belly and pressed it against his heart. Tom screeched. Wailing like a banshee, the cat launched itself at Ginny. She twisted out of the way just in time.

As Tom made the leap from the couch to the floor, a black wraith, stinking of sulfur, exploded out of his back and spiraled toward the ceiling. Ginny caught it with DarkFire in a shower of purple sparks and sulfuric smoke, but just before it died, the demon took shape.

There was no disguising the twisted face, the sharp teeth, or the long, curving claws. This was most definitely a demon, hiding in plain sight within the body of Tom the cat.

The smell of sulfur filled the room. The three of them paused, caught in the sudden stillness and the foul stench. At that moment, Ginny's aunt walked into the room.

"Markus? What is that awful smell? Oh! Ginny? When did you get here?"

"Aunt Betty. Uh . . . good morning." Ginny shot a frantic glance at Alton.

He raised his hand and swept it slowly in front of her eyes. Aunt Betty smiled, turned around, and went back into the kitchen. Then Alton turned to Markus, who was holding Tom against his shoulder, stroking the fat cat's silky fur. "Is your cat okay?"

Markus frowned. He lifted the cat out in front of his face and stared at him. Tom hung there like a fat rag doll and purred. Smiling, Markus brought him back to his shoulder. "Yeah. He's fine, but what was that thing? How'd you get rid of it? And how'd you get rid of Mom? She's usually like a dog with a bone when there's something going on. She wants all the details *now.*"

Ginny glanced at Alton and carefully slipped DarkFire into her scabbard. "Alton and I really are government agents and what he just did to your mom is a special form of hypnosis. Demons are invading Sedona and it's our job to get rid of them. That's why I came down here, Markus. You guys are my cover and I'm trusting you not to say a word to anyone."

Markus stared at Ginny, glanced toward Alton, and stared at Ginny again. "Holy shit. I thought you were making that up." He swallowed and held on to Tom. "I won't say a word. I promise. Is there anything I can do?"

Alton nodded very seriously. "There is. You've got Ginny's cell phone number. Call if you see something suspicious. Let us know immediately, but don't get near creatures you suspect might be possessed. They're very dangerous."

Ginny wrapped her fingers around his wrist and gave him a comforting squeeze. "Thank you, Markus. We'll be in touch."

Chapter Ten

Ginny managed to hold on to the giggles until they'd pulled away in the little blue rental car. "This would be a lot more effective if we could shoot out of here in the Batmobile, or leap into the air and fly away like Superman. Somehow, rolling away in a Ford Focus doesn't have the same impact."

Alton's confused frown just made her laugh harder. It took her a moment to get things under control. "When this is all settled down, and if you plan on hanging out on Earth, we need to rent some movies, make a ton of popcorn, and catch you up on popular culture. For now, though, what's next?"

He still looked a little confused, but then he merely shrugged and sat back while she drove. "Boynton Canyon, I imagine. I want to check the vortex and see what, if any portals, exist there."

"Boynton Canyon it is. But food first."

This time he smiled. "I do like the way you think."

Ginny already knew Alton liked breakfast burritos, so she pulled through a drive-in window. They loaded up on stuff they could eat along the way.

As Alton was unwrapping his second burrito, he glanced toward a small strip mall and shouted, "Stop!"

Ginny hit the brakes and pulled to the side of the road. "What's the matter?"

Alton swallowed and pointed at a drugstore. "Does that store sell condoms?"

Ginny couldn't believe she was blushing. Not after what they'd been up to last night. "Well, yes, but . . ."

"Take me there." He swallowed the burrito in a couple of quick bites. "I need some money." He held out his hand. Ginny fumbled in her purse, grabbed a twenty-dollar bill, and handed it to him.

"I'm not going in there with you."

He grinned, swallowed, wiped his face with a paper napkin, and then leaned close and kissed her. "You don't have to. I've discovered that the young women who work in stores are always very helpful."

He got out and walked across the parking lot. Ginny didn't even want to think about all those helpful young women, especially with Alton shopping for protection. A few minutes later he returned with a large plastic bag. "What did you buy?"

"I told you. I wanted to buy condoms." He opened the bag.

She looked inside and giggled. "Two boxes of extra large? My goodness. You are an optimist, aren't you?"

He tossed the bag in the backseat, looked at her down his long nose and raised one dark eyebrow. "I'm following your advice. I merely want to be prepared."

He sounded so serious it threw her for a loop. Recovering, she quipped, "Are there Boy Scouts in Lemuria?" Alton didn't answer. When she tried to reach him telepathically, there was absolutely nothing there.

Now why would he be blocking her? Sometimes she was so sure she knew this guy, but at other times he totally confounded her. She turned her attention to the road and tried to ignore the oversized hunk in the seat beside her. It wasn't easy.

There was hardly any other traffic as they passed through

neighborhoods that grew more and more rural, until Ginny was driving past small ranches spaced out along the two-lane road.

"What are those?"

She glanced to her right, saw what Alton pointed at, and pulled over to the side of the road. The fenced and irrigated pasture was unnaturally lush and green for desert country, but she knew it wasn't the thick grass that had attracted Alton's attention.

She leaned across him to get a better look out of his open window. "I think those are Spanish fighting bulls. They're bred for the bull ring in Spain and Latin America, where they live like kings until they're old enough to fight against matadors, guys who dress weird and carry very sharp swords. It's pretty ugly—the matadors stab the bulls in a ritualized battle in front of an audience until the bull dies in the ring."

Alton turned and stared at her. "They kill these beautiful animals for sport? These creatures will die?"

Ginny shook her head. "Not here. Bullfighting in this country is illegal. These are probably some guy's hobby, more like pets."

Alton nodded. He seemed fascinated by the small herd. "They look placid enough, but their horns are quite impressive."

"That they are. Impressive and very sharp." She checked for traffic and pulled out onto the road once again, but she noticed Alton's gaze stayed on the grazing cattle with their long, curved, and deadly looking horns until they were out of sight.

He remained quiet, staring out the window as they wound along the two-lane road until they reached the parking lot at the trailhead in Boynton Canyon. Ginny checked her watch. Considering all they'd done this morning, she was surprised it was barely eight o'clock.

Other than her little blue rental car, the parking lot was

empty. Gray clouds hung low in the sky and a cool wind was beginning to blow. Ginny grabbed her day pack and a bottle of water, checked to make sure her scabbard was adjusted comfortably, and then followed Alton along the well-worn trail.

"Do you feel anything different here, Ginny?" Alton paused a few steps ahead of her.

"No." She glanced nervously around, noting the wind-shaped red bluffs and unusually twisted juniper trees. "Should I?"

Alton shrugged. "The energy in this vortex is supposed to be a blend of masculine and feminine. You never did ask me about girl vortexes and boy vortexes."

He didn't look like he was joking. Ginny folded her arms across her chest and stared at him. "Are you flirting with me, Alton?"

He shrugged, but he didn't smile at all. "Maybe a little. Don't I need to?"

He seemed terribly serious for such an odd question. "It never hurts," she said. But they continued on in silence, only pausing while Alton consulted his map.

"This way," he said. They veered off to the left. When Ginny tried to connect her thoughts to his, again there was nothing where she expected Alton to be. Instead, she felt as if she'd run smack dab into a wall.

Alton couldn't shake the uneasy sense he was being watched, and it wasn't by the gorgeous woman walking along the trail behind him. No, it was an all-over uncomfortable sense of something *wrong*.

He'd been blocking Ginny most of the morning, mainly because he wanted to think about the fantastic time they'd had together last night and he certainly didn't want her tagging along on such personal impressions. Now, though, he was glad he'd been keeping her out of his thoughts.

It had started with the bulls and a strange uneasiness he'd felt when he saw them. He'd never been prone to premonitions and didn't think of himself as all that imaginative, but the feeling had grown stronger, even after they'd left the bulls behind. Now he sensed something about this gorgeous canyon with the red rock bluffs and the gray sky hanging overhead that had his skin prickling and his nerves on edge. The last thing he wanted to do was make Ginny as nervous as he was feeling, though he really missed her comforting thoughts in his head.

He hadn't realized how quickly he'd become accustomed to her subtle but constant presence. Just as he'd grown used to HellFire. Maybe the sword could tell him what was going on.

HellFire? Is it just me, or do you sense something here is not right?

I wondered if you were ever going to ask.

He definitely wasn't in the mood for attitude. *Just your impressions of the canyon, HellFire. Please. I don't need a lecture.*

Well . . . all right. I feel it as well, but there's no stench of demon. No sense of anything specifically evil. More of an unrest, as if the spirits walk uneasily in this place.

Spirits? Demons were bad enough. Now he had to worry about spirits, too? He glanced over his shoulder. Ginny was about five paces back. She stopped when he did.

"Something wrong?"

He shook his head. "I don't know. What do you think? Do you feel anything at all that you shouldn't?"

She gazed at the rock bluffs on either side of them and frowned. Then she slowly shook her head. "I'm not as relaxed as I'd like to be. Maybe it's those girl and boy vortexes you were talking about." She flashed him a quick, if uneasy, grin. "Maybe they're not getting along."

He knew his smile was a pretty halfhearted attempt.

"What does DarkFire say?" The feeling seemed to be growing, the sense they should be anywhere but here.

"I'll ask." She closed her eyes, reached over her shoulder, and stroked the jeweled hilt rising above the scabbard. Then her eyes flashed open. "She says be prepared to fight. She doesn't know who or what, but to be ready."

Ginny drew her sword.

Alton nodded and drew HellFire as well. They walked another hundred yards or so, and the sense of wrongness grew. Dark clouds swirled overhead. The soft shush of wind through the canyon and the harsh caw of crows in the distance were the only sounds beyond the scuffle of their boots on the rocky trail.

"Alton?"

The uncertainty in Ginny's soft call brought him to an immediate stop. "What?" He spun around.

She stood behind him and stared up at the sky. He followed her gaze and his heart practically stood still. Where moments ago there'd been only rain clouds, the sky was thick with dark shapes circling above them. The crows they'd heard weren't the only black birds gathering. Others with longer wings and ugly, naked heads dipped and swerved soundlessly on the rising air currents. Birds by the hundreds, soaring and gliding above them in a dark circle that rose high into the threatening sky—a veritable tornado of birds.

Yet none of them made a sound.

"What in the nine hells are they?" He realized he'd tightened his grasp on HellFire. The sword quivered in his hand, as if anxious to act.

Wide-eyed, Ginny slowly shook her head in what had to be utter disbelief. "I recognize crows, ravens and turkey vultures. Some of the smaller birds might be blackbirds or starlings, but they don't usually circle together like that. There have to be almost a thousand birds up there."

She took a few steps and closed the space between them,

but she kept her head raised, her eyes on the growing flock overhead. "This is freaky. It reminds me of an old Hitchcock movie—*The Birds*. For what it's worth, that one did not end well." She touched Alton's arm. "How far to the portal?"

Alton glanced at the map he'd shoved in his pocket and looked around for landmarks to help him get his bearings. "This way." He grabbed her hand again, but now they ran along the trail until it came to a fork with a sign that said VISTA TRAIL.

"It's not much farther." Still hanging on to Ginny's hand, lungs heaving with the short, hard uphill run they'd made, he raced along the fork to the right. "We're close," he said.

A raven dove at them, screeching like a banshee straight from hell. Ginny ducked just in time as it slashed inches from her face with a beak filled with rows of sharp teeth and wickedly curved claws at the end of each toe. "Crap," she said, turning Alton's hand loose and holding DarkFire high. "I was afraid of that. They're demons."

"We'll fight later. This way." Alton grabbed her free hand and tugged. "That spire over there is called Kachina Woman. The knoll with the vortex must be"—he laughed—"right in front of us. There, where the rocks are piled? Someone's left a marker."

"You sure we'll be better off inside? Isn't that where these suckers are coming from?" Ginny trotted backward, still watching the circling birds.

"Inside they should still be harmless mist. Besides, if they're using a portal here to come through from Abyss, we could fight possessed birds forever and never kill all the demons. We need to close the gateway first."

A turkey vulture shot out of the sky, vicious beak extended and red eyes glowing. Alton pushed Ginny down and bent over her, protecting her with his body. The bird hissed as it passed overhead. As soon as it took off, Alton clambered up the side of the small knoll. He ran his hands over the sandstone face until he found the portal. "Here! Ginny, hurry up. They're coming!"

He leaned down and reached for her. She grabbed his hand. "Hurry!" he shouted, and hauled her up the side of the rock just as a huge phalanx of screaming birds headed straight for them. Alton shoved Ginny through the portal first. He tumbled in behind her, along with half a dozen screeching ravens.

The cavern was filled with the stench of sulfur. Dark wraiths streamed through a seething red portal. Ginny immediately went after them with DarkFire and the screams of dying demons echoed off the walls. The stench of their burning souls polluted the close air inside the cavern.

Alton battled the birds, but on his own it was more difficult to stop the possessed creatures without harming them. At this point, all he could do was keep them away from Ginny.

"I need to close the portal. There's no end to them," she cried. "What do I do?"

"Command DarkFire to shut it. She'll know." He shoved a raven aside, but not before it managed to leave a trail of bleeding slices across his forearm. Even their claws were demonic—long and sharp and probably worthless for perching.

Perfect, however, for ripping and tearing.

He sensed the surge of energy in the cavern as Ginny focused DarkFire on the portal. The banshees already through the gateway screeched and screamed, as if they understood what Ginny was doing. Alton knocked another bird aside and quickly reevaluated his opinion of mindless demons.

These obviously knew they needed that portal. The wraiths began to gather, piling one upon the other, taking shape as they'd done in the Shasta vortex. Alton shoved another attacking raven aside and slashed HellFire through the demon mist. All those he connected with burst into flame and died, but others flowed in to take their place.

He felt a burning slash across his shoulders and knew

he'd taken a direct hit from a raven, but his focus now was protecting Ginny, giving her the chance to close the portal. She held DarkFire in both hands while the sword's dark fire covered the shimmering gateway in the rock.

Glowing in shades from deep purple to an incandescent green, DarkFire slowly but surely melted the portal shut. Demons on their way through were immediately destroyed. The ones already in the cave screeched and cried out, their voices growing louder, more frustrated as their gateway to Abyss melted away, as more and more of their evil brethren died.

When it was done, Ginny spun about and grinned at Alton with a triumphant look on her face. It quickly faded when she saw the blood. "Good Lord! How badly are you hurt?"

"Later." He shook off her concern. "It's going to take both of us to handle all of these. I'll knock them down and drive out the demons. Don't let any get away if you can help it."

"I'm ready." She took her position behind him as he swung at an attacking raven, knocked it to the floor, and held it down with HellFire's sharp tip. The demon immediately escaped from its avatar, but Ginny was there. With a single slash of her sword, the demon burst into flames.

They repeated the moves on the rest of the birds. Alton quickly gathered up the birds, filling his arms with dazed ravens and carrying them through the portal. They were beginning to recover their senses by the time he set them gently on the ground outside, but the sky was clear of their brethren.

Which meant that untold numbers of demon-possessed birds were most likely now winging their way toward Sedona.

It was such a strange feeling to be alone in a cavern filled with demon wraiths. Ginny glanced toward the portal and willed Alton to return. She wasn't afraid, which was weird enough . . . crap. If anyone had told her just a couple of days ago that she'd be armed with a crystal sword, fighting demons inside an energy vortex somewhere in Sedona, she'd have thought they were certifiable.

She slashed through another dark wraith and wrinkled her nose against the sulfuric stench. Then another, and another. She'd positioned herself in front of the portal that led out of the rock, but she was afraid a few of the demons had still managed to slip by her. Hopefully Alton would catch them outside.

She sensed movement and turned to her left. The demons were gathering again, coming together to form a huge, seething creature with arms and legs and long, sharp teeth. All still made of mist, but she couldn't see it as a harmless wraith.

Not beneath DarkFire's illuminating light. Their demonic features were made much too obvious. Out of curiosity, she stuck her hand into the dark mass of demons. Other than feeling icy cold, there was no substance to the joined creatures at all. She slashed DarkFire through the middle and smiled with satisfaction when a dozen demons burst into flames and sparkled away into nothing but stinking smoke.

Suddenly Alton was beside her. "You doing okay?" he asked.

"I am," she said, lunging forward and catching two demons as they tried to circle around and get past her. "How are you?" She risked a quick glance. "You're still bleeding."

He slashed HellFire through a pair of dark wraiths. "I'm okay. Most of the cuts are on my back and shoulders. They don't hurt as much if I can't see them."

She laughed. Only Alton . . . "What about the ravens?"

"They flew away. That's what took me so long. I waited to make sure they could fly. I didn't want something to get them while they were helpless."

"What about that huge flock?"

HellFire glowed as Alton slashed through another gathering of demon mist. "The birds are gone. It seems they lost interest once we disappeared through the portal. Unfortunately, I have a bad feeling they've headed toward Sedona."

"You're probably right." Ginny slashed through the last of the demons within sight. Alton leaned on his sword beside her.

The smell was making it difficult to breathe, but Ginny searched the entire cavern. She didn't see any more portals or demons. They'd killed over a hundred before she lost count.

Best of all, she and DarkFire had closed the gateway. She stepped close to admire her handiwork. Alton looped a long arm around her shoulders. "Beautiful, Ginny. It's completely destroyed. You did it perfectly."

Ginny lifted DarkFire. "No, the credit goes to DarkFire. All I did was hold on for the ride."

Alton sheathed his sword. After a moment, Ginny did the same, but when she turned to walk toward the portal, Alton drew her into his arms. "Ginny, I am so sorry. Once again, I must apologize. I never would have sent you here if I'd realized the danger." She felt the warm caress of his lips against her hair and didn't know whether to laugh or rip his shirt off.

Laughter won, and then it took her a minute to catch her breath. Alton stared at her because he obviously didn't have a clue what was going on.

She leaned back in his embrace and held his face in both palms. He was frowning, which made her laugh even harder. "Alton, you can be such a jerk. Quit worrying! You're the one who's bleeding, damn it!" She dragged him close for a quick kiss, and backed away before he could deepen it. "I wouldn't have missed these past days for anything. My life has changed in such wondrous ways, and I'm having more fun than I ever imagined. None of this would have happened if you hadn't sent me to Sedona, and the only thing that would make it better is if Eddy and Dax were here."

He smiled at her. Then he leaned over and gave her a quick kiss. This time, Ginny was the one who tried to make it last, but Alton pulled away. He straightened up and looped his hands around her hips. "Then it appears we need to call them," he said. He stared at the melted wall where the portal from Abyss had allowed untold numbers of demons to enter Earth's dimension.

After a long moment, he shook his head. "We need to check the other portals—the one by the airport and the other at Cathedral Rock. Then we have to hunt down the demons who've made it through. There were at least a thousand birds out there, Ginny. That's a thousand evil souls at the very least, and right now, only two of us."

Ginny checked the fastenings on her scabbard, grabbed Alton's hand, and tugged him toward the portal. "And you think two more demon hunters will make a difference?"

Gazing about the small cavern, Alton merely shook his head. "It's going to have to," he said. "They're all we have unless my people decide to join the fight."

With that depressing thought hovering between them, Ginny and Alton stepped through the portal into a downpour. Rain boiled out of the seething clouds and water raced in muddy streams across the rocky ground.

Ginny took off down the trail at a full run with Alton right behind her. The situation was dire—Alton was bleeding from dozens of cuts and scratches, they were both getting soaked, and they were outnumbered by demons.

Yet for some stupid reason, both of them laughed as they ran through the rain, all the way back to the car.

Ginny's laughter—in fact, her entire good mood—ended the moment they got back to their rooms when she followed

Alton into the bathroom and helped him peel his shredded shirt off his shoulders.

All the way back in the car, she'd thought most of the dark splotches on his flannel shirt were rainwater, that the wounds the possessed ravens had inflicted were nothing more than scratches.

She'd been dead wrong. His dark red plaid shirt was torn to ribbons and drenched with his blood. Bits of fabric were actually buried in the deeper cuts, where at least the flannel had helped staunch the bleeding. Ugly gashes stretched across the top of his shoulders and along his left forearm, the one he'd used to protect his face from the attacking ravens.

"Oh, Alton. I had no idea." She felt like crying as she threw his shirt in the sink. His crimson blood smeared against the white porcelain made her feel even worse. Her hands shook as she grabbed one of the pristine white towels off the rack next to the sink, soaked it in warm water, and began dabbing at the deeper cuts. Most of them were no longer bleeding, though as she washed the caked blood away, some continued to seep.

Alton pulled a small makeup bench close to the counter and sat there while Ginny cleaned away the blood. Even though she knew her amateur first aid had to hurt him, he never said a word. It made her feel sick inside, to see him injured and bleeding.

"You need to see a doctor. Some of these are really deep." She rinsed the towel once more, wrung it out, and watched the blood-stained water swirl down the drain. As she turned to clean more of the cuts, Alton grabbed her wrist.

She stared at his long, pale fingers wrapped around her arm and wondered if he could feel how badly she was trembling.

"Please. Don't be upset. It probably looks a lot worse than it is." He raised his arm and studied the bloody scratches.

Then he smiled and shook his head. "See? They're not that bad. I don't need a doctor, Ginny. Eddy stuffed some bandages in my pack, if you want to use some on the deeper cuts, but I really don't need them. Lemurians heal quickly, remember?"

She sighed, shaking her head with dismay. "I didn't know you'd been hurt this badly. I feel terrible. I was treating it as a big game, like it was all for fun, and you're bleeding all over the place. I can't believe I was laughing all the way back to the car! I'm so sorry."

"Now you're being the jerk." For some reason, his gentle laughter made her tense up. "If you'll recall, I was laughing, too." He pulled her close until she gave in and sat on his lap, though she certainly wasn't able to relax.

She could, however, disagree with what he'd said. "I should have been more aware you were hurt. This happened because you were protecting me. You always remember to watch out for me." She shook her head so hard her wet pony-tail slapped the sides of her face. "I was so caught up in the fact that I was actually inside the rock fighting demons with my own sword that I think I got a little carried away."

He laughed again and hugged her. "It was pretty exciting. I think you had a right to be a little carried away."

She dabbed at the bloody cuts on his forearm and decided they weren't quite as bad as they'd looked, but she still felt guilty, as if she needed to do something to atone. She hated the fact he'd been hurt protecting her. Hated feeling guilty over his cuts and bruises and bloody slashes.

Yet even as she worried, she felt panic rising. How had she allowed him to become so important to her so quickly? When had he started to matter so much? They hardly knew each other and yet she was sitting in his lap, dabbing at his wounds like they'd been together forever. She was worrying about him as if he was her responsibility, as if they were actually involved in a really serious relationship.

Which they weren't. She didn't do relationships. She didn't let guys matter to her, because the minute she did they started demanding things she wasn't ready to give. Even though she'd known him only a few days, already she realized that Alton was everything she'd ever wanted in a man, which was exactly why she shouldn't be getting so close to him.

Men never hung around, no matter how perfect they might seem at first. They got what they wanted and then they left, or they started making a woman's decisions for her, taking away her sense of control, her choices, her life. No way was she going to get involved with a guy to the point where he wanted to take over her entire existence.

No way was she willing to give up everything she'd worked so hard for—her sense of herself, her independence, her control.

It wasn't going to happen.

Except, she had a terrible feeling it was happening already. Whether she wanted it or not, her life was changing. It had been changing since the night she'd been cornered by a demon-possessed concrete statue of a bear, and rescued by a drop-dead gorgeous guy from another world.

If she really thought about what had happened to her since that moment, if she closely examined what they'd done last night when they made love, or this morning when she'd fought demons with a powerful, magical sword, she'd probably end up hiding in a dark corner somewhere, babbling like an idiot.

Life was never going to be the same. Most of what had happened was totally out of her control, but part of the fault was hers—she'd broken her own rules. She'd laughed when he bought all those condoms. Why hadn't she thought about the implications of Alton buying two big boxes? She should have known what he was thinking, but instead she'd let him inside her shields, those barriers she'd kept up around her heart since she was just a little girl.

She and Alton had made love last night, and it had been unlike anything she'd ever experienced in her life. She'd never be content with any other man, not after a night with him. He'd set an entirely new standard, one no one else could ever come close to meeting.

Even more frightening were all the other changes in her once perfectly normal, comfortably boring life. This morning alone, she'd run from demon-possessed birds and found shelter inside an energy vortex. She'd fought demons with her own sentient crystal sword. She'd used DarkFire to close a portal between dimensions.

Ginny Jones didn't do things like that. At least she never had before Alton, but she wasn't just plain old Virginia Jones anymore. She was an immortal Lemurian with a sexy lover and an important job.

"Oh, crap!" She slapped her hand over her mouth.

Alton's head shot up. "What?"

"I have to be back at Shascom by Saturday. That's where I work as a nine-one-one dispatcher. My vacation's over Friday and I'm on swing. That means I have to work late afternoon until eleven."

Alton's fingers gently caught her chin. He was smiling broadly when he turned her to face him. "Ginny . . . think of what you're saying! It's impossible. You must tell them you're not coming back. Your work with me is more important."

"What?" Ginny's skin flushed hot and then shivered icy cold, and she could swear she heard her heart pounding in her throat. She wrapped her fingers around Alton's and set his hand back in his lap so she could finish cleaning the cuts. She couldn't look him in the eye, so she busied herself dabbing at the blood. "You're a terrific guy, Alton, and I know this battle is important, but I can't quit my job. I've been there for seven years. I'm good at what I do. How do you expect me to support myself?" She laughed, but she knew he could tell it was forced.

"Why do you worry about supporting yourself?" He shook his head. "I have money. You said the diamonds were worth a fortune. We'll sell them as we need them. Earning money to live on should be the least of your worries. We have a war to fight."

She slipped off his lap and stepped back, out of his reach, aware she was shaking her head so hard she probably looked like one of those stupid bobble-head dolls. "No, Alton. It doesn't work that way. I support myself. I'm in charge of myself. I don't take money from a man—not from you, not from any man."

"I don't understand." He leaned back on the bench and folded his arms across his chest. "You didn't mind taking the money to pay for this room. How is that different?"

"This is for one week, Alton, and you sort of owe me for this one because you're the only reason I came to Sedona, re-member? One week, that's all, and I'm okay with that, but now you're talking about the rest of my life. If I'm immortal, that's a damned long life. I've got a job so I can take care of myself. That's important to me. I take care of me. You don't."

He smiled at her like she was a complete idiot and shook his head in total denial of everything she said. "In Lemuria, a man cares for his woman. He makes sure she wants for nothing, that anything she needs is provided for her. She in turn cares for her man. She makes his home . . ."

Ginny slashed her hand through the air. " . . . a calm and peaceful place where he can relax. I know. You told me all about women in Lemuria. Well, I may be Lemurian, but I was raised human and in our world we're equal partners— when we're partners." She paused and took a deep breath, spun around, and paced across the room. She really needed to put some distance between them.

"We're not really partners, Alton. I'm not your woman.

We hardly know each other. Three days ago, you were practically a stranger to me. Three days is not enough time to build a relationship, much less a partnership."

If she hadn't been so busy making her point, she might have been paying closer attention, but it suddenly dawned on Ginny that Alton had gone very still, that anger practically radiated from him in waves.

"I see. So, saving your life doesn't count."

She'd never heard his voice sound so perfunctory, his words offhand yet very precise. He leaned forward and rested his elbows on his knees, tilted his head, and steepled his fingers beneath his chin.

Blood continued to run down his forearm. It soaked the towel in his lap. He ignored it, but she couldn't stop staring at that steady stream of crimson blood. Blood he shed from wounds he'd gotten protecting her.

She stood perfectly still, frozen in place, feeling smaller and more insignificant with each word he said.

"So . . . if what you're saying is true, then saving your life, making love with you . . . we were not building a relationship. Taking you to my home, to Lemuria, sharing the discovery of your heritage—that didn't count either, I guess. Sharing your joy when you received DarkFire, fighting shoulder to shoulder with you against demonkind . . . not even when I held your hand and we ran through the rain, both of us laughing." He shook his head. "All these things we did together. I must have misunderstood. I thought these were the things couples did as they built a relationship, as they learned to care for each other. I guess I was wrong."

She folded her arms across her chest so he wouldn't see how badly her fingers were shaking. Everything he said made her feel like an utter fool, which made her dig in her feet and defend her defenseless position even more. "It's not like anything that's been going on with the two of us is even remotely normal, Alton. We've been thrown together under such strange, extraordinary circumstances, that—"

Her cell phone rang. She'd never been so glad to hear that stupid thing in her life. She clamped her mouth shut, spun away from Alton, and dug through her pack.

She answered the call, unbearably aware of the way Alton watched her. Even more aware of his thoughts battering at her mind as she kept him out. Kept him away from all those twisting, screaming fears that were racing through her mind.

She ended the call and looked at him. "That was Eddy. She and Dax are waiting in the parking lot at Bell Rock. I'll go pick them up." She didn't invite him. Didn't want him with her. Not now. She couldn't handle it if they were stuck close together in that stupid little car.

Alton nodded as if everything was perfectly okay, as if he wasn't absolutely furious with her. "You do that, Ginny. You run away and get Dax and Eddy. I will wait here."

She nodded, a short, sharp jerk of her head. "Fine. I'll have the front desk send someone to open up the other half of the casita. That way Eddy and Dax can stay with us. And, for your information, I am not running away."

Except she was. As fast as she could get her skinny butt out of here. And maybe, just maybe having her best friend here to talk to would help her figure out why she was so horribly confused—and, why the conversation she'd just had with Alton had left her feeling like pond scum.

Chapter Eleven

It was less than ten miles but took a good twenty minutes to get to Bell Rock from the resort. By the time Ginny pulled into the parking lot her head ached and she was beginning to feel physically ill from the confusing thoughts bouncing around in her mind.

Eddy and Dax sat together on a red sandstone boulder waiting for her. The first thing she noticed was the fact they were holding hands. How come Eddy hadn't had any trouble figuring out her feelings for Dax?

Ginny rolled to a stop. Eddy and Dax got in. Eddy took the cramped backseat and Dax filled up the passenger seat beside Ginny. Any other time she would have been laughing hysterically at the sight they made, all of them squished into the little car. At the moment, nothing seemed funny.

"Okay, Ginny. Give. What's the matter?"

Ginny glanced over her shoulder as she backed out of the parking lot and caught Eddy's eyes boring into her. "It appears you haven't lost your touch," she said. "Later, okay? We've got more important things to discuss."

Eddy nodded, and Ginny filled them in on the upsurge of demons in Sedona and the possessed birds attacking them at the Boynton Canyon vortex. She didn't mention her fight with Alton. She couldn't, not if she wanted her eyes clear enough for driving.

By the time they got back, the adobe casita already had been opened up to allow access to the second bedroom, where Dax and Eddy dumped their things. Dax grabbed a cold beer out of the refrigerator and met Alton on the front porch, but Eddy cornered Ginny on the small back deck off Ginny and Alton's bedroom.

Ginny glanced up nervously as Eddy opened the bedroom door and stepped out onto the deck. She flashed Eddy a nervous smile. "Where's the dog?" she asked. Anything to avoid the inevitable.

Eddy took a seat beside Ginny. "She stayed with Dad. She can sniff out demons really well, and we didn't want to leave Evergreen totally unprotected. Dad can get in touch with us if there's any sign of demonkind around town."

She grabbed Ginny's hand and squeezed. "Okay, now that we've got BumperWillow out of the way, what's going on? Alton looks terrible and you're not much better. What's the matter?"

Ginny opened her mouth, shut it again, and then took a deep breath. "I'm not positive, but I think I'm the matter."

Eddy frowned. "Oh. Okay. That makes absolutely no sense at all. Explain?"

Well, crap. If she couldn't even explain it to herself, how was she going to . . . ? *Crap, crap, crap.* She dove in. "I'm starting to care about him too much. He's making decisions for me, about me, and I've been letting him do it. I can't stop thinking about him." She waved her hands helplessly in front of her, realized what she was doing and clasped them firmly together in her lap. "See? Look at me! I'm acting all girly, like a nervous female without a thought of her own. That is not me. I won't let it be me!"

Eddy's soft chuckle wasn't what Ginny wanted to hear. "C'mon, Ginny. Alton's not the controlling type. I've never seen him do or say anything that wasn't fair. Are you saying he's pushing you to do things you don't want to do? Has he been mean or unkind to you?" Eddy leaned forward in her chair and gazed steadily at Ginny.

It was impossible not to meet her serious stare. Ginny shrugged. "It's not that so much, though he keeps talking about how Lemurian women don't fight, how their entire goal is to make their homes a calm and peaceful place for their men. Look at me! Can you see me playing the little woman, taking care of hearth and home?"

Eddy laughed. "Not exactly. You can't cook and you're certainly not what anyone in their right mind would consider the peaceful type. I'd put you over in the chaos-and-crisis column."

Ginny leaned back and folded her arms across her chest. "So, do you see my problem?"

Eddy shook her head. "Not really. Alton's not about to insist you act like a typical Lemurian woman, Ginny. For one thing, he knows you were raised on Earth and think like a human woman. An independent human woman. Besides, you've got a sword. The fact you're carrying DarkFire means you're destined to be a warrior, not a housewife. Even Alton has to accept that. Is he telling you he doesn't want you to fight?"

Feeling more like an idiot, Ginny shook her head. "No."

"Does he try to keep you out of danger? I mean, does he get in the way of you doing what you're obviously destined to do?"

"No." Grudgingly, she added, "He said he liked fighting shoulder to shoulder with me. We fought really well together today. The birds I told you about? They really cut him up badly, but he kept them away from me long enough that I was able to close the portal to Abyss."

"Wow. Is he okay? I didn't even notice he was hurt." She folded her arms across her chest. "But that's not why you're upset, is it? Ginny, what the hell is really wrong?"

Ginny grabbed both of Eddy's hands and squeezed. How the hell could she put her problems into words? All the fears, the way she'd felt when she realized how badly Alton had been hurt while he was keeping her safe. Her eyes burned with incipient tears. *Crap.* She did not want to cry.

"Everything's wrong," she said, and damned if it didn't sound like she was crying. She sniffed and cleared her throat. "Alton's wrong. Eddy, can't you see it? Everything about the man is perfect! He's absolutely gorgeous. He's strong and brave and he protected me so I could do my job. He made love to me last night and it was so wonderful. I've never felt the way he made me feel, but I don't want to feel this way!"

Eddy's soft chuckle grated on her nerves. "Ginny, you are not making one lick of sense. The man is perfect and that's what's wrong? Explain. Please. I'm all ears."

Eddy squeezed her hands and Ginny felt like an even bigger idiot, but she had to make Eddy understand. "I don't want to care about him. I don't want him to be perfect. Don't you see? It's like I'm getting sucked into a relationship with a man who's everything I've sworn I never wanted but still everything I've ever dreamed about. He's arrogant and self-assured. He's rich and he wants to support me. He expects me to quit my job and fight demons with him, and I've only known him for a few days. I can't make decisions like that when I don't even know him. What if he's not really what he seems like now? What if it's all a lie and he turns out to be just like every other loser I've dated?"

"Alton's not a loser. He's everything you think he is and more. Can't you trust him? Can't you give the guy a chance?"

"I have to be back at work on Saturday. I'm not ready to quit a job I've worked at for seven years after knowing a guy for less than a week. I don't want to end up being one of those women calling nine-one-one because her life's turned to shit."

Eddy sighed. She turned Ginny's hands loose, stood up, and leaned against the deck railing. "Look . . . when I met Dax, I didn't want to believe he was as perfect as he seemed, but we had a pretty big problem that had nothing to do with whether I had time to get over my hang-ups and fall in love. He only had a week before he was supposed to lose his borrowed body and return to the void. In other words, he would be dead."

She gazed off toward the desert. Shocked, Ginny realized Eddy's eyes glistened with tears.

"I spent half that week trying to figure out if I really believed what he was telling me, and I almost lost him. By the time I realized I was head over heels in love with the man, that it was worth loving him even though I knew I was going to lose him, our week was almost over."

She turned toward Ginny. Tears fell. They left silver tracks down her cheeks as she softly added, "Then I did lose him. I saw him die, Ginny. I held his hand. His body grew cold and I knew he was dead. A miracle brought him back, but during those long minutes, when he was dead and I was left alone . . ."

"So what are you saying?" Ginny crossed her arms tightly, protectively, across her chest.

Eddy brushed the tears away with a swipe of her hand. "I'm saying you're a fool if you don't take what Alton's offering you—a chance to explore a relationship with a perfect man. Don't waste a minute worrying about what might happen. We're in a battle that's so much bigger than any of us. We're fighting demons, Ginny. Creatures from another dimension hell-bent on destroying not only us but our entire way of life. We could all be dead by the end of the week. Do you want to spend what time you've got with

Alton debating whether he's as good as he seems? Good Lord, Ginny. That doesn't make any sense at all. You're smarter than this."

Eddy stared at her for a long, silent moment. "And another thing," she said. "Alton gave up his home, his family, his friends—he gave up everything to fight a battle that isn't even his, and you're worried about a stupid dispatcher's job?" She shook her head as if she couldn't believe how foolish Ginny was acting. Then, without another word, she shoved herself away from the railing and went inside the casita.

Probably in search of Dax. Ginny watched her walk away with a terrible ache in her heart. She and Eddy had been best friends since they'd been old enough to have friends. They had grown up on the same street. Ginny was two years older and little Eddy had followed her around like a devoted puppy.

Never, not once in all the years they'd known each other, had Eddy ever called her a fool. They'd been through boyfriends and heartache together. Eddy'd been there when Ginny's parents died—first her dad from a heart attack and then her mom just a couple years later from cancer—just as Ginny'd been there for Eddy when she lost her mom.

Like sisters, they'd supported each other, loved each other, argued with each other, but never once had Eddy criticized Ginny's actions. Not like this. She wasn't sure how to take it. Wasn't sure if she should be hurt or thankful that Eddy loved her enough to tell her the truth.

Knowing Eddy, that was the way it was meant. She was so damned honest she didn't know how to lie, but where did that leave Ginny? She couldn't just give in to Alton, quit her job, and let him make all the decisions and take over her life, because that's the way it worked. Once a guy was financially responsible, once he got a woman's heart, he took everything. She saw it time and time again.

As a 911 dispatcher, she'd seen the result of controlling men who became abusive. Domestic violence accounted for way too many of the calls she handled, and it always seemed to start when a woman turned over her life to some guy.

But Alton's not abusive or controlling. He's definitely not just some guy.

"Crap." He was so much more than that, which was, of course, the reason she was having all this trouble. If he was just any guy she could walk away without a problem, but he was so far beyond any man she'd ever known.

He'd already saved her life at least once, and today he'd ended up slashed to ribbons while he was keeping her safe. She still hadn't finished bandaging his cuts, and she knew she owed him an apology. But she wasn't going to quit her job. She was going back to Evergreen on Friday night and she was going to show up for work, as scheduled, on Saturday at three.

She wasn't ready for more. She wasn't!

Alton was just going to have to deal with it.

He'd felt Ginny's confusion ever since she'd returned with Dax and Eddy, but he had no idea what to say or do to make things better. Now he sensed her drawing closer, though he couldn't read the roiling thoughts that were flashing through her mind. He wished he understood her better, but obviously something was getting lost in translation.

He most definitely did not understand women.

Dax gave him an encouraging smile and even Eddy stroked his shoulder as she walked past him and flopped down in Dax's lap. Alton wished he and Ginny had a relationship as easy and comfortable as Dax and Eddy, but those two had known each other longer.

Almost two weeks, now. Maybe that was the secret. Did

he have to be patient and wait for Ginny to fall as hard for him as he'd already fallen for her?

She stepped through the open door and all his patience went the way of demon mist. Nine hells, she was something. Even standing there looking so confused and unsure of herself, she took his breath. He'd never dreamed he'd be attracted to a powerful woman, a warrior as strong and true as any man he'd ever known, but when he saw Ginny now and thought of how she'd looked in battle today, swinging Dark-Fire with all the grace and skill of a seasoned fighter, he'd wanted to pick her up, throw her over his shoulder, and carry her off to their bedroom.

Which would probably really make her angry. Dax had tried to explain what it was with human women, how their physical strength might not be equal to a man's, but their sense of purpose and their desire to control their own destiny was every bit as strong.

If that was what Ginny wanted, he'd do his best to comply, but it wasn't going to be easy.

"Alton?"

He nodded, acknowledging her greeting.

"I wanted to apologize."

Now, this was more like it. He sat up straighter. "Yes, Ginny?"

"I'm sorry I didn't finish bandaging your injuries. If you'd like, I can do them now." She stood there with her hands folded in front of her like a rebellious child trying to behave, and then she apologized for not bandaging his wounds?

They were already healing, without the bandages. What about an apology for denying their relationship? For denying him? He took a deep breath and slowly exhaled. "My injuries are almost healed. There is no need to concern yourself."

Then he stood up and brushed past her on his way into the house. It took all his strength not to grab her as he walked by, but he decided it was more satisfactory to leave her standing there with a perplexed frown on her face.

He almost laughed when he heard her exhale in frustration as she asked Eddy, "What'd I do?"

He wanted to tell her. Wanted to go back out there and grab her by both hands and say what was in his heart, that he wanted her to care as much for him as he already did for her.

But that wasn't what Ginny wanted to hear. She'd already made it perfectly clear she didn't want him. Didn't want his money, didn't want his protection, didn't want a relationship of any kind.

She was right when she said they hardly knew each other, and the few days since he'd first seen her fighting for her life were but a blip along the way for a man who counted his life in thousands of years, but he'd known from the beginning. He'd seen her and he'd known she would be important to him, even before he thought they had any chance at all.

He'd also known she was going to be nothing but trouble.

Even when he was the immortal son of the chancellor of the Council of Nine he'd been fascinated by the human woman who would have been nothing more than a commoner in Lemuria.

Was that it? He stopped dead in his tracks. Of course it was! He felt like such a fool. Why hadn't he considered her feelings since so much had changed? She'd nailed him. He *was* an arrogant jackass, setting himself above her when he'd first noted the impossibility of any kind of relationship between them. Now she'd discovered she was not only immortal, Ginny was a descendant of Lemurian royalty.

While he, once the son of Lemuria's ruler, the only child of the chancellor of the Council of Nine, was no one. Lower than the lowest of the common people. Disowned by his own father, an exile from the only home he'd ever known. What could he offer a woman like Ginny? She was a woman of royal blood. An immortal who carried crystal. He couldn't even offer her his honor. That had been stripped from him as well. He was no one, not even a citizen of the world he loved. Was that it?

She was so far above him now, there was no way in the nine hells he could ever dream of courting her. He'd been so caught up in the passion of the moment, he hadn't even considered their change in station. He should have known it would affect her feelings for him, as it should. A woman of Ginny's stature would want an equal as a mate, not a loser like him.

He would have laughed if he hadn't felt like crying. Instead he continued on through the casita and went out through the back, vaulted the low deck, and took off through the desert. Maybe a good, brisk walk would clear his head. A walk anywhere as long as it took him far from Ginny.

But what about tonight? They'd be sharing a room again. The same room with memories of their lovemaking filling his heart and soul. He walked faster, putting distance between him and an unattainable woman as his long legs carried him out into the Arizona desert.

The resort's version of room service looked better than anything Ginny'd seen in any upscale restaurant. She went in search of Alton while Eddy and Dax set the table for lunch and put the food out.

He wasn't in the bedroom, though his scabbard with Hell-Fire lay atop one of the beds. She checked the bathroom, but the towels were dry, so he hadn't been in the shower. She cast her thoughts and searched. There was no sense of him. None at all.

She went back into the kitchen. "I can't find Alton. He's not in the casita and I don't see him outside."

"He can't have gone far. He was here just ten minutes ago." Dax gave the plates of food a longing glance. Then he went toward the back deck and gazed out over the desert. Ginny and Eddy stood beside him. Gray clouds heavy with rain boiled over the horizon and framed the red bluffs in stark relief.

One area seemed to seethe and swirl, rising and falling on the horizon. As Ginny watched, the darkness came together and dove, then swept high into the sky again. She opened her mind and sensed him then. Alton. He was out there, unarmed.

And the birds were back.

"Grab your swords. Follow me!" She snatched her scabbard from the back of the chair where she'd hung it earlier this morning, slipped it over her shoulder, and checked the buckle. Then she raced into the bedroom and grabbed Hell-Fire out of his scabbard.

She slammed one hand on the top rail and vaulted over, hitting the ground beyond the deck with Dax and Eddy right behind her.

"What is it? What do you see?" Eddy caught up and ran beside her.

"That black formation. Those are the birds, the ones possessed by demons that attacked us earlier. I'm not sure, but I think they're after Alton. Hurry. There's no place out here for him to take shelter."

Dax put on an extra burst of speed and quickly outpaced them. As they drew closer, it was obvious the birds had someone or something cornered against a huge saguaro cactus. Dipping and diving, their banshee cries carried on the sharp breeze that whistled through the sagebrush and over the red bluffs.

Finally they could see Alton. He'd grabbed a length of scrap iron and was using it to swing at the birds as they dove at him, attacking in an almost military precision. Dax skidded to a stop, raised his hands, and shot a powerful blast of icy air at the demonic flock.

Hundreds of birds dropped. The rest wheeled away, spinning above the blast of freezing air. Ginny tossed Hell-Fire to Alton. He grabbed the sword without a word and immediately pressed it to the stunned birds littering the ground in front of him. One by one, dark smudges of demon mist escaped from each bird. Ginny and Eddy caught the wraiths with their crystal blades and filled the air with the sulfuric stench of dying demons.

Dax blasted the second wave of birds, dropping hundreds more to the ground. With Alton driving the demons from their feathered hosts and Eddy and Ginny killing each one as it tried to escape, they worked their way through the fallen birds and destroyed each demon before it could go in search of a new avatar.

Ginny lost track of the number of times she swung Dark-Fire through demon mist. Each one showed its true demon self, flashing fangs and claws in the seconds before it died, but they all died—just as all their avian hosts survived.

By the time the birds were gone and the demons destroyed, Ginny's arm felt like a lead weight. She glanced at Alton. He leaned on HellFire and stared at her. "Are you okay?" she asked.

He nodded. "Other than feeling pretty stupid. I can't believe I came out here without HellFire. They were on me within minutes, almost as if they were lying in wait."

Ginny took a deep breath and willed her heart to stop pounding. "They might have been." In fact, they probably were, but she didn't want to think about that.

"Let's go back and eat." Dax slapped Alton on the arm. "C'mon. We left a lot of really good food on the kitchen table."

"Is it as good as Ed's cooking?" Alton sheathed HellFire and followed Dax. Eddy and Ginny walked beside them.

"Nothing is as good as Dad's cooking." Eddy flashed him a grin. "But this looks like a close second."

They laughed and teased one another all the way back to the casita. Ginny did her best to take part, but she couldn't stop thinking about Alton. About what Eddy had said about the dangers facing them.

There'd been a moment, that very brief moment when she'd realized Alton was alone in the desert, unarmed and under attack, that she'd known she would risk anything—*anything*—to keep him safe.

Including her freedom?

Yes, she admitted. *Even that.*

But what about her heart? Ginny Jones was never going to fall in love. She flat out refused to make herself that vulnerable to any man.

But then she glanced at him, walking beside her with that sexy, long-limbed stride of his and the cocky smile on his perfect lips, and she wanted him. Wanted him so badly she felt like screaming.

No, damn it. She refused to allow it. She was not going to fall in love. Not as long as she had anything to say about it.

The four of them stood beside the little blue Ford Focus and stared at the car. Ginny cocked an eyebrow at Eddy, who was obviously having a hard time fighting a case of the giggles.

"What's so funny?" Ginny bit the inside of her cheek.

"It's awfully small," Dax said, bending over to peer through the open window on the driver's side. "The three of us barely fit. How are four . . . ?"

Eddy snorted. "Reminds me of the circus where about ten big clowns all climb out of an itsy-bitsy car after it pulls into the ring."

Alton shook his head. "I'm not sure how big a clown is, but I have a feeling the four of us won't fit in this."

"If you guys knew how to drive, Eddy and I might fit in

back, but there's no way I'm turning either of you loose with any car I'm responsible for." Ginny reached for the door. "Alton, you're taller than Dax, so you take the passenger seat. Dax and Eddy will have to squeeze into the back. It's less than ten miles to the car rental place. I saw it when we drove through town."

Ginny waited to get into the car until the others had managed to squeeze into their seats. There was much shuffling and good-natured cursing as they rearranged long legs as well as scabbards and swords. Ginny maintained until the other three were situated, but as she buckled herself in, she made the mistake of glancing up and catching Alton's twinkling green eyes staring directly into hers.

The humor in his gaze did it. She'd been so tense all through lunch, so unwilling to let down her guard. He'd moved his seat as far forward as he could to make room for Dax and Eddy in the backseat, but now, seeing him squished into the small front seat with his long legs folded tightly and his jeans-clad knees poking up in front of the dashboard was just too much. Laughter bubbled up out of her chest and exploded in a burst of giggles.

She leaned her forehead against the steering wheel and let the laughter flow. Alton's deep chuckle was quickly joined by Dax's and Eddy's unrestrained laughter and the tension melted away. Finally Ginny raised her head, turned toward Alton, and caught him smiling at her, laughing with her, and she knew.

Whatever happened, she and Alton would figure it out. If they could laugh at the stupid stuff and deal with the tough issues, they'd get through whatever came their way.

Even the convoluted feelings that seemed to affect every thought Ginny had, every move she made?

Even those. They could be friends. They could care about each other without falling head over heels in love. Without all the issues that went along with a deeper, more emotional relationship. All it meant was keeping things on an even keel. Remembering that she was an independent woman who had done well without a man in her life for the past thirty-one years, who could continue to succeed with a man as a friend, not the other half she'd need to complete her whole.

She was already whole. A woman complete unto herself.

And don't you forget it.

With that admonition planted firmly in mind, Ginny got her giggles under control, wiped the tears from her eyes with both hands, and then started the car. First things first.

They definitely needed a bigger car.

"Okay." Ginny handed her cell phone to Alton. He tucked it into her bag as she smiled at Eddy in the rearview mirror. "Watch for Airport Road. The same company where I got this car has an office at the Sedona airport. The guy I just talked to says he's got a Yukon. It's a big four-wheel-drive SUV that should be perfect for us."

Eddy leaned forward. "How are we going to pay for it? You can't keep sticking things on your charge card, Ginny. That place we're staying in must be costing you a fortune."

Alton interrupted. "That would be my department. I grabbed a handful of diamonds when we were in Lemuria and we sold a couple to a jeweler."

Eddy's mouth fell open and she grabbed his shoulder. "You mean he didn't ask you where they came from?"

Alton shrugged. "He was more interested in paying us a fraction of their actual value and getting us out of his shop."

"There's our turn." Ginny flashed a glance at Eddy as she made a right onto a side road. "No thanks to my navigators."

"Sorry about that, but I'm still trying to figure out how you were able to sell loose diamonds and not get arrested." Eddy laughed and sat back in her seat.

"There was a little Lemurian compulsion involved."

Ginny flashed a quick glance at Alton, but Eddy didn't seem appeased.

"Alton? Didn't it bother you to know he'd cheated you?"

Alton thought about that a moment. He knew enough about human currency to recognize the value of the perfect stones and the fact the jeweler had definitely made out better on the deal, but Alton and Ginny had still gotten more money than they needed. And he had played what Ginny referred to as his Lemurian mind games on the man.

Alton turned toward Eddy and shrugged. "He gave us enough to pay for the room and to rent the car. Enough that we won't need to sell more diamonds for many months. My compulsion helped him accept our explanation, and the deal worked for us as well as it worked for him. Plus, I still have many more stones."

"And here I'm totally frantic, wondering how I'll pay bills if I'm not writing for the *Record*. I gave notice this morning before we left for Sedona."

Ginny parked the car in front of a small building. "You quit your job?" She frowned at Eddy and then shot a quick glance toward Alton.

He kept his features as expressionless as possible. The decision whether to leave her job was one Ginny needed to reach on her own.

"I did," Eddy said. "And Harlan was less than pleased, but I really didn't have a choice. It's not like you can ignore a demon invasion, but at the same time, I'm totally freaking out about what I'm going to live on."

Ginny nodded. "So true, Eddy. No one ever explains how superheroes pay the bills, but that's not going to be a problem for us. For one thing, I'm not quitting my job."

Alton held back a frustrated sigh and turned back to Eddy. "I've put more than enough money in Ginny's account for all of us." He glanced at Ginny and wondered what she would think of his offer. "If Ginny doesn't mind, we can take some of those funds and transfer whatever you need to your account."

Ginny frowned at him. "Why would I mind? It's your money. Do whatever you want with it. I think it's a great idea, Alton."

He merely nodded.

"Really?" Eddy flashed him a big grin. "Wow. That would definitely make a difference. Thanks. And Ginny, good luck on the job. I couldn't do it, not with all the interdimensional running around we've been doing."

"You say that like you're just hopping a Greyhound from one town to the next." Ginny slowly shook her head.

Alton picked up a few scattered thoughts, mostly about all the changes in her life, how unbelievable everything seemed. Maybe, once it felt real to her, she'd understand she couldn't go back to the life she'd once had. It was gone. Forever gone.

Just as his had forever changed. Had Ginny even once considered how much he'd given up?

Ginny climbed out of the car and held the door for Dax. Alton did the same for Eddy. Ginny's thoughts filtered into his head as Eddy slid out of the small backseat.

Thank you, Alton. I hadn't realized what a huge favor you'd done all of us. The money from the diamonds really does make this a lot less stressful.

He wanted to laugh, but he merely nodded. The money was nothing—merely one more weapon in their battle against demonkind, and there was no way anyone could take the stress out of hunting demons. Still, he couldn't hide the pleasure her telepathic message gave him. She'd been blocking him since earlier today. Hiding her thoughts so successfully, he'd not had any idea at all what she was thinking.

For that matter, he still didn't, but at least she'd reached out, if only to be polite. That had to be an improvement. As

Ginny led them into the car rental agency, he opened his mind to her, searching for more of her thoughts.

He slammed into a seething wall of fury.

There was no sign of Ginny. No, what he found was pure evil. The demon king was back, and he was very, very close.

Alton reached for Dax, linking their thoughts as gently as he could. He didn't want the demon to know he was aware of his presence.

Dax? Do you feel it?

He's nearby, isn't he?

He is. Tell Eddy to be alert and I'll warn Ginny. We need to find out where he is, what avatar he's taken.

Dax nodded and slipped an arm around Eddy's waist. Alton stepped up close beside Ginny. *I sense demonkind nearby, possibly the demon king. Dax and I are going to search for him. Rent the vehicle. Don't worry about us. If we have to, I'll use a compulsion to hide our activities.*

Ginny nodded, turned, and gave him a quick kiss on the cheek. "Be careful." Then she walked away from him.

Alton stood there, bemused by the soft kiss that seemed to shimmer over his cheek, and wondering why she confused him so. Then Dax lightly punched his shoulder.

"Don't even try and figure them out." He nodded toward the women and then turned back to the door they'd just entered. "Demons are a lot less complicated. Let's go."

Alton followed. "You're telling me you don't understand Eddy? Even now?"

"Not a bit." Dax grinned at Alton and stepped out into the bright sunshine.

"But, how . . . ?"

"I follow her lead. I listen to her heart. I love her." He stopped and stared directly into Alton's eyes. "Do you love Ginny?"

His question brought Alton to an immediate stop. "Love?" He shook his head. "I don't know." He glanced back toward the small office building shimmering in the afternoon glare. "At first I was concerned because I was Lemurian, an immortal, and she was . . ." He shrugged. "Nine hells, who am I kidding? I saw her and I was drawn to her. She's brave and beautiful and smart and funny, but she was human and I thought maybe we could spend time together, though not anything serious or truly important."

"And now?" Dax had turned and continued walking, heading quickly down the road they'd driven in on.

Alton followed. "Now I know Ginny is not only Lemurian and immortal, she's also of royal blood." He laughed, aware of the bitterness in the sound. "I thought her a lesser person and I find now that I'm the lesser one. I am an outcast, an exile from the only world I've ever known. Even if I were to love her, she would not want one such as me. So, whether I love her or not can't really matter one way or the other."

"You're thinking like the spoiled son of the Lemurian chancellor. Think like a man interested in a woman, if you are. Because you once put yourself above Ginny and believed she was not worthy of you, now you think she'd do the same." Dax sent him a look that was much too perceptive.

"I don't understand. Social standing is an important part of relationships." Alton paused again as the sense of demon grew stronger.

"Think of what you're saying, my friend. I'm an ex-demon. Eddy was a newspaper reporter. We didn't ask to be thrown together, but we were. We didn't expect to fall in love, but we did. Do you think she questioned my origin or I questioned hers? We were both too busy trying to stay alive, hoping to enjoy the one week we thought was all we had together."

Dax turned and gazed toward a small saddle in the nearby hill. "When you love, it is the object of your love who matters. Not where they came from or even what they are. It's who they are. Ginny is a brave and giving soul, an independent young woman who has been thrown into a battle without any warning at all. Remember, you chose to join this fight. Ginny didn't. Don't push her, but don't underestimate her, either."

Alton rested his hand on Dax's broad shoulder. "How, my friend, did you grow so wise so quickly? You've been human for less than two weeks."

Dax gazed at him with eyes that had seen too much. "In my short span on Earth, I've fallen in love, I've watched those I love fight to the death. I've died and been reborn." He laughed, but there was very little humor in the rough sound.

"All of those things tend to force you to focus on what counts. I learned that love is what counts. Only love." Dax blinked, tilted his head, and turned away. Walking quickly, he headed across a small parking lot toward the saddle. "It's up here," he said, increasing his pace to a jog.

Alton had no choice but to follow. His mind seemed to spin with what Dax had said, but he'd have to study those ideas later. The sense of demon was growing stronger, as was the pulse of energy—a powerful masculine energy emanating from the nearby rise.

Ginny'd said there was a vortex near the airport. This must be it, but it appeared the demon king had found it first.

Chapter Twelve

The big, bronze-colored SUV looked a lot more practical than her little Ford Focus, at least for hauling around a large ex-demon and a very tall Lemurian warrior. Ginny stood beside their new rental and searched for Dax and Alton. "Do you see them anywhere?" She glanced at Eddy.

"I don't see them but I'm in contact with Dax. They're climbing up to that small saddle, just over there." Eddy pointed toward a shallow dip in the surrounding hills. "There's another vortex up there. Dax thinks it's where the demon king might be."

"C'mon." Ginny climbed into the driver's seat while Eddy got in beside her. "I wish Alton and I were clearer with the telepathy. I'm getting better at finding him, but I really can't tell what he's thinking most of the time." She pulled out of the parking spot and drove back toward the main road.

"It'll come with practice." Eddy giggled. "Sex helps." She blushed dark red and turned away. "Park there."

Ginny ignored the comment about sex, pulled into the parking lot, and found a space for the Yukon. Suddenly she felt anxious, as if something bad was going to happen. She scrubbed at her arms. "Do you feel anything?"

Eddy opened the door and jumped out. She adjusted

DemonSlayer so that the sword was perfectly placed for a quick grab. "That anxiety is how you're reading either the sense of demonkind or the energy of the vortex. I feel it more specifically now, but at first it was mostly a vague sense of something really horrible about to happen."

"You nailed it. This is all so new to me. I can't always interpret what I'm sensing or feeling." Ginny locked the doors, shoved the keys in her pocket, and followed Eddy. She hated this, the sense that her body was picking up messages, but it was like they were in a foreign language and she couldn't read them.

Yet she knew they were important. Knew that their lives could depend on her understanding of the warnings given. The feelings grew stronger as they climbed the hill, the sense of anxiety, of something terrible about to happen.

Her teeth were actually chattering, and it had to be at least eighty degrees outside. Ginny opened her mind to Alton and immediately felt his presence.

Ginny? We're in the saddle above you. Follow the twisted juniper trees. They'll lead you to us.

Thank goodness she understood Alton's words for once, if not the other signals buffeting her mind and body. She glanced at the trees alongside the trail. Their trunks were twisted, as if someone had wrung them out like wet rags. A shiver ran along her spine at this visible effect of the power of the vortex. Her sense of apprehension grew and icy shivers raced over her spine.

Alton and Dax waited in a narrow saddle between low hills of red rock. The sun was warm but a brisk wind lifted biting sand to scour exposed flesh. Eddy immediately went to Dax and took his hand, as if to anchor herself. Ginny decided it was time to swallow her pride. When Alton reached for her, she gratefully grabbed his hand. There was something about this place that made her want to be anywhere else but here.

"Where's the portal?" Eddy studied the town of Sedona stretched out below them.

Dax shook his head. "We're not sure. The sense of demon is strong here, but we can't smell them. I've asked Demon-Fire and he's not sure if there's an actual gateway here or not." He rubbed his hands over his arms. "I can feel the bastards. I'm certain they're close."

Ginny glanced at Alton. He shrugged. "I can't find a portal either. I can tell you, though . . . I don't like it here."

The hill to your left, Ginny. Look there. DarkFire's soft tones filtered into her thoughts. Ginny stared at a small hill, hardly more than a bump to the left of their position. With a slight tug on Alton's hand, she headed toward the rise.

"Where are we going?"

"DarkFire told me to look at the hill on my left." She pointed. "I think she means that one."

The others followed. Ginny's sense of anxiety grew, the feeling that they should be anywhere but here in this place of power. None of the other vortexes had affected her this way. She'd battled actual demons without experiencing the dark sense of foreboding that seemed to pervade this whole area.

The snick of crystal on leather caught her attention, and she knew Dax had drawn his sword. Alton set HellFire free, and Eddy grasped DemonSlayer in her right hand. Another, stronger shiver raced along Ginny's spine as she freed Dark-Fire from her leather sheath. The sword quivered in her grasp, and she knew DarkFire was anxious for a fight.

An idea crept into her mind, one she knew must have come from DarkFire. "Let's try the power of our swords." She held DarkFire high. The crystal glowed with its impossibly dark light when the others touched their crystal tips to hers. A blast of amethyst flame burst from the center, rose high, and then shot as if fired from a cannon, straight toward the windblown red rock.

Purple light bathed the surface and disappeared into the

hillside. Dax stepped forward and placed his left palm against the spot. His entire arm slipped neatly through the rock. He'd found the portal, exactly where their swords had marked it with their fire.

"I have a bad feeling about this." He pulled his hand free and glanced at Alton. "Why don't just you and I take a quick look inside?"

A spark of anger flashed through Ginny. Didn't Dax think she and Eddy were strong enough to fight?

But Dax wasn't through. "Then, if something goes wrong, we'll have backup." He leaned close and kissed Eddy. "It wouldn't be the first time she's saved my ass."

"Mine, either. Ginny? Is that okay with you and Eddy? We'll step through, check it out, and return within two minutes to let you know what we've found. If we don't come back in that time span, you'll have to come in with the knowledge that there's probably something really nasty on the other side."

Her thoughts were still spinning, interpreting this new reality, the one she didn't expect. Both Dax and Alton were treating their women as trusted fighters, as warriors equal in strength and cunning to their own. Their trust made Ginny think seriously before she replied.

"I don't like this. I'm not sure why, but something feels wrong." She thought of how she'd felt when Alton had been out there in the desert with possessed birds attacking him from all directions. There was no demon stench around them now, but that didn't mean the bastards weren't in there, waiting.

"I don't like it either, but I'll feel better with you and Eddy as backup. We'll be careful, but you take care as well." Alton gave the surroundings a quick check. Then he leaned down to kiss her. He paused, as if he wasn't quite sure of the reception he'd get.

Ginny raised up on her toes and kissed him hard and fast. "You be careful." It was an order he'd better obey.

* * *

Dax stepped through first. Alton followed, mere seconds behind. The cavern pulsed with deep red light. There was no portal visible, nothing leading to Shasta or Atlantis. Nothing that seemed to lead to Lemuria or even to the worlds of Abyss or Eden, but the sense of something *other* within this vortex was strong enough to have Alton and Dax taking up a defensive mode and turning, back to back, to study the small enclosure.

Light flashed from both their swords, illuminating the area, turning the red glow to a deep yellow. Alton peered into the corners, glanced around the few stalactites hanging from the ceiling a good twelve feet above them. "I don't like the way it makes me feel," he said, "but I can't see anything in here other than that weird light."

He focused on his sword. "HellFire? Can you sense anything? Is demonkind nearby?"

The sword glowed, almost as if in thought. "I sense evil, but it is all around. There's nothing specific and yet I know danger exists. It is everywhere, but nowhere in particular."

"It's got to be coming from somewhere. Should we call the girls?"

Alton nodded. "I'll get them. Ginny's sword might be able to help. DarkFire illuminates things in ways the other swords can't."

He slipped out through the portal just as Ginny and Eddy prepared to enter. "What's up?" Ginny's eyes flashed tiger-bright.

"Come on. We're not sure, but be wary. It's really strange in there." Immediately he turned and stepped back through the portal. Ginny followed with DarkFire clasped tightly in her hand. Eddy was right behind her.

They passed through the portal and entered the vortex.

Dax was gone.

"Where is he? Where's Dax?" Eddy stepped into the small space and quickly spun about.

"I just left him." Alton's heart thudded in his chest. His lungs burned with each sharp gasp for air. He lifted his crystal blade high. "Where is he, HellFire? What's happened to Dax? Do you sense him? Do you feel DemonFire? Are they here?"

"Draw DarkFire."

Ginny held her sword high at HellFire's terse command. Her blade flashed with dark light. The hideous faces of thousands of demons burst into view, shadows intertwined throughout the cavern, camouflaged within the very structure of the rock, so thick they looked as if they were part of the stone itself.

A glint of blue flashed through the seething mass of dark wraiths. With a horrifying scream, Eddy leapt toward the bulge against the far wall and slashed through the clinging mist.

Demons screeched and hissed and died. Ginny and Alton were right beside Eddy, burning through the demon mist that somehow held both Dax and his sword prisoner beneath their roiling, writhing bodies. The stench of sulfur polluted the air as demon after demon died, and their ear-splitting shrieks echoed off the walls, but as Eddy or Ginny or Alton managed to free an arm or a leg, more demon wraiths rushed to hold Dax immobile.

"Can you reach him, Eddy? Can you hear him?" Alton ran his blade carefully across Dax's torso. Demons burst into flame.

Eddy's sobbing breaths echoed in the small space. "No," she cried. "There's nothing. No sense of his mind. I can't reach him at all. Hurry!"

Ginny swept her sword through masses of demons and they died horribly, shrieking and wailing, but they weren't dying fast enough. Enough survived to keep Dax as their prisoner.

Alton's sword flashed and twisted and more demons died, yet the truth remained—from everything they'd learned of demonkind, this shouldn't be happening. Demons were mist, mere ghosts in this dimension, wraiths without power or strength. Somehow they'd managed to capture a powerful warrior. It should be impossible, yet they held Dax against the cavern wall, immobile and apparently unconscious.

Alton hoped that was all that was wrong. Dax couldn't be dead. Not in such a brief time. He'd only left him for a few seconds—not even a full minute. He wore the phoenix tattoo. Didn't that ensure his immortality?

Eddy fought like a woman possessed. Her sword flashed and demons died. Still more came, but where were they coming from?

Ginny's sword not only dealt death, it showed them the true nature of the demons, their actual appearance as they looked on Abyss—foul, ugly creatures with fangs and claws and shimmering scales. Here, though, they'd only existed without substance or strength. How could they hold a man as strong as Dax?

How could they hold a crystal sword?

Alton glanced around the small space, searching for some sign of the portal. Somehow demons were slipping into this dimension, but he couldn't tell where they entered. The walls were covered in demons, clinging like slime mold to the red rock. More crawled across the ceiling overhead, undulating like dark smoke through and around the stalactites, all of them heading for Dax.

So many had died that their ghostly bodies began to litter the floor with black soot, yet Dax remained trapped. Frantic, unsure how to rescue his friend, Alton thrust his hand into the demon mist and managed to wrap his fingers around Dax's cold right arm. He pulled with all his strength, yet Dax seemed frozen. His arm remained clasped against his body. DemonFire was wrapped in fingers gone white with the strain of their grasp.

Alton sheathed HellFire so he could use both hands. He reached through the icy chill of the massed demons holding Dax against the wall of the cave and managed to wrap his long arms entirely around his waist. He latched his long fingers together against Dax's lower back. Then, using the wall for leverage, he braced one foot beside Dax and slowly pulled.

Ginny's and Eddy's swords slashed all around Dax, killing the wraiths that seemed to connect him to the wall. Dax was limp, his dead weight beginning to lean forward into Alton's embrace. His head wobbled loosely on his shoulders, his eyes were closed and his features slack. Alton couldn't tell if he breathed or not. If he still lived.

More demons died and their hold on Dax seemed to loosen, yet still Eddy and Ginny fought on. Alton continued to pull, yet something held Dax. Something powerful refused to give him up.

Eddy moved to one side and Ginny to the other. Ginny raised her sword and DarkFire's light flashed through the space between Dax and the solid wall of the cave.

Something large and dark rose up, a creature of boiling black mist and too many long, snaking arms. Arms that grasped Dax and continued to hold him. Light from Ginny's sword bathed the creature and his features sprang into full relief.

This, then, must be the demon king. Hideous beyond belief and as tall as Alton, as powerfully built as Dax yet still an insubstantial wraith here in Earth's dimension.

Or was he? Two sets of multi-jointed arms with clawed hands wrapped around Dax's waist as the demon pulled his captive close once again. Ginny swung her sword, but the crystal passed through the dark body. Eddy stabbed deep and hard, but there was no spark of dying demon, no stench of sulfuric smoke.

"Why doesn't it die?" Alton hung on to Dax, frantically tugging him away from the demon. At that moment, Eddy and Ginny pressed their swords together, deep within the demonic mist.

Sword points met—dark crystal to light. Energy flashed. The creature screamed, but it wasn't a cry of death. The banshee screech bounced off the walls, reverberating and growing in volume. It was a sound of fury. Pure, unadulterated rage that filled the cavern.

Then, without warning, the creature suddenly turned Dax free, swirled like a miniature tornado, and streaked upward, through a portal no one had seen, a narrow, glowing gateway to Abyss, hidden within a dark cleft in the stone overhead.

Dax lay on the littered floor of the cavern with Demon-Fire beside him. The crystal blade was dull. Dax's chest rose in fits and starts. He made strangled, gasping sounds as if he wasn't getting any air. Eddy leaned over him, listened for his heart, and then blew air into his lungs. Again, and then again, until he coughed, gasped, and then sucked in a huge breath.

He took another, and then another, and his chocolate-brown eyes flashed open, flickering wildly in obvious confusion as he slowly returned to consciousness.

"DemonFire?" Dax's hoarse whisper brought an answering glow from the crystal sword. Dax touched the blade and sighed. "He's all that kept me alive," he said. "The spirit in my blade shared his life force with me."

Stunned, Eddy sat back on her heels. Alton knelt beside Dax and helped lift him to a sitting position. Ginny stood back, away from the three of them. *I'm staying here,* she said. *We need to close the portal, but not until we know Dax is safe.*

Alton raised his head and gazed at her. She was absolutely lovely, standing beside them, a powerful warrior with her sword clasped in her right hand. He felt pride in what she'd done, even though he'd had no hand at all in her abilities. He was proud just the same. Both she and Eddy had proved themselves once again as women worthy of carrying crystal.

Carefully, with little sign of effort, Alton lifted Dax and carried him through the portal to the SUV. Ginny was sure Eddy wanted to remain beside her ex-demon lover, but she opted to stay with Ginny and help her close the portal to Abyss. It took them only a few minutes working together to seal it entirely.

The red glow disappeared. Even the stench wasn't as bad, though Ginny wondered if maybe they'd just fried some of their scent receptors during the height of the battle. "Let's make a quick pass and make sure we got all of them."

Eddy nodded, but she moved as if on automatic pilot. They quickly checked walls, ceiling, and floor, making certain the demons were gone and the gateway to Abyss sealed shut.

Together, Ginny and Eddy stepped out of the vortex. The anxious sensation was gone. Ginny drew in a deep breath of clean air as they walked the short distance down the hill to the SUV. Dax was sitting up in the backseat, a little woozy, but at least he was conscious. Eddy crawled into the back beside him, wrapped her arms around his waist, and burst into tears.

Feeling close to crying herself, Ginny got in and started the engine. Eddy slowly got her emotions under control. Alton was quiet, sitting beside Ginny, staring out the passenger window. His thoughts were entirely closed to her. He didn't speak all the way back to the casita.

Ginny unlocked the door while Alton and Eddy helped Dax inside. Not a word was said as they separated and went to their rooms to bathe. Somehow, it was most important to wash the stench of demon from their bodies before they sat down and tried to figure out what they'd just experienced.

It was a rather subdued group that met around the dinner table a couple of hours later. Ginny'd ordered dinner from the restaurant on site and they chose to eat inside at the kitchen table rather than out on the beautiful deck with the view of the desert at sunset.

Somehow, after Dax's brush with the demon king, it was more comforting to sit at the small table within the solid walls of the little adobe casita. More relaxing, knowing that a demon-possessed creature wouldn't be showing up unexpectedly during their meal.

At least not unless one knocked on the door.

Ginny toyed with her wineglass while Eddy passed around the plates of enchiladas, beans, and rice. A bowl of fruit sat in the center of the table for all of them to share, and under any other circumstances, they'd probably be drinking margaritas and having a party.

Not tonight. Alton reached for Ginny's hand and she wrapped her fingers in his. His hair was still damp from his shower, hanging long and loose over his shoulders. Ginny thought about running her fingers through the damp, silky strands, but she didn't have the energy. She felt absolutely lethargic after a long soak in a very hot tub—her mind as well as her body still numb from the battle this afternoon.

It was so much easier not to think about anything. Not to let her thoughts wander down the torturous trails of the utterly impossible, of demons and Lemurians and Dax's beginnings. Of talking crystal swords and other worlds in dimensions apart from this one.

Of the fact Eddy'd actually quit her job and embraced her new reality—not only as a demon fighter, but as the forever partner to a man she'd known for less than two weeks.

No wonder Ginny'd slept so soundly once they'd returned this afternoon. She'd needed to escape a reality that seemed more impossible every day. She'd crawled out of the tub, dried herself, and slipped into a soft terry robe. There'd been no question of lying down on her own bed. She'd joined Alton on his. They'd stretched out together and held hands the way they were holding on to each other now. He'd been her anchor then.

He was her anchor now.

They'd talked for a while, lying there on the big bed in the room darkened with a heavy shade that shut out the late afternoon sunlight. Alton had filled Ginny in on more of the details of his week with Dax and Eddy, a week of terrifying battles and even some laughter as they'd discovered all the different kinds of creatures demons had possessed.

Killer garden gnomes? Check. Mrs. Abernathy hadn't been off the mark at all when she'd called 911 the night Ginny was working dispatch to report that a garden gnome had eaten Twinkles the cat.

Impossible but true.

Ginny'd finally learned the truth behind the battle in Evergreen when demons had taken on cemetery statuary as avatars and marched against the townsfolk in what had turned out to be an almost epic battle orchestrated by the demon king. It had actually seemed humorous when Alton told it. Humorous until Ginny considered the danger behind each act the demons had committed, each amazing and terrifying sign of the accelerated evolution of their abilities.

Even more terrifying had been the full story of that last battle on the flank of Mount Shasta. How the three of them—Eddy, Alton, and Eddy's father—had sat beside Dax's dead body and felt him grow cold as time passed, knowing their friend and fellow warrior was truly gone. His return to life had been no less than a miracle, though even that had been eclipsed by the replication of Alton's sword.

Out of HellFire, DemonFire and DemonSlayer were born, and the war against demonkind had truly begun.

So many things had changed that day. Willow had lost her body and taken up residence in Bumper the mutt, Eddy and Dax had achieved immortality, and while Ed's mortality hadn't changed, the bad hip that had crippled him for years was totally healed.

The oddest thing in Ginny's mind as she'd finally drifted off to sleep was the fact she believed every word Alton told her. Demons were real. Earth was the fulcrum that kept other worlds in balance, and she really was an immortal Lemurian, charged with defending more than one world against demonkind.

Never in her wildest dreams . . .

In truth, her dreams had never been this wild, and her life, by comparison, had been merely a shadow of what she was living now. As unbelievable as today had been, it hadn't been unusual, at least when she compared it to her new reality—a reality that had changed forever the night that stupid concrete bear cornered her behind the garbage Dumpster, and she'd been kissed by the most beautiful and amazing man she'd ever known.

She glanced at their hands, at the way her dark fingers entwined with Alton's fair ones, at the strength in his hand, the muscles in his forearm, and she mentally dragged herself back to the small kitchen, to the friends surrounding her at the table. To the amazing fact it was all real. All happening to Ginny Jones, Shascom 911 dispatcher.

What a weird day it had been. Today's attack on Dax had been totally unexpected . . . but at least Dax was safe. Ginny raised her head and caught his dark-eyed gaze and she thought of the first time she'd met him, when Eddy had introduced him as an old college friend in that little coffee shop in Evergreen. Was it only a week and a half ago? She'd liked him immediately without even realizing who or what she was actually meeting.

With that memory firmly in place, the present rushed back into focus. They could have lost him today, and while she would have lost a friend, Eddy would have lost the man she loved. The one she'd promised to love for all time. It was a sobering thought. One Ginny wasn't prepared to dwell on, especially with Alton's fingers clasped so firmly in hers.

She let go of his hand, picked up her wine, and lifted her glass. "To Dax," she said. "May you always stay safe, no matter how dangerous the fight."

"Hear, hear." Eddy leaned close, kissed Dax's cheek, and clinked her glass to his beer bottle. Alton joined them. They all sipped at their drinks. Then, one by one, they set their glasses down and an uncomfortable silence hovered over the small group.

Ginny couldn't stand it a minute longer. "Does anyone know what happened today? From what you've told me, that wasn't normal demon behavior, if there is such a thing."

Dax nodded. "It certainly wasn't what I expected. The second Alton stepped through the portal and left me alone in the cavern, the demons attacked. I've never seen anything like it. They practically exploded off the walls. We hadn't seen them because they'd somehow taken on the shape and color of the stone, but they flew at me like an explosion of black mist. It was too fast for DemonFire to warn me. There was enough force behind their attack and enough substance to the creatures that they caught me off balance. It felt like a harsh wind picked me up and threw me against the back wall."

"But what was that thing holding on to you?" Ginny covered his big hand with hers. "It didn't look anything like the other demons. It was huge, and it was one entity. I'm sure of that. Not a collection of demons trying to appear as a single beast." She shook her head. "It was real, real ugly. A hideous face. Scales, long fangs, and what looked like four multi-jointed arms with hooked claws even on the joints. Yuck. Definitely ugly."

Dax raised an eyebrow, nodded, and glanced toward Alton. "You guys got a better look at it than I did. I could feel it—feel at least four scaled arms around my waist, the strength in muscles and bone. It wasn't just mist. Was it the demon king?"

"I think so," Alton said. "But if it was, it's more dangerous than we realized. Tell Ginny what you learned about the demon king when you were in Eden. It might help explain why we have reason to fear him."

Dax nodded. He glanced at Eddy and the look in her eyes spoke volumes. Ginny knew they must be thinking of that terrifying time when Eddy thought Dax was dead, when they couldn't find their tiny will-o'-the-wisp companion, Willow.

Dax's voice was rougher than usual. He squeezed Eddy's hand and exhaled a frustrated breath of air. "I've told you how I was originally a demon from Abyss. Well, the one we're fighting now began in Eden. He had it all—he was a creature of Paradise, but he threw it away. They told me he was the only son of one of their leaders, a young man of uncommon beauty and impeccable lineage. They banished him because he embraced the darkness. He was sent into the void as punishment for his evil acts, where he should have remained forever entombed, except he was recruited by leaders of Abyss—leaders I didn't even know existed—and turned into a demon."

"You had no idea your world had rulers?" Ginny tried to imagine Abyss, a dimension of total chaos and unadulterated evil. What kinds of creatures ruled such a place?

What kind of creature would choose Abyss? Even the void sounded preferable.

Dax shook his head. "No. I was merely a nameless demon, one of untold millions of creatures who exist merely to survive at all costs. I wasn't concerned with kings or rulers. My biggest worry was not getting fucked or eaten by someone bigger or smarter than me. Our recruited demon, however, never actually existed among the masses. He was transformed while still in the void and given the body of a demon."

Frowning, Dax stared at Ginny. "It almost sounds, from your description, that he got my old body. If I ever actually see him, I'll let you know if he looks familiar, but I was a pretty scary guy, once upon a time."

Eddy leaned her cheek against his shoulder. "Love, you're still a scary guy. Anytime you doubt yourself, just ask me."

"I'll try and remember to do that." Laughing now, Dax planted a kiss on top of her head. "Anyway, it appears he was sent to Earth as head of an invasion force, but he lost much of his intelligence and the knowledge of his purpose in the transition from banished Edenite to mercenary demon. Unfortunately, it seems he gains it back the longer he's on Earth."

"But he just went back to Abyss. Shouldn't that make him lose what he's learned?" Ginny looked to Alton for confirmation, but it was Dax who answered.

"We don't know for sure he even goes back to Abyss. He started out in the void. Maybe that's where he returns. Maybe the rules don't work the same for this guy. He wasn't born a demon. He was sent somewhere once before when Eddy destroyed his gargoyle avatar. He seems to have returned this time as an even stronger entity." Dax stared at his clasped hands, both of them wrapped around one of Eddy's. When he raised his head, the look in his dark eyes left Ginny feeling chilled to the bone.

"He directed the attack on me in the cavern. When he grabbed me and held me against the wall, I felt his teeth at my throat. Smelled his foul breath on my face. He was more than just mist. He felt solid. He shouldn't—not in this dimension. I tried to break away, but I had no strength. I still feel weak. I think he was somehow siphoning my energy, absorbing it much as he did from the demons he took at the battle in Evergreen. If it hadn't been for DemonFire sharing his own life force, I don't know if I could have survived even that brief an attack."

"Are you certain?" Alton leaned across the table. He held his fork in his hand as if he'd forgotten he was planning to take a bite of his enchilada. "If that's true, Dax, we've got an even bigger problem than we thought. Do you think the other demons have that ability, or is the demon king unique?"

"The others were able to shove me into the demon king's grasp, but only the demon king was stealing my energy." Dax shook his head. "It was the weirdest sensation, as if my energy were spiraling up and out of my body, like it was being sucked out of me. At the same time, I felt the pulse of power from DemonFire, small amounts at a time, not enough to interest the demon king, but enough to keep me alive."

He pulled his T-shirt collar aside, showing the smooth column of his throat. "I think the demon king is like an energy vampire. His mouth was against my throat, though he didn't pierce my skin with teeth of any kind."

Eddy ran her fingers over his skin and shook her head.

"See?" Dax said. "Nothing. Not a mark. Not even a bruise. There aren't any marks on my body, either. As tightly as he held me, I should have bruises, even scrapes from the talons."

Dax released the cotton band and it settled back against his neck. "I felt him. His scales, his claws. He was very strong and my ribs still ache from the way he held on when Alton was pulling me away, yet there's no visible sign of his touch." He shook his head, as if denying the lack of evidence.

Ginny glanced from one somber face to the other. "How long before you think he'll be back?" She took a bite of enchilada, hardly tasting the spicy flavor, but she chewed anyway. They all needed to eat—they'd need all the energy they could get to fight this threat.

"A couple of days at the most. It's been less than a week since Eddy sent him back to Abyss." Dax turned and gazed on her with such pride it made Ginny's stomach do a strange little flip.

Dax and Eddy had only known each other a week and a half, and yet they seemed so sure of themselves, of their feelings for each other. How did you know when the guy was right? When the time was right? Ginny couldn't believe Eddy'd quit her job! As much as she hated Harlan, Eddy'd loved writing for the paper.

Almost as much as Ginny loved working at Shascom as a 911 dispatcher. She felt as if she actually did things to help people, like her job mattered.

And demon fighting doesn't?

She blinked. What was DarkFire doing in her head?

You are a warrior now, Virginia Jones. It is your destiny to fight demonkind. You have strength and intelligence, and you have me. Your position in your world can be handled by another. This one can't. Only you can wield DarkFire. Do not squander the gift presented to you by Daria the Crone. Do not keep me away from this battle I long to fight.

DarkFire's presence faded from her mind, but her admonition left Ginny rattled. She turned and frowned at Alton. He was taking another bite of enchilada, but he turned with his fork poised halfway to his mouth and frowned right back at her. "What? Why do you look at me that way?"

"Have you been talking to DarkFire?"

"Of course not. Your sword only speaks to me with your permission. Why do you ask?"

"No reason," she mumbled. "No reason at all." *DarkFire, too?* Feeling horribly outnumbered, Ginny switched gears. "Okay, if it's going to take him a couple of days, we might have more help by then. That's when Alton and I are supposed to meet Taron inside the portal at Bell Rock. He should have word of the Council of Nine's plans."

Alton finished his meal and shoved his plate aside. "That's true, but we can't count on their help. Unfortunately, as long as my father is the council leader, they're going to listen to him, and he has no desire to do anything his son might suggest."

Dax seemed obviously perplexed by Alton's comment. "Are you saying he would condemn an entire society to prove his point? He'd let demonkind win rather than accept that you might be right in this instance?"

Alton merely shrugged, but Ginny knew how badly his father's narrow attitude hurt him. She covered his hand in hers. He gave her a quick, sad smile. Then he sighed and turned his attention to Dax and Eddy.

"Dax, why don't you and Eddy stay in tonight? Get your strength back so you'll be ready to go out when we patrol the area tomorrow. Ginny? Would you be willing to take me into town? I think we need to look around Sedona at night when demonkind tend to be more active. I want to know if they're still taking over pets. We haven't heard from your cousin or the vet. I fully expected a call from at least one of them by now."

Ginny folded her napkin and set it next to her plate. "I think that's a good idea." She turned to Eddy. "Are you guys okay with that?"

Dax was the one who laughed. "You're kidding, right? You're asking if I want to stay here and sleep? It sounds wonderful."

Eddy punched his arm. "Actually, he's been eyeing that big-screen TV and the remote control." She rolled her eyes in dramatic fashion. "He's discovered the joys of reality TV."

Dax frowned. "I'm merely trying to learn more about Earth's culture in the twenty-first century. My body's original owner died over sixty years ago. I have a lot of catching up to do."

Ginny snorted, covered her mouth, and did it again. "Sorry, but this conversation just struck me as totally unreal. We're sitting here in this ritzy little resort in Sedona, Arizona, paid for by stolen diamonds from Lemuria, talking about fighting demons and Dax's borrowed body and reality TV. Don't you think it's just a little bizarre?"

Eddy stood up and grabbed her plate and Dax's. "Tell me about it. What's really freaky is that my father has never been happier. Every weird legend, every myth he's studied or crazy tale he's heard is suddenly coming true. It's given the man a new lease on life."

"Ya know, I miss your dad." Ginny grabbed the rest of the dishes and carried them to the sink. All they needed to do was scrape the dishes and leave them in the sealed carrier for housekeeping to pick up off the front porch.

"I miss him, too, but he's home with BumperWillow for company. I'm going to call him in a bit."

"Tell him hi for me." Ginny turned and leaned against the counter, well aware of Alton's silent perusal of her. She opened her thoughts to his and found only impressions of contentment as he watched her. She'd not expected thoughts as comforting and calm.

"Will do. You guys be careful." Eddy poured herself a glass of wine and grabbed another cold beer for Dax. "We'll be thinking of you out there battling demons while we're sipping our drinks and watching the moon rise over the desert from our lovely room in this luxurious resort."

Laughing, Ginny pushed away from the counter. "Thank you so much. Your concern overwhelms me."

Alton waited by the door with a hopeful expression on his face and the keys to the Yukon in his hand. "No," she said, grabbing her keys as she walked past him. Laughing, Alton shrugged his broad shoulders and followed her out the door.

Chapter Thirteen

Ginny drove slowly out of the resort grounds. She glanced at her cell phone for messages. Then she handed it to Alton. "Call Markus. See if he's seen anything unusual."

Alton took her phone, found Markus's number, and punched the key. There was no answer. He left a brief message and then handed the phone back to Ginny. "Now what?"

"Wasn't this your idea?" She laughed. "I guess we drive. Open the windows. Keep your senses alive to anything that feels wrong." She slanted what should have been just a quick look in his direction. Light from the dashboard reflected off the curve of his chin and the sharp line of his nose. His hair was dry now, hanging like pale yellow silk over his shoulders and pooling in his lap. Damn, but she was jealous of that hair. Why was it the guys always got the beautiful, smooth tresses? She loved that he'd left it unbound. His black T-shirt was tucked into his jeans—it stretched over his muscular chest as if it had been painted on him.

She had to force her attention back on the road stretching out in front of them. *Concentrate, girl. Pay attention.* "I felt the demons at the airport," she said, though she hated recalling that awful feeling. "It was a horrible sense of something really wrong, like a slow-motion anxiety attack that just kept building and getting worse."

Alton's big palm covered her right knee and she smiled at him, then quickly looked at the road ahead. "I wasn't sure if it was the vortex I was sensing or the demons, but once we went through the portal I knew it was demons making me so anxious."

Alton nodded. "I sensed them as well, but I'm wondering now if it was the lesser demons we sensed, or the demon king. I've never noticed that kind of physical reaction before, but this was a feeling of something truly evil."

"Maybe it's because he truly is evil. Think about it. A demon that's born a demon, that's always a demon, is acting true to his nature. In Abyss, he's not evil, he just is. As Dax said, his only concern was staying alive, so the demons invading Earth's dimension aren't inherently evil—they're merely acting the way they're supposed to act—like demons. The demon king, though, was once a creature in a world without evil, so for him to choose the darker side means he consciously chose to be bad. Doesn't that make him worse than a natural-born demon?"

Alton's burst of laughter caught her by surprise. "What?"

"Ah, Ginny . . . If I'd had any doubt that you were Lemurian, your argument just now would have convinced me of your true nature. Lemurians live for the debate. You're a natural."

She chuckled. "Eddy's always said she hates to argue with me because I refuse to lose even when I'm wrong." Grinning broadly she added, "Of course, I'm never wrong."

"I'm glad you told me. I'll remember that when we disagree." Alton settled back in the comfortable seat and smiled as if he were enjoying his own private joke. At her expense.

"You say that like it's not going to happen."

Alton cocked one expressive eyebrow and rolled his head to one side to watch her. "I was being facetious. I imagine we'll disagree many times in the many years ahead. Don't expect to win every time. It would be bad for my self-image."

Many years? Would they really be together for many years? How could Alton say that when they'd known each other such a short time?

She really didn't want to think about that right now. No, she just wanted to check around Sedona for demons and then get back to the casita and sleep. Except where was she going to sleep tonight? In the same bed as Alton? And if they slept in the same bed, would they make love again?

Just thinking of the possibility made her stomach clench—but was it nerves or expectation? Ginny glanced Alton's way, but he was staring out the window as they sped toward town. She wondered what he was thinking, but when she searched, she came up against a solid wall blocking his thoughts. Turning her attention to the road ahead, she drove through the darkness toward the lights of Sedona.

Alton hadn't felt this relaxed in ages. There was something about Ginny Jones that seemed to make him feel complete in a way he'd not been in thousands of years. It didn't make sense, really, since she'd certainly not committed herself to him. They'd made love only that one night and she certainly didn't treat him with the respect and deference a Lemurian female traditionally offered to her mate.

Which, he'd finally decided, was part of the attraction. Ginny deferred to no one. She was tough and outspoken and fearless in battle, as aggressive on the battlefield as she'd been in his bed. There was a lot to be said for a tough, self-confident woman.

At least he finally understood why Dax loved Eddy so—she was his equal, a woman to stand beside, to count on, not one to treat like spun glass. Eddy was a woman worthy of respect.

Just like Ginny.

She drove slowly once they reached Sedona. At the intersection of Highway 89, she stopped for the red light and then turned left into town. Traffic was quiet—not nearly as heavy as it had been during the daylight hours. It was still comfortable out, so they drove with the windows down.

Alton fiddled with the radio. He was quickly growing to love the different kinds of music he could find with the mere flip of a switch. For all their advanced technology, Lemurians had nothing to compare to the music humans made. They couldn't.

Good music was passionate. It stroked the emotions.

He stopped at a country-western station, listened a moment, and then sat back to enjoy a slow, sad ballad about lost love and missed chances.

Ginny laughed. "You always go for the most depressing music, Alton. What's wrong with something fast and sexy? Some of these songs just make me wanna cry."

"That's because they make you feel emotions." He steepled his fingers beneath his chin. "I was raised in a society where emotions are frowned upon. In Lemuria, it's all about logic, about the common good. Humans are all about passion and emotion, about getting in touch with their feelings." He sighed. "I envy you the life you've led, the freedom to enjoy emotional highs and lows, to feel sadness and joy with equal measure."

Ginny was quiet for a long time, staring straight ahead as they slowly drove through town. After a couple of blocks, she softly sighed. Her voice was so quiet he barely heard her.

"I know it sounds great in theory, Alton, but emotions aren't always a good thing. I still feel horribly sad when I think of my parents and how much I miss them. I'm scared to death of the changes in my life right now." She stopped at a red light and turned to stare at him.

"Most of all, I'm really terrified of what I feel for you."

She shook her head. "I don't want to feel all twisted up inside, unsure of how you feel about me, afraid of what I'm beginning to feel for you."

The light changed and she pulled forward, but her soft words hung in the air between them, emphasizing the charged silence.

He had no answer for her. Dax had asked him if he loved Ginny. How could he know what love was if he'd never felt it before? He liked her. Liked being with her, admired her, but *like* and *admire* weren't necessarily love. His lack of response only added to the silence between them.

A silence that didn't end until they heard a blood-curdling scream. Ginny hit the brakes and skidded to a stop at the side of the road. "Do you hear that?"

"C'mon!" Alton jumped out of the SUV, drew HellFire, and raced back the way they'd just come. Traffic continued past them on the road as if no one else heard the terrified screams. Alton skidded to a quick stop in front of a narrow alley, slid around the corner, and ran down the dark passage between two buildings.

Ginny's feet pounded the sidewalk behind him. He held his sword high. HellFire's brilliant glow illuminated the shadows, spotlighting an older woman cowering in a doorway, surrounded by huge gray rats.

He saw seven of them, though others might be lurking in the shadows. Their eyes glowed blood red. Naked ears lay flat against ugly heads. It took Alton a moment to place the odd clicking noise echoing around him—it was the rhythmic snap of teeth as the rats closed in on their prey.

She was wearing shorts and hiking boots. Her legs were bleeding from a dozen deep scratches, though Alton was relieved to see she didn't have any visible bites. She looked about sixty or so in human years. Her gray hair framed her face in a wreath of curls and frizzy tangles. She grasped the broken handle of a broom in both hands and held it like a club. The rest of the broom lay just beyond, along with the bodies of two dead rats.

"Don't worry about finesse," Ginny said. "I hate rats."

"Whether you hate them or not doesn't matter." Alton swept his loose hair over his shoulders to get it out of the way and moved around to the other side of the advancing circle. "If you kill the living avatar, the demon will take its life force. The last thing you want to do is feed demons. It's better to force them out and kill them in their mist form."

"Damn. I was afraid you'd say that." Ginny touched Dark-Fire to the first rat. It screeched and rolled over. The demon shot straight out of its belly in a dark swirl of stinking mist. Alton swung HellFire. The demon burst into flame and disappeared in a thick cloud of sulfuric smoke.

Another rat, another demon gone. Then another. Suddenly Ginny sensed a movement to her left. She spun around as a large black cat launched itself from the top of a pile of boxes. Ginny slapped it down with the broad side of her blade and Alton forced the demon from its body. Ginny swung DarkFire through the screeching wraith and watched with absolute satisfaction as the black mist burst into flames.

The cat sat up and shook its head, hissed once, and raced away. "Ungrateful beast." Ginny turned her attention to the rats once more. "The least he could have done was hunt a few rats."

Only four of the creatures remained, but they continued to circle in front of the woman. She'd moved to the top step. Trembling, she hung on to the door, watching wide-eyed.

Advancing slowly, Ginny and Alton methodically destroyed the rest of the demons. The stunned rats wobbled to their feet, blinked with beady but normal rat-colored eyes, and scattered. The woman stared as the last of the vermin disappeared into the shadows.

Then she focused on the light from the two swords. Slowly she moved down the three steps, but she didn't turn loose of the broom handle. "What the hell happened? There've always been rats in the alley, but never once have they come after me."

Ginny sheathed DarkFire and stepped forward. "Are you okay?"

The woman nodded and glanced at her legs. "I scratched myself when I fell. I was trying to get away from them." She pointed at the dead rats. "Those two came flying out of the dark and scared me half to death. I knocked them both down before I had a chance to think about it, but the broom snapped in two."

She grabbed the short banister beside her and hung on. Her entire body shook as she stared at the dead rats. Then her head snapped up and she looked at Alton as if she were seeing him for the first time. Her terrified gaze settled on his sword. "Who are you? Are those lightsabers you're using? I've only seen those in the movies." She reached for HellFire.

Alton quickly pulled the blade out of her reach and slipped it into his scabbard. He checked Ginny's sword to make sure her glamour was in place. Then he swept his hand across the woman's eyes. She blinked owlishly and looked down at her legs.

"Oh, wow! How'd I do that?" She touched one particularly deep scratch and then looked up at Alton. "Who are you?"

He ignored her question. "We heard you scream. My friend and I came to see if you needed help. Are you okay?"

Still somewhat dazed, she nodded. "I'm fine. I must've fallen. I'll need to clean these up, but thank you. It's nice to know someone will still stop and help a person."

She gazed into the shadows and shuddered. "Weird," she mumbled. "Just weird." Then she turned, opened the door to the back of the shop, and went inside.

Alton gazed at Ginny for a long moment. A sound caught

his attention and he turned quickly, drawing HellFire. *Nine hells.* He quickly sheathed the sword.

A small crowd of onlookers had gathered at the far end of the alley, obviously drawn by the woman's screams just as Alton and Ginny had been. Alton grabbed Ginny's arm and they walked quickly toward the group. As they drew closer, Alton realized they were mostly teenagers and young adults.

At least a few of them had been drinking. "Hey, man." One who'd obviously had too much, a tall, lanky kid, stepped forward. "Cool sword."

"Sword?" Alton gave him a confused look. "What sword?"

The kid frowned. He looked at Alton's hands. One clasped Ginny's arm, the other hung at his side. He shook his head. "I was sure I saw a sword." He looked over his shoulder at his friends. "Man, I need another beer," he said. Then he spun around, stumbled, and laughed. "Make that two."

He took off down the street with his buddies laughing and teasing him. Alton watched the group go with his thoughts in turmoil. He wasn't thinking of the demons or the fact they'd just saved a woman from an unprecedented attack, one that almost seemed too organized for demons as they knew them.

No, he was thinking of what it was like for young humans. The friendships they had, the opportunities to go out in the world and do stupid stuff, to take chances. To learn and grow and experience life in all its wonders, even if that wonder was nothing more than hanging out on a street corner with friends.

The best memories of his life were of his times with Taron when they were still children, but then their world had changed and they'd been thrust into a life without any challenges at all. A life so tightly directed they'd never had the chance to grow, to find out what they were capable of.

And what had he done with the life he'd had? Disappointed his father. Left his mother without the one child she'd been able to have. Abandoned his world, his people, and any chance at redeeming himself to his family and friends. Had he made the right choice when he'd left Lemuria? Would his sacrifice make any difference at all, or was he merely using this battle against demonkind as an excuse, a chance to see what there was beyond the only world he'd ever known?

He was still learning. Still discovering who and what he was. Even Ginny knew more about living than he did. She'd lived more in her thirty-one years than he had in all the long centuries of his existence. What did he have to show for his long life? What had he done to make his mark on his world?

"Alton? Are you okay?"

Ginny's soft question dragged him out of his dark thoughts. Pulled him away from a lifetime of regrets and worries about his future—if he even had a future.

"I'm okay," he said. "Just thinking about a lot of stuff I can't do anything about."

Ginny squeezed his hand and hugged his arm close against her side. "I know. Life's like that. Lots of questions and not nearly enough answers."

They quietly walked away from the alley and back to the SUV. When they reached their vehicle, Ginny paused and stared at Alton. "I wonder where the demons that were in the rats she killed have gone?"

He shook his head. "I don't know, but odds are they've got the life force of the rats to give them more power. Demons are definitely growing more aggressive, but rats?" He rolled his shoulders. "Nasty things." He gazed around the area where they'd stopped, in a part of town filled with small shops, restaurants, and bars. A few tourists wandered from store to store and most of the businesses were still open. "Let's walk," he said. "Can we leave the vehicle here?"

"It's fine here. I actually parked legally."

She flashed him an uncertain smile and slipped her hand

into his. They walked along the sidewalk like the rest of the people enjoying a balmy evening in the desert. Alton searched her thoughts and found the same disquiet he felt within himself.

Sometimes he wondered if he and Ginny were more alike than he'd thought. Maybe Ginny was the answer to his questions, if he only knew what they were. Was Ginny as confused as he was?

Sounds of laughter filtered out of a small bar they passed, but it was the country-western music that brought Alton to a stop, made him back up, and drew him toward the sound. He gazed in through the open door. Once his eyes adjusted to the gloom, he realized the place was filled with young adults around Ginny's age, all gathered in couples or groups. They were laughing and talking and doing all the things young couples in this world did to get to know each other.

It wasn't this free in Lemuria, but even at their more formal gatherings the objective was the same. Spend time together, see if the person you met would make a proper mate, a potential parent to the child you hoped to have one day. Here it was called dating. He understood the concept, how human men and women interacted as they grew to know each other.

He glanced at Ginny and wondered what it would be like to go on a date with her. Would it hurt to take a moment for themselves, just the two of them?

Feeling absolutely reckless, he leaned close to Ginny's ear and whispered, "Hey, sweet thing. Can I buy you a drink?"

She giggled and leaned against his arm. Then she gazed up at him with a look of pure adoration that he knew was absolutely fake. "Can you afford a girl like me?"

He blinked and straightened up. That certainly ruined his line. "Well, no. I gave all my money to you."

She laughed, hooked a finger in the waistband of his

jeans and tugged. "C'mon, cowboy. I'm buyin'. It is, after all, your cash." She winked. "How's that work?"

"Works for me." He looped an arm over her shoulders and they stepped into the shadows. There were at least a dozen young men lined up along a wooden bar. Light reflected off of various bottles and glasses along the wall. Most of the tables were filled with couples or groups of single men or women sitting and drinking, talking and laughing.

The noise level dropped as he and Ginny walked through the door. Alton was immediately aware of the avaricious looks some of the women gave him. Any other time he might have enjoyed the attention, but tonight he only wanted Ginny. She clung tightly to his arm. He wanted to think she was staking her claim, but he figured that was only fantasy.

Still, he couldn't help but wonder if she ever gazed at him in such a covetous manner. If she ever looked at him as if she were mentally undressing him. He doubted it. Not Ginny. She had more pride, unlike these ladies. Some of the women they passed looked like they wanted to eat him alive.

One particularly busty blonde tried to make eye contact, but Alton quickly glanced away. Luckily, the music that had caught his attention when they'd walked by was still playing.

"I thought I knew this song." He grabbed Ginny's hand and dragged her over to the colorful machine in the corner that seemed to be the source of the music. "What is this? Is it like the radio in the car?"

"No, silly." Ginny leaned over and read a list of titles across the front. "This is an old-fashioned jukebox. I haven't seen one of these for years. Look—it's actually flipping real records. Wow . . . Johnny Cash and *Folsom Prison Blues*. I haven't heard this one for a while."

"It was on the radio in your little blue car. That's how I recognized it." He turned and caught Ginny looking at him, but she was only curious. At least he didn't think she was imagining him naked, and since her thoughts were blocked he couldn't really tell.

Her thoughts were always blocked, it seemed.

"It's an old song," she said, glancing at the list of titles once again. "I used to know all the words."

He nodded. "I've only heard them once before, but the lyrics made me think of my life in Lemuria, when I knew there was a whole other world outside and I was stuck inside a mountain with nothing to look forward to."

She raised her head and her tiger's eyes seemed to look right through him. "You thought of Lemuria as a prison? For all those years?"

He shrugged. "Not always. When I was younger, shortly after our continent sank beneath the sea, I was excited about our new home. When I was old enough, I helped with some of the early construction, but then it was done and there was nothing. No challenge, nothing to dream of. It became even more of a prison after I began sneaking out and visiting your dimension. The personal freedom here made me realize how much more there could be in a man's life. When I heard this song on your car radio yesterday, it reminded me again of how I felt within the stone walls of our world. Earth was the train, forever moving, knowing freedom."

His words drifted off as the song ended. Ginny continued to stare at him and her look was one of timeless wonder, as if she might finally have started to understand more of the man he was and not just the man he preferred to show her.

But was that a good thing or bad? He'd never been close to anyone other than Taron, never really shared his more intimate feelings and thoughts. Maybe it was a mistake to let Ginny get too close. She'd already said she didn't intend to stick around.

She had her job to go back to, a job she seemed to think was more important than fighting demons, than saving the world . . . than him.

Nine hells . . . he hoped his mental barriers were strong. They could still communicate, but he didn't want her wandering around inside his self-pitying thoughts. Another song came on. The same singer, but with a totally different sound. Something about naming a boy Sue? Alton tried to make sense of the silly lyrics, but he couldn't give them his full attention. Not when Ginny was so close, her eyes focused solely on him.

He reached out and touched her hair. Her dark curls were springy beneath his fingers, so unlike the straight, smooth feel of his. Hers had life and energy, just like Ginny. They fit her. Everything about Ginny fit. She was perfect, exactly as she was, a woman comfortable in her own skin.

"Son of a bitch!"

Ginny pressed close. Alton focused on the group of young men at the bar. He recognized two of them. They'd been part of the small crowd watching from the end of the alley when he and Ginny took care of the demon-possessed rats. He'd left them all with a compulsion to forget, but the tallest one had been particularly inebriated.

He was the one who'd shouted the curse, though he sounded more frightened than angry.

Alton grabbed Ginny's arm. They edged over so he could see the guy better. His compulsions generally worked really well on drunks. They didn't have the mental clarity to fight his suggestions, but there was something weird about this guy.

He was there, wasn't he? He looks familiar.

Yes, Ginny. I want to watch him. Something's not right.

I agree.

She moved with him and they took two empty stools close by the young man. He was leaning over the bar now, staring at his mug of beer and mumbling incoherently. His shoulders jerked, his legs twitched, and there was obviously something very wrong about him. The bartender was serving another customer, but he was definitely keeping an eye on this one.

Even his friends seemed to have noticed something was wrong. A couple of the guys had their heads together, but they kept their focus on the drunk. Suddenly he straightened up, screamed as if the gates of hell had been flung wide, and lunged toward Alton and Ginny. He swung his arm around and caught Ginny hard on the shoulder with a round-house punch.

She flew off the stool before Alton even had time to react. He caught her before she hit the floor. The guy's buddies were all over him. Within seconds they'd grabbed his arms and pinned him against the bar.

"I'm okay." Ginny shook her head and tried to sit up, but Alton held her down between the legs of their barstools while the battle for control went on over their heads.

"Stay down. I have a horrible feeling that I know where those two demons pumped up with the life force from the dead rats went." Alton pulled HellFire from his scabbard.

Despite his orders, Ginny scrambled to her feet and grabbed DarkFire. Five men were trying to hold the drunk, but he managed to shake them loose one by one whenever they grabbed an arm or a leg. The bartender was on the phone, calling for help.

"Now, before the police arrive." Alton stepped forward and waved his hand over the group of men as they struggled with the drunk. All five suddenly turned the tall kid loose. He shook them off, completely unaffected by Alton's compulsion. His eyes glowed red. He snarled a curse and the sharp points of his teeth glowed in the reflected light.

Alton leapt forward and pressed his crystal blade against the drunk's chest. The kid jerked and his body went totally rigid. His arms flailed, his mouth opened in a soundless scream.

Then another piercing screech poured out of his mouth,

along with a thick, black mist. Ginny caught the wraith with DarkFire's blade and it burst into amethyst sparks and sulfuric smoke. A second dark cloud shot out of the man's mouth and Ginny got that one as well.

The drunk stared blindly at Ginny. His eyes rolled back in his head and he slowly crumpled. Alton grabbed him before he hit the floor and eased him slowly to the ground. Ginny quickly sheathed her sword and Alton managed to get Hell-Fire in the scabbard before the sound of sirens and screech of tires warned that the police were pulling up out in front.

Alton quickly set a compulsion over everyone in the bar. He knew it wouldn't last, but hoped it would at least give Ginny and him time to escape.

He grabbed her hand and slipped out through the door just as the police raced toward the bar. Alton and Ginny stepped to one side and the two officers ran by them without seeming to even notice they were there.

"What'd you do? How come they didn't even look at us?" Ginny frowned and stared over her shoulder at the bar as Alton dragged her down the sidewalk toward the SUV.

"I used the same glamour on us that we use on our swords. They were so intent on getting inside the tavern that they weren't looking for us, so they didn't see us."

"Oh. I never would have thought of that." Ginny wrapped both her hands around his left arm and matched her steps to his. "Well, Alton. I must admit . . . you certainly know how to show a girl a good time."

He snorted. He couldn't help it, and it made her laugh. "Good times like that we can do without." Then the reality of what they'd done slammed through the adrenaline rush that had him practically giddy with relief. "You know what this means."

Ginny's smile disappeared. She nodded. "That's the first human possession we've seen." She stopped and frowned at

Alton when they reached the SUV. "But he was drunk, Alton. And there were two demons filled with the rats' life force."

"I know, but remember, they're evolving. When they first showed up, it was inanimate objects of the earth. They could only take over stone, metal, or ceramic. Then they moved to family pets and wild animals, and I was with Dax and Eddy when we discovered they're taking on plastic avatars. That's still of the earth, but definitely processed."

"From rats to humans is a pretty big leap to make so quickly, even if it was a drunk human."

Alton opened Ginny's door for her. She climbed into the Yukon and buckled herself in. He stood there in the open door, watching her as she latched the seat belt over her trim hips, but his mind was spinning a thousand directions at once—and not a single direction was good. "In some ways," he mused, "that's even worse. Two demons working together were able to take over a human's mind and body. That's more than an evolution of abilities—it's showing more conscious thought. More cooperation."

"Well, we knew they were beginning to cooperate when they started bundling together in the cavern and turning themselves into über-demons."

Alton backed away and shut her door, but he leaned his elbows on her open window. "I know. It's another step forward for them, though. And it means none of us are safe, if they develop the ability to possess someone who's sober."

Ginny's eyes opened wide. "How do we fight that?"

Alton shook his head. "I don't know, but we need to figure out something. I have a feeling the gloves, if there ever were any, are off."

He circled around the front of the Yukon and climbed into the passenger seat. Ginny flashed him a tired smile. "I take it you're not interested in more barhopping?"

He shook his head. "No. I'm worried about Cathedral Rock. There's another vortex there, which means there might be another portal allowing demons through. We've closed the portals at the airport vortex, Bell Rock, and Boynton Canyon, but we haven't even checked the one at Cathedral Rock."

Ginny stuck the key in the ignition and turned to smile at him. "Let's worry about it tomorrow. I'm not too concerned about that one."

"Why not?" Alton paused in the process of fastening his seat belt. The big grin on Ginny's face seemed out of place with the current discussion.

"Because Cathedral Rock is a girl vortex." She started the engine and eased out into traffic. "Remember that discussion we never had about boy and girl vortexes? Well, I read about them. The actual source of the vortex is on the creek at a place called Red Rock Crossing. It's got lots of feminine energy. You know—kindness, compassion—the good things women are known for."

"I see." Alton bit back a smile. He settled into his seat and watched Ginny while she navigated the narrow streets on her way back to the road that would take them to their rented casita, back to Eddy and Dax and, hopefully, an uneventful evening. "So you think the demons might avoid this particular energy source?" He chuckled when Ginny flashed him a wide-eyed, innocent look.

"Well, wouldn't you?" She blinked. "All that sweet goodness should be absolute poison to any right-minded demon."

Alton rolled his head to one side and played along. "It might, Ginny m'love, if all feminine energy were nothing but sweet goodness, and if there were such a thing as a right-minded demon. There's no such creature."

She turned and headed out the rural road that would take them home. Then she deadpanned, "You're such a killjoy, Alton."

He leaned back in the seat and folded his arms over his

chest. In his best Johnny Cash voice he said, "I know, but when you've got a talent, you learn to work it."

Her soft laughter shivered over his shoulders as he settled back for the short ride. The evening hadn't gone anything like he'd planned, but they'd worked well together. They'd made a difference, and they'd learned more of their enemy's abilities.

In battle, at least, they were a perfect team.

And now they were headed back to the casita where all he could think about was the fact they'd be sharing a room again tonight. He stared at the headlights sweeping over the road ahead and carefully blocked his thoughts.

No wonder they'd not gotten very good at their telepathy. They spent more time blocking thoughts than sharing them. He wasn't certain he wanted to think about the implications of that, the fact that they still didn't trust each other with their deepest thoughts, but at some point in the not too distant future he and Ginny really needed to learn to communicate.

Of course, they'd need to learn to trust each other, even when they weren't surrounded by demonkind. That might be the most difficult lesson of all.

Chapter Fourteen

Ginny parked the Yukon in front of the casita. There was a light in the main room but the rest of the little house was dark. Her mind had been spinning all the way from town, and she really wished her thoughts didn't keep bringing her back to the same crappy conclusion.

Alton reached for the door handle. She put her hand on his arm. "Wait." She glanced toward the house and back at Alton. His face was hidden in shadow, but light from the front porch reflected in his eyes.

"What's wrong?"

"Dax. I'm worried about Dax." She shifted around and leaned her shoulder against the back of the car seat. "Today he said the way we described the demon king sounded like we were describing his demon body, the one he gave up. What if it is his body? What if the demon king has targeted Dax? Maybe there's still some sort of link between the ex-demon part of Dax and the body he used to have, and maybe that's why he's the one the demon went after today. Not because he was left alone near the portal, but because he's more susceptible to the demon's powers. Does that make sense?"

"Unfortunately, yes." Alton shifted around and faced her.

"I wasn't thinking of that so much, but I have been worried that, in his weakened state, Dax might be easier for a demon to possess. If demons could take him over, they'd have his demon powers along with his considerable strength. He's not himself right now. What happened today weakened him."

Ginny sighed. "I hadn't thought of that, but that's another part of the same problem. We need to talk to him. He's got to be aware of the danger he could be facing."

"I agree." Alton leaned his head back against the seat. "Dax is my closest friend, besides Taron. We have fought together and faced death together. I don't want anything to happen to him."

"I don't want anything to happen to any of us. C'mon." She got out of the Yukon and followed Alton into the casita. Eddy was sitting by herself in the front room with the television on.

"Hi, guys." She waved them to a couple of empty seats. "It's not looking good. Demons have hit the nightly news."

Alton sat beside her on the couch. Ginny took a seat on the footstool in front of him. "What's going on?"

"Unexplained animal attacks. The local shelter is full, but after a couple of hours in the cages, vicious animals are suddenly just fine. Ravens swarmed a couple of outside restaurants, attacked customers, and broke windows. A few of them were killed running into cars or getting shot by armed citizens. Toxicology tests show nothing unusual, though there're reports of some sort of toxic chemical being released." She turned and shrugged. "Oddly, people say it smells just like sulfur."

"Go figure." Ginny shook her head. "I wish we knew how many were left out there."

"Demons?" Eddy sat back and stretched her long legs out over Ginny's lap. "More than we had in Evergreen, I think."

"Alton! Look . . . that's the bar we were in tonight." Ginny scooted forward as the newscaster described the fight in one of Sedona's more popular nightspots.

"The young African-American woman who was attacked left the bar before police arrived. Witnesses didn't recall if she'd been injured or not, but everyone has mentioned the sulfuric odor." He raised his head and sniffed the air. *"I can still smell it. It's very faint but it reminds me of the smell of striking matches. Everything appears calm now, but toxicology tests are being run to determine whether some sort of hallucinogenic chemical is responsible for the strange behavior of local animals and now, a visiting tourist. Back to you . . ."*

"Ginny! You were attacked? Are you okay?" Eddy grabbed her hand and gave her a quick once-over.

"I'm fine." Ginny shrugged and pulled her hand free of Eddy's grasp. "Really. He caught me in the shoulder, but there wasn't much power behind his swing. I don't think the demons had very good control of him."

Just then Dax wandered out of the bedroom. His hair was mussed and he looked half asleep. "What's going on?"

Eddy waved at the screen. "Demon attacks made the nightly news and Ginny and Alton were in a barroom brawl. Just the usual."

"We're fine, Dax." Ginny stuck her tongue out at Eddy. "Eddy's exaggerating."

Dax sat down on Eddy's side opposite Alton and gestured at the television where the news had moved on to sports. "They know they're demons?"

"No, but they're going to figure out something's not right before too long." Eddy grabbed his hand. "How are you feeling?"

"Better, but still not up to full strength." Dax linked his fingers with hers and turned to Alton. "What did you guys come across in town? Other than a fight in a bar."

"He really knows how to show a girl a good time." Ginny elbowed Alton's thigh.

Alton ignored Ginny. "We came across rats," he said. "Demons had taken over a bunch of rats and had a woman cornered in an alley. She'd killed two of the rats but the others were moving toward her in formation and a crowd had begun to gather."

"Alton and I took care of the rest of the rats and demons," Ginny said, "but the demons that escaped before we got there took over a human." She focused on Dax. "He was drunk, so his defenses were down, and the demons had probably grabbed the life force when the rats died, but still, there were two demons working together in him. They didn't seem to have much control, but Alton says it's a sign of their continuing evolution."

Dax leaned back in his chair. "That's not good. A human? If they can control a human, they've definitely evolved."

"The question is," Eddy asked, "what are they evolving to? Do they have a plan?"

Alton shook his head. "The only one who appears to have a plan so far has been the demon king. Are we still in agreement that he was drawing lesser demons to this dimension for their energy?"

Shrugging, Dax glanced toward Eddy. "He was definitely absorbing their life force during that fight in Evergreen," he said. He turned back toward Ginny. "If we destroyed an avatar and the demon got free in the form of that black, wraithlike smoke, the demon king would pull the wraith toward him and inhale it."

"And he'd get bigger and stronger almost immediately," Eddy added. "That's when we realized he wasn't actually gathering a demon army. It was as if he needed the demons stored in this dimension for his personal use. To stay here, they needed an avatar. When he needed their energy, he'd set up a situation where the avatars were broken and the demon's soul set free, at which point the demon king was able to siphon off their energy. He needed to catch demons in their mist form before they could be drawn back to Abyss."

"At first, we were actually helping him." Alton glanced toward Ginny. "We'd destroy an avatar, but sometimes missed the demon. Then we realized they were drawn to him, like metal to a magnet. It was scary to watch. Every time he swallowed down another demon, he got stronger, more lifelike. At first his avatar—the gargoyle—was stone. By the time we fought him on Mount Shasta, he was alive— supple, breathing, and bleeding."

Dax was shaking his head. "If you can call that acidic muck leaking out of him blood. Pretty nasty stuff. The biggest difference now, though, is that those lesser demons were mindless creatures. Pure energy, definitely evil, but there didn't appear to be any real cognitive thought involved in their actions. Now we're seeing intelligence."

Eddy wrapped her fingers around Dax's hand and frowned. "Dax, you said that the longer the demon king remains in Earth's dimension, the more of his intelligence he regains. Could the same thing be happening with the lesser demons? Obviously, if the demon king was originally an intelligent creature from Eden, he's got more to start with, but what of the lesser demons? What do you know of them? What kind of demon were you?"

Dax stared down, as if he focused on their linked hands. "I probably started out as a lesser demon long ago, but by the time I was cast out, I had become a fairly formidable creature. I know I was intelligent enough to question my existence, but, for whatever reason, I retained my intelligence when I was given this body by the Edenites."

"But, you had to learn to use it, just as the demons are learning to use their avatars." Eddy touched the side of his face. "You learned very quickly."

Dax smiled, turned, and kissed her palm. "If you'll

recall, I had Willow feeding me info the whole time. I had my powers and knowledge stored in the tattoo, and I still had the remnants of memories from the human who first owned this body." He smiled. A smile that was all for Eddy. "Plus, I had you."

"That you did." Eddy curled her fingers against his lips.

Ginny watched the emotion flare in Dax's eyes, noticed the dreamy look in Eddy's, and felt a tight clench in her stomach. She wondered what they were remembering, what shared events had drawn them so close so quickly.

They'd known each other less than two weeks, yet they loved as powerfully as if they'd been together forever. Ginny wished she had Eddy's certainty. Wished she understood her own feelings better.

Dax seemed to catch himself, as if he suddenly realized he and Eddy had an audience. He glanced at her. "Things have changed, though. The demons have changed, and they're doing it without any help that we know of, unless the demon king is somehow able to affect their behavior." He turned his attention to Ginny and Alton. "Alton, remember how you described the demon king, as if he looked the way I used to? Eddy and I are wondering if I was targeted, if he . . ."

Alton glanced at Ginny and they both nodded. "Great minds think alike," she said. "Alton and I were wondering the same thing, if maybe the fact he's got your old body makes you more susceptible to his demon strength."

"Exactly, and it's got me worried." Eddy leaned against Dax's shoulder. "I want to get this guy back to Evergreen for at least a couple of nights, away from that soul-sucking bastard. Dax needs to recuperate before we face him again. He's tried his demon powers, but he's definitely not at full strength."

Dax's expression was almost sheepish. "I know I'm not

carrying my weight, but Eddy reminded me I haven't had this human body very long—and I was dead just a few days ago."

Eddy's eyes sparkled with unshed tears. "I don't ever want to go through that again. You're not a cat. I don't think you get nine lives."

"She's right." Alton nodded and reached for Ginny's hand. His long fingers wrapped around hers and he squeezed. "It looks like we'll be fighting demons for a while. We'll need you at full strength."

He dropped her hand and stood up, as if he had too much energy to sit in one spot any longer. "Look . . . Ginny and I were planning to check the vortex at Red Rock Crossing tomorrow, the one near Cathedral Rock. There might be a portal there that will get you to Mount Shasta, and if there's one to Abyss, I want to close it. Tomorrow morning okay with you?"

Dax gazed at Eddy for a long moment. Ginny wondered if they communicated silently. When Eddy nodded and stood up, tugging Dax with her, Ginny was certain of it.

"Works for us. Get us up early." Eddy wrapped both arms around Dax's waist. "I hate to leave you guys here on your own, but he needs to stay away from that damned demon. Just long enough to get his strength back."

"No problem." Alton turned away and stared out the window toward the dark desert.

Ginny watched Dax and Eddy leave. When the door to their room closed, she turned to Alton and caught him watching her. Irritation rolled off of him in waves, and he was frowning. She raised her chin, folded her arms across her chest, and stared right back at him. "What's wrong?"

He let out a frustrated gust of air and glared at her. "Everything's fine. Just perfect. You're going back to that important job of yours while I hang around and fight a bunch of fucking demons by myself. Other than that, I'd say it's all good."

A bolt of panic flashed along Ginny's spine. "Taron's coming Friday. He's got a crystal sword, right? Just tell him you need his help. He'll stay."

"Not quite." Alton shook his head. "Taron's got crystal but it's not sentient. Besides, we need his voice, not his sword. He's the only link we've got between us and the council and we need him there. Communication, Ginny. You know that—it was your idea. It's the only reason he's coming, to fill us in on what's happening in Lemuria. He can't stay."

It felt like the room was closing in on her and it was hard to breathe. Her heart pounded unsteadily in her chest and her damned hands wouldn't stop shaking. "I have to go, Alton. I don't want to lose my job. I don't . . ." She stood up, clutched at the scabbard with DarkFire, and hugged it against her chest, against her pounding heart.

There was no glow at all from the dark crystal.

"So you've said." Alton grabbed his scabbard and his voice had gone cold and flat. He stared down that long patrician nose of his like she was nothing but scum on the sole of his boots.

"Think about this, Ginny, when you worry about your damned job—I gave up my home, my family, my entire world to join this fight. And no, I'm not complaining, but I sure hope your dispatching job's worth it."

She cringed beneath the lash of his gaze, the condemnation in his voice. "You chose this fight, Alton . . . I didn't. I . . ." She swallowed back the lump in her throat. How could she defend an indefensible position? "Where are you going? Aren't you coming to bed?" Damn. She hated sounding so needy, but she was scared and pissed off and he didn't seem to understand what was going on in her head at all. And she didn't want to be alone. Not tonight. Not after all the changes in her life—changes she had no control over, changes that made her feel like a volcano ready to blow its top.

Alton shook his head. Obviously he didn't want anything

to do with the original bitch on wheels. "Later," he said. He had his hand on the door like he was ready to bolt. "I need some air." He stepped out through the sliding glass door and quickly shut it behind him.

Ginny stared at her reflection in the glass. Alton's cold rejection left her feeling nauseous and light-headed. She'd been so sure he wanted her with him tonight. So positive while they were driving home that he was thinking of sex, of making love.

At least, that's what she'd been thinking of, when she wasn't worrying about Dax, or about keeping her mental shields up. She'd imagined what it would feel like to crawl into that big bed with Alton and just do the deed until they both quit worrying about demons and her job and what exactly was going on between the two of them. Quit worrying and fall asleep.

Only it looked like she'd been alone thinking along those lines. Obviously their minds weren't nearly as synchronized as she'd thought. Ginny stared at her reflection against the dark glass a moment longer. Then she picked up her scabbard and her silent sword and went into the bedroom by herself.

Alton sat in the darkness on the back deck, cocooned by the quiet night sounds of the desert. An owl hooted nearby. In the distance, a coyote howled. Crickets chirped from their hideouts beneath the deck. Bats squeaked overhead as they hunted on the still night air. All normal nighttime noises.

Not a single banshee scream among them.

Slowly he slipped HellFire out of the scabbard, laid the sword across his lap, and stared at the glowing crystal blade. He was filled with questions, but Taron wasn't here. Taron, who'd been his anchor in so many ways for so many, many years.

Taron. Alton chuckled. He could almost hear his buddy telling him to pay attention. To be aware of the world around him, or in Taron's phrasing, to get his head out of his ass. So pragmatic and focused—so aware. Taron was the one who always had the answers. The one Alton counted on.

He'd thought he could count on Ginny the same way, but now he had his doubts. He didn't understand her well enough. Was she too complex, or was he just stupid?

He ran his fingers over the shimmering crystal. HellFire had become his trusted companion. He wondered . . . could the sentience within the sword help?

Ginny hadn't hesitated to ask DarkFire, and DarkFire had answered. Alton swallowed back his fears. A man shouldn't be afraid of the weapon he carried, but Alton had feared this sword for most of his life. It had been the constant reminder of his failure as a man, as a warrior.

And then, when it finally chose to speak to him, it had generally been insulting. Probably served him right, that he carried a sword that still didn't respect him. He was a man without honor. Now, a man without even a family name.

As if Taron whispered in his ear, prodding him to take a leap of faith, Alton made his decision. "HellFire? Are you awake?"

The soft chuckle surprised him. "I am always awake. What troubles you?"

Now that was the question. Alton wasn't certain he wanted the answers for what truly troubled him. His feelings for Ginny felt like an open wound, too tender to probe. Instead, he asked, "Who were you?" He ran his fingertips along the blade. "DarkFire was a warrior named Daria. Who were you before you became spirit? What is your story?"

The blade pulsed dark blue, then light, then dark again. Alton wondered if he'd somehow insulted HellFire's spirit. It wasn't like he had a set of rules to follow. How to talk to one's sword without screwing up? He wished.

He could have sworn HellFire sighed.

"I was called Justice. Like you, I was the spoiled son of one of Lemuria's leaders. I was a sycophant, foolishly proud of my position as a parasite upon the world as a whole. I existed with the same sense of entitlement you had for so long. I believed Lemuria owed me a living. I was young and handsome, and I enjoyed every unearned moment. Until the demons came."

Frowning, Alton stared at the blade. He hadn't expected an answer like that, though in retrospect, he knew he deserved it. Knew HellFire described him perfectly. "Am I still that way? A parasite? The spoiled son with a sense of entitlement?" Alton thought of the person he'd been when he first left Lemuria. Hadn't he changed even a little?

"I would not speak to you if you'd not moved past your childish ways."

Childish? A man grown, one who'd lived thousands of years? He'd laugh, except it was too true to be funny. He sighed, accepting. "Why did it take me so long, HellFire? What was I lacking? I left everything I knew to fight demons, yet you refused to speak. What was I doing wrong?"

"The same things I once did. Your motives were not pure, though another sword might have recognized your growth sooner than I did. Since I saw myself in your actions, I knew you could be so much more if properly challenged.

"You left Lemuria because you were bored. The chance to fight demons was a diversion for you. The excitement of going into battle was all about you—your needs, your wants. You could have stopped the demon gargoyle on many occasions, but you were unwilling to risk your safety. Instead, you put Dax and Eddy at risk by your cowardice."

HellFire certainly wasn't mincing words. Alton felt the heat in his face and knew his humiliation must be showing. The sword was right. He'd been afraid each time they fought the demon, and he'd pulled back. He'd been terrified during that last big battle on Mount Shasta. As difficult as it was to say the words, he admitted his fears to HellFire.

"Ah, but in that battle, even though you were afraid, you didn't falter. You attacked."

Alton snorted. "A lot of good it did. The damned gargoyle just about crushed me. I'm surprised it didn't kill me."

"Yet knowing you might die, you attacked to save Eddy and her father. To help Dax. You failed, but you were willing to give your life for your friends. Do you recall your thoughts at that moment, Alton? It wasn't all about you. It was about keeping others safe. You finally showed me that you have what it takes to carry crystal."

Alton stared at the glowing blade for a long time. The sounds of the night ebbed and flowed about him and he thought of the battle he'd fought, how frightened he'd been.

How angry he'd been, to think they might somehow lose, that demonkind might actually overrun an innocent world. Nothing else had mattered then. Not his life, not how terrified he was or the chance he probably wouldn't survive. He hadn't felt particularly brave when he'd attacked the gargoyle. No, he'd been desperately afraid, not only for himself, but for his friends. He'd been willing to do anything to save his friends and his people.

Anything, including risking his life.

But he'd failed and the gargoyle had completely overwhelmed him. He'd been unconscious when Eddy had grabbed his silent crystal sword and decapitated the gargoyle. She'd faced death to save her father, to avenge Dax's death, and she'd succeeded. No wonder her sword had spoken to her from the beginning.

And Dax! He'd actually died—horribly, painfully. He'd thrown himself on the gargoyle, knowing he couldn't possibly prevail. He hadn't, and the gargoyle had killed him.

Thank the gods Dax had been given another chance.

Alton wondered if Dax remembered those last moments

when the demon had broken his body—snapped his spine as if it were nothing more than a twig. Ed had given Alton the gruesome details later, when they'd had time to talk about those last frantic, frightening moments. Alton had missed the worst and the best of it—Dax's death, Eddy's selfless bravery.

He'd been unconscious. Not a very brave participant in that one big battle, but it had changed him forever. He'd come away from it believing in himself for the first time in his very long life. Believing in his value as a Lemurian, as a man.

It had given him the courage to face his father, to stand up to the Council of Nine. He hadn't even faltered when his father had publicly disowned him. He never would have been brave enough before that battle.

That was the first time he'd truly been tested—and he'd passed. There'd never been a reason to doubt Dax's bravery. Knowing he had only one week to live, Dax had sacrificed everything for the cause. In that respect, Alton's first opinion of his friend had been right—Dax had more honor and integrity than any man he'd ever known.

He ran his fingers along the sharp edge of the crystal blade. "HellFire? You said you were like me, a spoiled young man with a sense of entitlement. What changed you? What was it that turned you from that worthless parasite into a warrior brave enough to be reborn in a crystal sword?"

"My death changed me." The light of the sword dimmed. "I fought a battle we had no hope of winning, but my stand allowed some of our citizens to escape to safety. I didn't intend to die that day, but that was my path."

"You sacrificed yourself so that others might live." Alton felt the burn of tears in his eyes. "A truly brave act."

Again he heard the soft chuckle. "It was both a brave and foolish act. I was terrified. My actions were those of a coward with no other choice than to act bravely. If I'd fought a smarter fight, I could have survived and gone on to fight another day. As it was, I died less than a week before the demons were finally vanquished. All these thousands of years I've waited for my rebirth. It's about time you got it right."

This time it was Alton who laughed. "I never claimed to be the sharpest sword in the scabbard."

"No, Alton. That is my job. Your job is to help build a stronger force to take up the battle against demonkind once again. There are so few of you. Go to Ginny. You must convince her to stay. Without her courage and strength, without DarkFire, our chances of success against the demon invasion are slim. Their leader is a new malevolence, something we've not seen before. Something I still don't truly understand. It will take a powerful force to defeat him. Without DarkFire's unique talents, without Ginny . . ."

Alton sighed. "But how? Ginny is determined to follow a path of her own choosing. How can I hope to change her mind?"

HellFire shimmered brightly. "You must give her a reason to stay that is within her grasp. The concept of saving many worlds against demonkind is too much for any mind to comprehend, but there are other reasons for her to stay, for her to risk everything. Think of how you have focused yourself in this fight. Think of the adjustments you've made in your own goals. Then ask yourself—do you love Virginia Jones?"

The blade went dark and silence closed in around Alton.

Alton stared at the sword. What did loving Ginny have to do with anything? *Nine hells.* He had no idea if he loved her or not. How could he know if those feelings tearing him up inside were really love? Love shouldn't hurt this much.

Except he knew, in the deepest, most private part of his soul, that HellFire had been right about everything else. Alton's motives had been entirely selfish when he first left Lemuria. Thinking back to his feelings at the time, he'd seen helping Dax and Eddy escape from the Lemurian prison as a grand gesture on his part, a chance to find some excitement to liven up his dull life.

So why had HellFire asked him if he loved Ginny? What an odd question. Or was it? Hadn't he realized from the first time he saw Ginny that she was the one he was fighting for? Not for Lemuria, not for Earth or the people of Atlantis and Eden. No. It was Ginny who mattered. Ginny's safety, her future.

By focusing on Ginny, he'd been able to face a battle beyond anything he'd ever imagined possible. He'd discovered strengths he hadn't realized he possessed.

What if he were to put the battle against demonkind into words that made more sense to Ginny? Show her something to focus on besides worlds she barely believed in, people she didn't know. If she realized how Alton felt about her, how much she meant to him . . . He shook his head. First he needed to get his own thoughts in order before he tried organizing anyone else's.

Still, he had to admit that maybe HellFire hadn't been so far off the mark after all.

It came to him, then, what had been different about the conversation he'd just had with his crystal sword. No snark. None at all. HellFire had spoken sincerely, as if they were comrades of long standing. As if Alton were an equal.

Justice. His name had been Justice, and he'd been young once, and spoiled. And then he'd died, though he'd obviously redeemed himself with his death. Alton stroked the silent blade with his fingertips, imagining the young man HellFire had once been. Then he picked up his sword and carefully slipped it into the scabbard.

An errant thought filtered into his mind. Had Justice ever been in love?

The blade remained dark.

"Well, Justice. It appears it's up to me to convince Ginny

to stay and fight. Is loving her the key? Is it really something so simple?" He shook his head, chuckling softly. "Like love is simple? Nine hells. If I screw up, lose track, and forget, please remind me it's about the fight and it's about Ginny. About winning against demonkind for the good of all. That it's not about me."

The blade flashed a quick spark of blue, almost as if Hell-Fire winked at him.

Alton stared at the scabbard. "Though it would be nice if all this could happen without me having to die first, don't you think? I'd like to hang around and reap the rewards of victory, if there actually is such a thing against demonkind."

There was no response from the sword.

Alton stared at the tooled-leather scabbard and thought about their strange conversation. Then, with one last look across the dark and silent desert, he went inside.

Alton paused in the bathroom doorway after his shower. Ginny slept soundly, but she'd chosen the bed he'd slept alone in the night before. Her arms were tightly wrapped around his pillow, her face buried in its soft depths.

He wished he understood women better, but he hoped it was a positive sign.

Standing here, warm and relaxed from the shower, Alton opened his mind to Ginny's and gently entered without leaving any hint of his presence. He found her sleeping thoughts unguarded, her dreams open and filled with questions.

He folded his arms across his chest, leaned against the doorjamb, and wandered through her most private images and ideas without any sense of trespass whatsoever. He'd gained a pretty strong feeling of entitlement while he'd stood there beneath the biting spray, his body aching with need for the darkly beautiful woman sleeping so soundly just beyond the bathroom door.

Entitled, because he'd finally admitted that she'd stolen his heart. He wasn't about to let her get away with it—not without giving her own to him in return.

He wanted her smile—the one she shared with him and no one else. He wanted her touch, wanted the warmth of her long, lean body close to his. He wanted the joy of her laughter.

But even more, he wanted Ginny's trust.

It was more than a feeling—instead, it was a powerful sense of the inevitable that Ginny was meant for him, just as he was meant for her.

It seemed counter to the lesson he felt HellFire'd been trying to give him, but at the same time, Alton knew these potent feelings went deeper than merely satisfying his own desires. He wanted to satisfy Ginny's. He wanted her to stay, not only to fight demonkind, but because she'd discovered exactly what she needed to fill all those empty spaces in her heart, to make her life complete.

Somehow he had to convince her he was the one. That only he could fill her emptiness, just as she filled his.

It wasn't easy to admit he'd never be whole without Ginny in his life. HellFire had forced the issue, but it was something Alton had sensed from the very beginning, from the moment he'd seen that beautiful woman with the tiger's eyes fighting off a demon-possessed concrete bear with nothing more than a scrap of wood. He'd known even then she was special.

Of course, then his concerns were a little bit different. He was still hung up on his rank in Lemurian society and the fact he was immortal while Ginny wasn't.

All that had changed pretty dramatically when he'd been disowned the same day they'd discovered Ginny was a descendant of Lemurian royalty. Which meant that all the issues keeping them apart weren't issues anymore. So why wasn't he any happier about it?

For one thing, that sleeping beauty in his bed obviously didn't feel the same way about him as he felt about her, not if she was so willing to take her beautiful, shapely butt back to work this weekend. Unfortunately, he didn't think there was much he could do to change the way he felt, and he had no idea how to convince Ginny.

What a mess. He'd never imagined love could be so confusing, if that's what this was really all about. Was this love? This sense that nothing in his life would ever be right again if Ginny wasn't a part of it? The powerful pressure that squeezed his heart and forced the air from his lungs when he thought of her returning to Evergreen without him, when he imagined going on in this battle without Ginny at his side?

He was incapable of imagining life without her beside him. Not behind him, as a proper Lemurian mate would be, but next to him, shoulder to shoulder, whether it be fighting demons or, if they were ever so blessed, raising a child. When he thought of his future, he thought of it with Ginny.

She was his future. She was also very much his present.

What else could he call it, if not love? What did Ginny call it? She was every bit as confused as he was. He confirmed that little tidbit of information even now, tiptoeing through her sleep-bemused thoughts.

Then he found something that stopped him cold.

It wasn't the job calling her back to Evergreen—it was her fear of a future she didn't understand. Her fear of committing herself to a man who'd not promised her anything beyond the next fight. No wonder she clung to the familiar security of her work. He'd offered her nothing.

Nothing at all.

Of course, what did he have to offer a woman like Ginny? His heart? She already had it, even though he'd not said the words. He'd hardly admitted them to himself. She was, after all, Lemurian royalty and he was nothing more than the exiled son of a pompous jackass.

Have you already forgotten our conversation, Alton? It's not all about you. . . .

He almost laughed out loud. Generally HellFire waited to be addressed before making comments, but in this case, the warning was welcome, and right on the mark.

It wasn't about him. Right now it was all about Ginny. It was about her needs, her desires, and her fears.

He'd been brave enough to face a demon-possessed gargoyle. Was he brave enough to accept that this horrible, wonderful, terrifying feeling he had was love, and then face the woman he loved? Brave enough to lay his heart out for her to mangle and stomp on as she saw fit?

Nine hells, he hoped so.

He stepped back into the bathroom and hung the wet towel over the shower rod. Then, naked, aroused, and still damp from his shower, he quietly walked across the room and crawled into bed beside Ginny.

She turned to him and rooted against his chest as if she wanted to bury herself inside him. Alton wrapped her slim body in his arms and drew her close. He tucked her head beneath his chin and rubbed his cheek against her springy curls. Her scent was all warm woman and invitation, but she slept so soundly he didn't want to disturb her.

Nine hells . . . he was disturbed enough, all by himself. How does a man with nothing tell a woman who has everything—who *is* everything—that he loves her? How does he convince her that she needs him every bit as much as he needs her?

They'd been together such a short time. How could he possibly trust desires he didn't really understand? He'd never felt this way about any woman before. He'd never known the same sense of expectation—of desire or excitement— in his entire life. It wasn't all about sex, though he had to admit that the thought of burying himself in her hot, wet sheath had him so hard he ached. No, it was something else altogether, a feeling that the disquiet he'd lived with for most of his life had finally found the calm he'd not even known to search for.

The feeling of having traveled for countless miles before finally stumbling upon the perfect oasis, a flowing spring that offered salvation to his weary soul and brilliant color to a life lived in nothing more than shades of gray. It was such a simple thing, really, now that he admitted it. Now that he allowed himself to accept it.

He loved Ginny. She gave him hope. She was hope, and he'd felt hopeless for so very long.

Never again.

With that promise uppermost in his mind, Alton closed his eyes and willed himself to sleep.

Chapter Fifteen

The faces were pure evil. Twisted, loathsome things coming at her from all directions—horrific creatures beyond even her worst nightmares.

Demonkind.

She stood alone—all alone except for DarkFire. She grasped her crystal sword in her right hand and planted her feet firmly. She knew she had to fight, had to protect . . . someone. She wasn't sure whom she guarded, but she knew it was important.

Knew she could not afford to fail.

She called out to DarkFire, but the crystal didn't respond. The voice was silent. The shimmering crystal blade had gone dark and dull. She stared at the flat, dark blade, shocked by DarkFire's silence.

The creatures loomed closer. Voice or no voice, she had to fight, but why couldn't she lift her sword? Her arm had no strength, her hand no sense of touch. As she stared at her fingers clutching the hilt, DarkFire fell from her grasp. When the sword hit the ground, the crystal blade shattered. The sound of breaking crystal echoed, repeating over and over like waves against the shore growing louder, more strident with each repetition.

She stood there, alone in the darkness with a broken sword, an arm without strength, a hand that had failed her, and she was more afraid than she'd ever been in her life. Terror washed over her, fear unlike anything she'd ever known, but it wasn't the advancing demons that frightened her, or even the sword that lay in scattered shards of amethyst across the dark floor. No. Her fear was based on something worse, something beyond the monsters, more than shattered crystal.

She was alone. Isolated by her own choice, set apart to fight or flee by her own design. DarkFire was gone— destroyed now, her sentience lost because Ginny had been too cowardly to commit. Even Alton had abandoned her and turned away in disgust. She'd proved herself unworthy in so many ways. She no longer deserved to carry crystal. Even worse, she'd shown herself unworthy of love.

Her life was empty and the demons were coming, but she had no strength left to fight, no will to continue.

No strength, no help, no hope. The demons were all around, but this was the choice she'd made. She'd done this to herself.

She'd chosen this path. Chosen it all on her own.

Ginny lay there in the darkness as reality slowly pulled her free of the nightmare. Her arm was numb, probably from sleeping on it. Something big and heavy held her down. She should have been terrified, but she was warm and cozy and it was still dark in the room. Instead of fear, she felt protected as she rubbed her face against a solid, warm wall of . . . Alton?

Blinking, Ginny struggled the rest of the way out of sleep, away from a dream of horrific creatures and fears that were even more terrible to imagine. Thank goodness Alton was here, his body close and warm, the weight of his leg across her thighs the physical proof he'd not really turned away.

Only in her nightmare, in the deepest fears of her subconscious mind.

But what of DarkFire? Would the sentience in her sword abandon her if she refused the challenge she'd been offered? What kind of coward walked away from sentient crystal, from a battle that was nothing less than a holy war pitting the powers of good against the encroachment of pure evil?

I did. I have.

Good Lord.

No wonder Alton was disgusted with her.

Or was he? Would he be here beside her if he didn't still like her at least a little? What if he didn't? What if he'd finally realized what a fool and a coward she really was?

She'd never really thought of herself as a needy person, but right now, Ginny needed. Forget pride, forget fear, forget everything that might deter her from her goal. She needed Alton, but she wasn't sure how he felt about her.

Crap, she wasn't even certain how she felt about him! She liked him a lot, but she didn't know if she loved him. Did that really matter? She didn't have any promises that either of them would live through the coming battle against an unthinkable foe, but if her dream had taught her anything, it was that she had to get her priorities straight.

DarkFire had nailed it perfectly. There were other women who could handle her dispatcher's job at Shascom, but only Ginny could wield DarkFire. Only Ginny Jones had the strength and the ability to carry the dark crystal sword, the only sword they knew of that showed demons in their true guise.

It was time to stand up in spite of her fears. Time to act like a grown-up, which meant she must accept DarkFire's challenge. Somehow she needed to find the strength to face the evil that was coming, to stand against the threat of demonkind.

She needed the strength to take a chance, to take control of her own future. But first, she had to admit that, for all her bravery and all her tough words, she needed the man who slept beside her.

It was definitely time for that.

The question was, could she open herself enough to allow him inside those private recesses of her heart? Inside her mind? No man had ever touched her heart, not like this. No man had ever made her feel needy and uncertain. It terrified her even as she felt tempted by the strength of his arms, seduced by the honesty of his character and by the innate goodness of the man.

He treated her as an equal even though he came from a world that looked at women as lesser beings. He'd never tried to hold her back, had never asked her to be less than she was. He'd been proud of her fighting strength, proud of her ability to carry crystal. Not once had he treated her as if she didn't matter.

Because, to Alton, she did matter. She mattered greatly. No one—man or woman—had ever held her in such high esteem. She had no doubt of that, but was it enough? Enough to change her life, to give up all she'd worked for, what she was familiar with?

Not if you're a frickin' coward, it's not.

Is that what this was all about? Was she just too big a coward to take a chance on whatever was building between them?

Ginny Jones isn't afraid of anything.

Well, not usually, but this was all new, unexplored territory. Not just fighting demons—this meant accepting love.

Giving herself over to love.

There. She'd labeled it, the thing that had her so freaked out. Was it fear of falling in love that held her back? If that was it, she was a bigger coward than she'd thought.

She drew in a deep breath and inhaled his scent, the warm, sleepy smell of shampoo and soap and man. Tears filled her eyes, unexpected and unwelcome. What the hell was wrong with her?

"Ginny?"

Alton's drowsy mumble tickled her ear.

"Hmm?" She nuzzled his chest and quickly blocked her thoughts. Damn. Had he been snooping around in her head?

"Are you okay?"

His words were clearer, his body suddenly taut, muscles tense and hard.

"I'm fine. Go back to sleep." She forced herself to relax.

His long fingers stroked along her flank, over the curve of her buttock. Her hips tilted of their own volition, bringing her belly up close against his rising erection. He fit tightly against the swell of her stomach, a burning brand she couldn't ignore—didn't want to ignore.

"I'm awake now." He nuzzled the soft skin beneath her jaw and nipped her throat with sharp teeth. "I want you, Ginny. I need to be inside you. I want to taste you and touch you and make love to you."

He punctuated his soft whispers with kisses that traced the swell of her breast and ended when his lips fastened around her tightly puckered nipple. He sucked hard, drawing it into his mouth.

She arched her back and cried out. His teeth scraped the sensitive tip and his fingers stroked her flank. He moved to her other breast, suckling and licking, pulling the nipple painfully tight between his full lips. She concentrated so intently on the way his mouth ravaged her breast, she lost track of his roaming fingers.

But not for long.

His tongue pressed her nipple against the roof of his mouth at the same time his long fingers slipped beneath the elastic waist of her panties and slowly but certainly plundered the cleft between her legs. Two long fingers, stroking deeply inside while his thumb made tiny circles over her clit.

She whimpered as he teased her, as he showed her what her body was capable of feeling. All so new, so unbelievable. She wasn't like this—she'd never been this responsive, her body so sensitive, her heart so unguarded. His mouth and lips, teeth and tongue, and probing fingers took her to the precipice and over before she even realized what he'd done. Gasping, arching her back, Ginny pressed her breast against his mouth and clamped her legs around his wrist.

Her whimper became a cry, the cry a soft scream of surprise and completion. Writhing within his tender hold, she didn't know whether to press close or pull away from so much, so fast. He held her there, caught in the midst of an orgasm that wouldn't end, carrying her through wave after wave of sensation until her body shuddered with its final release.

Not until her spine lay flat against the mattress once more did Alton release the pressure on her nipple and gently lick the sensitive tip. He eased his fingers out of her, swirling them in damp circles over her sensitive clitoris as he slowly pulled his hand out of her panties.

Her hips jerked in response. Alton's laughter was strained when he leaned close and kissed her mouth. Then he rolled away and she heard a sound that could only be Alton ripping his way into one of the boxes of condoms. A moment later he rolled back to her, hugely erect, fully sheathed.

She expected him to penetrate her immediately, but he scooted down between her legs and slipped his long arms beneath her thighs.

Ginny raised her head and glared at him. "What are you doing?"

He looked up and smiled at her from between her raised knees. "Something I've wanted to do since the first time I saw you." His palms slipped under her butt.

She tried to shove her knees together. His wide shoulders held them apart. He leaned close and blew a soft little puff of air over her damp and swollen folds. Her hips jerked in response.

"Hold still." He was laughing softly. Ginny tried to squirm out of his grasp but he held her in place without any effort at all.

Held her in place, dipped his head low, and slowly ran his tongue in one long lick between her legs. She giggled, embarrassed and flustered and a little bit afraid. She had no idea what to expect, how to act, what to do. He swirled his tongue around her sensitive little nub and then speared her deep, licking and suckling as if he loved every taste and all the different textures of her feminine parts.

No one had ever done this with her before. No man had tasted her so intimately. She should tell him to stop. Really. It was too personal, too much, too soon. She hardly knew him. She'd never know him well enough to allow him to do this.

He licked and sucked and explored with teeth and tongue and lips, and she wanted to die. She should be embarrassed. She was embarrassed . . . she was so close to coming and his tongue felt so amazing that if he'd suddenly decided to quit she was sure she'd scream and pull him back down between her thighs to finish what he'd started.

Then he wrapped his soft lips around her clitoris and sucked, exactly the way he'd suckled her nipple.

Ginny screamed. Arched her back, thrust her hips forward, and screamed again. Laughing softly, Alton moved over her body, covered her mouth with his and she tasted him and more—she tasted herself.

Her first thought should have been *how gross, how disgusting,* but it wasn't. Not at all. This was something shared, a taste so intimate she wanted to cry, a climax so perfect she sobbed with the pulsing, quivering ripples still racing through her body.

Once again Alton shifted his position, moved his long, lean body over hers, and pressed the broad head of his penis against the mouth of her vagina. Slowly he surged forward, filling her, stretching her inch by full inch, sliding along sleek, sensitive muscles until he was buried deep inside.

He held perfectly still, giving her body time to adjust. He was huge and the size of him made her burn, but she remembered when they'd done this before, how the burn had quickly eased and the pleasure of his size and his skill had taken her places she'd never expected to go.

She'd thought it could never be better than it had been that night. She was wrong. This time she felt a connection to Alton she'd not known before, a sense that they were meant to be together, meant to love each other.

Almost a sense of destiny.

If only she knew for certain how he felt. His muscular body covered hers, warming her, protecting her. His long, silky hair draped over them both and tickled her shoulders and breasts like a thousand tiny fingers across her skin, enclosing the two of them in shimmering golden strands.

He turned her on, he made her feel safe, and she knew without a doubt she wasn't going back to Evergreen. Not yet. Not until this fight was finished. Not as long as Alton needed her by his side.

Slowly rolling his hips, he stroked her, deep and full, and her body rippled and clenched around him, holding him close, loving him. Still, there was a sense of something missing, a feeling there should be more between them. A connection she'd somehow missed. Slowly she raised her lids, looked into his beautiful emerald-green eyes, and knew exactly what that was.

For the first time since she'd learned of her Lemurian heritage, Ginny consciously lowered her mental barriers and opened her thoughts. She chose trust, and with that one small step, she opened herself entirely to the man who made love to her so perfectly. She shared her fears, her needs, and most of all, she shared her love.

She felt him connect, felt the wonder of his love, and her body shivered in reaction. He was as fearful as she, as unsure of her feelings toward him, but so very certain of his for her.

Ginny raised her hand and traced the curve of his jaw and the sharp ridge of his eyebrow. "I love you, Alton. I'm not sure how or why it's happened so quickly, but I can't deny what I'm feeling."

His eyes sparkled with unshed tears and his beautiful face wavered in front of hers. Dear God, she was crying, and it made her feel so stupid, to be making love with this gorgeous man and weeping for absolutely no reason whatsoever.

He leaned close and kissed her lips, kissed the tears that leaked from her eyes and rolled into her hair. Whispered against her temple, kissing her between every word. "I love you, Ginny. I can't explain it either, but I know how I feel, what I feel." He chuckled softly, and still he kept up that perfect rhythm, filling her over and over with each slow and powerful thrust.

His thoughts were as open to Ginny now as if she read a printed page. Open and full to bursting with feelings neither one of them could deny or even put actual voice to. Her nerve endings were all on fire, her heart pounded out a wild tattoo within her chest, yet her mind was calm, open, and gloriously, unbelievably free.

Free, yet filled with Alton. She knew now how he worried, how he'd felt so undeserving of her love. Knew that he'd once been selfish and self-centered, that he'd looked down on her as a lowly human female, as nothing but trouble, yet couldn't help but be drawn to her, as unsuitable as he thought she was.

"So, I'm unsuitable, am I?" She frowned, or tried to, but he was kissing the sensitive skin beneath her ear and it was impossible to even fake being angry.

"So terribly unsuitable," he said. "Extremely unsuitable. Wrong in every way." He nipped her earlobe and tugged. "I think that's part of your allure. It's what caught me from the very beginning. Your unsuitability, your amazing spirit, your bravery and your beautiful tiger's eyes." He kissed her lids, she tilted her hips, he drove deep and hard, and suddenly her heart was thundering in her chest, her back arching as she lifted to him, reached for him with her body, with her heart, with her mind.

This time her orgasm started slow and deep, a hot coil of energy radiating from her womb to her toes, to her fingertips to the sensitive peaks of her breasts. Alton wrapped his arms around her waist, lifting Ginny, rearing back on his heels. Her legs tightened around him, her heels locked tightly at the small of his back, and she pressed her cheek against the hard wall of his chest.

Powerful heated spasms filled her. Muscles rippled and pulsed and her body enfolded his, holding him deep inside, contracting around his heat and length, forging a connection unlike anything Ginny had ever experienced in her life. Alton's strong arms held her close, their bodies shuddering as each of them drew deep, gasping breaths of air. Finally, Ginny's muscles all went limp as the last spasm slowly faded away, as the heat and rush of climax gave way to enervation.

Alton's chest shuddered beneath her cheek. Ginny raised her head and gazed drowsily into green eyes sparkling with laughter. "I think I want to sleep now. Why are you laughing at me?"

He chuckled softly and nuzzled the top of her head with his lips. "I'm laughing at both of us. At how stupid and stubborn we've both been, at how perfect we can be. I love you, Ginny Jones. No matter what happens over the coming days, don't ever doubt my love."

She planted a kiss just above his heart. "Never, Alton. I

promise. Now put me down. I need sleep, preferably without nightmares."

Laughing softly, he slowly withdrew. Ginny stretched out on the bed, totally replete and unbelievably relaxed. Vaguely, she was aware of Alton bathing her with a warm washcloth, of his big body settling in beside hers.

Of his lips brushing her temple, her chin, the corner of her mouth, before he lay back. The night was dark and still and the man she loved slept beside her. Wrapped in his arms, Ginny slept without dreams.

Alton awoke in a cold sweat. He fought the instinctive urge to jump out of bed and search for whatever it was that had disturbed him. Instead, he lay perfectly still, listening to the silence of the predawn hours.

Ginny slept quietly beside him. Her nose was pressed against his shoulder and the tousled tangle of her hair tickled his chin. He opened his senses to the darkness. Something was off but he couldn't tell what.

HellFire? Would the sword answer him, sheathed and stored in the corner where he'd left it?

I am here, Alton.

Thank the gods! *Is anything wrong? I have a sense of something not quite the way it should be.*

After a brief pause, HellFire said, *I sense evil. Something moves within this dwelling. Something that does not belong.*

"Ginny?" Alton leaned over and brushed his lips across her brow. "Ginny, wake up. Something's wrong."

Her eyes flashed wide, barely visible in the darkness. "What's the matter?"

"I don't know, but HellFire agrees. Get something on, grab your sword. I don't want to open the door unless we're both armed."

She nodded and slid out of bed. He heard the rustle of her

clothing as he was slipping into his jeans. A moment later, DarkFire burst to life in a brilliant flare of amethyst light. He slipped HellFire out of the scabbard and rested his fingers on the doorknob.

Ginny? Are you ready?

Ready.

She rested her fingers on his hip. Slowly, Alton opened the bedroom door. The stench of sulfur was thick in the main room separating the two bedrooms. Ginny held her sword high, but there was no visible sign of demons.

Alton flipped on a light and the room was bathed in a soft glow. Everything looked fine, though curtains flapped at an open window. The screen was still in place, but he remembered shutting the window against the evening's chill.

He glanced over his shoulder and nodded to Ginny. Quietly the two of them moved across the room to the door that led to Dax and Eddy's room. Alton listened at the door, glanced once more at Ginny, then turned the handle and shoved.

The door flew open and Alton raised his sword to illuminate the dark room. The stench of sulfur almost flattened him. In HellFire's blue glow he saw Eddy trapped against a corner wall, surrounded by a thick, black mist that seethed and boiled around her. Her eyes were wide, her mouth moving as if she screamed, but no sound escaped.

Dax still lay on the bed, struggling beneath more of the stinking mist that somehow held him prisoner. Only his right arm and one foot were visible beneath the mass of demons in the light from Alton's sword. Ginny slipped in beside Alton and flipped the light switch. The dark shadows seemed to draw back, as if afraid of the brightness, but they didn't leave.

Ginny held her sword high, and suddenly the mist took on shape and form. Hundreds of lesser demons grappled with Eddy. Their hideous faces leered and twisted arms and legs and prehensile tails held her arms at her sides, covered her mouth, and kept her captive. More of the disgusting beasts held Dax down, but the largest one, the demon king, straddled his chest. He covered Dax's face with his in a disgusting parody of a kiss.

Alton lunged at the creature with HellFire. He slashed through the wraithlike body with his sparkling crystal blade, but the demon rolled away unscathed. He didn't appear to be injured or damaged at all. The lesser demons stayed in position, still holding Dax to the bed.

Alton took a quick look over his shoulder to see where Ginny'd gone. She'd grabbed Eddy's sword, DemonSlayer, and held the leather scabbard in her left hand while she slashed at the demons holding onto Eddy with her right. DarkFire glowed. Screams rose as demons flared into brilliant flashes of flame and died, but their banshee wails seemed to embolden the demon king.

As Eddy reached out of the boiling, seething mass of demons, DemonSlayer leapt from the sheath and into her grasp. The demon king rushed for Alton with his four powerful arms spread wide. Alton feinted and dipped to his left, grabbed Dax's sword, and loosed DemonFire from the scabbard. He swung HellFire at the demon king and forced him back from the bed, away from Dax.

Alton swung again. Once more the creature twisted out of the way and evaded the blow, but Alton now had his back to the bed, between the demon king and the ex-demon who was Alton's friend.

"Dax? Can you hear me? Reach out with your right hand. I have your sword." Alton glanced down between blows, saw Dax's fingers twitch, and managed to slip the jeweled hilt into his hand. Dax took DemonFire from Alton, gave a mighty yell, and rose up from the bed. Demon mist scattered in all directions. Others clung to his body, writhing and twisting over his bare flesh, almost as if they tried to form a cage about his torso.

Dax lunged to his feet, still covered in demonkind. Shaking like a big dog, he quickly dislodged the filthy creatures. Alton swung HellFire through the wraiths as they slowly floated to the ground. Dozens burst into flames and sparks.

Dax swung his head around. "Where's Eddy?"

"She's fine. I've got her." Ginny's shout came from the far corner. "Don't let that bastard get away."

Alton glanced toward Ginny's voice and saw Eddy standing beside her, sword in hand. The women were fine. The air around them was filled with the sparks of dead and dying demons. Eddy and Ginny appeared to be working their way across the room, killing demons as they came.

The demon king was nothing more than black roiling mist beneath the bedroom lamp and the light of DemonFire and HellFire. Swinging and slashing through the mist, their swords seemed to disrupt the creature, but for some reason they couldn't kill him. He surged and then recoiled, like black smoke in a capricious wind, constantly evading a killing strike and then reforming once the blade had passed.

"How the nine hells do we kill this bastard?" Alton swung once more, but the darkness reformed behind the slashing blade.

"I don't know. He's getting stronger. He managed to siphon off more of my energy." Dax was breathing hard and his strikes were not as clean.

"And here I thought you two were just making out." Alton slanted him a quick grin. Dax rolled his eyes and jabbed DemonFire completely through the wraith.

A flash of amethyst light caught the edge of the mist and turned it into a twisted, scaled arm. Ginny moved even closer and held DarkFire overhead, illuminating the beast beneath her sword's violet glow. The entire demon king burst into view. It towered over them, all scales and talons and slavering fangs—hideous beyond belief, a vision of evil incarnate.

"Holy shit." Dax took a quick step back. "It's me! That's my old form. There were none like me. The bastard's definitely got my old body, my demon form."

Alton caught the look of horror on Eddy's face, the anger in Ginny's eyes, the confusion in Dax's expression. "It's not you now, Dax. Whatever you were before, you're not that thing anymore. But he's after you. You're his target."

They circled the hulking creature. It was larger now than it had been earlier in the day, when it had trapped Dax in the vortex. Now it pivoted on powerful multi-jointed legs with clawed feet and reached out with four powerful arms tipped with vicious claws. Always it watched Dax, reached for Dax. Saliva dripped from a mouth filled with razor-sharp teeth, and curved horns protruded from its forehead.

Its eyes glowed with an unholy light and a terrifying intelligence. It knew what it wanted. It wanted Dax.

"I want to know how it got here. We saw it go through the portal to Abyss, but that portal's been closed." Alton drove his sword into the creature's body. Black mist swirled around the blade, reforming after the crystal passed through. But the creature kept glancing at Ginny's glowing blade as if he feared it, pivoting and spinning away from the dark violet light.

Whenever it escaped the glow, the demon king became mist once more, yet it still remained untouched by their swords.

"There's got to be another portal." Ginny stepped closer and held DarkFire high. The demon king lunged in her direction. Without hesitation, Ginny lashed out.

The demon shrieked and recoiled. Sparks exploded where she'd hit him with the blade. "Interesting." She flashed a brilliant grin at Alton. "He doesn't like DarkFire." She lunged forward and slashed at his torso. The demon king twisted and evaded the blade. Again and again Ginny went for the kill, but each time she managed nothing more than a nick and a spark. The sharp stench of sulfur told them she'd wounded the beast, but not seriously enough to stop him.

Alton stood at Ginny's side with his sword at the ready, but there was nothing he could do, not if Ginny's DarkFire was the only blade that could kill the damned thing. Still, watching her fight was amazing. She danced around the demon and her crystal sword flashed almost faster than the eye could follow.

The demon king roared his anger, but he backed steadily away from Ginny's assault. His eyes flickered from Dax to Ginny, to the flash of her sword. She forced him into a corner. Alton caught her eye. *What if we go at him together? Maybe the strength of two swords?*

Ginny nodded. *Ready?*

"Ready!" Alton leapt toward the demon king as Ginny drove her sword deep. It screamed, a horrible banshee howl, and leapt into the air, away from the dark-light glow of Ginny's blade. Out of the violet light, it once again appeared as formless mist that suddenly swirled into a violently spinning tornado of black, sulfuric smoke. Spinning faster and faster until it was little more than a midnight blur of stinking mist, it flew through the open bedroom door and out toward the window in the main room.

With a loud *whoosh* the demon hit the screen and disappeared into the early morning darkness.

The room seemed unnaturally quiet after the creature escaped. Ginny leaned on her sword, blowing as if she'd run a mile. Alton checked to make sure she was okay before turning away to see if Dax and Eddy were all right.

Dax sat on the edge of the bed, breathing hard, with DemonFire grasped in both hands. Eddy stood next to him with her arm wrapped around his shoulders. There were fresh tear tracks on her cheeks. The room reeked of sulfur, but the demons were all gone, presumably destroyed by Ginny and Eddy's attack.

Alton knelt in front of Eddy and Dax. "What the nine hells happened in here? How'd they get in?"

Eddy shook her head. "Through the window, I guess. We were both exhausted. Dax was asleep before I even got out of the shower, but the fight earlier had already taken so much of his energy." She shuddered. "I didn't awaken until I was already covered in demonkind. When I tried to get to my sword, they trapped me against the wall." She shook her head, a short, sharp jerk of utter frustration, and wiped the tears from her face with the back of her shaking hand. "I couldn't break free."

Alton pondered that a moment. He hadn't thought demons in this dimension capable of such an attack, especially without avatars. Once again they'd proved him wrong. "How'd they manage to hold you? They're just mist, aren't they?"

"Yeah. Right. Toughest mist I ever saw." Eddy slowly sheathed her sword. "They look like smoke but there's substance there. They're not like they used to be. I remember passing my hand through them before and they felt like cold smoke."

She swept the tousled hair back from her forehead. "They still look like smoke in regular light. I couldn't see their demon shapes without Ginny's sword, but I could feel them. When they had me covered, I felt scales and claws. They couldn't bite or scratch me, but they were certainly capable of holding me down." She took a deep breath and shuddered. "The worst of it was the fact I was screaming and cursing for all I was worth, but there was no sound. None at all. I knew you guys couldn't hear me. God, that was so scary."

Dax slipped an arm around her waist and leaned his head against her belly. "I couldn't see you. I was buried in the damned things. Thank goodness you're okay." He planted a kiss on the bare strip of skin between her cami top and cotton pants.

Then he raised his head and focused on Alton. "We know that the demon king was once from Eden, that he was intelligent and evil. He seems to regain more of his cognitive abilities every time we see him. Now that I know for certain he's got my old demon body, I'm wondering if I'm the only one he can siphon energy from."

Ginny sat down on the edge of the bed beside Dax, but she looked up at Alton. With Dax weakened, he felt as if more of the weight of this battle had fallen on his shoulders. At one time, he might have taken pride in their trust. Now it terrified him. This fight was not going as well as he'd expected. Not at all.

Ginny's question confirmed it. "Are you sure it's just energy he wants? Could he be after something more?" She turned toward Dax. "Your life force, whatever it is that makes you immortal and gives you your powers. Could he be stealing that?"

She leaned close and kissed Dax on the cheek. "Nothing personal, Dax, but you look like shit. A lot worse than you did this afternoon at the vortex. I think he's taking some important stuff from you. We need to stop him before he gets any more."

Eddy nodded. "I agree." She laughed, but it came out sounding like more of a sob than anything else. "I want to get you home for some of Dad's cooking." She wrapped both arms around Dax's shoulders and rested her chin on top of his head. "Hell, I just want to get you home. I'll feel safer back in Evergreen."

Dax tilted his head and kissed her. "We have demons to fight, Eddy. Staying safe isn't how battles are won."

"I know, but going into battle when you're not fit isn't how to win, either." She raised her head and stared at Alton. Her dark-brown eyes were swimming in tears, but she didn't give in to the emotions that were obviously choking her. "We'll go with you like we planned this morning and find a portal back to Evergreen, either at Red Rock Crossing or Bell Rock. We just need a couple of days. I promise we'll come back by Sunday. I know Ginny's got to go back to work in a—"

"No." Ginny interrupted, shaking her head. "I'm going to call Shascom and tell them to find a replacement. I'm not going back. Not until we win." She wrapped her fingers around Alton's.

He almost wept with relief.

"What?" Eddy's mouth hung open. "You've been there forever. You love your job. You swore you weren't going to quit."

Ginny shrugged. "Sort of like you said you weren't going to quit the paper?" She laughed. "I think it's finally sunk in—this is a lot more important."

Eddy wrapped her arms around Ginny and hugged her tight. "I am so glad you've finally come to your senses!"

"Gee, thanks." Ginny hugged her back. "I love the way my best friend in the whole world backs up my decisions."

Laughing, Eddy patted her head. "That's what friends are for, right?"

"What? To drive me crazy?"

"Well, that among other things." Eddy's expression sobered. "I'm really glad, Ginny. It's the right decision. I know it's not an easy one, but it's the right one."

Ginny nodded. Then she grabbed Alton's hand and hung on like she'd never let go. "This all happened so quickly. It took awhile before I realized there's a lot more going on than just some big adventure. It's a war we can't afford to lose." She lifted DarkFire and stared at the glowing blade. "The Crone is the sentience in my sword. She lived so long, waiting to give DarkFire to me. Then she gave me immortality.

I feel like an idiot now, but it took me awhile to realize the responsibility that came with her gifts."

Dax slipped an arm around her waist and gave her a quick squeeze. "We can't do this without you, Ginny. It appears only DarkFire has any effect on the demon king, and he's the one we need to defeat."

She nodded. "I know. Do you have any idea how scary that is?"

Alton pulled her into his arms and hugged her close. "Yes, Ginny. I know exactly how scary it is. I was terrified, watching you go after that bastard."

She kissed his chin, leaned back in his arms, and grinned at him. "I notice you didn't try to stop me, though. Thank you for standing beside me, for trusting me."

Alton laughed. "Trusting you? Nine hells! I was hoping you'd kill the damned thing for me. I'm beginning to think the warrior women of Lemuria were a lot tougher than the men. I wish I knew what happened to them, but that's probably why their history's been hidden. The fragile male ego couldn't handle it."

Both Eddy's and Ginny's swords flashed brilliantly and then the blades went dark. Alton stared at the fading glow on Ginny's sword and shook his head. "I'm not saying another word. Not a single word."

HellFire glowed within his grasp. "That's probably an excellent idea, Alton."

"What do ya know." Eddy flashed a huge grin at Alton. "No snark this time." Laughing, she and Ginny sheathed their crystal blades.

Chapter Sixteen

Alton pulled Ginny close after they crawled back into bed. It wasn't even four yet—too early to get up, too late for any really restful sleep. Unfortunately, he was way too wired to sleep at all. The images from the battle they'd just fought kept flitting through his mind like scenes from a movie—Dax covered by demons with the demon king sucking his energy or life force or whatever out of him, Eddy held against the wall by the mass of demons, and Ginny, his beautiful Ginny, spinning and twirling like a dancer, striking out against the demon king as if she enjoyed every minute of the fight.

Thank goodness she'd chosen to stay, not only because he couldn't bear to lose her, but because it was painfully obvious she was the best weapon they had to defeat the threat posed by the demon king.

A shiver ran along his spine. He hated to think of the danger this could expose her to. The thought of Ginny battling that monster . . . He wrapped his arms around her and held her even closer.

She nuzzled his chest and planted a kiss above his heart. "I thought you were asleep."

"You're kidding, right? I only came back to bed so Eddy and Dax would try and get some sleep."

Ginny sighed. "I know. I'm worried about Dax. Whatever that thing is doing to him, it's not good. He looks awful."

"Dax will be fine. Once he gets back to Evergreen and takes a day to catch up on food and sleep, he'll be himself again." At least Alton hoped that was true. The demons were growing stronger by the day, but there were only four warriors armed with crystal, and they were all tired and frustrated. And Dax! What had the Edenites been thinking, to send one man against demonkind? Poor Dax hadn't had a chance on his own. Alton wished there was some way to contact the Edenites, to find out if they had any ideas how to vanquish the demon king.

That strange creature was, after all, one of them, an inhabitant of Eden, so evil he'd been kicked out and exiled to the void. Too bad he hadn't stayed where he belonged.

Ginny's fingers swept along Alton's flank and settled on the curve of his butt. Arousal seared him with her touch and he felt himself stir in response. They'd made love for hours last night. He'd been worried about her, wondered if she might be too tender this morning to . . . *Nine hells!* What was she doing?

She'd scooted down his body while he'd been lying here worrying. Now her soft lips trailed across his belly and lower, to the sensitive crease between his thigh and groin. Her tight curls brushed the length of his cock as she nibbled and kissed her way around all his suddenly alert parts.

Warm, wet lips traced a path over his belly, down to the base of his erection. He fisted both hands in the soft blankets and groaned when she trailed kisses his full length, all the way to the weeping tip.

"Ginny? What the nine hells do you think—" He gasped as her lips encircled the crown and she drew him deep inside the sleek, wet heat of her mouth. Her tongue and lips and teeth held him in place, and all conscious thought disappeared like demon mist on the wind.

She knelt between his thighs and curled her slim body in a graceful arc to take him in her mouth. One hand cupped his sac while the other encircled the base of his shaft, holding him in place so he wouldn't choke her with an uncontrolled thrust of his hips.

As if he had any control left! Her mouth was so perfect, the sensation of full lips, stroking tongue, and sharp teeth taking him right to the edge where she held him on the precipice, teasing and tormenting him until he knew he couldn't take any more.

Carefully she rolled his balls within their sac with one hand. With the other, her long, strong fingers applied pressure around the base of his erection—just enough to keep him from coming, even if he'd wanted to.

He didn't. Not yet. Not until he'd found his place deep inside Ginny. She slipped him out of her mouth and blew a soft breath of air across his damp tip. He shuddered and arched his back, but met only the chill morning air. He heard the sound of tearing foil and almost lost it when her fingers wrapped around him once again and held him still.

Slowly Ginny rolled the condom over his sensitive length.

Then she was moving over him, straddling him, sinking down on his erection and taking him deep inside. Her sleek thighs locked against his hips and powerful vaginal muscles rippled over his full length, drawing him in, taking him home.

Ginny was his home, the one woman he would ever need, the only one he could ever love. Now, with her thoughts and heart open, he shared her deepest needs, her fears, her love.

Last night had been their debut, their first time together with the knowledge they loved each other. Today was a confirmation, the proof that what they'd felt before was real and true, that they could fight the evil facing them, so long as they faced it together.

Alton wrapped his arms around his lady love and rolled her over. She smiled up at him as he filled her. Her thoughts, so simple and yet profound, filled his mind.

I love you, she said. *I will always love you.*

As I love you, he replied. And then her body tightened in his arms and he set himself free to join her. Together they soared, and together they tumbled over the edge.

Ginny was the last one into the kitchen after finally crawling out of bed and taking a quick shower, but she'd slept so soundly after making love with Alton she hadn't even heard him get out of bed. As revved up as she'd felt after the fight with the demon king, she hadn't expected to sleep at all.

Dax looked up from his newspaper. "G'morning. Alton's out on the deck."

Ginny nodded and poured herself a cup of coffee. "Where's Eddy?"

"Talking to her dad. He's going to drive up the mountain and meet us near the portal." Dax shoved the paper across the table to Ginny. "People are beginning to notice things."

Ginny looked up from her cup. "What kinds of things?"

"Strange animal behavior, birds attacking pets and people. They've discounted rabies. Now they're talking about some new virus, or maybe toxic poisoning of some kind. So far no mention of demons. Are you sure you and Alton can handle stuff here if we leave?"

Ginny glanced at the paper. The articles were small, more like stories used as filler. At least they hadn't made the front page. "We'll be fine. You need to get stronger. You still don't look like yourself."

"He's not." Eddy stepped out of the bedroom, leaned over, and kissed Dax on top of the head. "I got into bed naked after the demon fight this morning, and all he did was hug me, roll over, and go to sleep. I'm definitely concerned."

Ginny snorted. "I imagine so. Did you call nine-one-one?" She slapped her hand to her forehead. "Crap. That reminds me. I need to call Shascom and tell them I'm not coming back to work."

Eddy pulled Ginny's cell phone off the charger and handed it to her. "Do it now. I have a feeling today's going to be really, really busy for you guys."

She took her phone out to the back deck. Alton was sitting on a long, low bench beneath the shade with HellFire on his lap. Ginny leaned close, kissed his cheek, and sat beside him.

"I need to call work and give notice, effective today." She punched in the numbers and made her call. It took no more than a couple of minutes to end a career she'd spent the past seven years building. When she completed the call, she stared at the phone in her hand.

"You okay?" Alton slipped an arm around her shoulders and tugged her close.

"I am." She leaned her head on Alton's shoulder and thought about how it felt to be unemployed after so many years on the job. It felt weird, to be honest. She'd once seen her job at Shascom as the door to her future. A good, solid job with a steady income and hours she could count on, maybe going back to school to study law enforcement if she could save enough money.

She wondered how fighting demons compared to life as a sheriff's deputy. "My supervisor said if I ever decide to come back, to let him know, that he didn't want to lose me. That was nice of him. I need to stop by next time I'm in town and fill out some papers and empty out my locker, but that's it."

Alton planted a kiss on her temple. "Thank you. I know it wasn't an easy decision, but we need you. I need you."

Ginny leaned back so she could look him square in the eyes. "I need you, too. You're right. It wasn't an easy decision. Thank you for understanding that." She stared off into the distance a moment and then she flashed him a wide smile. "It was my only choice. I love you." She grabbed his hand and stood up. "C'mon. We need breakfast, and then we need to get moving."

Ginny's cell phone rang as she was turning onto Highway 89. Alton took the call while she watched for the exit leading to the vortex at Red Rock Crossing near Cathedral Rock.

Alton's burst of laughter had everyone staring at him. By the time he ended the call he was wiping tears from his eyes.

Ginny turned left onto the narrow road that led to the vortex. "What's so funny?"

"That was Dawson Buck, the veterinarian we met the other day." He turned in the seat so Eddy and Dax could hear him. "I used a mild compulsion on him so I could explain the demon possession without raising too many questions, but he'd had a clinic filled with demon-possessed pets. Once the animals were caged, though, the demons fled. I asked him to let us know if he had more brought in."

"And?" Ginny slowed down as the road narrowed.

"And, he's figured out a way to catch demons, but now he doesn't know what to do with them."

"What? How?" Dax leaned forward.

"He says he's using his shop vacuum. When the demons slip out of a caged pet, he's somehow sucking them up into plastic bags and popping them into the freezer. He said they turn into little black ice cubes, but he's not sure if they're dead. He wants us to stop by later and take care of them."

Eddy giggled. "Demon cubes? Wonder how they'd taste in a margarita? Run them through the blender with a little tequila, add some triple sec and lime juice, salt around the rim of the glass . . ."

Ginny pulled up to the park entrance, paid the fee, and drove on in. She went as far as she could, parked the Yukon, and turned in her seat. "Don't demons have issues with salt?"

Shrugging, Eddy turned to Dax. "I don't know. Is salt a problem for you?"

"Only if there's not enough on my steak." Dax unfastened his seat belt. "What are we looking for at this vortex?"

"He can be such a poop." Still laughing, Eddy got out of the SUV and gazed at the surrounding country.

Alton and Ginny joined the two of them. Ginny glanced at a map she'd picked up in one of the local shops. "This way." She grabbed Alton's hand and tugged him down a trail that followed the creek.

"Actually," Dax said, "demons do have issues with salt. It's a pure substance, whereas demons are impure beings. If you're in fear of demons, make an unbroken circle of pure salt around the interior of a room or around your bed when you're sleeping. They can't cross it."

"Now he tells me." Eddy snorted. "Why didn't we do that last night?"

"Because demons aren't supposed to be able to do what they did last night. They shouldn't have that kind of strength in this dimension. Not without an avatar." Dax hugged Eddy close as they walked. "I'm sorry. I really am. We have to quit underestimating the bastards."

Ginny turned and walked backward a few steps. "Well, obviously demonkind has interacted with humans before, or we wouldn't have so much mythology about them. Some-one, somewhere had to learn the stuff about salt keeping them away. Every religion has demons." She laughed. "Where would Hollywood be without demons?"

Dax nodded. "Occasionally a demon will manage the

crossing from Abyss to Earth and maintain his demon form, but it's a rare occasion; it takes an unusually powerful demon with old skills, and they'll try to possess someone as quickly as possible before getting sucked back into the void. What's happening now is unprecedented, the way they're coming in such huge groups, the evolution of their abilities. The demon king, or whatever the hell he is." He shook his head. "I wish we had more information. It's like the rules keep changing but no one has thought to update the playbook."

"Just like a man," Eddy said, hugging his arm. "Human for just a few days and he's already making sports analogies. Don'tcha love it?"

"Playbook or not, they're definitely stronger at night. That's when we're seeing them without avatars." Alton glanced around. "I wonder where they go during daylight?"

Eddy gazed up at the clear sky. "They appear to be in the birds and other animals during the day. I wonder if they leave the avatars behind now, once it's dark? Could the ones that came after us last night have spent the day inside animal avatars?"

Ginny shuddered. "That makes way too much sense."

Alton stopped everyone with a wave of his hand. "Do you feel anything here?"

Ginny was the first to look at him with a big smile. "It feels good. Almost as if we should all be happy."

Eddy frowned. "You're right. How weird. Usually when we get close to a vortex, I begin to sense demonkind and I get really anxious."

Dax stepped closer to the creek. The cliffs rose high above them at this point, blocking the view of the beautiful monument known as Cathedral Rock. "The vortex is here. I sense it, but there's no scent of demons. Interesting. They've been at every single one we've found so far."

Alton hugged Ginny. "Ginny can answer your questions."

"Me? How so?" She frowned at him.

"Remember what you said about girl vortexes? That this one is known for its feminine energy? Only goodness exists here." He leaned close and kissed the frown off her face. "And we all know how sweet you women are. Filled with nothing but goodness and light."

Laughing, Ginny stepped close to the wall of the cliff. "Obviously he doesn't know me very well." She slanted a look at Eddy. "Or you, either. Goodness and light. Right." She ran her hand over the cliff, searching with all of her senses for the portal. She really wanted to find it on her own, if only to prove to Alton that she was learning to handle her new skills.

Her hand slipped through the stone. "It's here," she said. She reached for DarkFire and pulled the sword free of her scabbard. The others unsheathed their swords. Together, they stepped through the portal and into the heart of the vortex.

Alton wasn't certain what he expected, but the tiny cavern with only two small portals wasn't it. One led directly to Bell Rock, just a few miles away. The other appeared to link to Lemuria. There was no scent of demon, no sign of other gateways to other worlds. Just Lemuria and Bell Rock.

"I expected more," he said, holding HellFire high to search for other portals. "Cathedral Rock feels so powerful, but there's not much here at all. I wonder why?"

"I can answer your question."

"HellFire?" Alton turned the sword so that the crystal blade faced him. Not that HellFire actually had a face or even a mouth or brain or anything else remotely functional, but he always felt better conversing with the spirit that lived in the crystal if he was looking at the blade.

Go figure. "Explain, please. I'm curious."

"During the last eruption of Mount Shasta, when the people of Lemuria relocated to Sedona, this portal was put in place as a secret route back to Lemuria. It was used by members of the Council of Nine."

"But how could they go back? Wasn't Lemuria destroyed by the eruption?"

"No, Alton. That fear was propagated by your father and other members of the council. Lemuria is not in the same dimension as Mount Shasta. The volcano's eruption had no effect on your world, only on the exterior portals. There was no reason to leave your home."

Alton's legs felt like they might fold beneath him. He leaned against the cavern wall and stared at the glowing blade. Eddy, Ginny, and Dax waited silently while he tried to figure out exactly what HellFire was telling him. "Why?" he asked. "It doesn't make any sense. Why would my father want to uproot an entire people, move families and all that was familiar to them to this place in the desert?"

"Your father wasn't always the head of the Council of Nine. The move to Sedona was entirely political, all designed to strengthen his position as chancellor. It had worked for him before when Lemurians abandoned their sinking continent. He used that first move and the chaos that ensued to subjugate and then purge the women warriors from Lemurian society, as well as usurp the power of the man who was then the leader—his own father."

"I've never heard any of this. Couldn't anyone stop him?"

HellFire's glow pulsed and faded. "Your father rules by fear and lies. Lemurians love debate, but they are a trusting people. No one questioned him. He stepped into the role of leader by virtue of his forceful nature. The move unsettled the status quo and further strengthened his position. Now no one risks crossing him."

Alton straightened up. "Why haven't you said anything about this before?"

HellFire shimmered. "We may only give knowledge in

its proper time. I am sorry. There are powerful limits on what we may share."

"Well, shit and nine hells." Alton glared at the blade. "If that's true, someone has to stop my father. He's the reason our people won't join the fight against demonkind, isn't he?"

HellFire pulsed a brilliant blue and fell silent. Alton stared at the gateway to Lemuria. Only a few steps and he could be home. He could find out for himself what lies his father was spreading.

Ginny wrapped her fingers around his forearm. "Not now, Alton. Wait until we speak with Taron. He'll meet us at the Bell Rock vortex in a few hours. Dax needs to go back to Evergreen, not to Lemuria."

He wrapped an arm around her waist and hugged her close. "You're right. That doesn't mean I don't intend to have a heart-to-heart discussion with my father. He has a lot to answer for."

Dax clapped a hand on Alton's shoulder. "I agree. It's beginning to sound as if he's using his position for the good of Artigos, not for the good of Lemuria."

"I think you're probably right." Alton took another look around the small cavern. He couldn't think about his father right now. Didn't want to even consider some of the terrible things he'd done, and for what? What was his motive? Why would one man force an entire civilization to pack up and move? Of course, Alton couldn't figure out how he'd convinced them to do it, either. None of this made sense and his mind seethed with questions, but Ginny was right. This was not the time. He stared at the two portals for a moment, then turned to Eddy and Dax. "Do you want to go straight through to Bell Rock from here?"

Dax glanced at Eddy. She shrugged. "We might as well," she said. "Dad will be on Mount Shasta to meet us in about an hour. It'll take us at least that long to walk down the mountain to the spot where he'll be." She turned and hugged

Ginny. "You guys be careful, okay? And call me as soon as you talk to Taron. We're all going to be really anxious to hear what he's got to say."

Ginny grabbed Alton's hand. "Let's go with them. At least as far as Bell Rock."

Alton nodded. "Sounds good. Do you have everything you need?"

Eddy patted the bag hanging from her shoulder. "All in here." She grabbed Dax's hand and stepped through the portal. Ginny and Alton followed right behind them.

Within a few steps they'd popped out into the energy vortex in Bell Rock. The difference was noticeable the moment they left the purely feminine energy of the vortex at Red Rock Crossing. Here, where masculine and feminine energy was in balance, there was neither a sense of joy nor fear. Instead, Alton felt energized and ready for whatever he might need to face.

"The seal is still holding." He ran his fingers over the melted stone that marked the portal to Abyss. "I closed this the first day I arrived."

Dax sniffed the air. "There's no sulfur stench at all. They haven't made a new gateway."

Eddy gazed around the large cavern. "I don't see any others that might lead to Abyss. Ginny, you closed the one in Boynton Canyon, right?"

Ginny nodded. "I did."

"Okay, that's Bell Rock, Boynton Canyon, and the one at the airport. There wasn't a portal to Abyss at Red Rock Crossing, so unless there's a vortex we're missing, that should be all of them." Eddy looked from one to the other. "Agreed?"

"Which means the only demons we should need to worry about are the ones that are already here—and the demon king, who doesn't appear to need a portal, which is just plain scary." Dax took a deep breath. "So, how many is that?"

"A bunch," Alton said. "Hundreds, at the most, a dozen or so at the least, including the demon king. There was a huge flock of possessed birds that got away, though we did kill an awful lot of demons early this morning."

"Yeah, but the vet is still seeing possessed animals at the clinic," Ginny added.

Alton agreed. "We need to get over there. I can't wait to see how he's catching and freezing the bastards."

Eddy stood on her toes and kissed his cheek. "You do that. I'm taking Dax home. We'll be back in a couple of days. Sooner if he's feeling better or if you need us, but call as soon as you talk to Taron." She turned and gave Ginny a big hug. "And be careful. Don't take any chances."

Laughing, Ginny hugged her back. "You're kidding, right? You're leaving me here with this crazy Lemurian to hunt demons and telling me not to take chances? A little late for that, don't you think? Go. Now. Give your dad a big kiss for me. Dax? Get healthy and come back." She gave Eddy a slight shove toward the portal to Mount Shasta.

Dax grabbed Eddy's hand and they stepped through the gateway and disappeared. Ginny stared at the pulsing color that marked the portal and sighed. "She's the best girlfriend I've ever had." She leaned her head against Alton's shoulder. "But I realized today, you're my best friend. You know me even better than Eddy does."

Alton wrapped his arm around her waist. "Thank you." He kissed the top of her head. "I feel the same about you. It's a good feeling, but I understand your feelings for Eddy. Though Taron is my oldest male friend, I've grown closer to Dax because of what we've shared. I worry about him. He needs to regain his strength before he fights the demon king again."

Ginny tugged his arm and turned toward the portal that would take them back to Red Rock Crossing. "I know. I just hope the demon king hasn't followed him back to Evergreen."

Alton stared at the portal Eddy and Dax had just passed
through. He took a deep breath and let it out in a long, slow
sigh. Reassured there was no stench of demon about, he
followed Ginny through the portal that would take them
back to the Red Rock Crossing vortex at Cathedral Rock.

They checked the vortex at Cathedral Rock one more
time. Nothing at all. No sign of any other gateways beyond
the one to Bell Rock and the other to Lemuria. Ginny felt
Alton's anger even without telepathy—thank goodness they
wouldn't be seeing his father anytime soon. She didn't want
to think about what that meeting would be like.

They left the vortex and walked the short distance back to
the Yukon. It was cool and clear out today. The air smelled
fresh and clean. No scent of sulfur, no hint of demons.

Ginny stopped beside the car door. "We've got time to go
see the vet."

Alton nodded, but it was obvious his mind was on other
things. He climbed into the passenger seat without a word.
Ginny got in beside him and stuck the key in the ignition.
Before starting the engine, she turned and stared at him until
he raised his head and returned her steady gaze.

"Alton, you're not your father," she said, shaking her head
for emphasis. "You have no control over the things the man
has done, and no reason to feel guilty about his misdeeds."

He looked away, stared straight ahead, and sighed. "I can't
believe he is so obsessed with power that he's willing to destroy an entire civilization. I don't understand it. He's got to
be stopped, Ginny. Whether he's my father or not, the man
has to be stopped."

She stared at him long enough that he finally tilted his
head and looked at her once again. "I agree, Alton. And I
imagine you're going to be the one to stop him. I just don't
want you to feel guilty for doing what has to be done."

"Thank you." He reached across the console and wrapped his fingers around her arm. "If you're beside me, I believe I can do anything." His lips quirked up in a half smile. "Now let's go check out Dr. Dawson Buck and his demon cubes."

It was almost noon by the time they reached the clinic. Ginny parked in the back and she and Alton walked around to the front door. The CLOSED sign was up. "They must shut down for a lunch break." She knocked sharply on the door.

Dawson Buck opened it almost immediately. Ginny'd forgotten how attractive the man was in his own quirky way. He was tall and lean with unkempt, shaggy dark hair, neatly trimmed beard, and a definite twinkle in his dark blue eyes. The creases beside his mouth and the laugh lines around his eyes said a lot about his sense of humor.

"I'm glad you're here," he said, stepping back and inviting them in. "This is good timing. The staff's gone to a luncheon for one of my employees. A bridal shower." He laughed. "Thank goodness they don't expect me to show up." As he talked, he headed toward the kennel in the back of the clinic with Ginny and Alton right behind him.

There was a large chest freezer against one wall. "I have this for animals that need to be preserved for testing, or for the occasional client who wants their pet stuffed or freeze-dried."

"Freeze-dried?" Ginny shook her head. "Stuffing Fido is bad enough, but freeze-drying?"

Dr. Buck chuckled. "It sounds a bit macabre, but they actually look okay when they're done right." He raised the lid on the freezer and pulled out a cardboard box. "I've been keeping the little bastards in here."

He opened the box. Inside, baggies filled with little black chunks of ice were neatly stacked in rows.

"Wow." Alton shook his head. "That's fantastic. You must have fifty or sixty of them."

"You're good. Fifty-seven, actually. I got the last one

yesterday. Haven't had any new patients brought in today, and neither have any of the other vets in town, or the animal shelters. Everyone's aware of the strange animal behavior and we're all sort of keeping up with each other, though I haven't mentioned demons." He laughed and shook his head. "Enough of my peers already think I'm nuts without that. I'm wondering, though, if we've got most of them."

"Wouldn't that be nice." Alton reached for one of the baggies and set it on the tile counter. "Let's see if this works." He carefully opened the sealed plastic bag and dumped the frozen demon in the sink. It clunked and rattled just like a regular ice cube.

Ginny drew her sword as Alton pulled HellFire out of the scabbard.

The vet stepped back out of the way. "Where the hell did those come from? I didn't even see them when you walked in."

Ginny flashed him a quick grin. "They're magic," she said. "You can only see them if they want to be seen." She almost giggled when Dawson Buck merely nodded, as if magic made perfect sense. Of course, in her new reality it did. She wondered if Alton's compulsion was still working on the man.

DarkFire flashed a brilliant violet light over the frozen demon. All its demonic features were exposed, twisted and frozen in a dark parody of evil.

The vet hissed a soft curse and stepped back. "Holy shit. If I'd known how nasty they looked, I might have thought twice about trying to catch them."

"They're definitely ugly." Ginny held DarkFire in place, almost mesmerized by the disgusting creature lying frozen against the white porcelain sink. "They only show their true colors in the glow from my sword."

"Let's hit this together and see what happens." Alton's words snapped her back to the present. He touched HellFire's sharp point to one side of the frozen demon. Ginny tapped the other side with DarkFire's tip. The demon sizzled and burst into a shower of blue and violet sparks and sulfur stench. The steam dissipated almost immediately. Only the foul odor remained.

"Now that we know that works . . ." Alton shoved the box toward the vet. "Doctor Buck, why don't you open the bags and dump them in the sink. We'll get rid of all of them before your staff returns."

"Call me Dawson, and there's no rush. Lunch is at a good Mexican restaurant that serves the best margaritas in town. I don't expect anyone to show up for a couple of hours. Besides, they'll all be next to worthless when they get back." He grinned. "I've left the afternoon schedule free."

Ginny glanced at Alton and they both cracked up. All Ginny could think of was the demon margarita Eddy'd been joking about earlier, as one after one they sent the frozen demons sizzling and sparking away to the void.

Ginny zapped the final demon with DarkFire and carefully slipped her sword back in the scabbard while Alton cleaned up the used baggies. They reeked of sulfur.

"Throw them in here. This is for toxic waste." Dawson opened the lid of a heavy-duty waste can and Alton threw all the used baggies inside.

"I want to see how you trapped them." Alton rinsed his hands off in the sink. "I'm really impressed. I never would have thought of using a vacuum."

Dawson dragged a big shop vac out from under the counter. "I just stick the possessed animal in one of the smaller pens. It only takes a minute or two before the demon realizes it's trapped, and it pops out of the critter. I imagine they're looking for an animal that's not caged, but the minute I see the black mist hovering in the air, I suck it up with the vacuum, grab a baggie, put it over the nozzle and reverse the airflow. That blows it into the baggie, I seal it shut and toss it in the freezer."

"Amazing." Alton slapped him on the shoulder. "Be sure and call us if you come across more. Ginny and I can come back and get rid of them."

"Sounds good." Dawson shoved the vacuum back under the counter and walked them to the door. "Can you tell me what's going on? Where they're coming from?"

Alton shot a quick glance at Ginny. Silently, she replied, *He deserves to know, don't you think?*

I agree.

Alton paused by the door and gazed out at the quiet street that ran in front of the clinic. His thoughts were wide open to Ginny, the fears he had that this could all end if the demon invasion were successful. He looked directly at Dawson when he explained what they were involved in.

"The balance between good and evil is tipping toward darkness as demons move into this world. Ginny and I are part of a very small group fighting demonkind. We've closed the local pathways into Earth's dimension, but the battle's far from over. We can't let any of them escape, and those we've not caught are growing stronger by the hour." He placed a hand on Dawson's shoulder. "Be careful. They've already possessed at least one man we're aware of. Be alert when you're around them."

"Why are you keeping it secret? Shouldn't the army be brought in?"

"We can't risk it," Ginny said. "They'd come in with guns blazing. Every death in the fight against demonkind, even of cats and birds and dogs, means another soul lost and more energy for the demons."

"Imagine the panic," Alton added. "People would see demons in everything. It would feed right into the demons' plans. They thrive on chaos."

Ginny laughed and bumped him with her hip. "Imagine

explaining you." She smiled at Dawson. "Alton's not human. He's actually from another dimension. One of our guys is an ex-demon in a human body. I'm not fully human, and there's a dog hosting the spirit of a will-o'-the-wisp that can communicate telepathically."

Dawson's eyes got bigger with each little bit of information they shared. Finally he sat down on his desk and started to laugh. "I was going to say thank you for trusting me, but now I'm wondering if I really want to know all this. My staff already thinks I'm nuts. Harmless, but nuts."

Dawson held out his hand to Alton. "I've got a million questions that I hope you'll be able to answer for me someday. I promise to keep all this to myself." He laughed again as they shook hands. "Hell, if I tried to tell anyone what you've just told me, they'd have me committed. I wouldn't believe a word of what you've said if I hadn't seen those little bastards myself."

He stood and walked them to the back door of the clinic. "You've got my number. If there's anything at all I can do to help, call me. Anything. I mean it."

Dawson closed the door behind them and Alton and Ginny walked back to the Yukon and took their seats.

"I'm glad we told him," Ginny said. "I don't think he'll say anything."

"I agree. Sometimes you have to learn to trust people." He caught Ginny's eye and she smiled at him. They were both living proof that trust didn't always come easy.

"What next?" Ginny stuck the key in the ignition.

"I think we need to check with Markus."

"Markus? What for?" She backed out of the parking place and headed toward the neighborhood where her aunt and cousins lived.

"Because we're secret government agents and we need to keep him informed. Besides, there's a really good taco stand on the way to his house." He flashed her a bright smile. "Unfortunately, I don't think they serve margaritas."

"Gotcha." She pulled a pout. "I just hope I'll survive."

"I hope we both do," Alton added.

She turned her head and caught him looking at her. He wasn't smiling anymore.

Chapter Seventeen

While they ate lunch, Ginny called ahead to make sure Markus was home. He met them outside, sitting on the front porch steps with Tom in his lap. When Ginny parked the Yukon at the curb, Markus set the cat down and walked quickly out to meet them. He didn't even give them time to get out of the SUV.

Alton rolled the window down. "Hey, Markus. What's up?"

Markus looked over his shoulder. Then he quickly glanced at the house. "Probably not a good idea for you guys to come in."

"Why not?" Ginny leaned across Alton to talk to her cousin. "Is something wrong?"

Markus let loose a dramatic sigh. "Everything's wrong. Aunt Betty's convinced you brought the devil to Sedona. She's blaming you guys for all Tom's weird shit, and whenever one of the twins acts up, now she says they've got the devil in them." He made his voice all high and squeaky and said, "All this bad shit's because of your cousin Ginny and her weird friend."

"What?"

"Shush." Alton bit back a laugh, but Ginny's shriek made his ears ring. He held her hand and listened to her grumble before asking Markus, "Are the twins okay? They're not acting possessed, are they?" When Markus shook his head no, Alton asked, "Why would she blame us? I don't get it."

"There's all kinds of crazy shit going on. Pets attacking their owners, some guy in a bar going berserk and talking in a weird voice, a lady in town said she was attacked by rats that stalked her like they knew what they were doing. It all started the day Ginny arrived."

He shrugged and gave Ginny an apologetic smile. "Mom knows you were adopted and she never could figure out how your folks could take in a baby when they didn't know anything about her background. She always said they were asking for trouble taking in a stray kid, and now she says you're probably a demon child."

"Aunt Betty said that?" Ginny sat back in her seat. Alton turned around and caught the look of utter devastation on her face. His first reaction was to punch Markus in the nose, but he controlled himself and concentrated on Ginny.

"Your aunt doesn't know what she's talking about." Alton leaned close and kissed her. "She's an idiot."

"For what it's worth, I agree." Markus leaned on the open window. "I tried to tell her she was talking crazy, but she won't listen to anything. That's why I haven't called you. I didn't think it was a good idea for you to come here, at least until whatever's going on stops. In fact, I'm glad I caught you just now, before you actually knocked on the door and freaked Mom out entirely. We're all okay, Tom's just Tom, and the twins are their usual spoiled-rotten selves." He smiled apologetically at Ginny. "If they get extra rows of teeth or their eyes start to glow, I promise to call."

Alton glared at him. "You do that, Markus."

Markus slapped the roof of the Yukon and backed away. "Yeah. Ginny? I'm sorry. I shouldn't have said that. Mom's, well . . . she's just Mom. I probably got my big mouth from her."

"Yeah." Ginny's audible sigh broke Alton's heart. "We'll see you around. Be careful. Call if something comes up."

"Will do." He stepped back up on the curb.

Ginny drove away from the house. She'd wiped all the expression from her face, but Alton could feel the sadness flowing off of her in heavy waves of pain. Her voice sounded totally flat when she asked him, "Where to now?"

He stared at her a moment, wondering how he could make things better. Nothing came to mind. "Let's make a quick drive through town," he said. "Then we can check the Boynton Canyon vortex again. Maybe go by the one at the airport. I want to make sure all the portals we've sealed are holding."

"Okay. The airport first. It's closest."

Her voice had totally lost its spark. Alton wanted to strangle Markus, but the kid hadn't realized what he was saying.

"That explains so much."

Alton leaned back in his seat and watched Ginny. "What explains what?"

"What Markus said. My mom and his mom were never very close even though they were sisters. I always thought it was their age difference, but it could have been over things Betty said to my mother about me."

Alton nodded. "Markus should have kept his big mouth shut."

Ginny laughed. "'Discretion' and 'Markus' are never used in the same sentence. He says what he thinks, generally before he actually thinks it. He's always been that way."

She clammed up, turned at the light, and drove down the highway that led to the airport. After a minute she patted his leg. "Alton, I have no doubt that my mother and father loved me. I was their only child. They chose to adopt me and they were such good parents. Even though they were older, they loved me and did the best they could for me. Look at it this way—Markus has had to live with my Aunt Betty all his life. I was the lucky one, don't you think?"

Alton leaned over and planted a quick kiss on her cheek. "No, sweet one. Your parents were the lucky ones."

"Thank you."

The rest of the trip to the airport was made in silence. Alton wondered about Ginny's thoughts, but he decided not to intrude. In some ways he couldn't help but feel jealous. Ginny had loved her parents and they'd loved her. She was proud of them and she missed them, but she'd always have such good memories.

He wished he could say the same. He loved his mother, but it was hard to respect a woman who'd stay with a man like his father. She'd chosen to remain his mate all these years, no matter how Artigos had treated her or their only son.

Had she known about the other stuff? What in the nine hells had his father done? What was the man thinking when he forced an entire civilization to give up a home it had finally grown comfortable in, after their traumatic move from the original continent of Lemuria?

And what was his plan now? With demonkind attacking and the future of all life balanced on a razor's edge, what could his father possibly have in mind, that he was willing to sacrifice so many worlds, so many lives?

Alton hated to think of Ginny hurting over her cousin's thoughtless words, but even more, he hated wondering what his father might be planning. What the man had in mind. A showdown was coming, and as much as Alton loathed the idea, he was afraid it was going to be more personal than he'd ever imagined.

He was going to have to face his father. Not as the man's son, but as the one who would somehow remove Artigos from his position as the head of the Council of Nine.

Artigos was powerful. He was canny—a smart man without morals or ethics to impede his actions. But why? What would make an intelligent man turn on his own people, his own family—his own son? He couldn't do more to help demonkind if he'd tried.

A chill raced along his spine. Could that be it? Was Artigos literally in league with the devil? Had his father somehow, during his long life, become the tool of demonkind?

It would explain so much. Alton had to find out. Then he had to face the man who had been his father.

They walked back to the Yukon after checking out the vortex near the airport. Ginny reached for Alton's hand and wrapped her fingers around his. He'd seemed distracted most of the morning. At first she'd thought it was because Dax and Eddy were gone, but now she was almost certain it was over the information they'd gotten from HellFire this morning.

It was bad enough that Alton's father had disowned him, but it might be so much worse. She'd been in Alton's thoughts, following his convoluted mental process as he'd worked his way through his father's transgressions. Could Alton be right? Was Artigos somehow in league with the creatures of darkness? She glanced at Alton and figured she'd be distracted, too, if she'd suspected such devastating information about one of her parents.

"Are you still up to checking out the vortex at Boynton Canyon?"

Alton nodded. "It shouldn't take us long. There was no sign of demonkind here, and I'm hoping that one will be just as clear. Then we need to rest a bit before we meet Taron. He's due around sunset."

Ginny unlocked the Yukon and opened the door. She glanced up at Alton, standing beside the SUV, staring off into the distance. When he didn't answer her, she said, "I think you need to learn to drive."

He turned and stared at her. "What?"

She smiled. At least this was taking his mind off his father. "You need to learn to drive the Yukon. If anything were to happen and I couldn't drive, I'd want to know you could get us away safely. There're plenty of roads out here without much traffic. Do you want to give it a try?"

He grinned and held out his hand. She dropped the keys into his palm and they traded sides of the car. She crawled into the passenger seat and made a big show of buckling herself in safely and pretending to put on a crash helmet.

Alton did the same. She watched while he inserted the key, checked to make sure the gears were in Park, and started the engine. Then he shifted to Reverse and slowly backed out of the parking space. With a flourish, he shifted to Drive and headed for the main road.

"You act like you've been driving for years. How?"

He flashed her a bright grin. "I've been paying attention. Taron always tells me I don't pay attention like I should, so I've made a point of watching you."

He braked at the stoplight and smiled at her again. "I've discovered it's very easy to pay attention when you're the subject I'm supposed to be watching."

She blinked, aware of a warm glow that seemed to heat her from the inside out. She was still thinking of his words when the light changed. Alton signaled and turned right, back onto the main road. He drove down the highway as if he'd been driving for years. Within minutes he'd turned again, onto the road that would take them back to the Boynton Canyon vortex, and then to their little casita at the resort.

After a few minutes, Ginny realized she'd totally relaxed. "You're really a good driver. You even remember to signal. I'm impressed."

He flashed her a bright grin. "Thank you. You should be." Then he turned his full attention back to the road, frowning with intense concentration as he drove along the two-lane highway.

He slowed as they passed by the green field where the fighting bulls were pastured. It was a large herd, but they grazed peacefully on the lush grass. Their horns shimmered in the bright sunlight. One huge bull raised his head and watched the Yukon as they slowly passed by. After a moment, he lowered his big head and returned to munching on the grass.

"I think we've just been dismissed by the lord of the pasture." Alton chuckled. "Those things fascinate me. They're huge and they look like nothing but muscle." He accelerated and they continued on past the herd. "With attitude," he added. "They've definitely got attitude."

Ginny laughed, and with her laughter tension flowed out of her. What a morning they'd had. She slanted Alton another quick glance and sighed. Talk about attitude! Alton had it in spades, but his was well deserved. He looked so good sitting beside her, all broad-shouldered and long-limbed and so damned *male.* How a guy who was as flat-out pretty as Alton, with all that gorgeous long, blond hair and perfect bone structure could epitomize everything masculine made absolutely no sense at all.

But somehow, Alton had it nailed.

Even now, wearing a black T-shirt that stretched over his muscular chest and tucked into his tight-fitting jeans, he only needed the horse to pass for a cowboy, or a motorcycle to look like he belonged on a Harley. He'd braided his hair this morning into a single long braid that hung down the middle of his back. With his baseball cap on, he looked like a regular guy—a regular drop-dead gorgeous guy.

His green eyes sparkled and with the hair pulled away from his face, his sharp cheekbones, the line of his jaw, and his long, straight nose looked like something a sculptor might create. She thought of him the way he'd been this morning, lying beneath her when she'd straddled him, made love to him. How he'd flipped her over so effortlessly and taken her even higher.

She sighed again.

Then she thought of the demon king and the danger facing them, and all the tension came flooding back.

"Don't."

She turned to him, blinking. "Don't what?"

Alton shook his head. "Don't worry. Enjoy a few minutes without worrying about what's coming next. You look so gorgeous sitting beside me with stars in your eyes. Much prettier than when you've got your eyebrows all tied in knots."

"Stars in my eyes? Me? Ha!" She sat back in her seat and folded her arms across her chest. "I never have stars in my eyes. That's for dreamers."

Alton merely grinned as he pulled off the highway and turned down the road leading to the Boynton Canyon vortex. He parked the Yukon in the lot, turned off the ignition, and stuck the keys in his pocket. Then he turned in his seat and rested his arm against the back. "You had stars in your eyes this morning when we were making love. I looked up as you straddled me, when you took me deep inside you, and I saw them. Brilliant stars in those tiger's eyes of yours. Don't ever lose them."

His soft words left her speechless. He leaned over and kissed her and her eyes filled with tears. *Damn him.* She kissed him back, but she'd never been so afraid in her life. She'd gone and fallen in love and they still had a war to fight. She'd never had so much to lose before, never wanted anyone as much as she wanted Alton.

Immortal they might be, but what kind of future awaited them? She kissed him again, almost desperately, but she knew he understood. His eyes hinted at the same desperation she felt as they slowly broke the kiss.

Together they got out of the SUV and hiked up the canyon

to the vortex. One more to check. Then they had to hope they'd found all of them.

But how many demons were left? How many had already made it through from Abyss to Earth? There were other vortexes around the country. Did they contain portals between Earth and Abyss? As the two of them hiked the trail to the energy vortex, Ginny kept glancing at the sky. The last time they were here, they'd been attacked by possessed birds, but no birds circled them now.

Who knew what the afternoon would bring.

Hopefully it would bring Taron with some good news for a change. But what about Alton's father? There were just too many things that could go wrong, too many variables out of their control.

Alton reached for her hand and wrapped her fingers in his. "C'mon. Let's check this place out so we can get back to the casita."

She was going to ask him what for, but then she glanced up and caught the glint in his sparkling green eyes and knew exactly what was on Alton's mind. Warmth flowed through her at the promise she saw. She didn't hesitate when he tugged her toward the portal.

This time, the air inside the cavern was free of demon stench, musty and dry as caverns should be. There was no lingering scent of sulfur and the melted stone where the portal had once led to Abyss hadn't been tampered with.

Alton ran his fingers over the glassy rock. "No sign of demons here. Unless there are other vortexes we're not aware of, I think we've got them stopped, at least for now."

"So it's a matter of finding the ones that are already here?" Ginny ran her fingers over the melted portal. "Where do demons go in the daytime? I wonder how many are left?"

"I wish I knew. The demon king knows where we are, though. I have a feeling he's going to come to us. I imagine he'll bring his army with him."

* * *

Ginny folded the last of the laundry she'd done while they waited to meet Taron. She poured a couple of glasses of iced tea and took one to Alton.

"Thank you." He took a long swallow and then set it aside to go back to his project.

"What are you doing?" Ginny curled her legs and sat on the floor beside him.

Both HellFire and DarkFire lay side by side on the couch. Alton sat on the floor and leaned against the couch with Ginny's scabbard in his lap. "Oiling the leather. It keeps it supple, so it won't crack."

"Where do you get leather in Lemuria if you don't have animals? In fact, where do you get your food without farms to raise stuff?"

"Everything we need is brought in from other dimensions. Lemurian tradesmen handle the commerce."

"But what do you trade? What kind of product can you offer?" Ginny ran her hand over the supple leather and wondered what kind of animal it had once covered.

Alton laughed. "Remember those diamonds? We have an endless supply of precious gems and metals. We spend them carefully so the markets aren't flooded in any one world, but that's the basis of our economy. They're so prevalent in our world that they're worthless to us, but valuable in every other dimension."

"But who does all the work? I was there such a brief time, but all I saw were security guards in blue robes and the rest of the people wearing white and sort of hanging around. Who cleans and cooks and teaches school?" She laughed and leaned her head against his shoulder. "I guess I want to know where the people like me are."

Alton leaned close and kissed her. "Ginny—there's no one like you anywhere. You're unique."

"That's no answer. I have this image of dark little drones working in the bowels of the earth. Do you have a working class?"

Alton shrugged. "Yes and no. Our technology is so advanced that there's very little we have to do to make things work. We learn by absorbing information while we sleep and then we test our knowledge in discourse and debate. We pick up our meals at food centers, and those who are interested in the economy and other worlds take positions where they deal with those things."

"What about you, Alton?" She cupped the side of his face in her palm. "What have you prepared for?"

He turned away and shook his head. "I've been groomed to take my father's place, but when one is the son of an immortal ruler, there's not much hope for job advancement."

"How'd your father get his title?"

Alton raised his head and frowned. "I don't know. He's been the head of the Council of Nine as long as I can remember, and his father before him. I honestly have no idea what became of my grandfather or how my father took over the position."

Ginny nodded. Then she gazed directly into those beautiful emerald-green eyes of his and made a suggestion she hoped she wouldn't regret.

"Maybe you need to find out."

Alton drove out to Bell Rock just before sunset. Ginny'd just handed over the keys as if she expected him to take the wheel, and he sure wasn't going to disagree. Lemuria was such a small world and there were so few citizens that there was no need for mechanized travel.

That was definitely a huge mark against his home. Driving was wonderful. No wonder Ginny had hesitated over letting him handle the Yukon.

The parking lot was empty. Dark clouds billowed high in the western sky and hid the last rays of the setting sun. A cold wind raised dust devils across the asphalt lot. Ginny zipped her hoodie sweatshirt and tucked her hands in the pockets. Alton zipped up his windbreaker and wrapped an arm around Ginny's shoulders.

The weather here could change from hot to cold in a heartbeat. With the sun already gone behind the red rocks, it was definitely chilly ahead of what appeared to be an incoming storm.

"Do you think Taron will be there?" Ginny slipped out of Alton's embrace and headed up the trail.

"If he's not already there, I expect him within the hour. Our time seems to coincide with Lemuria's, though sunset in a world without sunlight is a fairly abstract concept."

Ginny flashed him a big grin. "So how do you tell time?"

He stopped and frowned at her. "We have clocks." Then he laughed. "Sorry. I didn't mean to sound insulted. Our light works on a twenty-four-hour clock, just as it does in Earth's dimension. It's a carryover from when we were part of this world. We have our sunlight during day and darkness at night. The artificial light illuminating our world covers the full spectrum of the sun so that we get the necessary nutrients our bodies need. It's all very scientific."

Ginny waved her hand across the wide horizon. "What about storms and clouds? Do you have rainbows and seasons? How can you stand it, not having the surprises that nature gives us on a daily basis?"

"We don't have earthquakes or tornadoes. Our people don't live in fear of hurricanes or typhoons, of freezing to death or dying from the heat. I think it works both ways."

Ginny stopped and turned around. She stood above him on a smooth red slab of sandstone with the towering form of Bell Rock behind her, and when she planted her hands on her hips she practically screamed her exasperation. "But when are you tested, Alton? How do you know if you can meet a challenge if you're never faced with one? When life is perfect, there's no need to be brave, no reason to stand up for anything. What keeps you sharp and alert? I think I'd go nuts."

He reached out and grabbed her hand, brought it to his lips, and kissed her fingers. "You're right. And I was going nuts, which is why I chose to leave it all and join Dax and Eddy in their fight against demons. Our perfect world isn't enough. It's not healthy for people to live without challenges. We need to be tested if we're to survive. The demon threat is testing us now. I hope I can take that message back to my people. I'm going to have to if Taron doesn't bring us good news. Somehow we need to convince them that they're going to have to fight if they want to continue. We can only hope they pass the test."

Ginny nodded. She wrapped her fingers around his and tugged him up on the rock with her. They hiked the rest of the trail in silence.

Alton spotted the portal first and pressed his hand against the smooth rock. When it passed through, he tightened his grip on Ginny and the two of them walked through the portal into the vortex. Taron waited just inside.

"Taron. It's good to see you, my friend."

Taron reached for Alton and the two of them embraced. He nodded in greeting to Ginny, but his expression was somber.

Too somber for good news. Alton sighed. "I guess there's no need for me to ask if you've been successful."

Taron shook his head. "There's no arguing with fools, but even more discouraging is the news I'm hearing from Roland and other members of the Guard."

"They have their swords. What does the council want to—"

"The members of the Council of Nine, led by your father,

wanted to take the crystal swords away from Roland and his men."

Ginny's eyes flashed. "They can't do that!"

Taron chuckled. "They figured that one out very quickly, when the soldiers refused to give up their swords and the entire guard backed the men. The people are standing behind the soldiers, and the men of Lemuria are digging their own crystal swords out of storage and carrying them proudly."

Alton clapped Taron on the back. "This is a good thing. Maybe the members of the council will get their heads out of their butts and—"

Taron interrupted. "Don't count on it. Alton, there is more going on here than merely your father's stubbornness. Rumors are flying ever since the Crone made her appearance. Rumors of the women warriors who fought during the DemonWars, and what happened to those women."

Alton glanced at Ginny, and then again at his friend. "What are you hearing?"

"That they were purged from Lemurian society. Enslaved and sent to work below in the mines. Rumor has it their daughters toil there still, guilty of nothing more than their birthright, as the children of good and loyal warriors."

It felt as if a shaft of ice had replaced his spine. Alton couldn't even look at Ginny when he asked the question he knew must be burning in her mind as well. "Who was responsible for that purge? For such horrible treatment of brave citizens."

Taron's sigh and the shift of his always steady gaze to a point beyond Alton's shoulder was all the answer he needed. "My father?"

Taron nodded. "It appears so."

Ginny interrupted. "Does the Lemurian Guard know of these women warriors?"

"It seems they do, now." Taron shrugged. "Roland said

he's heard rumors for years, but had no way of following up on anything without going through proper channels. His paperwork never went anywhere. He finally made a search for himself, breaching the lower levels in order to see where the prisoners were kept, how they fared."

Alton folded his arms across his chest, as much to still the sudden trembling in his limbs as to give himself a moment to calm his racing heart. "And what did he find?"

"Women. Young women working the mines as slaves. Their mothers, those brave women warriors, are all gone, but their daughters live on."

"Alton?" Ginny's fingers tightened around his forearm. "We have to do something. We can't leave them like that."

He nodded, covering her fingers with his. "The Lemurian Guard is sworn to protect the citizens of Lemuria, and that includes the Council of Nine. The only way we can successfully bring about change in a peaceful manner is with a coup at the top."

Taron coughed and cleared his throat. "That's not going to be easy with your father in command."

Alton nodded. "I agree. Easy or not, my father has to be stopped and a vote taken to choose a new council—one that includes women. Taron? This fight I'm in now consumes me. What does the council say about joining our war against demonkind?"

Taron shook his head. "They want no part of it. They've lifted the charges against you and Ginny, much to your father's dismay, but as far as helping with this fight? Their decision is to bury their heads beneath their blankets and hope the demon threat goes away."

"That's probably because all their warriors are working as slaves." Ginny glared at Alton. "You want soldiers? I imagine the women you're talking about are the ones you need, which means you're going to have to deal with your father first."

She folded her arms across her chest. "I didn't like him from the moment I saw him."

Alton wrapped his arm around Ginny's waist and laughed. Taron looked at him as if he was absolutely nuts. Maybe he was, but only a nut would consider organizing a rebellion of women slaves on one world in order to fight demonkind on another.

And wasn't that exactly what he was planning? "Well, Taron if you have a plan, I need to hear it now. We have work to do." He glanced at Ginny and caught her smiling, but she was still in his mind and knew exactly what he was thinking. "That includes you, Ginny. Where do we start?"

Chapter Eighteen

She'd never been more proud of anyone than she was of Alton at this moment. He didn't hesitate, even when faced with overthrowing his own father. Even though none of them had any idea where to begin.

Ginny reached over her shoulder and withdrew DarkFire. Alton's eyes lit up and he reached for HellFire. They lay their crystal swords side by side on the rock outcropping. "Dark-Fire, are you aware of the women who toil in Lemuria's caverns, the daughters of your fellow warriors?"

DarkFire pulsed a deep violet: "It is the shame of our people, that our women warriors were treated as criminals. Their daughters are the innocent victims of one man's hubris."

Ginny glanced at Taron first and then Alton. There was no doubt what man DarkFire spoke of.

Alton didn't flinch. He touched HellFire's blade. "What happened to the crystal swords the women once carried? Do they still exist?"

HellFire glowed with a soft blue light. "They were confiscated and destroyed by members of the Lemurian Guard loyal to the new council. Their sentient spirits were cast out."

Taron stared at HellFire's blade. "Do those spirits still exist? Could they inhabit other swords?"

HellFire pulsed blue. DarkFire's violet glow flickered and sparked, and it was DarkFire who answered Taron's question. "We believe they could. There are one hundred daughters laboring in the caverns. One hundred daughters of brave women warriors. The spirits who once inhabited the mother's swords would welcome the daughters."

Alton sat back on the outcropping beside the swords. He glanced from Taron to Ginny. "Where in nine hells are we going to get a hundred crystal swords?"

HellFire shimmered blue. "DarkFire and I are needed to battle demons on Earth. Taron, take your sword into the deepest caverns, those forged of crystal far beneath the mines where the women labor. Carry food and water for one week. Remain beside your weapon. Be prepared to do as it asks."

DarkFire glowed violet and her voice sent shivers along Ginny's spine. "Taron, your blade awaits you now. At the end of one week, you will carry the newly replicated crystal swords to the women. The blades will know their mates. When all are armed with crystal, your course of action will be clear."

Alton rested his hand on Taron's shoulder. "Can you do that? Spend a week in the crystal caverns by yourself?"

Taron smiled at Alton. "I've heard of them, but I've never been that deep before. If I can find them, I'll do whatever it takes. HellFire said to be prepared to do what my sword asks. That means it's going to speak to me." He shook his head slowly, adding softly, "Finally, after all these years."

Ginny shook her head, but she couldn't quit grinning. "If we know we have an army of a hundred brave warriors coming to join us, I imagine we can hang on for another week. Eddy and Dax will be back in a day or two."

She stood up and sheathed DarkFire.

Alton slipped HellFire back into the scabbard. Then he reached for Taron and the two men clasped hands. "This wasn't the meeting I expected. It was so much more. I'm not sure how I'm going to get my father out of his council seat, but trust me when I say that I'll do everything I can."

"What of the Lemurian Guard?" Taron glanced from Alton to Ginny. "They've sworn a loyalty oath."

"Exactly," Ginny said. "An oath to Lemuria. I have no doubt they'll realize, just as Roland and his men did, that Lemuria and the council are two separate things. I think the current council is headed for a change."

Alton looked toward Taron. "We've learned that when Lemuria was relocated to Sedona during the last explosion of Mount Shasta, it was a totally unnecessary move. The members of the council were continuing to travel by a secret portal back and forth between Sedona and Lemuria. We have no idea why, but now that we know there were women laboring below all that time, women who remained behind unharmed by the eruption, it's hard to trust any of our council members for anything."

Taron shook his head in disgust. "They have a lot to answer for. Why would your father turn against his own people?"

"I have my suspicions," Alton said. "When I know more, I'll share everything with you."

A scrape of feet on rock had everyone spinning toward the Lemurian portal. Roland of Kronus, the sergeant of the Lemurian Guard, stepped into the cavern. He saluted Taron and bowed his head to the others. "You must return now, before the watch changes. It's easier to move you through when I'm sure of the men under my command."

"Thank you, Roland."

"Thank you, Taron. And good luck." Ginny held Alton's hand while the two Lemurians slipped through the portal. Then she glanced at the tall Lemurian standing by her side. "Wow," she said. "Definitely not the meeting I expected."

Alton slipped his arm around her waist. "Ginny, I had no

idea. None at all, but the story of the enslaved women explains so much. Why we have no history of women warriors. Why there's no obvious reason for our women to be so terribly subjugated in what should be a free society." He bowed his head. "DarkFire blames it on one man's hubris. She had to have been speaking of my father."

"Probably." She sighed. "I don't know. We have as many questions as answers, at this point." Ginny tugged him toward the portal leading out of the vortex. "Like what happened to your grandfather, and why your father would want to be rid of the women who were such brave warriors. And why he orchestrated the move to Sedona. That's one I don't get."

"I know." Alton paused at the gateway and took a deep breath. Then he let it out and sighed. "Ginny, there's another question you asked me this morning, one that I wasn't able to answer."

Ginny glanced up at Alton, expecting a smile.

He was frowning. "What's that?" she asked.

"Where demons go during daylight." He shook his head. "I'm not certain, but I think I have an idea."

Ginny was frowning as well when she followed him out of the vortex, into the Arizona night.

Alton used the light from HellFire to guide them down the trail skirting the flank of Bell Rock. Within fifteen minutes they'd made it back to the Yukon. Ginny held on to his hand the entire way, but neither of them spoke during their brief hike.

Alton opened the passenger door and Ginny climbed in without question. As he pulled out of the parking lot, Alton glanced her way. She stared straight ahead, frowning. Softly he asked her, "What are you thinking?"

She shook her head. "I don't know what to think. I've

been so focused on the demon threat that it's hard to switch gears and realize we have an issue that's almost as big and every bit as important, waiting for us in Lemuria."

He couldn't help smiling. "We? It sounds as if you're taking on the women's fight as your own."

"Well, of course I am." She tilted her head and stared at him. Her eyes glinted in the darkness, reflecting the lights from the Yukon's dash. "I'm Lemurian, I carry crystal, and I'm a woman. Why wouldn't I feel it's my fight?"

Her words, spoken with such frank conviction, settled warmly against his heart. "Thank you, Ginny." He glanced at the dark road ahead, then looked her way once more. "I mean that. Thank you very much."

"I don't get it." She leaned back against the seat with her arms folded across her chest. "Why are you thanking me? What for?" She was still frowning and she was absolutely beautiful.

Alton turned his attention to the road when he spoke. "For embracing your Lemurian heritage, even though it appears it's not one you have any reason to be all that proud of. For seeing the women warriors' fight as your own." He glanced her way again. "For being exactly who you are. I love you. Never more than at this very moment." He turned his eyes back to the road. "I'm very proud of you. Proud to know you stand beside me."

"Always, Alton." Her soft laughter sent shivers along his spine. "It may have taken me awhile to figure it out, but there are no doubts in my mind. Not anymore."

Ginny unlocked the door to the casita and walked in ahead of Alton. She went straight to the refrigerator and grabbed two cold beers, popped the tops on both, and flopped down in a chair at the kitchen table. Her mind wouldn't stop spinning—where should they begin? How in the hell were they going to get rid of the demon king and manage a coup in Lemuria on their own?

Who in the hell was she trying to fool? Ginny grabbed her cell phone and handed it and one of the beers to Alton as he walked into the kitchen. "Call Dax. Tell him what's going on."

Alton took the beer and the phone. "Good idea." He took a big swallow of beer, hit the speed dial for Dax, turned on the speakerphone, and set the phone on the table between them.

Eddy answered. "What's up?"

Alton sighed. "More than you want to know." Then he explained all that they'd learned from Taron. "So . . . any suggestions?"

"Wow. That's some story. And you're right. There could be a connection between what's happened in Lemuria and the demon threat on Earth. Dax actually has an interesting theory."

Dax's deep voice rumbled out of the speaker. "Hello, Alton. Eddy and I have talked about your father, how he came to power around the time the demon wars ended. Isn't that when he took over?"

"Yeah. It was during that period when the wars were ending and we were evacuating to Mount Shasta. Why?"

"Why did you have to leave Lemuria?"

Alton flashed a quick "save me now" glance at Ginny. She had a feeling he was tired of explaining his father to everyone, especially himself.

"Your story," she said, shaking her head. "You tell it."

He sighed and began, but she realized how painful it must be for him. He was, after all, condemning his own father with each retelling.

"There was a series of devastating earthquakes," he said. "Our scientists concluded the continent was sinking into the sea. The war was just ending, our civilization was foundering and everything was chaos. The move was made very quickly."

"Could Abyss have been behind the earthquakes? Was there any hint these were not natural phenomena?" Dax's question hung in the air between Ginny and Alton.

"Not that I know of," Alton said. "But I was just a kid. I wasn't aware of a lot of what was going on."

"Wait a minute." Dax's and Eddy's voices filtered through the phone, but they were obviously speaking to each other. Ginny thought she heard Eddy's father make a comment. Then Eddy came on the line.

"Alton, this might sound way out there, but what if Abyss was behind the destruction of Lemuria? What if somehow the demons were able to infiltrate the council, maybe even affect your father's decisions. Dax says there are all kinds of demons. If it's a lesser demon, it might not exert full control, but it could influence the way decisions are made. It sounds as if there were a lot of drastic changes in Lemurian society, especially in respect to the treatment of the women warriors and the status of women. They were all made relatively quickly. This doesn't sound like a natural progression."

Alton took another swallow of his beer. "My mother said my father changed very quickly, from someone idealistic and loving to the man he is today."

Ginny frowned, remembering Gaia's comments. "Actually, she said he lost his soul. I remember thinking that was a strange way to describe her husband, but a wife would recognize a change like that before anyone else. She wouldn't have had a reason to associate it with demon possession, but if that's the case, how do we tell? Wouldn't our swords have sensed the presence of demonkind in Artigos?"

"Not necessarily." Dax sounded thoughtful, as if he pondered all the different aspects of demonkind. "Over time, if a demon remains within a corporeal host, it melds almost entirely with what is essentially its permanent avatar. The relationship becomes symbiotic—one can no longer exist without the other."

"Which means that if we try and remove the demon, the host dies?" Alton's question hung in the space between Evergreen and Sedona.

There was a jumble of conversation from the Evergreen group. Then Eddy answered. "Possibly true. If your father has been possessed long enough, it might require his death to destroy the demon."

Dax interrupted. "But if you kill a man to free the demon inside, you've just given the demon a powerful life force to take with him when he possesses another. You could create an even stronger and unknown enemy by destroying the one you know. I would encourage attempting to remove it, or at the very least, imprisoning your father so he can do no more harm."

"I will not kill my father." Alton's comment left no room for argument. "I'll help remove him from his position of authority, but I won't kill him."

"That's good." Dax left little doubt either. "We'll think of something, Alton. For now, concentrate on finding the demon king. Eddy and I will be back tomorrow around noon."

Tomorrow? Ginny shot a quick look at Alton. "Dax, are you sure you'll be okay by then?"

Eddy answered for him. "He'll be fine. Dad's been stuffing food down him since we got here and he's beginning to fidget. Plus, he can't keep his hands off me. I think he's healed. We'll see you around lunchtime." She laughed.

Ginny heard Dax grunt. *I think she punched him,* she said to Alton.

He probably deserved it. Alton laughed. "We'll see you tomorrow. Call when you want us to meet you at Bell Rock."

Ginny ended the call and plugged the cell phone into the charger. "What now?"

"We walk down to the restaurant and get something to eat and then we get some rest. We'll make sure the windows are tightly closed so we don't have any visitors. From the lack of demon activity today, I'm wondering if the demon king is on his own, or close to it."

"What about all the birds? There were hundreds of them circling you the other day."

"We've destroyed hundreds of demons since then. At least two or three hundred last night when they attacked us here in the casita. We would have seen some hint of demon activity today if there'd been any still around. Remember, the portals are all sealed, so there aren't any new ones coming in. I'm beginning to think there aren't many demons left in Sedona at this point."

"I prefer not to take chances." Ginny stood up. "Unless he got sucked back into the void, which I doubt, we know the demon king is still hanging around. Look, I'm hungry, I'm tired, and I'm in desperate need of a bath. I want a shower and some clean clothes before we go down for dinner." She kissed him briefly as she walked past him toward the bathroom. "And I want your promise we're going to discuss anything but demons during dinner. Got it?"

He tried to catch her for another kiss, but she evaded his quick grab. Then she paused in the doorway, raised her eyebrows, and waited. He sighed dramatically. "Got it," he said.

With a quick bump of her hips, Ginny left him sitting in the kitchen, nursing the end of his beer and wondering about the fate of Lemuria and Earth and everything in between.

Hand in hand, Alton and Ginny walked back to their casita after dinner. The restaurant had been less than half full this evening and their meal and service were both excellent. Ginny'd dressed in a flowing red skirt and a white camisole top with tiny little buttons down the front. She had her wild hair braided and tamed and tucked up on top of her head, and she'd finished off her outfit with some really high-heeled red sandals that made her long legs look even longer. Her full lips were painted the same deep red as her skirt.

He hadn't been able to take his eyes off her all evening. They'd had a quiet dinner and talked about everything but what lay ahead of them. Alton decided it was a pretty nice way to spend the evening—dinner with a beautiful woman who would most likely be sharing his bed in a very short time, and a conversation that did not include any life-or-death issues.

Now, though, with the dark desert night all around, he faced the fact they needed a course of action, sooner rather than later.

In one week, the daughters of the women warriors would rise up and expect to reclaim their place in Lemurian society. He tried to imagine how the people as a whole would react. Somehow he needed to prepare the citizens of Lemuria for the changes destined to come. You couldn't just bring an entire army of angry young women armed with crystal into an established society ruled by men and turn them loose.

They had been treated terribly, as had their mothers. It was too late for the women warriors of old, but their daughters deserved their freedom—and so much more. Yet the introduction of all those young women was bound to cause a huge shift in their fragile civilization.

The balance of men to women, for one thing. So many men who'd not thought of marriage because there were so few women among them would suddenly be faced with an entirely new group of females, but these females were not going to be the typical subservient women Lemurian men had grown to expect.

No, they were going to be strong and tough and a lot more like Ginny.

"Nine hells." Alton stopped dead in his tracks, looked at

Ginny, and burst out laughing. When she returned his look with one brow raised, he laughed even harder.

"What?" she asked. At least her lips were twitching.

He took a deep breath and got control of himself before he started giggling like a schoolgirl. "It just came to me that when the women rise up, armed and angry and ready to claim their place in Lemurian society, it's going to be like turning an entire army of Ginnys loose on my unsuspecting world."

Ginny glared at him. "You say that like it's a bad thing. Explain yourself, bud!"

There was definitely a twinkle in her eye.

"Let's just say it's going to come as a shock to the average Lemurian male."

Ginny wrapped her arms around his waist and smiled up at him. "Are you still in shock?"

"I am," he said. "And loving every minute of it. However, I am not your typical Lemurian male."

"I know," she said, standing on her toes to plant a kiss on his lips. "You're so much more." She nuzzled her cheek against his chest. "So how do we break it to those average Lemurian males that women have rights, too?" Backing away, she gazed at him with a more serious expression. "Actually, I hadn't thought about what a huge shift in behavior this is going to require. American men have been faced with liberated women for over fifty years and they're still not all that cool with it."

"No one wants to change the power structure when they're on the top. It's going to take planning and a lot of diplomacy."

They walked on to the casita. The evening clouds had blown through and the air was comfortable. Alton sat on the top step and pulled Ginny down beside him.

"So, what's your plan?" she asked.

"We'll wait until Dax and Eddy are back. In the meantime,

we'll watch out for demons and make sure things are okay here. I think it's dangerous to divide our attention right now. First we need to concentrate on defeating the demon king. I think our fight with him will come sooner rather than later." He stood up and tugged her hand. "Let's go in. I'm beat."

She blinked slowly and pulled her perfect lips down in a pout. "Oh. I was hoping you weren't too tired."

Alton tightened his grasp on her hand and pulled her slowly to her feet. "I'm never too tired for that," he said. He tugged and she came into his arms, curled her long, lean body against his, and kissed him.

He leaned over, grabbed both their swords and scabbards, and followed Ginny inside.

Ginny checked the windows while Alton made certain the front door was securely locked. He left HellFire by the front door and Ginny set DarkFire by the back door. The sentience within the swords never slept, and they'd decided to try using them as an early alarm system.

Ginny swept her fingers over the softly oiled scabbard and thought of all the changes her life had gone through in just a few short days.

Of all of them, the most important was Alton. She glanced up and saw him standing in the doorway, watching her with a funny little half smile on his full lips. "What?"

"You're beautiful." He shook his head. "Every time I look at you, I see something else about you to love. You look absolutely gorgeous in red, did you know that? Your skin glows and your eyes sparkle." He stepped closer, so close she had to raise her chin to see his face.

He was so much bigger than her, so much more powerful, and yet she'd never known a more gentle man. He reached out and ran the backs of his fingers over her cheek, down the side of her neck, and across her exposed collarbone.

When he reached her throat, his long fingers cupped her jaw and tilted her face perfectly so he could lean close and kiss her. His lips were soft and slick, and his tongue slipped between hers and brushed the sharp edges of her teeth, delved deeper, and stroked the sensitive roof of her mouth.

She moaned, and it was a sound of need and desire, of joy and even fear. There was so much ahead of them, so many things that could go wrong and sunder this perfect beginning to love.

A sense of desperation lanced along Ginny's spine. She threw her arms around Alton's neck and hugged him tight. He kissed her deeper, slipped his arm beneath her legs, and lifted her high against his chest. He kissed her again. Then he carried her down the hall to their room.

When he carefully laid her on the bed she looked up at him through eyes blurred with tears. Her emotions were churning tonight, but she and Alton hovered on the peak of great events—events that would affect them both for all time to come. Maybe tears were apropos, but she forced her fears away until they waited in the shadows, out of sight of the here and now.

Alton kicked off his boots and slipped off his shirt. He unbuttoned his jeans and slid them down his long legs. Then he stepped out of his pants and stood before her like a fair-skinned god. His hair hung loose in shimmering waves of pale gold and the muscles over his chest rippled with each breath.

She was still fully dressed, but it was so good, lying here and looking her fill at him. He was perfect, so tall and lean, with those long, strong muscles and the dusting of fine, golden hair across his chest and the tops of his thighs. The thicker growth over his groin was only a shade darker, a perfect setting for the absolutely beautiful erection thrusting high and hard against his belly.

He bent his knee and rested it on the bed beside her,

reached for her skirt, and slowly tugged it down over her legs. Then he unbuttoned the tiny row of pearls holding the camisole top closed across her breasts. When the seam parted and bared her breasts, a hiss escaped from his parted lips.

She'd not worn a bra tonight. His emerald eyes sparkled at the discovery as he spread the top apart and then carefully slipped it over her arms.

She wore nothing now but the tiny scrap of red panties. Not quite a thong, but not much more, they skimmed low on her belly and barely covered her pubes. Alton crawled over her legs and nuzzled her belly with his lips, nipped at the elastic on her panties, and tugged at them with his teeth. She lifted her hips and it seemed to be all the invitation he needed to pull them down over her legs and toss them aside.

Then he sat back on his heels and stared at her.

Again she gave him some attitude, rose up on her elbows, and said, "What? Just what are you staring at?" She had to bite the inside of her cheek to keep from laughing.

He cleared his throat, yet his voice still sounded gruff, almost as if he'd been overcome with emotion. "I'm staring at the most beautiful woman I've ever seen in my life." He leaned close and kissed her mouth, then her throat, and finally her nipples—first one and then the other. He tightened his lips around the one over her heart and sucked hard, pressing the tip against the roof of his mouth with the flat of his tongue.

She felt the draw all the way to her toes. He sucked harder, licking and suckling until she was writhing on the bed, her body growing wet and ready from nothing more than the pull of his mouth against her breast. He switched to the other one, sucking and tugging until she wanted to scream.

Then he turned her loose, dipped his head lower, and put his mouth between her legs.

Ginny screamed. He laved her with long, slow strokes of his tongue, dipping between her soft folds with the very tip, stroking, nibbling, and licking as if he couldn't get enough of her taste. Her body shuddered and jerked beneath his sensual assault. He slipped his warm hands beneath her buttocks and lifted her high. Her thighs rested on his forearms as he sat back on his heels and pleasured her, licking and nipping, using his tongue and teeth to take her higher, and higher yet again until she hovered there, crying out on the sharp edge of desire.

He raised his head and looked at her—she felt the heat of his gaze like a physical touch and opened her eyes. He hovered over her, his blond hair tangled over his shoulders, twisted around her legs and across her belly. His eyes smoldered with green fire and his lips and chin were shiny from her fluids. He licked his lips slowly, as if savoring her taste, held her gaze, and dipped his mouth closer to her. Then he sucked her clit between his lips and tightened down on that most sensitive bundle of nerves.

Fire sparked from his mouth to her spine and her heart stuttered in her chest. She arched her back, pressing herself against his mouth, sobbing with the power of the climax that continued to grow and expand with each thundering beat of her heart.

He lay her back down on the bed, sheathed himself to protect her, and slowly pressed the thick length of his erection between her legs. She was so sensitive she cried out, but she lifted for him, pressed her heels to the bed, and thrust against him as he slowly entered her.

Ginny wrapped her arms and legs around his long, lean body. She drew in his scent, the softness of his hair as it flowed over her shoulders and arms, the firm strength of his muscles rippling with each thrust of his hips. Physically it was all perfect, emotionally it was so right it scared her.

She'd never allowed herself to love like this; never had she been so vulnerable before. Loving Alton opened her to pain unlike anything she'd ever experienced. Their future was so terribly uncertain, she couldn't allow herself to dwell on what might be.

She had to live for now, for the wonder of these few moments when everything was perfect—when the world wasn't at risk, when their lives weren't in danger. This moment when their plans weren't hovering in the wings, waiting to ruin the perfection of this place in time.

She heard his heart pounding in his chest and knew it matched the rhythm of hers. She opened her heart and her mind and found herself there within the deepest part of his soul. She felt the coil of desire rising once again within her body and recognized its kindred spirit in Alton's.

This time when she hurtled from the top, she didn't fly alone. He was there with her, his heart and mind linked irrevocably to hers. And when it was over, when they lay on the bed, wrapped in each other's arms, their chests heaving with each labored breath and hearts still pounding in a wild rhythm, Ginny realized she didn't cry alone.

The tears in Alton's eyes blended with hers. The sense that every moment stolen could be their last, tempered by the knowledge that no matter what was to come, they had now, tonight, together.

Chapter Nineteen

Sunlight slanted across the bed. Alton blinked, and then blinked again when a dog barked nearby. Slowly he sat up in bed. Ginny slept soundly beside him, but the sun was high in the sky and if the clock was right, it was almost noon. He shook his head and looked again.

Definitely almost noon. He leaned over and kissed Ginny's shoulder. She twitched, as if she was trying to dislodge a fly. He kissed her again and she opened one bleary eye. "It's almost noon, my love. We need to get moving."

She popped up and shook her head. "Noon? When are we supposed to meet Dax and Eddy?"

There was a loud knock on the bedroom door and it swung open. Without waiting, Dax stuck his head in. Ginny shrieked and pulled the sheet up over her bare breasts. Alton made sure he was properly covered just before Eddy popped into the room. "You were supposed to meet Dax and Eddy around noon," she said, laughing. "It's noon and we're here."

There was a mad scramble behind them and BumperWillow came flying into the bedroom and jumped up on the bed. Ginny shrieked again and pulled a pillow over her face. The dog wriggled and barked and licked Alton and her tail was going a million miles a minute.

Ginny poked her nose out from under the pillow. "I thought you set DarkFire and HellFire up as sentries. How'd these guys get in?" BumperWillow turned and gave Ginny's face a big lick. Ginny screamed and ducked back under the pillow and the dog went back to work on Alton.

Laughing, he finally grabbed her by the shoulders and held her back from his face. "I'm glad to see you, too, beast, but settle down!"

BumperWillow barked again. *I missed you, Alton. I missed you a lot. We both did.*

Alton hugged the dog. "I missed you, too, Willow. And Bumper. So how'd you guys get here? And how'd you get past our sentries?"

Dax laughed. "You mean your swords? We're the good guys, remember? HellFire and DarkFire both wished us a good morning when we arrived."

"Great." Alton rolled his eyes at Ginny.

She giggled. "Well, it seemed like a good idea at the time."

Eddy sat on the foot of the bed and pulled Dax down beside her. Dax said, "We came back earlier than planned and popped out in the middle of your New Age meditation group, or one just like it. Anyway, they were just finishing up and gave us a lift here in a really cool bus."

Alton laughed. "I think I know the one you mean."

Eddy could hardly talk through her giggles. "We're talking psychedelic mid-sixties art and clothing—and people—but they were really nice and didn't seem the least bit surprised when we stepped right out of the rock. We're invited to a craft and music fair they're putting on this afternoon. It's just down the road, across from that ranch where the Spanish fighting bulls are pastured."

"Okay." Alton glanced at Ginny. "Those bulls remind me. I have a theory about the demons . . ."

Ginny frowned. "We haven't seen any since Dax and Eddy left. I know that doesn't mean they're all gone, but . . ."

Eddy and Dax immediately sobered. Dax wrapped his arm around Eddy's waist. "You probably haven't seen them because I think I'm their target at this point. The demon king has done all he can with the demons he brought with him. We talked it over with Ed last night and he agrees. The demon king needs me now, if he's going to get any stronger. Since it's my old demon body he's using, we think he's able to capture my energy and siphon it from this form into the one it's familiar with. At this point, we need to be alert, but we agreed—there's no need to hunt the demon king. Not when he's going to be hunting me."

"There's only one problem." Alton caught everyone's attention. "I think the demons are hiding out in the fighting bulls during the day. At least, I think that's where the demon king goes. If we go to that craft fair, we're going to be heading straight for the demon. He won't need to hunt very far."

Eddy fixed bacon and eggs in the small kitchen while Ginny and Alton showered. When Alton finally got to the kitchen, Dax handed him a cup of coffee and they wandered out to the back deck with BumperWillow right behind. Alton sipped his coffee and stared out over the desert. It was another warm, sunny day. Yesterday's threatening storm had never materialized. Today's blue sky created a perfect backdrop for the red rock formations.

"It looks so beautiful, doesn't it? Peaceful and absolutely perfect." He turned to Dax and grinned. "Have you thought of how we're going to stop this bastard?"

Dax shook his head. "It's going to take all of us. Ginny's DarkFire appears to be the most powerful weapon we've got, but it's stronger in tandem with another sword. It's almost as if her blade can focus the energy from ours. Eddy and I brought Willow along because she can sense demons before the rest of us. Maybe if we get a jump on this guy . . ." He shrugged.

Alton glanced at Dax and then returned his gaze to the desert. "I'm convinced he's spending his days inside the lead bull in that pasture just down the road. I'm not sure about the other bulls, but the big one there seems much too aware of us every time we drive by. Plus, it's like I'm drawn to him for some reason. HellFire can't tell for sure if he's there, but I have a feeling the demons are getting better at masking their presence."

Dax nodded. "If we go to that fair, it'll give us a chance to check and see if you're right. Let's assume you are. I'll feel better if we're all together, but we need to be prepared."

Eddy stuck her head out the door. "Come and eat. Breakfast is ready."

Alton followed Dax back into the kitchen. He felt a strange prickling along his spine, as if his senses had suddenly gone on alert. He glanced at BumperWillow. The dog didn't seem to notice a thing, so he relaxed and joined the others in the kitchen.

Still, he'd been feeling more suspicious of that bull since the first time he saw it. If the demon king was using it as an avatar during the day, could it somehow give him the strength to roam in his demon form at night? Maybe the fact it had taken on Dax's old body gave it an added boost of energy. It wasn't a true avatar because it was a wraith like the other demons, but it also had physical properties the others lacked.

It was so hard to know, especially since the rules of engagement seemed to change by the day. Alton glanced up as Ginny entered the kitchen. She grabbed a cup of coffee and took the seat beside him. When he took her hand in his, he felt her tension all the way through his body.

Something was going to happen today. He wasn't sure

what and didn't know how he knew what he knew, but the sense of dread that cloaked him suddenly had all of Alton's senses on alert.

Last night when they'd made love, he'd realized how very much he now had to lose. Of course, that was also more incentive to fight harder and smarter.

Come hell or demons, he was not going to lose Ginny.

Dax and Alton cleared the dishes away and Eddy wiped the table down. Ginny brought fresh coffee for all of them and took her seat beside Alton. "Do you realize this is the first time we're actually going on the offense?" Her gaze slipped from Eddy to Dax to Alton. "We've fought a defensive fight every time with the demons, at least since I've been involved. What do we need to do to be ready?"

Alton took her hand. "We have to find the bastards first. I'm guessing they're in the bulls. I could be wrong."

"Let's assume you're right," Eddy said. "We can't just go on someone's property and attack the livestock. How do we draw the demons to us?"

"If we go to the craft fair, it might bring the demon king out of hiding," Dax said.

"But then you're putting innocent people at risk." Alton shook his head. "We can't endanger innocent lives."

"Let's go to the fair, walk across the road to check out the fancy cattle, and see if we feel the demons' presence." Ginny squeezed Alton's hand. "Then if there's no sense of them, we can go to the fair and enjoy ourselves, and figure the demon king will find us here tonight."

"And if they're in the cattle?" Alton raised an eyebrow.

Ginny grinned. "We go to plan B."

"Which is?" He grinned back.

"You hit the entire fair with a compulsion while we kill

off the demon king and end the threat to all humanity. Seems like a simple enough plan to me."

"Oh, yeah," Alton muttered. "Real simple."

Dax pushed his chair away from the table. "Unfortunately, Ginny's idea is about the best we've got. I say we go and see what happens."

It seemed as if Ginny and Eddy had spent hours in the bedroom getting themselves ready for the fair. Alton sat next to Dax on the back deck and stared at the door to the casita, willing the women to finish up whatever they were doing so they could get this over with.

He'd never been to a craft fair, had no idea what one was, and was certain he wasn't going to enjoy it, but if it was being held near the bulls and if his theory about the demons using the bulls to hide during daylight was right, he wanted to go now, before it got dark.

"What do women do that takes them so long?" Dax glanced at Alton and shook his head. "They're both beautiful. What are they doing in there?"

Alton rolled his eyes and sighed. "I have no idea, but trust me. It'll be worth it. Ginny informed me that even though our main goal is hunting demons, this is still the first real date for either of them with either of us. They want to make it special."

"Hunting demons is a date?" Dax shook his head. "I don't get it. Even BumperWillow's been in there forever."

"Relax, Dax. They're all women. They seem to work on a different timetable than we do."

The door slowly opened. BumperWillow walked out and posed. She had red bows in her curly blond topknot and another one tied to her tail. Alton slapped Dax on the back and laughed. "See? What'd I tell you? She's gorgeous, don't you think?"

Ginny stepped through the door next. She wore the same outfit she'd had on the night before, but now her hair lay close to her scalp, braided in tiny dark rows and caught at the nape of her neck with red ribbon and white beads. With her dark eyes accented with a touch of makeup, she looked both exotic and mysterious.

Alton didn't even realize he'd stood up until he had her hand in his and had pulled her close for a kiss. "Breathtaking," he said. And she was. Absolutely stunning.

Dax's sharp indrawn breath had both Alton and Ginny turning to look at Eddy. Almost always dressed in jeans and a T-shirt, she was hardly recognizable in a flowing, gauzy dress that clung to her slim frame. Barely touching the tops of her knees, it shimmered in shades of dark blue, purple, and black. She wore strappy sandals that added to her height and made her long legs look even longer.

Ginny giggled. "My shopping trip in Phoenix paid off."

Eddy blushed and did a slow pirouette. "It's not really me, but . . ."

"You look amazing." Dax walked toward her, moving almost like a man in a trance. "Absolutely amazing." He glanced at Ginny. "What have you done to her? I can't take her out in public like this."

Eddy frowned. "Why not?"

Dax took her hands in his and slowly shook his head. "Because every man there will want you for himself."

Eddy self-consciously tugged one hand loose and touched her short, tousled hair. That was the only thing about her that really seemed familiar. Then, before the moment could grow uncomfortable, Ginny leaned past Alton and high-fived Eddy. "Looks like we did okay, eh, girls?" BumperWillow barked and the spell was broken.

Alton checked out their long legs and the sandals both women wore. "Can you fight in those shoes?"

Ginny scowled. "Better than you can in those pointy-toed boots, buster."

Eddy crossed her arms over her chest and leveled a long glare at both men. Alton held his hands up in defeat. They grabbed their swords, added a fresh compulsion to hide them, and climbed into the Yukon. Alton took the wheel and dangled the keys in front of Dax. "If you're good to me, I'll give you lessons one of these days."

Dax reached for the keys but Alton snatched them out of the way. Laughing, teasing, almost as if they were a pair of normal couples going off on a regular date with the dog sitting in the back, Alton headed for the craft fair.

A steady stream of cars pulled into a long driveway just across the road from the pasture where the bulls quietly grazed. Alton stared at the big animals as he pulled the Yukon into line. They looked just like what they were: big animals grazing in the sunshine. Nothing about them appeared at all threatening.

He turned his attention back to the fair. Multicolored flags flew along the drive. Dozens of people dressed in colorful costumes wandered about, selling everything from hand-carved toys to mysterious-looking foods that smelled absolutely mouthwatering.

Alton parked the Yukon in a big field that had been marked in neat rows, and they all got out. Ginny had tied a long red ribbon to BumperWillow's collar so that there wouldn't be any complaints about a dog roaming free.

"First let's check the bulls." Alton tugged Ginny's hand. Dax and Eddy followed and they walked across the two-lane highway, just another group of tourists curious about the huge bulls grazing so peacefully in the pasture.

BumperWillow stuck her nose under the fence and sniffed. The big bull stared at them, slowly chewing his cud. Some of the animals slept in the shade of a cottonwood tree, while the rest munched on the lush, green grass.

Alton shook his head. "No sense of demonkind at all. I was so sure they'd be here." He glanced at the dog. "Willow? Do you or Bumper sense anything at all?"

The dog barked. One of the bulls ambled close and sniffed noses with her beneath the bottom rail of the fence. Ginny reached over the top and touched the rough, black coat. A fly buzzed and landed on the bull. Muscles twitched and the fly took off. *Nothing, Alton. No lingering sulfur, no sense of demon.*

"HellFire? What about you?"

"Cattle. Nothing more, nothing less."

Shrugging off his disappointment, Alton tightened his grasp on Ginny's hand and turned away. "That's it, I guess. We might as well check out the fair." He'd been so sure.

They crossed the road and wandered through the tents and booths set up over an area that was even larger than the central plaza in Lemuria, which Ginny had already told Alton equaled the size of a football field.

He was still trying to figure out how football was played, though the sheer brute force of the game was enough to keep him interested.

Wonderful smells rose from a number of the booths and there was even a large, open pit with what looked like an entire pig spinning slowly on a spit over a fire. The event had the feel of a historical reenactment, with old-fashioned crafts and various art forms on display. Lots of the visitors and all of the participants wore brightly colored costumes.

None, however, were even remotely as beautiful as either Ginny or Eddy. Alton caught Dax's eye and the two men grinned at each other. Dax's thoughts slipped into Alton's mind.

You were right. It was worth the wait. I'm glad there were no demons here to spoil our date.

Alton couldn't recall when he'd had a more relaxing time with Ginny. Since he'd known her, there'd been one crisis after another. They'd either been in fear for their lives or trying to escape from or kill demons, and while the risk still existed, for this moment in time it was good to merely enjoy the company of the woman he loved.

Alton sniffed the air. There was no scent of sulfur, no sense of demonkind. Even Dax appeared to have relaxed enough to actually enjoy himself with Eddy. The two of them held hands and wandered from booth to booth with the silly-looking curly blond dog trotting along beside them. If there'd been any risk of demons at all, BumperWillow would be the first to notice, but she held her head high with her tail curled over her back.

All was well. He glanced at Ginny and she smiled at him. Better than well. Damn. She was so perfect it almost hurt to look at her. He swore to himself she'd always have a closet filled with red dresses and skirts and anything else that women liked—as long as everything was red.

Ginny in red stirred his senses. She took his breath with her beauty and dazzled him with her smile. He had to look away before he lost his composure altogether. He'd never, not in his wildest dreams, imagined feeling this way about a woman. Never dreamed he'd fall in love—or have that love returned.

Ginny squeezed his fingers and tugged him toward the next booth. Like a well-trained puppy, he followed. Dax and Eddy were just across the aisle from them. Eddy held up a beautiful scarf and draped it across her face so that she looked like a mysterious Eastern princess.

Dax tugged it down and kissed her. Ginny watched the two of them and laughed.

BumperWillow's hackles went up. Her lips curled back in a snarl. *Demon. I sense demonkind. I don't know where they are, but they're coming closer.*

Dax grabbed Eddy's hand and tugged her through the

moving bodies. They worked their way across the flow, toward Alton and Ginny.

Alton turned to Ginny. "Did you hear BumperWillow?"

"I did." She set down the wood carving she'd been admiring and stood on her toes, searching over the crowd. Just then Eddy and Dax broke through and joined them.

"Any idea where?"

Alton shook his head. "No, but I'm still betting on those bulls. Let's move back the way we came in, toward the front of the fair."

They threaded their way through the crowds of fairgoers, moving against the flow of bodies. Music was playing behind them at the far end of the fair, drawing the crowd toward a stage at the back side of the gathering. BumperWillow yipped when someone stepped on her toes. Dax leaned over and picked her up in his powerful arms, holding the fifty-pound dog as if she weighed nothing at all. Now they could move more quickly and BumperWillow had a better view above the crowd.

Someone screamed. The crowd surged against them. A shout echoed over the group. Another scream. "C'mon!" Alton grabbed Ginny's hand and broke into a run. People moved aside as he raced against the surging throng, toward the growing commotion.

Dax and Eddy followed right behind.

"The bulls are out." Eddy's breathless comment was punctuated by Dax's curse.

The stench of sulfur surrounded the herd of black bulls that milled about at the front of the craft fair, not far from the parking area. The biggest bull raised his head, sniffed the air and turned. He focused on Dax and bellowed out a challenge.

People screamed and ran from the area. A couple of men tried to herd the big animals back across the road, but they refused to move. Someone yelled to anyone listening to call animal control.

"No one's controlling those suckers," Dax said. He set BumperWillow on the ground and untied the red ribbon attached to her collar. "Stay close, my friend. Be careful."

Alton stared at the small herd. The sense of demonkind was strong now, almost suffocating. Where had the bastards been earlier? Had they somehow managed to mask their presence?

Obviously, because they were here now. Here and seething with power. This was not how he'd wanted to make their stand against the demon king, not how any of them had planned to fight. They were surrounded by innocent bystanders, people without a clue as to the threat that faced them.

At least the sun was still fairly high in the sky. The demons weren't at their peak strength.

BumperWillow braced her feet and stared at the bulls. First one and then another of the big animals turned to face the small group. There were at least twenty of the beasts, all of them heavily muscled with long, sharp horns. Their black coats shimmered in the sunlight. The largest animal pawed the earth and threw huge clods of dirt over his shoulders, but it was one of the smaller bulls that lowered its head and made the first rush.

Dax drew DemonFire as the bull picked up speed and raced toward him. Lightly he spun out of the way of the thundering beast, tapping the animal's shoulder with the tip of his sword as the bull charged by. Blue fire surged from the crystal blade. The animal stopped, shook his head, and stared at Dax. Two dark shapes floated free of its back. Eddy slashed through one with DemonSlayer while Alton caught the other. The demons burst into sparks and disappeared.

The bull lowered his head. Confused now, he pawed the ground, shook his head, and then trotted back toward his pasture on the other side of the road. The few bulls that had stayed behind bellowed a welcome.

Ginny glanced at Alton. "Do you always have to be right?" At least she was grinning. She nodded toward the small group of bulls still watching them so intently. "Keep an eye on that big guy. I think he's the demon king."

Another bull rushed, and then another and another, three huge bulls with their heads down, charging across the open space directly toward them. The ground rumbled beneath their feet. Alton heard Ginny curse her platform sandals, but she still managed to swing her sword, slap bulls with the glowing blade, and spin out of the way with grace and good effect as demon mist poured forth. It terrified him to watch her—terrified him and turned him on.

Damn but she was amazing—and one hell of a fighter. Within a few minutes, they'd destroyed almost a dozen demons sheltering within the four bulls.

This wasn't possession as they'd seen in the past. No glowing eyes, no demon teeth. It was almost as if the demons were merely using the bulls as places to hang out during the daylight hours. Hiding within their powerful bodies, somehow controlling them yet not taking full possession.

But why?

Alton spun to the side as more bulls charged. Bumper-Willow helped to keep them contained within a small area, nipping at heels and throwing her curly body beneath powerful hooves. Crystal blades flashed, and the stench of demonkind lay over the small area of ground that was now churned and carved as if it had been plowed.

A crowd had begun to gather as fairgoers filtered back toward the battle. Breathing hard, Ginny slanted a look at Alton. "They think we're part of the program."

"Beautiful girls and lots of action. Why shouldn't they?" He flashed her a wink but kept his attention on the biggest bull. There were only three others besides the big one left now. He had to presume they were possessed.

Or were they?

Alton glanced toward Dax. "Have you noticed? Their eyes aren't glowing. They haven't got demon teeth. Those demons that attacked us were in mist form. Could they merely be using the bulls as places to hide in daylight? Are they somehow drawing strength from the animals without actually possessing them? Maybe they don't need an avatar after dark anymore."

"More evolution?" Ginny asked.

"Possibly. Or learned ability? I imagine it takes a certain amount of power to possess a living creature. Merely hiding within a living shell . . . Could they be drawing on the bulls' life force? I need to know what their motive is."

Ginny took up a position near him. "We didn't sense them in the bulls. Neither did Bumper. Maybe that's their motive—hiding in plain sight."

Alton nodded. The explanation almost seemed too simple, but it had obviously worked. "I'm worried about the big one," he said. "He's waiting for something. You can almost hear him think."

One of the three smaller bulls rushed them. It went toward Alton first, then feinted and charged Eddy. Dax was on it. He slapped his sword against the creature's back and Eddy caught three demons with DemonSlayer as they escaped.

The crowd of onlookers cheered and applauded. Alton glanced at Dax. "Maybe you should take a bow," he said. Dax merely grunted.

There were two smaller bulls and the one large one left. The rest had trotted peacefully back across the road to their pasture once their demons were gone. Alton glanced over his shoulder. The crowd had moved closer. Parents held their children in front so they could see. "Get back," he said, waving his arm. "Get those kids out of the way. These things are unpredictable. They're dangerous."

"Great show," one idiot yelled. Someone clapped. Someone else blew on a horn and others yelled encouragement—some for the bulls, a few for the ones fighting them.

Alton looked at Dax and they both shook their heads. Didn't these people realize lives were in danger here? Ginny glanced his way and then turned around to the crowd. She held DarkFire high and yelled, "Get back, now. All of you." Purple fire shot from the blade and people moved back a few steps.

With a look of disgust, she turned away and stood beside Alton once again. "Stupid jerks," she muttered. "What now?"

Alton shook his head. "We wait and see what he does next. I'm afraid to make the first move. With three of them, we can't control what direction they go. I don't want anyone hurt."

"Can you use a compulsion? Send people out of the way."

"Yes. Why didn't I think of that?" Disgusted with himself, Alton turned and waved his hand over the crowd. After a moment they surged back and moved closer to the tents and booths. "That's better." He leaned over and kissed the top of Ginny's head. "I knew there was a reason I loved you."

She flashed him a bright grin. "What? Because I'm smarter than you?"

"Well, I wouldn't exactly say—"

"Alton! Look out!"

Eddy's shout spun them around as the two smaller bulls charged directly at Alton. He twisted to one side, slapped his sword down on the first bull, and ducked out of the way of the second. Ginny caught the demons from the first one and sidestepped the second. BumperWillow charged the second bull, raced beneath its belly, and came up under its throat.

Ginny swung DarkFire and slapped the blade between the animal's horns. The crystal flashed violet. Two demons shot out of its back, just out of reach of Alton's sword. They swirled high overhead and then shot straight for the one huge bull standing alone in the center of the field.

It bellowed, and as it stretched its neck out and opened its mouth, both wraiths shot inside and disappeared down its throat. The smaller bull that had been their temporary home shook his head, looked around stupidly, and trotted back across the road to join the others.

The huge bull that remained pawed the earth and lowered his head. Dust flew over his back; muscles rippled across his broad shoulders. The crowed had moved closer, but now, even without Alton's compulsion, they surged back out of the way.

The bull raised his head and his eyes glowed with an inner fire. It bellowed again, only this time there were rows of teeth, razor sharp and glinting in the sun, and the full-throated bugle was more the cry of a banshee than a fighting bull.

Alton, Ginny, Eddy, and Dax lined up and faced the creature. BumperWillow stood to one side, ears on alert, tail high. Dax looked her way. "You okay, Willow?"

I'm ready.

Dax grinned at Alton. "BumperWillow's just too big a mouthful. They know we're talking to both of them."

Alton shook the tension out of his shoulders and tightened his grasp on HellFire. "Works for me. Ladies? Are you ready?"

"Definitely." Ginny slanted him a quick look. *I love you. Don't you dare get hurt.*

The same goes for you.

Silence had fallen over the crowd, standing now at a careful distance. The bull lowered his head once again and pawed the ground. Sand and rocks flew over his shoulders. His powerful muscles bunched and rippled as he started forward, slowly at first, but building up speed as he got his massive weight in motion.

Alton felt the sense of evil grow, almost as if the creature projected fear and danger ahead of him. Someone behind them screamed. He heard the sound of shuffling feet, but he couldn't take the time to look. He had to hope people were moving back, out of the way and not into danger.

He glanced at the others. Dax and Eddy had moved to the right while he and Ginny took the left. Ginny stood bravely with her red skirt blowing against her legs and her sword held aloft. BumperWillow had moved and now stood her ground dead center between them, making herself the focus of the animal's wrath.

The bull raced directly toward the dog and then, in a split second that caught them all off guard, he twisted his huge body faster than any creature his size should have been able to move, lowered his head, and came up beneath Dax with his deadly curved horns. Eddy screamed and lunged with DemonSlayer but the crystal blade glanced off the bull's thick neck.

Dax grabbed the horn aimed at his belly and brought his knee up against the bull's snout, pushed and twisted and managed an awkward flip over the animal's head. Blood streamed from a shallow wound in his side, but he landed on his feet with DemonFire still clutched in his fist.

The bull shook his head. Thick streams of saliva dripped from his open jaws. He glared from Dax to Eddy and back at Dax once again. Alton slipped around behind the beast and BumperWillow charged the animal, barking frantically, going for his face. True to her pit bull nature, she baited the bull, teasing him with barks and growls and snapping teeth. At the last possible second, she jumped and clamped her powerful jaws down on the huge animal's tender nose.

He bellowed and shook his head, a sharp side-to-side jerk. BumperWillow hung on. Her back legs flailed as she reached for purchase against the ground, but the bull swung his big head high and then low, battering her muscular body hard against the dirt, knocking the wind out of the tenacious dog.

Still she hung on, until he jerked his head rapidly from side to side again. The sudden change in direction tossed her a dozen feet in the air. Someone in the crowd screamed. BumperWillow landed with a thud and a puff of dust, lying there in the dirt without sound or movement.

The bull spun quickly. Blood poured from his snout and his eyes glowed red, shooting angry sparks visible even in the daytime sun. His horns had grown longer and sharper— they glinted now like polished steel in huge, sweeping curves above his broad skull. Alton saw his chance and stabbed for the bull. He was willing to risk killing the creature if only to stop the demon's attack, but his crystal sword balked at taking an innocent life.

HellFire slipped off the thick hide in a trail of blue sparks, but a single puff of black exploded into the air.

"That's one of the demons it just absorbed." Dax reached high and caught the wraith with the tip of his sword. The mist exploded into stinking sparks, but his reach overhead left him exposed and vulnerable.

The bull swung its big head and caught Dax just beneath the ribs. He cried out, swinging DemonFire even as the bull gored him deep with another sharp jerk of its head. As Eddy reached for Dax, one of the bull's hooves caught her thigh and scored a long slash beneath her skirt. She twisted away as her leg crumpled beneath her, but she still managed to pull Dax free before the bull could force the sharp horn any deeper into his side.

Alton took a running leap and jumped on the bull's back as Eddy dragged Dax to safety. He couldn't tell how badly his friend had been gored, but the ground was slick with blood. Clinging to the animal, Alton swung his sword beneath the beast's throat.

The bull twisted away from the blade. It lunged and dipped, twisting like a whirling dervish, spinning faster than nature had ever intended. It was all Alton could do to hang on for the ride and try to avoid the thrashing swing of razor-sharp horns. Then the bull bucked high, came down stiff-legged, and landed hard on all four legs.

Jarred by the impact, Alton grabbed on to the horns with both hands to keep from flying off. HellFire flew from his grasp in a spinning arc and buried itself tip first into the ground.

Chapter Twenty

Fighting panic, Ginny quickly weighed her options. Dax was down and bleeding badly. Eddy's leg had a deep slash. BumperWillow was either unconscious or dead and Alton was clinging to the bull's back without HellFire. Ripping off her skirt, Ginny stood her ground in her white camisole top, black lace panties, and red platform sandals, waving the red fabric in front of the bull like a matador's cape.

She didn't know if demons liked red or not, but this demon-powered bull was putting his head down and blowing huge blasts of hot air from bleeding nostrils—thank you, Bumper. And he was glaring at the billowing red skirt.

Alton flashed her a thumbs-up and nimbly jumped from the bull's back. He reached for HellFire. The sword burst out of the dirt directly into his grasp. Alton held his weapon high and raced toward the bull. Just as he got within striking distance, the animal swung his head.

One of the long horns ripped into Alton's side and lifted him high overhead. Ginny screamed. She felt Alton's agony through their mental link as the horn sliced deep into his body. The bull swung his head and Alton tumbled over his broad back like a rag doll. HellFire once again landed in the dirt, but this time Alton lay beside his sword, unmoving.

Ginny searched for his thoughts and found nothing.

Then the bull charged.

Ginny stood her ground as best she could with her sandals sinking into the torn and shredded dirt. The bull lunged toward her red skirt. She whipped it out of the way as the animal passed and struck him across the shoulders with the flat of her blade.

A black wraith flew from between his horns—the second demon it had absorbed. Ginny lunged for it and barely caught the trailing end of mist. The demon burst into violet sparks as the bull raced by. Dirt flew when it twisted and slowed its huge bulk enough to turn and charge her once again.

She glanced toward Alton. Blood pooled around him but he hadn't moved. Eddy was on the far side of the field, kneeling beside Dax. Both of them were covered in blood, and BumperWillow still lay in the dirt where she'd fallen.

Ginny was alone and the bull was coming back. Her white camisole top was stained with blood and her bare legs were covered in mud and blood and saliva from the bull's last charge.

She linked with DarkFire and felt the power of the crystal pour into her as she faced the bull. The ground vibrated beneath her feet from his pounding charge and though he moved with the speed of a rolling freight train, he seemed to come at her in slow motion. Ginny stood her ground until the last second, then swung her red skirt to attract his charge. He lunged for the fabric and she ducked and rolled out of the way.

She came to a stop beside Alton. He lay in a crumpled heap in the dirt and blood poured slowly from a deep puncture in his side, but there was no time to check on him, no time to assure herself whether he lived or died. DarkFire seemed to vibrate within her grasp and she saw an answering glow in Alton's sword. Bending from the waist, Ginny swept HellFire up in her left hand. She put her head down and, with a glowing sword in each hand, raced across the field, as far from Alton as she could get.

She stopped in an open space, far from Dax and Eddy, farther from Alton and BumperWillow. She couldn't think about Alton now. Couldn't allow her mind to travel through all the terrible possibilities of whether the man she loved lived or died. *Focus.* She had to focus.

The demon king must be stopped—she was the only one left who had a chance to do it.

The bull paused in its attack. It lowered its huge head and stared toward Dax and Eddy on the far side of the field. Ginny was sure he weighed the odds of getting to Dax before Ginny got to him, because he swung his head around and lowered it, staring at her out of flame-red eyes.

Once more he pawed at the hard ground, throwing clods of dirt high over his back and shoulders. Blood still dripped from his torn nose, and saliva hung in long, nasty ropes from his jaws. He bugled his banshee scream and charged.

Ginny screamed even as she attacked. Running directly toward the crazed beast, she flung her red skirt over the bull's head and whirled out of the animal's way.

Bellowing its ear-splitting wail, the bull stopped and twisted his head, trying to dislodge the fabric that hung from his horns and covered his eyes. The sharp horns came perilously close to Ginny and he kicked out. One hoof caught her square in the chest. She grunted, gasping for air as she spun to the side with DarkFire raised high in her right hand, HellFire grasped tightly in her left.

Then she lunged forward and brought the flat sides of both DarkFire and HellFire down hard, right between the bull's horns. Power burst from both blades in a shower of amethyst and blue flames. The bull stopped as if stunned. He shook his head. Then, with a wrenching cry, the demon king burst forth.

Ginny lunged for the demon with both blades.

Caught in DarkFire's purple light, the huge, black wraith burst to life in all its demonic shape and form. Both blades passed through its legs and the demon howled in frustration. The bull shook his head again, but he couldn't dislodge Ginny's red skirt still twisted around his horns and covering his eyes. He trotted away with the demon struggling, half in and half out of his massive body.

Even away from DarkFire's light, the demon king was fully visible as a demon. A very pissed-off demon.

Still hanging on to both swords, Ginny raced after the bull. She leapt over the torn earth in a desperate dash to catch the demon king, but just before she reached him, he screamed a banshee cry and then with a horrible sucking sound, pulled his body entirely free of the bull.

She swung at the hideous shape with DarkFire. Sparks flew, but the wraith reformed as the one blade passed harmlessly through both his legs. She tried to reach him with both blades, but he was just out of her reach.

Moaning and screaming, the demon king hovered overhead for a moment, its four arms spread wide, its mouth gaping and fangs dripping saliva. Then with an even louder shriek it suddenly coalesced into a spinning tornado of sulfuric stink that collapsed in upon itself, growing smaller and smaller as she watched.

There was a tiny atmospheric *pop* and the demon winked out of sight. Seething with frustration and rage, unable to fully catch her breath, and absolutely exhausted, Ginny would have crumpled to the ground, but she knew that Alton needed her. Calling on her last bit of strength, she turned toward him with both swords dragging in the dirt.

It took her a moment to comprehend what she saw.

He had one hand pressed against his side and he was trying to sit up. Blood still ran from his wound, but he raised his head, caught her eye with a look that spoke volumes, and smiled at her despite his obvious pain.

He was alive. Energy surged and Ginny raced across the field on wobbly legs. She collapsed beside him. Alton reached for her and dragged her close. The warmth of his embrace and the love in his eyes was all it took.

She burst into tears.

He'd never seen anything more awe-inspiring than Ginny's battle with the demon king. Holding her now, loving her with all his heart, Alton had no doubt she'd saved all their lives. He glanced over her shoulder, to the place where Dax lay in the dirt.

Eddy and another man were bent over the ex-demon. Willow had dragged herself over to lie beside them. At least Eddy wasn't crying. Alton figured that was a good sign but he wasn't sure who was with them.

Right now, it didn't really matter. All that mattered was that Ginny was safe in his arms. Safe in spite of her bruises and her tears. His side hurt like the blazes, but as deep as the bull had gored him, he didn't sense that anything vital had been injured. Already he could feel his wound beginning to heal.

He brushed Ginny's hair back from her face. Her perfect braids had pulled loose, she was covered in blood and muck and dirt, and tears left dusty tracks over her cheeks. He'd never seen her looking more beautiful or wanted her so much.

He planted a soft kiss on her lips. She sniffed and turned away. He dug a handkerchief out of his pocket and she wiped her face and blew her nose. When the tears were gone, for now, anyway, she turned back to him. "Are you okay? You're bleeding. Let me help. . . ."

"I'm fine. And you? Ginny, you're absolutely amazing. You did it. All by yourself, you stopped that bastard. I think you sent him away for a while."

She sobbed and shook her head. "I couldn't kill him. I tried, but . . ."

"Ah, sweetheart. You were magnificent. Absolutely magnificent. C'mon. Let's go check on Dax." Slowly he rose to his feet, but Ginny was up before him and helped him stand.

She grabbed HellFire out of the dirt and handed his sword to him. Then she slipped DarkFire into her scabbard.

They helped each other across the field. Dawson Buck, the vet, was kneeling beside Dax. "Are you guys okay?" He looked at Alton's ripped shirt and torn flesh. "How bad is that? It's bleeding pretty heavy."

Alton shook his head. "I'll be okay. How's Dax?"

"Anyone else would need surgery, but he's something else. Literally. I think stitches might help. He said he doesn't want a doctor, but I can at least sew him up. I've got my kit with me, but I'll have to follow you back to your place." He glanced around. "It's illegal for a vet to treat a human."

Dax chuckled. "I'm not human. I'm an ex-demon. Alton's Lemurian. I doubt the licensing board covers us at all."

Dawson just shook his head.

Alton held tightly to Ginny. "Sounds good, Dawson. Let's get out of here. I need to do some crowd control first. Ginny, can you get the car?" Alton kissed Ginny's cheek when she nodded. He turned away and walked toward the crowd of curious onlookers, raised his hands, and let the compulsion flow from his mind through his fingertips.

Ginny headed toward the parking lot. Alton watched her walk slowly across the torn field wearing nothing but her stained camisole top, her tiny black lace bikini panties, and those silly platform sandals that made her long legs look even longer.

No one in the crowd seemed to notice. No, they were all talking about the great entertainment and what a wonderful show it had been. His compulsion had worked, but then with a vision like Ginny starring, it had to have been amazing.

Alton had to agree it had been a great show. They were all still alive. He went back and knelt down beside Dax again. His friend's face was pale, but his eyes were open. "I'll be okay," Dax said. "We need to get out of here before the authorities arrive. Is the demon king dead?"

Alton shook her head. "No. But damn, Ginny was amazing. She fought him with both HellFire and DarkFire. Neither blade was able to kill him, though she managed to send him somewhere. I don't know if he's gone to Abyss or the void, but he feels gone."

Just then Ginny pulled up in the SUV. She'd found the remnants of her red skirt somewhere along the way and had it tied around her waist, but when she climbed out of the Yukon, she still looked a little shell-shocked by what had happened.

Dax reached for her hand when she knelt down beside him. "I hear you were the hero of the day. Thank you."

She shook her head. "I couldn't kill him. Not even with both swords. And Dax, I could see him in his demon form, in your old form, without the light from DarkFire. Just before he disappeared, he was entirely visible. DarkFire wasn't close enough to illuminate him. I'm hoping I sent him to Abyss or the void, at least for now, but he's getting stronger. How do we stop him? There's got to be a way."

Dax didn't answer. He merely closed his eyes and clung to Eddy's hand. She looked at Ginny with tear-filled eyes and shook her head.

Alton and Dawson carefully loaded Dax into the SUV. Eddy climbed into the backseat beside him and held a towel they'd found in the Yukon over his deepest wound.

Alton didn't even ask for the keys. His side hurt like hell and he was feeling a little light-headed from blood loss. Ginny helped him lift Willow into the back. Still feeling dazed, they headed back down the road to their casita with Dawson Buck, the veterinarian, following close behind.

* * *

Ginny carried cold beer and a fresh plate of cheese and crackers out to the back deck. They were all bathed, their injuries tended and bandaged by the local vet, and the worst of their wounds almost completely healed by Willow. Even trapped inside Bumper, she hadn't lost her skills.

Dawson was still here, obviously fascinated by the stories Alton and Dax were telling him of the ongoing demon invasion and the lost women of Lemuria. Willow had parked her fuzzy butt against his leg and was shamelessly begging for treats.

"Thanks, Ginny." Dawson took the beer she offered and turned his attention back to Alton. "How many days do you think you have before the demon king comes back?"

Alton shook his head. "We have no idea. He could return tonight, as powerful as he seems to be growing, but we're hoping he's gone for a while. We think all the portals to Abyss are sealed, so hopefully he'll have to work harder to get back."

Dawson frowned. "How's that work? If the portals are sealed, how do they go home?"

Alton merely shrugged. They'd never quite figured that one out. "Somehow, they can be sucked back to Abyss or sent to the void without a portal, but they can't get back into Earth's dimension until they can find a functioning gateway. At least regular demons can't. The demon king seems to have his own rules."

"That's no good." Dawson took a sip of his beer.

Alton traced the condensation along the neck of his brew. "No kidding. Especially since he's targeted Dax, and with all the other problems we have to worry about, the demon king is the last thing we need. We still have to figure out how to deal with the mess in Lemuria. Taron's going to have the replicated swords ready in a week, according to DarkFire, which means it's imperative that we get my father under control before then."

Dax shifted in his seat. He was still obviously hurting, but at least he was able to move around since Willow and Dawson had treated him. "My suggestion is that we heal first and then worry about Chancellor Artigos. Eddy's covered in bruises and still has a pretty deep gash in her thigh, BumperWillow isn't any better, you've got a frickin' hole in your side that needs to close, and Ginny's a mess of contusions from that damned bull kicking her."

Dawson finished his beer and stood up. "I agree. You're all walking wounded right now, though it looks like you've got everything under control. At least no one appears to be bleeding." He chuckled softly. It was obvious he felt a bit like Alice after falling down the rabbit hole. "I hope you all have a good night and get some rest. You need it."

Alton stood up to walk him out. Dawson paused in the open door. "If there's anything I can do to help, anything at all, please call me. It appears this is more than just a battle between a few demons and a small army of demon fighters. You hold the future of worlds in your hands. It's a cause that affects more than any of us can imagine."

Alton nodded. "I know, and believe me, we will call on you. We need everyone we can trust. Thank you."

He stood in the doorway and watched as Dawson's taillights disappeared in the darkness. Then he softly closed the door and went back inside to Ginny.

It was barely dark when Ginny and Alton crawled off to bed. Alton decided on another shower. His puncture wound had closed and no longer bled, but dry blood streaked his belly and thigh.

Plus, he insisted he had to wash off the last of the demon stink. He seemed convinced his first brief shower hadn't done the job. Ginny couldn't smell any sulfur on him at all. She wondered if he was trying to wash away the fear they'd all experienced this afternoon, the risks they'd faced, the dangerous attack that had almost cost lives.

She watched him leave the room, but the bedroom felt horribly empty with him gone, so she quickly stood up and followed him into the bathroom. He was just reaching for the faucet to turn the water on when she softly closed the door behind her.

"Ginny?" He turned and his eyes were troubled.

She didn't want to know what thoughts filled his mind. Not now. Instead, she reached for his hand. "You're hurt. I don't want you to shower alone. I worry about you falling."

He paused with one hand resting on the shower rod and reached for her. She clasped his hand and stood there, feeling slightly self-conscious in her worn flannel pants and stretched cami top.

"I don't particularly want to shower alone, either." He watched her with such intensity that she felt herself blush.

Then, before she lost her nerve, she let go of his hand and slipped out of her clothes.

"Nine hells!" Alton moved toward her so quickly she almost jumped back.

"I had no idea. Ginny . . . love, you've been hurt worse than I realized." Lightly he brushed his fingers over the ugly contusions covering her ribs. The bull's hoof had caught her square in the chest. The dark and bloody bruise covered most of her torso between her breasts and navel in a horrible map of black and blue and red.

"Ah, Ginny. This is awful." He raised his head and gazed at her with troubled eyes. "Are any of your ribs broken?"

She shook her head. "No. Nothing's broken. It doesn't hurt. Not that much." She felt embarrassed for some reason and stared at her toes.

Alton lifted her chin with his fingertips. "Why won't you look at me? Ginny, what's wrong?"

She felt her throat close up, fought the burning in her eyes, and cursed the tears that suddenly spilled down her cheeks.

Alton wrapped his arms around her and gently hugged her close. "Why are you crying, sweetheart?"

"I thought you were dead." She sniffed. "I tried to reach you and there was nothing. No sense of you. Only the demon and the smell of blood and Dax so badly hurt and Eddy crying and BumperWillow lying in the dirt. I've never felt so alone in my life. Never."

"I'm sorry. I must have been unconscious for a few moments. Not for long. I came to in time to watch you." He leaned away and stared at her. "My gods, Ginny." He tilted her chin up with his fingertip. "I wish I had that battle on video. You were amazing. So powerful and self-assured. Absolutely magnificent!"

She gazed up at the wonder on his face, but all she could think of was how frightened she'd been. Frightened and angry at that damned bull for hurting Dax and Eddy, for goring Alton. She'd wanted to kill the bull and the demon inside, even though the bull was innocent. The demon wasn't, though. Damn him, he was still out there. Still trying to figure out how to steal Dax's energy and how to kill the rest of them. Was there any way to stop him?

Alton kissed the top of her head. Then he reached inside the shower and turned on the tap, stepped in, and carefully dragged Ginny under the warm spray with him. The warm water soothed her aches and washed away her tears. She ran a soft cloth over Alton's side and rinsed away the dried blood still caked there.

Even though he was healing quickly, she felt like crying again when she saw the size of the healing wound and knew how badly it must have hurt.

Alton gently dried Ginny with a soft terry towel before he

toweled himself off. When they went back into the bedroom, there was no question of what bed they'd sleep in. No hesitation when they pulled back the covers and crawled in together.

And even though they both were hurting, there was no question of what they wanted.

Alton fluffed the pillows behind him, leaned against the soft pile, and reached for Ginny. He drew her close and she went to him with the certainty that this was where she belonged. At his side, no matter what was to come. There was trouble ahead. She knew that as well as she knew her name. Unseating his father wouldn't be easy, but it would have to be done. She'd be there beside Alton, no matter the risk.

He cupped her face in his hands, drew her close, and kissed her. Then his fingers traced the swell of her breast and she felt his lips turn up in a smile against her mouth. "Ah, Ginny . . . I knew you were going to be trouble. Nothing but trouble from the start."

She ran her hands over his chest, and carefully rolled and twisted until she straddled him without brushing against his injured side. His erection was trapped between them, held in place by the soft, damp folds of her sex. She leaned over and pressed a kiss to his perfectly shaped nose. "I bet you forgot the condoms."

He chuckled and her body bounced with the soft rise and fall of his chest. He reached for the table beside the bed and held up a shiny foil packet. "Not me. I never make mistakes."

Ginny grabbed it out of his hand and tore the edge with her teeth. "I knew you were arrogant, right from the start. Arrogant and cocky and such a bossy know-it-all." She rose up on her knees until his erection sprang free. Carefully she sheathed his full, hot length. Then she lowered herself, but this time she positioned his shaft against her sex and slowly, so slowly took him deep inside.

They both sighed as she settled herself down over his full length. Alton wrapped his arms around her slim waist, nuzzled her neck, and kissed the side of her throat. "Did I ever tell you how much I love troublesome women?"

"No." She sighed as she adjusted to his size, to his heat and the amazing connection that linked them—body, heart, and mind. Then she slowly moved her hips in a gentle rhythm with his. "But I'd really love to hear."

Smiling, touching, kissing, laughing, and loving, he told her. In great detail. Over and over again.

And here's a special preview
from Kate's next sexy DemonSlayers title,

STARFIRE,

to be published by Zebra Books in April 2011!

Selyn pressed her back against the sharp stones lining the cavern wall and attempted to become one with the shadows. She listened intently as Roland's footsteps receded in the distance and faded into silence, yet still she waited.

They were too close to success to take any chances now. Too close—finally—to tasting the freedom that had forever eluded the forgotten daughters of the exiled women warriors of Lemuria.

Anger welled up inside, a harsh and biting pain reminding Selyn once more of her need for revenge, of her soul-numbing hatred for the people who had condemned her mother, her sisters—all of them—to lives of slavery.

Such was the reward mighty Lemuria gave its bravest warriors. Slavery until death brought release from toiling in the fetid mines far beneath the levels where the free folk lived. Toiling where the air was thick with the pollution of their labors, fouled by the seething anger carried within the hearts and souls of the Forgotten Ones.

Selyn clenched her fists and closed her eyes against the simmering pain of resentment. *Not now.* She could not allow herself the luxury of anger. Roland had cautioned her, and she would listen. He was a good man—one of the few good men she'd ever known. A true son of Lemuria, not one of the sadistic guards who kept the women imprisoned in the mines, and definitely not one of those damned aristocrats who thought themselves above the common folk.

No, Roland understood honor and integrity. His loyalty was to his world, not to the few who governed so unfairly. He'd become a good friend, braver than most because he had more to lose—a wife, a child, his position as a respected sergeant of the Lemurian Guard.

Selyn risked nothing. She'd long accepted the fact that as a slave, her life had no value. As a free woman—even if she were of the aristocracy—she would have no voice. Gods willing, that was soon to change. She remembered the stories her mother had told, and they gave her hope.

There'd been a time when women held positions of leadership as members of the Council of Nine, when mothers had fought demons beside their men as respected equals, and gender had neither defined nor limited status or personal autonomy

Finally, Selyn and the other Forgotten Ones sensed freedom.

Freedom and change, and a chance for revenge.

Roland of Kronus caught Alton's terse warning the moment he reached the upper levels of Lemuria. Damned telepathy was useless in the mines and useless between dimensions, but obviously it was working now.

This was a message he'd been dreading ever since the invasion of demonkind into Earth's dimension had begun. Alton's steady voice carried more assurance than Roland felt, but Alton had been raised to a life of privilege, destined to one day rule their world. It appeared he was finally getting his chance, but nine hells! The risk to all of them could not be denied.

We're moving against my father tonight, Alton said. *Ginny*

and I are hiding out in Taron's rooms until it's time to act. Artigos must be removed from the Council of Nine as soon as possible. There's no doubt he's possessed by demonkind. I need to have a firm grasp of the council before Taron arms the Forgotten Ones.

Roland nodded as he answered, considering their next steps even as he replied. The Forgotten Ones needed to know what was going on. Somehow he must locate Selyn without alerting her guards. Taron should be notified as well, though that would mean traveling even deeper into the bowels of Lemuria.

Taron had been far below and out of touch for days, creating enough crystal swords to arm each of the Forgotten Ones. He should have close to the full one hundred blades by now, each awaiting her owner.

One hundred crystal blades capable of sentience—alive with the souls of ancient warriors and Lemuria's most powerful weapon against the scourge of demonkind.

With the thought of the crystal blades in his mind, Roland replied to Alton. *I'm returning to the mines now. I'll inform Selyn that the timetable has been moved up, and contact Taron as well. I should be back before you move against Artigos.*

Roland also sent a quick message to his beloved wife. Chará was used to the long hours he kept, though she had no idea the danger he faced. There was no point in alarming her with the truth of his actions. No point at all. Sighing, he turned back along the dark tunnel, quickly retracing his steps, returning to the lower levels where the Forgotten Ones toiled.

The steady *drip, drip, drip* and the soft hum of overtaxed air purifiers were the only sounds Selyn heard as she cautiously pushed herself away from the cavern wall and moved silently through the darkness to the sleeping level.

With any luck she might be able to catch a couple hours of rest before her shift started, but she'd missed the evening meal and it would be a long time until she had another opportunity to break fast.

A hulking shadow suddenly filled the narrow passageway. Light glinted off pale eyes set in a massive frame a full foot and a half taller and three times wider than her own.

As usual, luck sucked. Selyn straightened to her full height, raised her chin and looked the guard in the eye. That alone should be enough to piss him off. If she could make him angry enough, he might even forget to ask why she was wandering along a passage so far from her cell.

"Ah, Birk. Fancy meeting you here." She folded her arms across her chest and hoped to the nine hells he couldn't see how she trembled. Showing fear was the same as giving up.

Selyn never showed fear. Never would she give up.

The huge guard didn't say a word. His fist came out of nowhere. The crushing blow to her cheekbone left her lying dazed and barely conscious on the ground.

He planted his hands on his hips and leaned over her. "So, bitch. You want to tell me what you're doing out here?"

Blinking back the shooting lights blinding her vision, Selyn shook her head.

He grabbed her hair in a meaty fist and jerked her to her feet.

"Ouch! Nine hells!" She twisted, but he grabbed her breast through the thin cloth of her robe and squeezed, digging his thick fingers into soft flesh.

"Ah!" Excruciating pain made her nauseous. Frantically, Selyn bucked and writhed, but his fingers only tightened on her breast and in her hair. She lashed out with her bare foot, connected just below his right knee.

Birk cursed. His leg buckled and he lost his grip on her

breast. Selyn jerked her head up as he fell and slammed him under the chin. Her long hair was still tangled in his fist and he pulled her down with him.

Scrambling beneath his massive weight she broke free, kicked again and caught him soundly between the legs. Birk roared in pain and clutched his balls, but her hair was still trapped in his fist and he jerked her head sharply down and caught her between his thighs.

Twisting, turning, Selyn struggled for freedom. Birk flipped her beneath him, clamping down on her head and shoulders with his powerful legs. Enraged, he tore his hand free of her hair and punched her with both fists, landing powerful blows across her chest and along her ribs.

She felt one rib crack, and then another. Gasping, unable to move or catch her breath, her vision clouded. She couldn't breathe, couldn't fight, could not give up. Not this close. Not with freedom only days away.

Blow after blow slammed into her ribs. Frantically Selyn sucked in a breath of life-giving air and tasted blood in her mouth. Darkness broken by fitful flashes of sparking lights closed in on all sides as the terrible pounding continued, yet somehow, she floated free, apart from the beating, as if she hovered in a separate space, beyond pain, beyond fear.

Maybe freedom would finally come as her mother's had—in death. Did it really matter anymore? Selyn no longer felt the blows, even as Birk continued to pummel her unresisting body.

A beautiful, achingly familiar face swam hauntingly just beyond her reach. With split and bleeding lips she whispered her mother's name.

"Elda?"

There was no answer, no sign of recognition, but it was okay. Her mother had found peace in death, and she'd been reborn to fight again. Reborn in the crystal sword called DemonSlayer.

Was that to be Selyn's path out of this hellhole? Through death? No matter. Not anymore. Giving in to the darkness, Selyn gratefully embraced the only freedom she had ever known.

At last.

Freedom, and darkness, and death.

As soon as he reached Selyn's level in the caverns, Roland cast out his thoughts. Always before, the young woman had responded immediately, even if he awakened her from sleep.

There was nothing. A great void where her active mind should be. He glanced along the shadowed tunnel and prayed to the gods he'd not be discovered. He had no business at this level. None at all, but Selyn should have answered by now.

He grasped his crystal sword and walked purposefully down the dark passageway. Calling silently for Selyn, he rounded a slight curve and stopped dead.

A body lay in the middle of the corridor. A woman's body. From the long tangled mass of her coal black hair and the coppery color of her skin, it could only be Selyn. Roland glanced both ways, saw no one, and raced to her side.

Her eyes were closed, her face battered and swollen, her slave's robe badly torn. Bloody saliva foaming at the corner of her lips was the only sign Selyn still lived.

Roland couldn't risk a call for help. The only ones strong enough to have hurt Selyn this badly were the guards who watched the Forgotten Ones. Selyn's trips to the surface must have been discovered, but how could anyone have done such a horrible thing? Roland had to get her out of here, now, and hope like the nine hells she lived long enough for him to get her to a healer.

Carefully, he gathered the broken young woman up in his arms and carried her down the dark tunnel. He reached the stairs without anyone spotting him, and began the long climb to the surface. He couldn't take her to anyone in Lemuria. Members of the aristocracy either did not know of the Forgotten Ones, or if they did, they refused to admit their existence. It would have to be someone on Earth.

Selyn was still alive, but barely, when Roland finally reached the upper levels and made contact with Alton. The young aristocrat didn't hesitate. He set his earlier plans aside and told Roland where they could safely meet.

Almost an hour later, Roland passed through the Lemurian portal that led directly into the energy vortex in Bell Rock, a large formation outside of Sedona, Arizona. Alton waited in the dark cavern with his woman, Ginny Jones, close beside him.

The Lemurian heir to the council took one look at the battered woman in Roland's arms and cursed, shaking his head in dismay. "Ah, Roland, my friend. How could this be?"

Roland was shocked to see Alton's eyes sparkling with compassionate tears—tears that reaffirmed Roland's decision to follow Alton no matter where he might lead.

Ginny gasped and stepped close. "Oh, my god." She lightly touched the pulse point on Selyn's throat and looked up at Roland. "She's still alive, but her pulse is so weak. Who did this to her?"

Roland shook his head. Anger, frustration and the strain of carrying Selyn so far had him blurting out, "One of the gods-be-damned guards, I imagine. They treat the women most cruelly, but I've never seen one beaten so badly."

"Will she live?" Alton's soft question calmed him.

He sighed. "I don't know. I'm sure she's got broken ribs, internal injuries. She's a tough one, though. She's still breathing."

Alton wrapped his arm protectively around Ginny. "I had no idea when you contacted me that she was hurt this badly."

He glanced at Ginny. "Do you think Dawson can help her? He's a veterinarian, after all, not a doctor for humans."

Ginny stared at Selyn so intently, Roland felt as if she were trying to force the injured woman to heal by the strength of her will alone.

"He's going to have to," she said. "Alton, we have to see if Dax and Eddy can bring BumperWillow. Willow might be able to help, but we need to hurry. Roland? Can you come with us?"

He'd not spent much time in Earth's dimension, and never here in Sedona. It was forbidden, after all, but a young woman's life was in his hands. "Yes," he said, gazing at the battered girl in his arms. "I can."

Alton led the way through another, smaller portal. They stepped out into a cavern almost identical to the first. "We just moved from one side of Sedona to the other," he said. He pointed to a shimmering gateway on one wall. "That's a secret portal we've discovered that leads directly to the chambers of the Council of Nine. I don't have time to explain it now, but do not use it to return. It's too dangerous. We'll go this way." He nodded toward another glowing portal. "We're meeting a friend of ours here who should be able to help the girl."

Lightly he touched Roland's shoulder. "I can take her if you're getting tired. He's got his vehicle waiting nearby."

Roland nodded. "I'm okay. Let's hurry." Even though his arms ached from carrying her, Roland didn't want to risk further injury by shifting Selyn to Alton's grasp. She hadn't stirred, but she drew soft, shallow breaths, proof she still lived. Thank the gods she was unconscious and unaware of her pain.

They stepped out into a star-filled night. Roland had seen stars once before, when he'd fought demons less than a week ago on the flanks of Mount Shasta, but he knew he'd never see them enough. Damn it all, but his people had lost too much when their continent sank beneath the sea.

They had survived these many millennia, but at what cost?

Lives without stars, without the warmth of the sun? Anger gave Roland strength for the short hike down a dark path. He was still grumbling to himself when they rounded a curve in the trail. Alton flashed his handheld light at a large vehicle waiting in the shadows. A tall, lean, dark-haired man climbed out and quickly opened the back door. Roland nodded without speaking and carefully slid into the wide seat with Selyn still in his arms.

Ginny took the seat just ahead. Alton got in beside the driver in the front. The two men conversed softly, but Roland couldn't hear what they said. Ginny remained quiet, though she'd turned and was watching Selyn.

After a short drive, they pulled into a well-lit yard with a low, sprawling building that appeared to be made of smooth stone. Holding Selyn as carefully as he was able, Roland quietly followed as the other three led him inside the structure. They walked down a long hallway into a brightly lit room behind a heavy set of double doors, where he finally laid his bruised and bleeding burden down on a narrow bed.

Finishing up after a long day at the clinic, Dawson Buck had been prepared for another quiet night at home when his cell phone rang. He'd certainly never expected to hear Alton's voice. When he'd recently offered to help his new friends in their battle against a demon invasion, Dawson honestly hadn't thought anyone would ever call.

He was, after all, merely human. What good could a mortal do among creatures who were not only immortal but capable of things he'd only read of in his favorite science fiction novels?

But when Alton told him that one of their kind was badly

injured and needed medical attention, Dawson hadn't hesitated. He'd quickly finished up the nightly feeding of his canine and feline patients, locked the doors to his clinic, and raced to the parking lot at Red Rock Crossing near the energy vortex at Cathedral Rock.

And there he'd waited. He'd had plenty of time to think about the changes in his life since that morning a little over a week ago when he'd arrived a bit late to work and discovered the clinic was already filled with dozens of animal patients, all exhibiting the same unbelievable behavior.

He knew his staff thought he was slightly nuts when he'd suggested the pets were all possessed by demons. Of course, he was well aware that the women who worked for him figured it was part of his charm. They loved to tease him about the fact he was so open to the odd stories about the land around Sedona and the energy vortexes that most folks thought of as nothing more than fodder for the tourist trade.

His Aunt Fiona had been the only one who truly understood him. When he was little and talked to his imaginary friends, she'd called him fey. As he'd grown older and lost himself in books with tales of the unusual and unexplained, she'd merely nodded and said he was learning to understand things that a lot of his real-life friends would never be able to see.

The imaginary friends had eventually faded away, cast out by a teen-aged boy's need to act like everyone else, but Aunt Fiona had understood. She'd told him that when he was ready, they'd come back.

Now, as he led this most amazing group of obviously mythical creatures into the small clinic he kept at home, Dawson sent a silent thank you to his long-departed aunt.

He could almost swear he heard her chuckling laughter and the soft, Gaelic lilt to her voice whispering, "I told you so, me boyo. I told you so."

* * *

Dawson glanced at his wristwatch. It was almost five—the time when he normally crawled out of bed—but he'd worked on Selyn most of the night. By now, he figured Alton and the big Lemurian guard he called Roland were probably sacked out on the couches in the main quarters of the house.

He hoped Ginny had gotten some sleep. She'd looked exhausted and a little bit numb from all the blood by the time they'd finished, but the poor girl's injuries had been extensive, and well beyond his training. He'd suctioned blood out of chest cavities for dogs and cats that'd been hit by cars, but he'd never done it for a woman with a punctured lung—at least, not until last night.

Dawson gazed down at the young woman now sleeping in the spare room of his home and hoped he'd done the right thing. He was a veterinarian, for crying out loud! He dealt with dogs and cats, birds, rabbits and the occasional hamster or guinea pig.

Not young, beautiful women barely clinging to life. What if he'd screwed up? What choice did he have? None at all, according to Alton. They couldn't take her to a human doctor, couldn't take her to one of their own healers. It had been Dawson Buck or no one. Her lung had been the most serious injury, along with bruising to her spleen and liver. Her cracked ribs would hurt like hell for awhile, but they'd heal. He'd stitched a couple of spots on her side where heavy blows had actually split her skin, but most of her injuries were bloody scrapes and bruises and contusions.

The darkly defined fingerprints on her right breast sickened him. More than once during the long night he'd thought of killing the one who did this to her. That was so unlike him. Dawson had never been the violent sort. He abhorred conflict of any kind, which was why he'd chosen animals as his patients. Dogs and cats were more *what you see is what you get* kinds of patients. They rarely came with baggage, and they didn't hold grudges.

Even now, he wasn't sure what he'd expected when Alton called, but it certainly hadn't been a beautiful young woman who'd been beaten nearly to death.

He rested his fingers on her shoulder, one of the few spots without the mottled black and blue and red from bruises. "Dear God. Let her live. Please, let her live." Taking a deep breath, Dawson tried to ignore the rapid pounding of his heart. For a brief moment, he thought of all the laws he'd broken by treating a female victim of an obvious assault. Any other medical doctor would have followed the law and reported this to the police. Another veterinarian would have made sure she was treated properly, in a hospital for humans.

Then he bit back a nervous laugh. Who was he trying to kid? She wasn't human. Maybe he hadn't broken any laws after all, but after he'd looked at all her injuries and realized how terribly she'd been hurt, Dawson had known there was no question at all as to whether or not he'd treat her.

Now he could only hope and pray that his efforts had helped and not harmed her. He gently touched a dark bruise on her cheek. Thank goodness the facial bone was merely bruised, not broken. Her bruises would fade, the ribs heal. Within a few days she should be feeling better.

But what of her state of mind? A beating this horrific had to leave more than bruises on the body. He'd learned that these Lemurians healed much faster than humans. They were obviously a lot tougher, too. Her injuries might have killed a human woman.

They would definitely leave emotional scars with a human, as well. He had no idea how a Lemurian might react to such horrible treatment. Alton said she was a slave.

Then he'd really confused the issue when he told Dawson that Lemurians were a free society, that they didn't believe in slavery. He, Alton of Artigos, the son of Lemuria's Chancellor, had not even known of the slaves' existence. Not until Selyn had bravely escaped her captors and told his friend Taron of their plight. And then, so as not to raise any alarm, she'd returned to her untenable captivity deep in the mines.

Obviously, there were things going on in Lemuria that were every bit as convoluted as human politics. And even more obviously, this young woman was unquestionably a hero.

Dawson carefully pushed her tangled hair away from her face and tucked the soft blanket around her badly beaten body. He couldn't bear to look at her injuries now. He'd done all he could as a doctor with the proper professional detachment his role required.

Now that he was finished repairing her injuries, he realized he saw her as any man would a beautiful woman. Those dark bruises and bloody contusions were a travesty, a horrible insult to such perfection. He'd never seen anyone as beautiful as Selyn. Even battered and bruised, she was lovely.

Never once in his life had he lusted after a patient.

Shaking his head with the convoluted stupidity of his thoughts, Dawson left the room, mumbling under his breath, "Of course not, you idiot. All your other patients have four legs."

Selyn drifted awake in a world of pain. Eyes closed, she took a moment to catalog the various parts of her body. Obviously, she had survived Birk's horrific beating, though she wondered if she'd be whole, even if her injuries healed.

She wriggled her toes, then her fingers. They worked. That was good. Slowly, cautiously she licked her dry, cracked lips with the tip of her tongue. Her chest ached and it hurt to breathe, but at least she could draw sufficient air as long as she did it carefully.

Taking another breath, she noticed the stench she'd long associated with her world was missing. Instead, the air lacked any discernible scent at all. Squinting through swollen lids, she saw cream colored walls and shelves neatly filled with books and jars and unfamiliar stuff. There were cabinets with closed doors and light streaming in through a window.

Window? She knew what windows were, but in the mines they looked out onto dark caverns and poorly lit passageways. Blinking, curious enough now to risk drawing attention, Selyn tried to sit up. "Nine hells and then some!" Gasping, she lay back against the pillow and tried to catch her breath.

The door flew open and a tall, lean man stepped into the room. "Don't move. You'll hurt yourself."

"I just figured that out on my own, thank you." Aware she wore nothing beneath the blanket, Selyn tugged the soft folds higher, almost to her chin. "Who are you? Where am I?"

He smiled. "I'm Dawson Buck. You're in my clinic, in Sedona, in Earth's dimension. Roland of Kronus brought you here last night, but you were unconscious." He shook his head and smiled even wider. "I wasn't sure you'd awaken this soon. You must be healing faster than I expected."

There were dimples in both his cheeks that were only partially hidden by his neatly trimmed facial hair. She'd never seen a naked man, but she'd been told that Lemurian men had body hair in places besides the tops of their heads, though rarely on their faces. She knew absolutely nothing about human men, but she found the dark hair framing this one's lips and covering his chin absolutely fascinating. Besides, it was easier to concentrate on the odd hair on his face and those delightful dimples than to think of what he'd just said.

She was on Earth? But how? Lemurians were forbidden

to leave their world, though she knew Alton of Artigos had crossed through the portal. But Roland?

"It was last night?" She wanted to sit up. She wanted her clothing and she wanted to get away while she had the chance. Earth! She'd dreamed of one day seeing Earth. Maybe she could disappear into one of the cities she'd heard tales about.

Disappear and never return.

Never have to face Birk or any of the other guards again.

Never hold the crystal sword Taron is replicating for me even now.

Selyn thought of her mother's spirit, bravely fighting demons once again as the sentience in the sword called DemonSlayer. Who would inhabit the sword Taron might have already finished making for her? What woman warrior would be her partner in battle? If Selyn left now, she'd never know.

She'd be forever a fugitive, trying to exist in a world where she didn't belong. No, she couldn't leave. As one of the Forgotten Ones, as the daughter of a woman warrior, Selyn knew she was honor bound to stay.